COULD IT BE MAGIC?

Paul Magrs was born in 1969 and comes from Aycliffe in County Durham. He is the author of two highly acclaimed novels, *Marked for Life* and *Does It Show?*, and a collection of short stories, *Playing Out*.

Paul Magrs

COULD IT BE MAGIC?

VINTAGE

07686156

Published by Vintage 1999

2 4 6 8 10 9 7 5 3 1

Copyright © Paul Magrs 1997

First published in Great Britain by
Chatto & Windus 1997

Vintage
Random House, 20 Vauxhall Bridge Road,
London SW1V 2SA

Random House Australia (Pty) Limited
20 Alfred Street, Milsons Point, Sydney
New South Wales 2061, Australia

Random House New Zealand Limited
18 Poland Road, Glenfield, Auckland 10,
New Zealand

Random House South Africa (Pty) Limited
Endulini, 5A Jubilee Road, Parktown 2193,
South Africa

Random House UK Limited Reg. No. 954009

A CIP catalogue record for this book
is available from the British Library

ISBN 0 09 926873 6

Printed and bound in Great Britain by
Mackays of Chatham PLC, Chatham, Kent

For Pete Courtie

With thanks to . . .

Joy Foster, Louise Foster, Mark Magrs, Charles Foster, Gladys Johnson, Gladys Magrs, Lynne Heritage, Nicola Cregan, Jon Rolfe, Antonia Rolfe, Brigid Robinson, Alicia Stubbersfield, Siri Hansen, Mark Walton, Daryl Spears, Sara Maitland, Dale Peck, Meg Davis, Jonathan Burnham, Sara Holloway, Claire Paterson, A. S. Byatt, Maureen Duffy, Georgina Hammick, Reuben Lane, Amanda Reynolds, Richard Klein, Lucie Scott and Jeremy Hoad.

One

In the shop the music they were playing was *Pan Pipes II*. Elsie loved that CD. 'Everything I Do, I Do It for You.' Across the cash desk Judith was leaning conspiratorially, messing up the magazines. Her hair was thick with lacquer and black dye, making Elsie shudder. Elsie believed in keeping yourself natural and nice.

'Number sixteen,' Judith repeated. 'The party's at number sixteen.'

Elsie pulled a face. 'I wouldn't want to go somewhere like that. I don't know them in that house.'

'Well, you have to go out on New Year's Eve, Elsie,' Judith insisted. 'You can't stay in and be miserable.' She felt awful saying that, but she'd been talking to someone about this the other day: Elsie needed snapping out of her misery. It was doing her no good.

'Ay, maybe I'll go out to this party.'

Behind her a queue was forming.

'Good lass!' Judith twinkled through her mascara. 'Now, what can I get you?'

Elsie decided she was drinking again. With Tom gone she had free rein. On the shelf behind Judith's head there was a row of gin bottles and they were the exact green of Christmas. The colour of the worst Christmas Elsie had ever known. It would be lashing out, buying a bottle of gin, even a smallish one, but it was cheaper than going out to a pub. At least going round someone's house saved you a bit of money that way.

'I'll have the cheapest bottle in the middle size,' she said, 'and four cans of Boddies for our Craig, and forty Benson and Hedges.'

Judith collected them all, loving the clink of the spirits bottles. 'Back on the drink then, pet?' she said wickedly.

'It's New Year, isn't it?' Elsie snapped.

Judith hadn't meant to sound judgemental. With her man away again, Elsie had nothing left but going back on the drink. They had taken him back into the home on Christmas Eve. He went in with his nerves about once a year. He was crackers, but he kept Elsie off the drink. What with him and her son Craig hanging about with a nasty set, Elsie had her plate full. As far as Judith was concerned, she was welcome to her drink.

'Are you off to this party then?' Elsie asked, softening. 'Have you been invited?'

'There's no invites, pet. It's all word of mouth. But yeah. Soon as I shut this place, I'm getting me glad rags on. All of Phoenix Court will be round there, I reckon.'

'Maybe I'll have a look in,' Elsie said. She liked it when the whole street got together. As she paid and packed her shopping bag, she missed the look Judith was giving her. The last party round their way had been at Judith's house. At that do Elsie was smashed, but she was holier-than-thou about alcohol when Tom was about. That night she had said she wasn't drunk, she'd been touched by a divine hand. Judith hoped she wouldn't make a show of herself tonight.

As Elsie bustled out, a spring in her step now as she crossed the scuffed lino, Judith decided that *Pan Pipes II* was too relaxing for this afternoon. She wanted something boppier in the background, Tina Turner or someone.

With all this frost the Yellowhouses looked almost beige. Icicles clung to eaves and satellite dishes and, as she cut through Sid Chaplin Drive, Elsie wondered that the vibrations from – where? Outer space? Other satellites? – didn't shake the icicles off.

It was this time of year on the estates that she loved best. She thought it looked picturesque. The rosehip bushes hemming play parks and car parks were icing-sugared. The

2

dark wooden fences of each garden had frost piped in neat, regular stripes. It wasn't muddy, either, which meant you could nip across the gaps without getting covered in clarts. The windows in the low-roofed, boxy buildings were warmly lit. She left her own lights on all the time and loved to come back to them. The downstairs windows were pebbled and thick. They made the light inside fuzzy, like a mirage indoors.

For almost two years she had been snug between the phone box and the main road, at the edge of Phoenix Court. She had managed to move away from the old, broken-down flats across town, behind the precinct. It was rough there and she hadn't been able to sleep because of the bother. Her doctor stepped in when she applied to the council for a transfer. They saw her right in the end and she landed up here, in the Yellowhouses. And it was a lovely street. They were all friendly round here. It was a pleasure to go visiting round the doors. By rights she should know everyone by now, but houses had been filled and refilled in the past two years. There was always something going on. Jane, the young woman who lived by Elsie, said, 'It's getting rough round here now. They're moving in the rough types from across town.'

Elsie looked stung.

'Oh, not ,you,' Jane said hastily. 'I meant all that lot coming over from the Dandy Cart. The council move them out of there for being trouble and then they shove them on our doorsteps.' Jane scowled. Elsie thought Jane scowled too much. Far too much for a young lass like her. She was what? Twenty-eight? And there wasn't a drop of joy in her. Everything seemed to get on her nerves. Elsie would think how she'd been at that age. That was the seventies, and she'd got up to all sorts.

Those were the years before Tom and God, even before Craig. Everyone she knew worked up on the industrial estate, assembling fiddly electrical parts in the Sugar Factory. All the lads and lasses from school were together

3

still, as if, on school-leaving day, they had walked out en masse, crossed the town, and walked into the factory together. For work they wore the same plastic hairnets and gloves and blue nylon smocks. They were all in the same boat. The lads kicked a ball about round the side of the factory building and the lasses smoked, standing by the doorways. Gossip and taunts would fly recklessly between parties. Reckless was the word, really. That was exactly how we carried on, Elsie thought. All the laughing on the production line, even the mocking and the bickering, it was all underlaced with a sexiness. It was a joke at the Sugar Factory in those years that everyone had had everyone else. So what if they had? Elsie thought back to all those faces in the early seventies; the lads with hair overgrown, unwashed-looking, big sideburns and tashes; the lasses still wanting to be Twiggy. They'd grown up together in the same small town. In a way it was no wonder they'd all *had* each other, if that was the way you wanted to put it. They were part of the same litter. Like animals, pulling and nuzzling at each other in unguarded moments. Send them out in a coach on bank holidays with crates of booze, to Redcar or Blackpool, or put them in a nightclub like the Gretna on the A167, and the inevitable happens. Gladly they would lose whatever inhibitions they had with each other. They would communicate everything they could, as quickly and breathlessly as possible.

There was an urgency about us, Elsie thought, passing through Catherine Cookson Close. At twenty-eight she'd had a list of fellers she still wanted to knock off. Was that wrong? When she told that to Jane, only recently, Jane had looked downright sniffy. She'd also told her that the pinnacle had been, in 1977, finding out on the day of the Queen's Silver Jubilee that Big Jim Burns, who she'd grown up with, wasn't called that for nothing.

Elsie wanted to ask, what was wrong with that? She'd had a lovely time, the day of the Silver Jubilee. Big Jim Burns was a copper and she kissed him patriotically in the

4

town centre and then took him back to her flat and there they fucked wildly for much of that afternoon.

1977 – the very number still glowed with the warmth of that June. She could still feel, if she thought hard, the press of his weight on her stomach and thighs. She could hardly open her mouth wide enough to get his thing in. Elsie wished she hadn't told Jane that bit. Now Jane looked at her as if she was a filthy old woman. Am I? Elsie thought. Here she was, at forty-something, getting all stirred up at the thought of a big policeman's big thing, carrying a shopping bag of drink back from the shops.

Jane made her feel disgraceful. That was the word. Yet Jane was no virgin. She had a seven-year-old bairn and no husband. What made her so prim? Anyway, they were pals, Elsie and Jane, and she shouldn't think ill of her.

Here she was. Turn the corner, where the puddles were frozen over black, and suddenly she was in Phoenix Court. Everyone's windows were lit up as the teatime gloom stole in. She counted off all the trees in the windows and felt sad that they would be coming down in a few days. She thought there was nothing sadder than Christmas ending. Maybe she'd be glad to see the back of this awful, lonely Christmas.

She stopped in the play park and looked across to number sixteen. All their lights were on and their tree seemed to be the biggest and most lavish in the street. There were shapes moving about behind the net curtains. They must be getting ready for the party. She could hear music coming faintly from within: 'Rhinestone Cowboy'. It all seemed inviting.

Before she went home to make some tea, Elsie thought she would check what her Craig was up to. She hadn't asked him yet, but she felt sure he'd see the New Year in with the lads. She just took it for granted. Most of Christmas he'd been with them. Her Craig, hanging out with the rough lads.

But look at him, when he was with his mates. If she was

5

a stranger, if she wasn't his mother at all, then she'd see no difference. Mothers could blind themselves, she knew, when it came to sons. But sons were men. They were full of blood and temper and that had to come out. From her bedroom window at night she could see across the main road, over Woodham Way, and sometimes she could see Craig, part of his gang, hanging around the streets. They would converge on the Forsyths' house. It was like a squat.

There was a car propped up, half dismantled, beside the fence of the Forsyths' house. It was painted scarlet with white flashes, like Starsky and Hutch's car. The lads were meant to be fixing it up for one of the Forsyth brothers, but Elsie never saw any car-fixing going on. They just stood around with their cans of lager and laughed long and raucously, fighting among themselves and playing the car radio as loud as it would go. Dance music night and day.

'Hip-hop,' Craig had snapped at her when she asked him, 'What sort of music is that?' 'Hip-hop,' he said, 'it's the latest thing.' It went right through her, the insistence of it, but she could see how it might appeal to the young. It seemed to go on for ever. Better than those songs that are over in three minutes flat, the ones she was used to. But when Craig said, almost belligerently, that his favourite music was hip-hop, her heart went out to him and he felt like her little lad again. Hip-hop and him with his broken, swollen, unmendable right foot. The one his stupid natural father had run over in a hired Transit van, the day he left them high and dry. Reversing down the street, still shouting at Elsie, he had driven over his only son. It was like a club foot, and the GP said he was lucky not to have needed a new plastic one, like Don off *Coronation Street*. That was her fault, not taking him for regular checkups. But going to the doctors gave her the heebie-jeebies. Craig would shout if he was in real pain and she would take him then. But then the doctor said there was gangrene and he was within a hair's breadth of losing the foot altogether. Elsie felt ashamed. When Craig's foot was unbound in the consulting room it was all misshapen. It didn't even look like a foot. It was like a big lump of gristle. Of course, this whole time, from his father running him over in the van, right until the present day, Craig hotly denied there was anything wrong with him. But he limped, he limped terribly. He was less steady on his feet than Big Sue round the corner, or Jane's stepdad, who had a wooden leg.

When you saw him from a distance, Craig looked fine. A fine figure of a lad, standing with all the other lads by the red Cortina, drinking their tinnies. In the summer they'd had a campfire out there and a barbeque. And it looked as if they were having fun. Someone said they were burning the body of a pit-bull that belonged to some other gang of lads. Elsie didn't think Craig would get involved in anything like that. He loved animals.

There was all that fuss, though, that August, when it was really hot, when the sweat stood out on you as soon as you went outdoors and everyone got fractious. The old couple in the bungalow by the Forsyths' house kept complaining about the lads' loud music from their Starsky and Hutch car. Elsie thought there was blame on all sides. The lads weren't doing anything so very bad. They were rowdy, but they were just showing off, for each other and for the few lasses who, stringy-looking and snapping gum, would come wandering past to eye the boys up as they took off their shirts and lifted weights and bricks and reddened their muscled bodies in the late sun. The lads were wrong to tell the old couple to haddaway to fuck. The old couple went too far, calling the police out three times and causing an almighty racket. And then, eventually, the storm broke. Elsie knew about these things from living in places rougher than this over the years: when the storm really breaks, it's the weakest who come off worst.

The old bloke went a bit doolally with bravado and he ran over to see to their radio himself with the baseball bat he kept in the downstairs toilet. The lads set their pit-bull onto him. His old wife watched, paralysed in their garden, as he was chased by the stubby black dog. It was a devil dog, like they said in the papers. She shook herself out of

7

her shock and tried to unlatch the gate for him. But he'd fallen down dead in the street already. He died of fright. 'He was a commando!' the old wife screamed at the lads. She was still screaming it when the paramedics were there and the lads had dragged and hidden their dog away. 'He was a commando!' at the top of her voice.

Elsie watched all this from her upstairs window, in a paralysis of her own. After the ambulance went, leaving the lads and their subdued dance music, she saw that Craig had noticed her watching their group. He stood at the back, uninvolved but implicated: the way he'd always been. His shirt was off and he had a broad, gym-toned chest that startled her almost as much as the sudden death in the street. He's got a proper man's body, she thought. At nineteen it seemed incongruous on him. As did his limp as he turned and went with the others into the Forsyths' dark house.

This afternoon Elsie stood by the red Starsky and Hutch car and paused before going in the Forsyths' gate. No one round here dared to knock on the Forsyths' door. All the women she knew thought she was mad, letting her son hang around with their gang. Elsie thought that it was all right, though. The women didn't understand. They didn't have grown sons. That Jane, Fran and Nesta would see, when theirs got to an age. You can't control them. Still, Elsie was relieved that the Forsyth brothers were away in prison. It was one thing hanging out with lads his own age, but she wouldn't be as happy seeing Craig under the influence of the Forsyth brothers, who must be in their thirties by now. They were in for burglary and the older one, Billy, had bitten off somebody's ear down the Burn.

The gate shrieked and clanged on its hinges behind her as she went up the garden path. The yard was in a dreadful state, with its rusted engine parts and old car batteries strewn on oil-blackened grass. Imagine someone tossing a match on that lot! Since the lads took the house over, the place had turned into a slum. They were living out their animal instincts, Elsie thought. She knocked on the kitchen door, wondering what Billy and Desmond Forsyth would say when they came back to the estates and saw all this.

One of Craig's mates – Steve, she thought he was called – came to the door. He had one of those home-made cigarettes in his mouth. She could tell it was drugs he had because there was a whiff of Schwarz spices, like her spice rack. Once, up the Sugar Factory, there'd been a craze on grass. They smoked it break-times, when the hooters sounded. Then Alison – what was her surname? Ginger lass from school – crushed her right hand on the production line when she went back to work stoned and Elsie kept off it after that.

This Steve was built up and beefy like the rest of Craig's gang. His skin was sunbed-tanned the colour of crème caramel. Elsie had tried that on her honeymoon in the big hotel at Scotch Corner. Her husband then, Craig's natural father, demonstrated how it would wobble like jelly on the plate and drool brown syrup down its sides. If you made a split in its skin with a spoon, it would heal itself seamlessly. This boy's flesh was precisely that buttery caramel shade, even on New Year's Eve.

'Yeah?'

Elsie rustled her carrier bag. 'Is Craig there? I'm his mam.' With this she reasserted her composure and authority. She wouldn't be outstared by this boy in his singlet and sweat pants. He had bleached hair grown long down his back, like one of the Gladiators. Like Craig himself, Elsie realised. That was what her son was setting out to be. He wanted to be like the Gladiators.

'He might be upstairs,' Steve said and drew in a deep lungful from his joint. The dark was coming in strong now and, Elsie thought, there was a sparkle in the air. She used to love New Year's Eve, but these past few years with Tom, he'd dissuaded her from having any fun. 'It's an excuse for the worst forms of licentiousness,' he sneered. He'd used his vocabulary on her. Once he had taught RE at, as he put it, 'secondary-modern level'. So that had put a stop to seeing in all the new years of recent memory. Tonight, the cold snap and the sudden dark, the weight of drink in her bag and the usual dance music coming out of the house behind Steve, all brought to mind for Elsie the idea that, if she really had a go, she could enjoy herself tonight. She asked Steve for a drag on his home-made ciggie.

'Fetch him, pet, would you?' she asked. There was an immediate kick from the joint. Her tonsils seemed to swell and the inside of her ears went prickly. 'Tell him his mum's brought him some tinnies.'

'Oh,' Steve said and turned to go. 'Listen – I'm sorry about your feller's trouble. Craig said something about it.'

Elsie shrugged and took another sip of that delicious, spicy smoke before giving it back to him. 'Just go and fetch Craig,' she said. When he went she stepped woozily inside the kitchen.

It was as filthy as she expected, though not as bad as some she'd seen. The sink was stacked as high as the taps with dirty glasses and plates and even foil dishes. The kitchen surfaces were atrocious with ashy dog-ends and smears of tomato sauce. That Steve had been making a sandwich for himself right on the side, no plate or chopping board. He might catch anything. Oh, but they're invulnerable at that age, Elsie thought, and forced herself not to go all mumsy. He was making himself a salad-cream and crisp sandwich. What kind of a meal was that? Elsie was planning to go home and have a microwave Balti. Put a lining on her stomach before she started drinking. She would hate to throw up in someone else's house.

She felt a pang of self-disgust. It was sharp and took a few moments to quell. Who was she, in her forties, to be planning a night out at someone's house, and taking precautions, making plans, not to vomit? Wasn't that sad? To be her age and to be carrying on as if she might well disgrace herself? The thought made her sad. What was saddest, she thought, was that there was no one here for her to be disgraceful *with*. It was never as bad if you had

10

someone egging you on to go daft and act as though you weren't middle-aged. You need pals about you, like Fran had Jane, or Judith had Big Sue. When they were all together, they didn't care if they were acting like kids and making a show. Simon and Sheila were married and they were each other's best pals. They had a laugh together. At the last Phoenix Court do, round Judith's, Simon had brought their karaoke machine and it was the life and soul of the party. I should have Tom, Elsie though miserably. Tom should be a laugh. He should be a sport. Look at Sheila and Simon – they were the street's dirty family, they always had that piddly smell about them. Why should they always have the nicest time? It was so typical, when Simon had the karaoke machine going, when his fat wife was singing 'Venus' and getting everyone to laugh, Elsie was throwing up in the downstairs toilet and Tom was solemnly patting her back and muttering prayers. He told her and anyone who cared to listen that Elsie was evicting foul spirits.

Waiting in the Forsyths' kitchen and catching sight of her own startled, blushing face in the cracked mirror, Elsie found herself thinking, I'm glad he's in care tonight. He's like an old fart. He's like my dad. I'm glad he's in the mansion on the hill outside Spennymoor. With deer in the snowy grounds and lovely walks. I'm glad he's in a bed next to a man who thinks he's Jesus. If he was here he'd only hold me back.

When she saw her face it was red with shame and the warmth of the kitchen. Look at all my lines, she thought dismally. They weren't even wrinkles, they were grooves. And I've warts, she thought: two of them, with wispy hairs. I look like a witch. The old image of a witch we had when we were kids. I've grown up to be an old witchy witch without realising it. And I've got a husband who's mad because he's disappointed and a son with a foot that will never get better. If I'm a witch, they'll all say I've put curses on them. I spoiled Craig's foot because I didn't take him down the doctors'. I thought they would take it off. I

11

didn't want them taking bits off his beautiful young body. It feels mine as much as his.

She could still think back to how they talked about his tied umbilical cord dropping off, days after delivery. Nineteen years ago, now. That withered end of skin, she thought, with sudden, peculiar clarity, is a piece of both of us. Whose is it, though? And maybe it's best that it dries up and dies and gets chucked away and then we won't need to decide where one of us ends and the other begins.

Footsteps upstairs. Her son was up there with who knew how many other lads and maybe lasses of his own age. It was like an adventure to them, having the run of this place, doing just what they wanted.

Elsie looked at herself again. Her hair had been auburn once and now it was threaded with silver. Tom called it salt-and-pepper hair and she liked that. There was more of the salt than ever these days and he was the one putting it there. Her pepper was thinning out. I'm losing my spice! she thought. Today she had her hair in bunches. I look like I'm pretending to be a child! What am I doing that for?

Then Craig was coming into the kitchen, in his tracksuit. 'Mam?'

When Craig wasn't home on Christmas Eve, he said it was because he'd been down the gym till closing and then he went straight to the Forsyths' house. They were having a Christmas party.

'Didn't you even think,' Elsie said, crying, on Boxing Day, 'that your poor old mother would want to see you on Christmas Eve?'

Haplessly he shrugged. 'I knew you would see me on Christmas morning. I knew I was coming home then. I thought that would be enough, Mam.'

She relented then, as she always did, content that he was doing his best, that he meant what he said. She had made him squirm with guilt *just enough*. He deserved the guilt, a part of it, she thought, because of everything she had gone through on Christmas Eve.

On the Thursday before Christmas, Tom had taken himself off to his bed. They had separate rooms now, which suited them both, because she found his religious paraphernalia gloomy and he had announced, quite calmly, in April, that the sins of the flesh disgusted him. He added that, even if they had been married, he still wouldn't want to sleep with her.

That suited Elsie, too. In her younger years she had been – what did they call it in the papers? Highly sexed. Her drive was high, that was it – but now she could take it or leave it.

Years ago, at the Sugar Factory, Elaine Francis once told her that you couldn't be too picky. Take what you can get. If you have standards that are too high, then you don't get any fun. You can't hang about waiting for Burt Reynolds. Old Elaine was crazy about Burt Reynolds. Take what you can, she cackled – she was like another mam to Elsie, a mother on the same production line – and you have yourself a nice time. Fellers are just fellers. One's as good as the next. You don't have to stick with them if you don't want. Give them a test drive! Give them a whirl!

So Elsie hadn't been too picky. You couldn't, in this life. Not in a town like Newton Aycliffe. Mind, she loved her town and, as the seventies went on, she found she loved the fellers here, too. Their bluff, slightly sour wit. Their pliable features and sometimes bulky Yorkshiremen's bodies. Or the stocky, proud forms of the fellers from Teesside. The allure and dark glamour of the broad Geordies, coming south. She was an expert.

She wasn't choosy, but she knew what she liked. Tom in his declining years – he'd never see fifty again – was a sight. He barely had a body to speak of, he was so thin. He dyed his hair the black of Kiwi boot polish and slicked it down with old-fashioned Brylcreem. It smelled of the fifties, of her uncles. He wore old suits. When he took to his bed, as he did at irregular intervals in the year, he'd pull the counterpane over his head and ignore her when she tried to be nice. He wouldn't get up to eat, to wash or to dress. He hardly got up to go to the toilet. As the days of not eating went by, he had to do that less and less and so he stayed under there, but he started to smell ripe and horrible. Elsie didn't even like to go in and check on him. The blinds were down and the room was a dusky pink. It smelled like Walter Wilson's cheese and deli counter used to smell, when everyone complained about it. On Christmas Eve he looked worse than ever. He'd been there three days and Elsie started to panic. Wasn't three days without eating fatal? Wasn't it the longest a human being could last?

'Tom,' she begged from the doorway. 'Tom, I'm worried about you.'

Slowly he rolled over to look at her. It was as if he could hardly be bothered even to do that much. His face was black with uncut beard.

Oh no, a small, rational, still sexy part of her mind thought to itself, I couldn't fancy him any more. I mean, I'm not choosy, but he's bloody awful.

'Leave me alone,' he said.

Elsie hurried out and, all the while, she was cursing Craig for not being there. If Craig was there and they had a car, they could bundle Tom inside, smother his protests, and get him to Casualty. Surely that's what normal people did. Of course, she thought, we can't do that. Instead, we have to have a terrible emergency. Tom has to die, or end up back in the loony bin.

She went outside and made a decision.

Elsie went straight to the most reliable person she knew. Fran lived opposite her, across the kids' play park. She was having tea on Christmas Eve with her husband Frank and her four kids.

'He's doing it again, Fran,' Elsie heard herself saying, in one breathless rush.

'Oh, he's not, is he?' Fran was the same age as Elsie. She knew everyone's business and kept it to herself. 'On Christmas Eve, too! That's awful.' Then she snapped into action. 'Frank, look after the bairns. I'm off over the way to see what I can do.'

Frank had a can of lager halfway to his mouth. 'But it's Christmas-time! The Santa van will be coming round in half an hour! We have to take the kids out to see Santa!'

Round the pine table the kids started to make a fuss, worried about missing Santa when he came in his van to their street. Fran silenced them with a look.

'I'll be back well before Santa comes. Now, Elsie, let's see how your Tom's doing.'

Frank gave his can a sceptical slurp as the women left. He's got a point, Fran thought, following Elsie across the park, I do let myself get too involved. She shuddered at the thought of what she might see when she reached Elsie's house.

All she saw, though, was a dirty old bloke lying in bed, too miserable to talk or acknowledge her. They stood at the foot of the bed.

'He used to look so dignified,' Elsie said. 'Didn't he?'

'Ay, he did,' Fran said. She'd always thought Tom had a shifty look about him, but she wasn't about to say.

'He'd hate it if he thought we were looking at him like this.'

She's talking like he's dead, Fran thought, fascinated. Then she saw that, to Elsie, he was as good as dead. She had written him off, not in a callous or underhanded way, but as if some pressing circumstance had made their love or enjoyment of each other impossible now.

Elsie said, 'We'll have to phone and they'll take him away again, won't they?'

Fran nodded. 'I reckon so.'

'I thought he'd be all right this time. We both did. We banked on it at one point. But look at him!'

'Do you want me to phone?'

'I worry that they notch it up. Like, three times caught and then you're out. Like rounders or cricket. Do you think they'll keep him in for good?'

'Don't worry about that now,' Fran said. 'We'll just get the doctor in first.'

'Will they come out at Christmas?'

'We can try.' Fran was heading back into the hallway, glad to be away from the smell of unwashed body.

'I want them to say he's no good,' Elsie was saying fiercely to herself. 'Really, I want them to keep him in for good.' She looked at his face then and realised that he might have heard her.

While Fran looked in the phone-messages book for the number she'd had to phone the previous year, she heard Elsie shouting out, 'Where's Craig? Where's our Craig?'

The GP arrived just after the council Santa came round in his van to see everyone from Phoenix Court. Fran dashed out for two minutes to be with Frank and the bairns as the council Santa passed round Swizzel lollies. Across the road, at the Forsyths' house, there was dance music blasting out, and Fran would have put money on it that Craig was over there. When Santa left she said she had to get back to Elsie, and would Frank put the bairns to bed?

He pulled a face. 'It's like when daft Nesta vanished, all over again,' he said, his voice going high in anger. 'You always get too involved.'

Fran tutted at him, kissed the bairns, and went back to see Elsie.

The doctor was there, a dapper little man in a dark suit, a sprig of mistletoe in his lapel and a twist of tinsel around the handle of his leather bag. In the kitchen he was insisting that Elsie stay at home and drink sugary tea. 'Come and visit your husband on Boxing Day,' he said coaxingly, 'and try to have a merry Christmas.'

Fran said, 'I'm a neighbour.' The doctor looked up and nodded at her.

'He's my common-law husband,' said Elsie sulkily.

'Yes,' said the GP as he straightened up. 'Well.' Then he headed out to the paramedics' van which, now that Fran stared through the window after him, had Tom under red blankets in the back. He looked strapped down. Blokes in overalls were looking down at him and closing the back doors. Then they were all gone.

'Do you want to stop with us the night?' Fran asked Elsie. Around them the house seemed dark and cold. The decorations Elsie had put up – ludicrous, oversized reindeer from Bob's Bargains Centre – seemed pitiful. 'You can't stop by yourself,' she added gently.

'I'll wait for my Craig coming home,' Elsie said, gritting her teeth. 'My lad will be home for Christmas. You better get back to your family.'

And that's all the thanks I'll get, Fran thought as she went for her coat. That Elsie's a hard one.

Elsie surprised her then. 'You're a star, Fran,' she said, clutching her mug of tea. 'Happy Christmas, pet.'

'I've brought you some tinnies to see the new year in,' she told him.

His face brightened as she pulled them out of her bag. She twisted her little finger on the plastic thing that held them together and sucked it when she gave him his gift.

'Ace,' he said.

'I thought they'd be the right thing.' She smiled. 'And I didn't think you'd be coming home to watch the New Year on telly with me.'

'Oh.' Now he looked pained. 'We're doing something here. Nothing much. Just a bit of booze. Sorry, Mam.'

She shrugged inside her winter coat. 'I'll let you off this time. I'm away out myself.'

'Yeah?' And look at him looking pleased, she thought. He looks like his natural dad. The same mouthful of flashing teeth. His neck strong like a china horse.

'It's a party at number sixteen,' she said.

'Penny's party?'

'Who?'

'Oh . . . she's the lass whose house it was to start with,' he said. 'Well, it was her mam's, but her mam ran away and Penny invited her friends to live with her.'

'Oh yes.' Now Elsie remembered the stories Jane had told her about Liz, Penny's mam, who disappeared with a bus driver. 'Nice lass, is she, Penny?'

He glanced down. 'She's all right.' He twisted a can free and popped it open.

'Have you taken a shine to her?'

'Who, Penny?' He smirked, hating being caught out like this.

'I'll have a look at her tonight,' Elsie said. 'Have a word and see if I approve.'

He tutted.

'Nah,' she said. 'That'd be good, that. A young lass with her own place. That's what you want.'

'Yeah, yeah.' He shrugged, tossing his hair – that Gladiator hair, as Elsie now thought of it. 'Look, Mam, thanks for the booze.'

All of a sudden she felt dismissed. It was time to go back to her own life. He was already in his.

'I saw Tom today.'

'You went all the way up to Sedgefield on New Year's Eve?'

'Someone has to.'

Craig looked down again. He had no intention of visiting his stepdad, and couldn't bring himself to tell her yet. 'How is he?'

'All right. He wants to come home already. Says he's fine again.'

'He's not, though, is he?'

'I'm not sure.' She hugged her carrier bag, with its freight of gin and cigarettes.

'Mam, man . . . he hits you.'

'Oh . . .'

'He's done it before and he'll do it again.'

She seemed to take a deep breath. She wanted to yell upstairs to Craig's pal Steve and get him to bring that funny fag back. She wanted to inhale spice again. 'Oh, let's not go on about him now, eh? I want a holiday from my life. Is that all right, pet? You can have one. You're having one all the time, aren't you?'

He shrugged. She grinned at him and touched his elbow briefly. 'No, that's great, Craig. I think it's great. Have a nice time. But I want a holiday too. Tonight I don't want to be thinking about what to do about Tom.'

'I wasn't the one bringing him up.'

'I know you weren't,' she agreed. 'But anyway. Listen, I'm going.'

'Thanks for the tinnies.'

'Happy New Year, pet.'

He opened the door for her. 'Ay. Same to you, Mam.'

Two

It was the year when they ate almost nothing but cornflakes. It was open house round number sixteen Phoenix Court and people came and went, throughout the year. To each new arrival, the fresh faces passing through, the old lags would say, 'You'll soon be eating cornflakes for breakfast, dinner and tea. And there'll always be crises in the middle of the night, and you'll sit in your dressing gowns, eating cornflakes.'

No matter whose turn it was shopping at Red Spot in the town centre, they always came back with a family-size box. They were cheap and they were homely. 'Well,' Penny said, 'what more can you expect? That's just what I am!' It was Penny who started the craze off in the first place. Last winter, when it was just her and Andy, she began the tradition of cornflakes at midnight. Gradually the house filled with strange faces, and they all wound up sitting there with breakfast bowls, crunching away.

My house, my traditions, she thought proudly on New Year's Eve. She had been making pizza for the party and the kitchen was full of steam and the comforting aroma of tomato sauce bubbling on the hob. The surfaces were dusted heavily with flour and the lopped-off corners of dough. There was a bottle of wine open already, and the carpet had flour trampled into it. Penny quietly poured herself some wine and gave a silent toast: 'To our house.' She tipped the glass and relished the bitterness of the wine. A year of having everyone around her.

Penny's mother had walked out a year ago. She had run away with her new boyfriend Cliff, a bus driver, shocking the street. How could she leave her daughter, a girl not even out of her teens? The women of Phoenix Court were scandalised, but they knew how wayward and glamorous Liz, Penny's mother, was. They knew she didn't fit in, she couldn't be a part of the normal life they had in this street. Of course she had to go exploring romantic pastures new, her swarthy, sexy boyfriend in tow. Word had it he'd whisked her away on a stolen double-decker bus that was meant to be headed for Newcastle. Good luck to her, most of the ladies of the Court had concluded.

They could also see how resourceful Penny was. She'd had a year alone, and even had a feller living in with her. That young bloke Andy, a skinny, rather pretty boy from Darlington. They were all up to that these days, having their boyfriends living in with them. Everyone was glad young Penny had some protection. For a while there was that other lad, Vince, but he was gone now. He was a teacher up at the comprehensive, so that proved everything was above board and moral. A teacher. For the summer there had been a whole load of students round there, down from Durham, cramming into the three-bedroomed council house. There'd been some noise, but nothing like what came from the Forsyths' house directly across the road. Now, though, come New Year's Eve, number sixteen was empty apart from Penny and her best friend Andy. They were throwing the house open for a party.

What a year! Penny thought. She'd liked having the students in. Her best friends among that lot were what they called crusties, which meant they wore dreads and tie-dye and smelled of wool. The smoked joints all day long and went from one music festival to another in a camper van borrowed from one of their mothers. They were all quite well off.

The summer had been an idyllic one, as far as Penny was concerned. They seemed to spend three months on pink candlewick bedspreads on the hillock of grass outside her house. Her new friends played in the play park and ran tearing about the place with all the little kids. The mothers from round there looked on disapprovingly for a while as Adele and Alan and Marsha, with their southern accents and scruffy clothes, helped the bairns to the top of the climbing frame, restrung the tyre swing for them and showed them how to roller-blade. Penny watched almost proudly as her crusty friends became an unofficial play scheme. The older girls had crushes on Sven, the blond Swedish boy. He had one of those crystal-clear accents, like someone out of Abba. Penny read novels, one after another – she read fifty that summer – and admired the fresh-scrubbedness of him. Sven was pink and golden and tall, but he was a microbiologist.

The only times away from the park and the kids and the sun on Phoenix Court was when they took Adele's mother's camper van to the music festivals. They vanished for weekends at a time. Penny went with them only once, to Glastonbury, which was nice enough, but she couldn't bear the toilet arrangements. She loved her tan, though, which seemed at its height at Glastonbury. She was the colour of Linda McCartney vegetarian sausages. So was Andy. Andy! Who'd been a Goth in his youth, he claimed.

Penny fetched out a pile of breakfast bowls, ready for the buffet. Was she really going to have cornflakes as part of the buffet? It was true that she found them comforting. They were one of her favourite things. But there was a danger that, when they came trooping in with their cans of lager and bottles of spirits, in their glad rags and ready to party, all her neighbours from Phoenix Court might think she was odd. Maybe she could just say that she expected the party to go on until breakfast-time.

There were noises of banging about upstairs. Andy was getting ready, having a clothes crisis. She hoped he was all right now. Earlier this afternoon Fran from over the way had been round. Fran was in her forties and careworn. Frumpy, Penny's mother might have called her in an uncharitable moment. She came to see if they wanted any help preparing the party. Penny thought that was good of her, especially since she was always busy with all her kids. She reminded Penny of the old woman in the shoe. Fran had been particularly pleased last summer that Penny's student friends had taken to looking after the children.

With Andy there this afternoon, Fran had made the easy mistake of asking if Vince was coming back for the party.

Andy's face had fallen. He said something about never knowing what Vince was up to, and disappeared upstairs. Penny hadn't seen him again all afternoon. He stayed in the narrow bedroom that he and Vince had shared for six months.

Fran looked as if she knew she'd hurt him, but wasn't sure how.

Penny said, 'They were very close. Vince just ran off in August and he's never been in touch with Andy at all.'

'Oh,' said Fran. She went back to blowing up the balloons. 'I thought it was something like that.'

Ever since Vince had gone, Penny had been working hard at keeping his name out of things. She hid the fairly regular cards that came addressed only to her. She fretted at night about whether to keep Andy up to date with Vince's doings, his new teaching job, his whereabouts. Andy pretended that he didn't care and hardly mentioned his lover's name. All that autumn he was angry.

Vince had made his announcement about his new teaching job on Penny's birthday. This was in August, and he had commandeered the crusties' camper van to take the household on a day trip to Lake Windermere. It was a drizzly, grey day. As Adele drove them over the Pennines, the others sat in the back laughing and drinking Montezuma.

Penny loved her birthdays because her mother had always put on a good show for her. It was the best day in the year. This was her first one without Liz, but her housemates – Vince especially – tried to make it up to her. News from Liz and her beau came irregularly. They sent back jaunty notes from the seaside resorts they were visiting, one after another, stitching a ragged hem around the country. Andy said to Penny, 'She's gone all devil-may-care,' his eyes wide with envy. Penny pointed out that Liz was always like that, and Cliff, the bus driver, only made her worse.

It seemed as if Liz was never coming back. Vince took Penny's birthday plans into his own hands. Although he would never say it, he felt responsible for her. He was her friend, and Andy's boyfriend, he lived in her house, but he was also her sixth-form English teacher. On the way to Windermere he watched her and took note of a certain strain as she laughed and drank tequila. It was as if she felt pressed into having a good time. She was enjoying herself for the sake of her friends. The house-mates, Vince knew, spent a fair deal of time speculating more or less wildly about Penny's mother. Neighbours gave them a few juicy titbits. They knew she had run off with a man. But there was also funny talk about her going off for a sex-change operation. Others said that she had already had it, that Penny's mam had once been Penny's dad. None of her house guests ever dared to ask Penny outright. The others suspected that Andy and Vince, as her closest friends, knew the full story, but they were loyal to her. Actually, Vince didn't know the details, but he knew that Andy did. Andy and Penny had become very close in the last few months. The conversations they had shared, and their dual role looking after the house and all its comings and goings, seemed, although he didn't want this, to drive a wedge between him and Andy.

Andy was settled here, now, with Penny and the others. Vince was a latecomer. He was out of place. He felt too prim for the cheerful mess and mucking in of the house on Phoenix Court. When he left his father's house, up by the school, moving out in desperation, it had at first seemed the perfect answer. He and Andy were doing all right. But they all preyed on his nerves, sitting about doing nothing, playing easy-listening music as loud as it would go, eating cornflakes and leaving towels on the floor. For months he

24

gritted his teeth and at least over the summer he had less work to do. But Vince knew he couldn't stay there for the winter term.

In August, when they sat on the pebbled shore at Bowness and threw chips for the grubby swans that came romping out of the shallows towards them, Vince was going through all this. He didn't mean to break the news that day, spoiling the already jeopardised birthday, but Penny had a way of tuning into things, even things she would rather not hear, and broadcasting them.

'I wish we could have brought you somewhere nicer,' he told her. They were all sitting in a row on the damp wooden breakwater. Andy sat on the other side of Marsha, Adele, Sven and Alan. He was picking scabs of mildew off the wood. The others were laughing at a fat teenager struggling at the end of the jetty to get himself into his kayak. When he sat down, he looked wedged inside, and there was something sticking up at the opposite end of the boat, making him appear to have six-foot legs.

Penny told Vince that she'd always loved it here. She remembered her dad bringing her to stay at the youth hostel when she was a kid. He'd been disgusted because they made them do chores to pay for their keep. He thought he was on holiday. And he thought the people who were staying there with them looked unkempt.

That afternoon they walked some distance around the lake's edge. They spent half an hour in a chintzy café, hidden between trees, where Andy upset a milk jug and laughed louder and longer than the others. 'I'm a bundle of nerves today!' he told the waitress as she wordlessly mopped the oil cloth for him.

Later their party crossed a wide field and climbed a series of rotting fences and dry-stone walls to get to a private beach. Vince led them straight to the most secluded and gentlest spot by the edge of the lake and the others were content to squander the rest of the birthday afternoon there.

Trudging through the matted grass to the lakeside,

Penny hooked up with Andy and asked him what the matter was. As usual he couldn't put it into words. He felt like something awful was happening, he said, but he couldn't be sure. Penny laughed and said that there was always something awful happening somewhere in the world, you could bank on it. Andy said, 'No, I mean, to *me*. I feel like you do having a tooth taken out with a freezing injection.'

'Oh,' said Penny.

Vince was striding ahead, leading Sven and the others to the quiet shore, briskly in control and jollying them along. Just like a teacher, she thought. He sounded hard and bright. It sounds like he's made his mind up about something. She kept an eye on Andy and he looked exactly like someone who had been put in his place. But not a cross word has been said all day, she thought. It was typical of Andy and Vince to have a row without exchanging a single word.

The wind and rain abated, but it was still cool. While they played unselfconsciously on the shore, they kept their coats on. Vince smiled and hissed something to Penny about wishing it was warmer, wanting to see Sven strip off and splash about in the lake. He had carried out this flirtation with Sven for several months, but they all knew it was a joke. Ever since the day Vince had been interrupted in the bath by Sven letting himself in for a pee, nonchalantly carrying on a conversation with the mortified Vince. But, Vince had confided later, the Swede had the most beautiful penis he had ever seen. And no, he couldn't say why. Andy had looked miffed at the time, but surely Vince's attentions to the bluff, resolutely straight Sven couldn't be narking him today? She knew there was more to this.

They stayed there until the last minute, when it started to pour and turn dark in earnest. Penny was content to sit on the shore and watch the others climb trees, hang from branches, skim stones, dash about. She watched them make a holiday out of her birthday. They did it expertly, with the ease of people used to pleasing themselves. Her house-mates were all in their early to mid-twenties and didn't mind playing at being children as much as she, in her late teens, did. Then Vince was sitting beside her on a flat rock, tugging up the collar of his purple suit jacket and brushing the sandy hair from his eyes. She thought that the two of them together must look like the Mock Turtle and the Gryphon. She kept this to herself, however, knowing it would derail Vince into a long, cryptic discourse on Lewis Carroll.

She said, 'You're going to go, aren't you?'

He looked across. 'I applied for a job down south. And I got it.'

'South.' She whistled. 'Does our school know?' Her heart was doing twenty to the dozen. She had provoked him into honesty and now she couldn't believe they were discussing this so blandly. She had asked him wishing only to be proved wrong.

'I won't go leaving anybody high and dry.' He had gone cold again, staring at the lake. Motorboats were slashing past in the near distance. You could see people sat on the back, holding wine glasses carefully and staring at Penny's birthday party on private land.

'But you're cutting your links with Aycliffe.'

'I think I have to, Penny.'

'I've known you would sooner or later.'

'I've loved living at number sixteen.' He smiled. 'If anything's kept me and Andy going past our sell-by date, it's having time together in the home you've made for us.'

She shrugged. 'Hey.'

'No, it's true, pet. You brought us all together. Look at the rest of them.' He nodded towards Sven and the others. Sven had his faded jeans rolled up to his knees, making a show of plodging out in water that would be freezing. 'They all love you. You have a gift for connecting people.'

'That's from you, teaching me E. M. Forster.'

He smirked. 'Right.'

'I wish you'd stay, Vince.'

'I know. And I'm leaving you in the lurch, mopping up after me. Andy won't be much fun for a while after I'm gone.'

'He's not going to be happy,' she said lightly as they both looked at Andy. He was self-absorbedly slinging stones into the brown water, trying and failing to make them skim. For that day he was dressed like someone out of Blur, or, as Vince pointed out, himself at the age of nine.

Vince was saying, 'I'm not flattering myself. I don't think Andy will be devastated to finish with me. But he's not going to be ecstatic, either.'

It seemed to Penny that she'd had almost a year of them charting their separate graphs of each other. They never had tallied and both had – if she were honest – worn her out. The treacherous part of herself gave a pang of relief at Vince's news.

'You never saw a future for the two of you, did you?' she asked.

'We met when we were seventeen. We thought we were the only two puffs in the northeast. So of course we mean a lot to each other now.' He gave a laugh that was almost mocking. 'Now that we're so sophisticated. Nah, we still mean a lot. But I don't know what he wants any more.'

Penny looked down. 'I've known him less than a year and he's changed so much in that time. He's become more . . . I don't know.'

'He's opened out,' Vince said. 'I suppose he's more amenable to people. I'm glad the two of you have become friends.'

She looked at him, thinking he was being sarcastic. But he wasn't. He felt that he was passing Andy on to someone. It was a relief Andy had someone there. Vince remembered being surprised at how solid a team Andy and Penny had become. He first saw it when he himself moved in, back in March. One Thursday night, hauling a few bags and boxes of essentials, Vince had at last left his dad's place. He found the squat's inhabitants eating bowls of cereal in the living room, watching *EastEnders* in a smog

28

of Benny Hedges. The household had just opened up to let him in and, even though it was to Andy's single bed in the narrowest room that Vince automatically went that night, he was treated by Andy and Penny as just another nonpaying guest. On some unspoken level they realised that Vince was, in his own blind way, passing through. Andy had seemed equivocal, almost diffident about his presence.

How to tell Vince that? Penny wondered. Vince who thought Andy clung to him and needed passing on from carer to carer. Vince who, thin-lipped and anxious, now seemed on the verge of changing his mind about moving on, suddenly fearful of upsetting Andy. Penny thought Andy was looking gorgeous that afternoon. His uncertainty and nerves brought up to the surface everything that was most endearing in him. When anyone talked to him he flinched and smiled shyly, struggling to join in with them.

Vince resolutely said, 'No. I do have to go south.'

She laughed when he came downstairs at last, dressed up for the party, because he was in a cowboy outfit. The least excuse and there he'd be dressed up as something. It was funny tonight, with him standing there in leather chaps and a red and black plaid shirt, because her song for the afternoon had been 'Rhinestone Cowboy'. She had played it again and again as she cooked and prepared.

Standing in the kitchen doorway, Andy adjusted his red bandanna, mystified by her laughter. He was often perplexed by what Penny and her friends laughed at. He assumed they must have college jokes, or jokes that went above his head.

Penny ran the tape back once more to play him the song. When it started, he realised the joke and relaxed.

She snorted. 'You were meant to be down here, helping with the party food.'

The heat in the kitchen went streaming out of the opened window, into the dark with the cigarette smoke. Outside there was a thin patter of snow starting up.

'Oh.' Andy shrugged. 'I had a crisis about what to wear.'

Last year the organisation of the Hogmanay party had been the same: Penny running about until the last minute. She'd be a drunken mess by the time the guests arrived. She'd forget to get changed again, too. Well, the guests could take her or leave her. Andy would always be immaculate, of course. She looked him up and down and decided that he made quite a sweet cowboy.

Our second party! she marvelled, and poured herself a second toast. Celebrating over a year of cohabitation.

Andy poured his own glassful, leaned across and kissed her cheek. 'Happy New Year,' he said, and she could smell his freshly washed hair under the bandanna. He lived in a borrowed room, signed on for income support and housing benefit, but he bought expensive shampoo, even with his hair shaved on number seven. She was glad he was dressed as a cowboy tonight. For an hour or more this morning he'd been digging through Liz's wardrobes in Penny's room. He tried on a couple of her dressy outfits. Tacky dresses, he called them, and he looked stunning in them, she had to admit. Penny wouldn't have refused him if he'd asked to borrow one for the party. At the same time she wouldn't have been altogether happy seeing him come downstairs done up as her absent mother. And the party guests might prove a problem. She wasn't sure how they'd deal with her house-mate in drag.

'Do you reckon we'll get everyone turning up?' she asked worriedly.

'Course we will. They love a good do round here, don't they?' He was distracted by the blinds rattling against the open window. 'The wind must be picking up. Should I close that?'

'We'll be getting a blizzard.' Oddly, the thought only made her feel cosy. She liked the idea of the house with a partyful of people trapped inside, a snowstorm raging out there in the estate. Imagine being snowed in and the party just going on!

Andy went to shut the window. As he did so, a sudden gust sent a black slip of paper spinning into the room.

'What's that?' He jumped back, slamming the window.

Penny picked it off the carpet. 'An empty After Eights packet.' She turned the black envelope over in her fingers.

'Oh,' Andy went to change the tape.

When Penny was little and couldn't sleep, she and her dad would eat After Eight mints in the kitchen at night. They would leave messages for each other pushed inside the packets, hidden in odd places. She looked inside this one, but there was nothing there.

We used the black envelopes from After Eights to tell each other the important things. It worked. The messages got across.

And it wasn't like dad was a bad communicator. He brought me up wonderfully. He knew the things to say. Some of the women I know, they were brought up knowing nothing. When they had their first period, they thought their insides were coming out. Dad told me everything. Sometimes sitting as we watched the washing machine thumping round all night. Sometimes roving miles in the car through the dark, sometimes via black envelopes. I suppose the ones in the envelopes were the ones we wanted to keep.

Keepsakes. It's a good word. I have a green After Eights box, I've kept for years. Like a tiny filing cabinet, crammed with messages on different coloured bits of paper. They're almost worn through with rereading. Funny what you keep. All the things dad told me. Then, when he became Liz, what she went on telling me. Things about me, things about her. I had this feeling that, when the After Eights mint box, when the tiny filing cabinet was full, then I'd know everything. My growing up would be complete.

It's full, all right. You can choose at random, pluck out an envelope, the box will still seem full. Inside, some precious sliver of wisdom or nonsense, still smelling of minty fondant.

That box caused a row between Andy and me. Not too long ago I found him in Liz's room, now my room, with the envelopes spread on the bed. I walked in and found him absorbed in them, opening out folded sheets and poring over the whole set. Greedy for the full story.

'I never worried about people going through my stuff,' I said. 'I let everyone live here and I never thought it would happen. I'm too trusting.'

Andy was trying to push the letters back in their pockets, to sort out the damage he'd done. I worried that he'd spoiled them, or ruined their order. He stammered apologies.

'I'm just nosy,' he offered at last. 'I see something like this and I can't help myself.'

'But it's my stuff! My private letters!'

'I didn't know that! Not until I found them!'

'You shouldn't have been here!'

'I was bored!'

'Bored? So you go rooting around in my stuff?'

He looked exasperated with himself. 'Yes!'

I laughed at him. 'Have you read all these?'

He sat back down on the bed. 'I've been reading them all afternoon. Sorry, Pen. But . . .' He shook his head. 'You're so lucky. To have all this. It's like all you need to know about life. Important things and daft things. But things you'd forget if they weren't written down. All about you and . . . your parent.'

So he knew the thing about Liz. Now he knew that she didn't start out as my mam. He'd read her letters beginning to end, and they started out signed at the bottom, 'love, dad.'

'Just call her Liz,' I said. 'That's what she wants to be called. If she ever comes back, that is.'

'I think she's an amazing person,' he said, which made me laugh again.

'Maybe she is.' I started packing away the notes. He'd laid them out very carefully, I saw, in precise order. Trust Andy to look after my things. 'Did I ever tell you . . .' I said. 'About Liz, when she was my dad and I'd just been born . . . and he took me out to look at the moon?' I tried to find the piece of paper where he'd written this down. One of the very early ones. 'He said we were both struck by lightning, and that's why I grew up with black fingerends and bad headaches.'

'How can you believe stuff like that?'

'When it's all you're told, you have to. And with Liz . . . you end up believing anything.'

'My parents didn't leave me anything much,' he said. 'They never got a chance.'

He'd already told me how they'd died. He was brought up mostly by his gran, is what I'd gathered. When he moved in here he brought hardly any stuff with him. Andy is someone who comes without baggage. Me, I've got baggage coming out of everywhere.

'But that means you're rooted somewhere,' Andy said. 'All this stuff is full of memories. It's your life and it means you belong.'

I wasn't convinced. 'But without it, I could up sticks and go anywhere. Like Liz did. Like you could, anytime.'

'It's easy to get rid of stuff. Just chuck it. That's what charity shops are for. Get rid.'

He knew I couldn't do that. Something ties me here. Not just waiting for my mam to come back.

I put away the box in her wardrobe. Among all her things. Wigs, roped beads and crusted, glittering fake jewellery. A selection of mandarin fingernails. 'Oh . . .' I said. 'You could guess from this lot that she's a tranny. What self-respecting woman would have a wardrobe like this?'

He chuckled. '*You* have now, pet.'

'Hm. So I have.'

Three

For years Mark Kelly had believed himself to be surrounded by people. His life was made too complex and
problematic by a constant stream of relations and friends,
and friends of friends. People crowded into his life and
pressed their concerns upon him. He had grown up
wanting to stand aloof, but always felt himself pulled right
in.

His ex-wife Sam had a thought or two about that.
'Crap. You love getting mixed up in it all. You're just
bloody nosy. You're more interested in what's going on
with other people than you are in your own family.' This
was one Saturday afternoon when he came to pick up his
eight-year-old daughter Sally. Sally watched the familiar
row go backwards and forwards. Nothing much changed
for Sam and Mark. Mark was still living in the flat in
Phoenix Court where they had all lived together. 'You
couldn't bear to leave that street,' Sam jeered. 'You think
too much of sitting with all those old women and their
tittle-tattle.'

Sam didn't think much of the inhabitants of Phoenix
Court. She thought herself a cut above. When Mark told
her that, she flew off the handle. She told him he didn't
know what he was talking about. He should have wanted
more, he should have provided better for his child and
wife. He should have been more ambitious. Couldn't he
see it was driving her mad, living on that lousy council
estate? Of course she wanted to be out and in a new
Barratt home near Darlington. She lived in one now, with
Bob, a policeman. Mark had to travel through Darlington
on the bus to pick up and drop off Sally at weekends. On

Sunday nights Sam would put their child in the bath and quiz her over what her father's life was like now.

Now Mark was living with no one. For a while there had been a man living there with him. Richard, who had befriended Sally and whom Sally talked about a lot when she returned home to her mam. Sam would listen pursed-mouthed to this, and could barely restrain a crow of triumph when, one day, Sally announced that Dad's friend Richard had returned to Leeds.

'Your little boyfriend's gone then, has he, Mark?' Sam said this as she pushed her daughter's arms into her anorak. Sally pulled free and put it on for herself.

'He wasn't my boyfriend,' said Mark, glowering. He didn't think his life was any of Sam's business now. Whoever came and went into his life had nothing to do with her. He, after all, never asked about her dopey policeman, did he?

Sam gazed at him as he stood in the porchway of her new Barratt home. She was surprised by a surge of affection and physical desire for this man. It was the way the light came in through the porch and lit up the many shades of blue of his tattoos. His all-over markings shone in that light. They reminded Sam of their years together. There was no one on this planet with a body like Mark's. 'Are you OK then?' she asked in a more subdued tone. He nodded, and took Sally.

This exchange had been quite recent. Mark had lost his lodger in the small flat. Sam and her policeman were taking Sally to the in-laws for Christmas. Mark would be alone for much of the festive period. He couldn't believe that his days would be empty of people. That wasn't like his life at all. On Boxing Day he had resorted to visiting his mother-in-law Peggy, who still lived nearby. He took a present for her new child Iris, who was barely two and walking about all over the place. Peggy could see how down Mark was. But she was glad of a quiet time, herself. Christmas two years ago, when Sally had been kidnapped and they'd all gone running about like mad things, was a mite too busy for her liking. She let her tattooed boy go, and watched him walk down the garden path through the snow. She felt fond of him, and sad for him. He was meant for better things. Peggy wondered if Mark in his mid-thirties thought that he'd spoiled his potential.

He was glad of this party tonight. At one point he was going to throw one of his own in the flat, but thought better of it. They'd all come snooping round, fascinated by how he was managing on his own. Luckily this do was on at number sixteen. The kids here were welcoming, he thought. That was how he thought of them, as kids. This was Mark in the second half of his thirties, looking at the inhabitants of number sixteen – Andy, Penny and their fluctuating roll call of hangers-on – and thinking, youth.

What a frame of mind to arrive in! Knocking on a door on New Year's Eve feeling old and alone. He forced an uneasy grin and knocked again. The music within was already fairly loud, so he couldn't be *that* early.

When Andy opened the front door, he was still laughing at something. To Mark he looked the picture of carefree youth in his check shirt, his cowboy outfit. It was very nearly an uncharitable pang of irritation that Mark tried to squash at the sight of his host. Andy looked as though he hadn't a care in the world. But at least he looked pleased to see Mark.

'Thank God for someone sensible!' Andy gabbled, shooing him into the hallway. It was still festooned with Christmas decorations, and a fresh load of balloons and streamers and holly hacked in armfuls from the Burn. Number sixteen was done up like a grotto and Mark's heart began to warm to the idea of a party. Coloured tissue paper covered all the lights and the air was scented with mulled wine and pizza. Andy was saying, 'So far we've had that mad Nesta, old Elsie from the corner, getting pissed already, and us. Nesta's brought her kids and she's feeding them all the finger buffet. Give us your coat.'

He led Mark into the living room, showing him off to

the others like a prize. 'Where's Penny?' asked Mark, and Andy explained that she was upstairs hurriedly repairing herself before the rest of the party arrived. Some of her student friends, who had managed to return for one night, were conscientiously milling and making conversation with the neighbours. As Mark was introduced, Andy went to answer the back door to Fran and Frank and their four kids. Dirty Sheila and Simon came in behind, with their son and depressed daughter. Andy wondered who told them all they could bring their kids. He looked at Nesta, who was forcing her dozy-looking daughters to eat more of the nibbles. She waved a corner of sausage roll under the nose of the baby in her arms. Andy thought that kid looked like a Martian. It was thin and pinched-looking. Nesta never took it out of the pram. The poor bairn lay on its front all the time and craned its neck like a tortoise. In its mother's arms for once, the baby's head was inclined backwards almost ninety degrees.

Andy looked across the living room as it started to fill up, and saw that Penny's student friends were staring at Mark. They had never seen him this close up before. Marsha, Sven, Alan and now Adele gathered around him and Mark let them, chatting politely, saying no, his daughter was actually with his ex-wife the night, and no, he hadn't come with anyone else, not even his mother-in-law, who was still one of his best friends. The house-mates and the neighbours seemed familiar with the sketchy outlines of his life. They knew he had been left alone over Christmas, poor Mark. They think they know everyone's business, Andy thought, and then, when they get that bit closer, when they get a glimpse of the full picture, then they see that it's different to what they expected. Duller or more complicated or more exciting than ever they thought. And who was prepared to go that far? To see the full picture of someone's life? Andy surprised himself, thinking this lucidly and bitterly so early in the night, only a few drinks down the line. There were hours yet to get disgusted about how committed people could or couldn't be.

And, like the others, Andy was staring at Mark's tattoos. Mark made no bones about them and, last summer, he had taken up jogging round and round the estate. Two circuits was a mile, he'd cheerfully tell anyone as he went streaking past, a blur of green and blue in his skimpy shorts and sleeveless T-shirt. He was the colours of a bad laser copy, parading himself at speed, thudding round the intricate streets. The neighbours would look up and think, There goes that tattooed feller with no shame.

But when you got close up – and this was the effect they were getting now – you saw all the fine detailing. Eyes painted on eyes, digits and letters, tarot symbols, fabulous horned and feathered beasts, fragments of clockwork and cartography, of texts and petals and microscopic creatures. No wonder they stared. Mark just seemed to drink in their regard and talked, talked easily. Andy was forming the opinion that the man was full of himself. He had these tattoos just to make a show of himself. That was fair enough: Andy wouldn't and couldn't find fault with that. But he instinctively distrusted anyone shamelessly extrovert. Now Mark was calling over and asking Nesta how she was, and Fran, and Elsie. Elsie needed no encouragement. Suddenly she was by their sides, the gin glass tilted to her mouth as she spoke, as if she was scared of someone taking it. Her pigtails waggled as she spoke.

'Hey, Mark, you'd better watch out!' She smiled. 'Frank's here.'

They looked over at Fran's tubby, ginger husband. He was unloading a carrier bag of tinnies and talking to their bairns.

'So?'

'Last I heard, he was still after you.'

Mark tutted.

'After you for what?' asked Andy, intrigued despite himself. He knew that Elsie made things up just to stir up trouble for others and interest for herself, but something in the way she disclosed things made you ask, 'And what next? What else, Elsie?'

'Frank thinks Mark's got a thing going with Fran,' Elsie burst out, tinkling the ice in her glass. ''Cause he was always over there on Tuesday afternoons.'

'We used to watch films on Tuesday afternoons,' Mark said with a shrug to Andy. Andy could have sworn he saw a blush in the gaps between tattoos. 'It's daft. People will talk about anything.' Mark was cross about the whole business, really, since the idle gossip had meant an end to video afternoons with Fran. They used to share a bottle of Country Manor and watch TV movies. The video shop down the precinct rented tapes of those cheapo weepies. They were usually true-to-life stories, about people with something wrong with them or lives that turn suddenly tragic. Both Mark and Fran loved them, especially the endings, where the screen turns black and captions go up to explain what has happened to the real lives of the real people since the events of the film. He blamed Elsie for stirring up the trouble, and thought about taking her to task about it now. She had got the neighbours talking about how Fran spent secluded indoor afternoons with Mark Kelly, her living-room blinds drawn, even in high summer. She spent days indoors with a man on the dole, while her own husband was out at work. But that was all over now.

Elsie asked, 'How's Sam and the new baby?'

Mark gritted his teeth. Was she setting out to be deliberately offensive? 'Last I saw of them they were fine.'

'That's his ex-wife,' Elsie mouthed to Andy. 'And the bairn's by her new feller. Bob the policeman, he's called, isn't he?'

'That's right,' Mark sighed.

'Eeh,' Elsie went. 'There's new life all over, isn't there? Things going on?'

Andy broke in, 'There's Jane coming in, Elsie. You're friendly with her, aren't you?'

Elsie whirled round to see Jane coming in wearing her best green dress, shoving her seven-year-old son in ahead of her. He was done up as a pageboy, in dicky bow and waistcoat. Elsie waved and hurried over, suddenly glad to feel surrounded by people she knew.

Andy knew Mark and Mark's tattoos from the gym. In the town centre there was a gym up the ramp, above Red Spot supermarket, and at the start of November it had become the place where Andy took control of his life. Inside it smelled of furniture polish and coffee and a not unpleasant tang of sweat. MTV played on thirteen tellies suspended from the ceiling and there was always this stilted pidgin English booming out between songs. In Completely Fit, the clientele consisted of unemployed young blokes, middle-aged women and professional people on dinner hours. They chatted and laughed and helped each other. Andy would have been shamed in a trendier or more competitive place, but here he slipped right into a work-out plan. Every morning, at eleven, he would wind down gently in the sauna in the basement, round the back of Red Spot's multistorey car park. At first it felt bizarre, sitting naked in a wooden shed, when just through the wall there were Cortinas and Capris jostling for free spaces. But he let the sharp heat and that funny, biscuity scent of the sauna soothe away his mid-morning anxieties. His complexion was marvellous these days.

Mark started at the gym just after Andy and it was here they first spoke, as if the intense, often boastful camaraderie of the gym was more convenient for conversation than their street. One morning Mark appeared to have trouble coordinating himself on the free weights. Andy stepped in and, in imitation of everyone else at Completely Fit, couldn't wait to offer advice. Everyone had their own little hints on how to do things right. Passing them on gave Andy a frisson, but Mark just lay on the padded bench, looking as if he wanted to laugh.

It was a bitterly cold December. It took half an hour to warm up for work-outs and longer again to cool down to go out. Andy lay in the sauna, thawing himself out gently, letting the spiced heat insinuate itself. The first time Mark joined him in the small, dimly lit cabin, Andy sat up in surprise and shuffled along to give him space.

'We're like battery hens,' Mark said, sitting down.

They talked and Andy stared and stared. He had trained himself not to look too hard at the men's bodies. Yet the sight of Mark drew him in.

Mark sat with his hands squashed under his thighs, kicking his legs against the wooden slats, chatting away. He sat like a kid in a boring school assembly, Andy thought.

He talked about his daughter Sally, who was in her first year at the juniors now. She had just been given her first biro and her first read-it-yourself book. Sally had been affronted: she'd spent the summer reading all of Edith Nesbit's books by herself. Mark complained about his lodger, who had done a moonlight flit in November; about his ex-wife and her policeman lover; and about his mother-in-law Peggy, who worried too much about his wellbeing. He moaned about these things in a funny, self-deprecating way. It was as if he was saying to Andy, Look, my life is a sitcom. Just listen to this! In August, he explained, in a car stalled at a garage on the way to Darlington, with the smell of petrol almost making him pass out, he single-handedly had to deliver his ex-wife's new baby by another man. Sam lay in the back of the car in the Texaco forecourt and yelled her lungs out at him. Why had he let her get knocked up by some copper? Listen to this, Mark said in the sauna, laughing at himself and telling the whole ridiculous story to Andy.

As he listened, Andy found himself staring at individual pieces of Mark's overall design. A Victorian clockface spanned a good third of his chest, the hands branching from the left nipple, which looked hard in the sauna's heat. Andy focused on this and realised that the clockface was drawn on to look cracked. Creeping through the jagged splits were lush jungle vines and between them blazed an azure sky. On the flat of his chest a parrot in crimson and gold perched on the hand set permanently at three o'clock.

And, because he couldn't stop himself, Andy slipped his glance down the flat stomach, pretending all the while to listen and concentrate, to Mark's prick lying squashed between his thighs. The end of his cock poking out seemed a faint chewing-gum pink beside the gaudiness of his outsides. A serpent twined the length of him, slipping along segments of ancient maps of coastline, sliced dewy fruit and the furled heads of lilies.

Andy looked back up and blushed, because Mark had seen him staring. Mark shrugged and said it was time for him to shower off: school was finishing soon and it was his weekend with his daughter. Through the porthole window Andy watched him shower and imagined the water running into the plughole tainted with his every colour. But it ran clear and Mark's tattoos showed up glossier.

They met daily and struck up a conversational ease and an ease with each other's bodies and nakedness. Even over the Christmas period they weren't too busy for the gym. Andy looked upon his work-out plan as a challenge, and having people who expected him there made him feel obliged to keep going. Mark was doing the same thing, he thought. More than once Mark had told him how pleased he was to get out of the house. He got the impression Mark anticipated a bleak Christmas so he invited him round to the house. Mark was pleased but said he had visits to make all round his split-up family. But here he was on New Year's Eve, stepping into the busying party, mesmerising everyone. Here was Mark wearing an excessively baggy Marksies jumper and jeans and all you could see of the real him was that bald blue head and the backs of his hands as he opened a can and started to drink it greedily down.

Fran was asking Nesta if she had seen Big Sue since Boxing Day.

'I've not seen nobody,' Nesta said through a mouthful of Battenburg. Jane was seeing to some cocktails with the clear plastic shaker-maker she'd brought with her and she rolled her eyes at Nesta. Across the buffet table Nesta's daughter Vicki was sneering at Peter, all dolled up in his frilly shirt and suit.

'She's still shaken up,' Fran said.

'Who, Big Sue?' asked Jane.

'Since them lads threatened her.'

'What's this?' All of a sudden Nesta was interested.

'She was on the bus coming back from the sales on Boxing Day,' Fran said. 'And these lads were baiting her. They sat on the back seat and took all her bags off her. They emptied them over the back of the bus and there was nothing she could do.'

'Never!' said Jane.

'Everything she'd bought in the sales, all over the back of the bus. And she'd been getting knickers and bras at BHS. They had them all out, laughing at them. Big Sue got off the bus in tears and came straight round mine. She left all her bargains on the bus. She ran straight off, she was scared of getting battered. The bus driver did bugger all. And the lads got right off on her stop. Well, you know the size of Big Sue. She just about killed herself, running from the bus stop to my house. She thought they were chasing her. But guess where they were going?'

'Where?' asked Nesta blandly.

'Over the road?' Jane asked. 'Was it that lot from over the Forsyths' house?' She knew fine well it was. They'd been nothing but trouble for months.

'Ay,' said Fran, glancing through the faces at the party, which was getting busier, the lights lower, the murmur of voices building. She looked at Elsie. 'Ay, of course it was that lot.'

As she said this her eye caught Elsie's and the way Elsie flushed red made it clear she was earwigging. If there was one thing Fran couldn't abide, it was earwigging. If you were told something in confidence or whatever, then that was OK. But listening in for kicks was the pits. Still, Fran was ashamed of making Elsie feel bad. Just one glance had been enough to make her blush. Why should Elsie be made to feel responsible for the lads over the road? Just because her Craig was a tearaway.

Fran mulled on that word, tearaway. It made her think of coupons out of magazines, of perforated edges. It was a soft word for hooligans, she thought.

Jane noticed Fran and Elsie's exchanged glance and she went weighing into attack. 'Can't you sort that son of yours out? They're like bloody animals over there. When are they going to get something done about them?'

Elsie opened her mouth and closed it again. Then she said, 'Our Craig has nowt to do with anything violent.'

'Yeah?' snapped Jane, giving her cocktail-maker a vigorous shake. 'If you ask me, they're all as bad as each other.'

'Let's just drop it now,' Fran said, wishing she'd never started this. 'It's a party.'

'Are they having a New Year's do over the road?' Jane asked Elsie.

'I think so,' was the surly reply.

'We can expect fireworks then,' Jane sighed. 'How long before they get guns and drugs and all sorts over there? God! It's like gang warfare.'

Elsie said again, 'Craig has nowt to do with the violence.'

But in the past year their estate had become a more dangerous place to live. Everyone was scared of the louche, raucous boys over the road and the free rein they enjoyed.

Nesta spoke up. 'But what about Big Sue? Where's she tonight? Is she too scared to come out?'

'Maybe I better go and call on her,' Fran said. 'Check she's still coming here.'

'It's bloody rotten that she has to have an escort,' said Jane.

'It's the way things are,' Nesta said glumly. 'In this day and age it's like having no laws.'

Elsie let out a yelp of outrage. 'Fancy you saying that, Nesta Dixon! It's not over a year ago you had everyone out searching for your dead body and there you were having saddo-masokinky sex with that young lad – God bless his soul – him who liked to dress up as an Alsatian!'

This turned a few heads, but most people already knew the tale. Nesta coloured and said that she was going round to see if Big Sue was all right.

'Honestly,' Fran muttered. 'People don't let you forget anything, do they?'

'Try this,' Jane said. 'It's a Monkey Gland.' It was bright pink, with too much Pernod.

'Do you know what you're like?'

Andy, standing framed in the doorway of Penny's bedroom, startled her as she was putting on mascara. She had never learned the trick of mascara, feeling it weigh too heavy and claggy on her lids. She wished Liz hadn't left without explaining the technique.

Penny was seated at Liz's dressing table with all the drawers open, the tins and boxes and tubes spread wide. Everything was mother-of-pearl: a gentler version of the colour of oil spillage on beaches. 'What am I like?' she asked Andy, amused by the way he slouched there with his bottle of alcoholic lemonade. He looked like he was at the saloon door. And that made her the bar-room belle, but she was in a minidress of peppermint green which crinkled and felt, to the touch, like sweet wrappers. She loved being in this dress, inside its several layers, like a chocolate lime.

Andy had already forgotten his first question to her and the reply took him by surprise. He shrugged and went, 'I don't know! I'm pissed!' Really, he just wanted to talk to her and say, Come downstairs. When he looked it seemed he could see every detail of the beautiful unguents and powders and pastes on the dresser. He licked his own lips as Penny applied a last smarmy, brilliant dash of lippy. To him she looked like . . . who was it? Snow White? No, Cinderella, in the Disney version, when she has birds and animals dressing her up and she never has to lift a finger. He imagined that this was how Penny was made ready, all the little creatures vanishing in a miraculous cartoon puff just as he came up the stairs and stood here to look.

Penny surveyed her finished self in the mirror that stood wide and high as the doorway itself. It was fringed with postcards from all over the place. There were cards from people who had lived at the house and moved away, cards from Liz and Cliff, from the resorts they had visited and, though Andy didn't know this, cards from Vince. Vince sent Miros, Matisses and Chagalls and Penny had alternated them with Liz's various 'Greetings from Morecambe!' or 'Sunny Scarborough!'

More than a wrapped sweet or a bar-room belle, Penny looked like a mermaid. Her newly hennaed hair was piled loosely on top of her head and the scarlet tendrils over her face looked plastered as if she had risen from the depths. Liking the effect, she dabbed her face with a bit of glitter and reached onto the window sill, plucking up the six dried starfish she had bought in Whitby. They were smaller than her palm and easy to pin into the soft mass of her hair. She stood and showed off to Andy.

'You're fucking mad!' He laughed. 'Starfish woman!'

She took his drink off him.

'Any fights yet?'

'No proper fist fights. Maybe a few sharp words. Some nasty looks. Mostly they're having a laugh.'

Penny went to look out of the window, at the whole of Phoenix Court being steeped ever more deeply in snow.

'Here's two more,' she laughed. 'They've come all dressed up, look.'

Andy saw his uncle Ethan and his new wife Rose struggling across the car park dressed as pirates.

Uncle Ethan was capitalising on his wooden leg, wielding it with aplomb, shouldering his navy greatcoat which had, for the evening, a gaudy stuffed parrot stitched to one epaulette. It must have been a parrot saved from the stock he'd given away when the taxidermist's closed. Andy was glad to see it come in handy. Or maybe his uncle had always harboured some desire to be a pirate. Maybe he was secretly pleased with having a leg like his. You could hear him now, throwing back his great, grizzled head and going 'Harr-harr, Jim lad,' and flicking up his eye-patch to make Rose laugh. Rose was dressed as Jim lad. Her navy breeks and striped Breton top seemed stretched to over-flowing. That she was in her sixties was something Andy often found hard to believe. She was a bright, brassy, infectious person. Even he could see how sexy she was. Her humour was all tits and bums and sauce and what made him laugh most was the way it mortified Jane, her rather uptight daughter. Rose was a scandalous presence whenever she came round Phoenix Court. Andy thought she'd done his uncle a lot of good.

'Who told them it was fancy dress?' Penny asked.

'We've all got to come dressed as something,' Andy said. 'Anyway. Maybe they've come as themselves. We have.'

There was a swift knock at the door and they realised that the party had spread upstairs, too. Mark's head popped round the door, startling them with its sudden inky blue.

'Uh,' he went. 'The phone for you, Andy. You better hurry, it's coming long-distance.'

Andy shrugged, on his way. 'Who do I know . . .?'

As he left the room, Penny got one of Mark's too bright grins. 'I've got a starfish on my right shoulder blade,' he said.

Silhouettes went darting by the windows. The curtains in the Forsyths' house hung in tatters, partially blocking the bright lights within. Dark figures massed, broke apart and loomed recklessly close to the glass.

Nesta watched for a moment from the street and then hurried on. The Phoenix Court party seemed almost sedate compared with the lads over the road. They weren't any less noisy, that wasn't it. The sound of the Brotherhood of Man ('Save All Your Kisses for Me') blasted as loudly from Penny's house as did the hardcore dance music from the lads' house. Yet Penny's noise didn't seem threatening.

That was the conclusion Nesta came to. The doors and windows of Penny's house were flung open and figures were out in the garden, getting cool air into stifled lungs. Red faces hung out of windows, calling and squealing. There were bairns running about and you could see Frank leaning in the doorway, eating from a jar of pickles and watching his kids play in the snow by moonlight.

But over the road the noise seemed menacing. It came thumping from a sealed house as if building up pressure. The house looked fit to burst open.

Nesta crossed the few hundred yards to Big Sue's bungalow. The field of virgin snow showed plainly that Sue hadn't left her door that night. She was too scared to walk past the Forsyths' house alone. Well, these days Nesta certainly thought of herself as a prouder and braver person and, in her own secret ways, she was. I may look no different on the outside, she found herself thinking as she banged on Big Sue's door, but I feel like I can do more. It isn't all so hard.

Big Sue's head poked out of the toilet window above. 'Is that you, Nesta?'

Nesta looked up, startled to see Big Sue without her wig on. A few soft strands hung past her face as she squinted into the gloom.

'Ay,' Nesta's face was stiff with cold. 'Lerruz in, man.'

Big Sue always made her own clothes and this made Nesta sorry for her. She would look at the thick curtain-material skirts the old lady wore and her heart went out to her. She'd tried to tell Sue she ought to . . . well, smarten up. To update her image. To do like they said on *This Morning* and have a make-over. Nesta had shown off her new leggings, saying Big Sue should have some. They always look smart. But Big Sue had her Singer, she said, and she could run up anything she desired or needed, quick as a flash, from oddments. What I like, she said beadily, on the day Nesta suggested a shell suit like hers, what I like is being self-sufficient. Nesta pointed out there was a warehouse on the industrial estate where you took your design of how you wanted your shell suit to look, and they would do it for you. She and Tony had tried it: eighty quid and they gave you a stencil of a little feller to colour in with felt tips, just how you liked. They'd had a lovely pair made.

'I'm happy how I am,' Big Sue insisted. This New Year's Eve she was wearing the same shapeless, mustard-coloured cardy and pea-green skirt. Impatiently she ushered Nesta in, locked the door again, and took her into the living room.

The one thing Big Sue never skimped on was hats. She had a marvellous selection of ones dating right back. She even wore them indoors, watching the telly. On top of her wig too, which must have been scratchy and hot with the heating on. Nesta had brought her one or two back from the car-bootie as presents, but she'd never seen Big Sue wear those ones. Tonight she wasn't wearing a hat. She sat on her swivel armchair in the centre of her living room with a completely naked head and, even though she was pretending to be as gruff and ordinary as ever, this was the biggest sign of her distress.

Wisps stuck all around the surface of her head. They put Nesta in mind of an Easter-egg-painting competition at school years ago. Nesta had messed up her display of three eggs. She'd been doing *Planet of the Apes*, but two broke in transit so that was the apes gone. She just did Charlton Heston, sticking his cotton-wool hair on with PVA. That went wrong too and his hair was reduced to shreds and patches of fluff. Nesta was bursting to tell Big Sue, You look like my Charlton Heston egg! But she held herself back, being too used to people just looking at her, baffled, when she said the first thing on her mind.

Nesta was the first person Big Sue had seen in days. Even plain, stolid, expressionless Nesta was a welcome sight. There were high spots of colour on her cheeks so you could tell she'd been on the cider already and her self-bleached, dry-straw hair was standing nearly on end. Why can't she put a brush through it? What irritated Big Sue most about Nesta was her eyes, which were never fully open. She looked perpetually on the point of nodding off and it made the older woman want to shake her.

'You have to come to the party,' Nesta was saying. 'It's an all right do.' On Big Sue's china cabinet her wedding clock bonged out eleven o'clock. 'All the street's turned up. You can't miss everyone. They've all asked after you.'

Sue's face crinkled into a smile as wide as Nesta's hand at the thought of being asked after. She was a broad, motherly woman who had never had kids, which always surprised Nesta, who'd had bairns without really thinking about it. When Nesta was having bairns it seemed to be in someone else's hands. Nowt for her to do but get passed pillar to post and that was all right. Nesta thought Sue's breasts under her hand-knit cardy must be colossal, like water-filled balloons. She wondered if she would finish up one day with breasts like that.

'I'll see,' Sue began. 'Maybe I'm not up to all them faces the night.'

When Nesta opened her mouth to protest, Big Sue held up her hand. 'Oh, you know, Nesta. When sometimes you can't imagine wanting to talk to anyone?' She gritted her small, square, yellow teeth and snatched a Regal from the pack by her side. 'Nesta, I just feel *shy*.'

Quite often people assumed that Nesta never listened to them, or that she never knew what was going on. Thinking her blithe or stupid, they never expected a clever or considerate response. As if the black of her thick mascara, the flaking gold and green of her favoured eyeshadow, obscured the world beyond her most immediate, selfish concerns. Sometimes Nesta saw more than people imagined, and she understood.

'Sue, I had this time . . . just before my trouble last year . . . and I couldn't leave the house. It's really horrible when you get like that. But don't give in to it. You know that, in the end, you have to get out and do things.'

'Oh,' Sue began, 'I'm not *housebound* –'

50

'Listen. I want to explain.' Nesta bit her lip. 'You know what got me out of the house in the end?'

'Was that when you had all that bother and disappeared?' asked Sue, being as tactful as she could.

'Hm. The only way I could leave my house was to go with that man. It was all I could do. To stay with him in the daytime in his house and then for both of us to dress up at night and walk the streets in disguise. Really . . . I didn't feel normal enough to be out in the day.'

That was the end of Nesta's explanation. It was more than she had told anyone in the year since her breakdown.

Big Sue said, 'It isn't that I don't feel normal, exactly . . .' She took a long drag on her Regal. 'And I don't feel altogether scared when I'm outdoors. Not all the time. There are some nasty buggers out and about and it pays to be careful, but I won't let them terrorise me. It's just, when I'm out, I feel exposed.'

Nesta looked at her friend and it seemed she was the same size as the chair she was sitting in.

'Come on,' Nesta said. 'Come out with me.'

'I'm not dressed.'

Nesta shrugged. 'My stepmam used to say, if you want to get ahead, get a hat.'

Minutes later they were trudging up the main road, linking arms as they sloughed off the drowsiness of Sue's gas-heated living room. Big Sue took small steps on the slushy path. She said of the Forsyths' house opposite, 'Look at them with their lights on, music blasting. I wonder if they've still got all my knickers and bras.' She had a brief flash of all them lads, running about indoors, playing the fool with her new underthings. 'They must be sick in the head.'

Nesta was turned the other way, squinting into the drifting darkness of Woodham Way. The road was almost smooth and unruffled. There'd been little traffic that night.

Big Sue said, 'Fancy driving a taxi tonight.'

Heading towards them, nosing determinedly through thick snow, came a big black cab. It ploughed blindly past the bus stop and, as it swept past Nesta and Big Sue, they saw that there was only one passenger. She sat in the back seat, staring at the houses of Phoenix Court. Her hair was golden and fluffed up proudly.

Then the taxi was gone.

Big Sue let out a great cackle. 'You know who that was, don't you?' She picked up her pace.

Nesta stared after the car. 'I think I do. Do you think she's come back for the party?'

The older woman grinned. 'Ha'way, Nesta. I reckon this do is gunna be a good 'un!'

Four

At number sixteen the party was well underway.

When the schmaltzy songs came on, Jane was in the corner, nuzzling another cocktail. Who was standing next to her this time? One of Judith's teenagers, listening politely as Jane bitched about everyone dancing. Sheila and Simon were hugging each other close in the middle of the impromptu dance floor. The song was 'Sometimes When We Touch' and they seemed to be mired in the carpet's swirling orange pattern. They stirred, hardly shuffling their feet, staring into each other's eyes. He's a skinny little thing, Jane was hissing to Judith's son, he has to crane his scrawny neck to see into his wife's eyes. He clung to her as if they were in a flood. His too tight jeans had a crotch that sagged low and his bomber-jacket sleeves were bunched up as his wife wheeled him slowly about. Sheila was gargantuan, with masses of kinky mushroom-coloured hair. Now he pushed his head flat to her breasts and she stared serenely out. Sheila watched their daughter slip quietly out of the back door.

'She goes collecting stones at night-time,' Sheila explained to Fran over her husband's shoulder. Fran was dancing with her own husband, but she felt forced into it. She gave Sheila a sickly smile. 'She makes her own jewellery, you know,' said Sheila proudly.

Jane's attention was drawn away from the happy dancing couples. Her mother Rose and her pirate lover wanted to talk seriously to her about something. All she remembered afterwards were their mouths working earnestly, through the love songs. She was nodding intently, as if taking in what they said. But talking with Rose was impossible with that bloody stuffed parrot staring her right in the eye.

Penny shuffled through to have her mermaid frock admired by Rose once more, and Jane was glad of the distraction. Rose was calling out, 'Oh, if I was still under twenty I would dress as a mermaid every day!'

Penny was telling them that she had nachos under the grill. 'You what, pet?' Rose was saying. 'What's that you've got?' Jane's mother had taken a shine to the motherless Penny. Of course Penny was so much more glamorous than Jane, Rose's natural daughter. And all Jane could think was, What on earth are nachos? When Penny showed them, they were like plates of crisps with cheese and tomatoes and olives, which Jane usually hated and these ones tasted of TCP.

'Ooooh!' Rose smacked her lips. 'Eating with our hands! This is like our cruise round the world!'

Penny filled the dining table with scalding hot plates of nachos and they all crowded round to eat with their hands.

'It's all right, pet, I'm not after one of your fancy cocktails.' Penny put the shaker back on the sideboard and smiled. She recognised the old woman as Elsie, but couldn't remember having talked to her before. She was a friend of Jane's, one of those nosy types who couldn't be bothered to actually get to know you before they knew all your business.

Elsie's eyes were pink and they settled uncertainly, speculatively, on Penny, as if she was after something. 'I'm just on the gin, if you don't mind,' and, almost shyly, she proffered her glass for a top-up.

Wasn't she an alkie? Hadn't Penny heard that somewhere? And wasn't she the one with the religious nut for a husband, the feller who reminded Penny of Dracula? He'd lope across the kiddies' play park and you'd make sure not to cross his path. Penny had even stood at a different bus stop just to be away from him. And, of course – she

54

recalled this as she hastily mismeasured the gin – Elsie was the one whose son was over the road with the bad lads.

'Ay,' Elsie said appraisingly. 'Our Craig's right about you.' She stared at Penny's dress and Penny thought for a moment that she, like Rose, would say she wished she'd dressed as a mermaid in her youth. 'Do you know our Craig? Have you met him yet?' Elsie was keen and rabbity, with urgent, pink-lined eyes, forcing Penny back against the dresser.

'Who's Craig?' Penny asked, and found she was looking for an escape. Something about Elsie set her teeth on edge. That overeagerness of hers and her humbleness. One thing Penny had learned from Liz was to keep your distance. Penny trusted to a certain reserve. She knew that the way she carried on seemed the very opposite of that, as if she threw in her lot willy-nilly with just anyone, but that wasn't quite true.

Now Elsie was staring into Penny's face as if she could see the future there. Maybe she could. She looks like a bloody witch, Penny thought, and then stopped herself. What if Elsie really can see what is coming? Penny wasn't prepared to dismiss the possibility. Her starfish bristled at the idea, she could feel them close to her scalp, mumbling their eager suckers on her dyed scarlet hair.

Pleased with her own circumspection, she beamed at Elsie, ready to start the conversation again. 'I was miles away, Elsie. I'm sorry. Was I rude?'

'It's that night,' Elsie said, stealing a glance at her watch. 'It's that night when we're prone to slipping off miles away, thinking about people.' Elsie rather startled herself with her own lucidity. There was a grasping sensation in her chest and she thought she was going to vomit, but it was a sob, a deep, sudden sob that took her as much by surprise as Penny.

Penny seized Elsie's glass of gin and found herself giving her a hug. That peppery hair in her nose made her think, This is how red hair ages. It was harsh against her face and smelled sour. She wondered if she would end up like Elsie, as if they'd met across the ages. Am I anything like her? Elsie was bawling now, right into the front of Penny's crinkly mermaid dress. 'Bathroom,' Penny said.

As she led Elsie there, through the massed bodies, squeezing between balloons and treading on beer cans, Penny was wondering, What if Elsie were to succeed? Surely she was here to matchmake. If she managed to get Penny and her Craig together, then what would happen? What if she and Craig married and got a kid and a council house here? Would Penny after twenty-odd years wind up the same as Elsie? Was it as easy as that? In the relative quiet of the bathroom she sat Elsie, still crying, on the toilet seat's pink cover. Penny poured her a cloudy, toothpasty glass of water. Was that the clean and simplified trajectory of a life? What other factors need she take into account? The marriage plot almost seduced her by its simplicity. She watched Elsie gulp the water down.

Suddenly Elsie tipped her head, as if it was far too heavy, into the bathroom basin, and bellowed until Balti and gin rushed out.

Here at the hinge between years – and these are tricky, rusted hinges that squeal perilously – you could easily slip, show yourself up, make a terrible mistake and lose yourself. Disappear as others have disappeared before you, Penny thought.

She then listened to Elsie pant out her story about Craig's poor foot and how it and his difficult young life had led him to get in with a bad crowd.

He needs a good woman.

Penny brushed all this aside, running the cold tap to sluice out the basin.

'I'm not going to be sick again,' Elsie said, grasping her arm. 'I'm trying to tell you about my boy.'

Andy had never travelled, but even as Vince started to describe it, in a tinny, exhilarated voice, he could see exactly what Paris on New Year's Eve looked like.

All Andy could say was, 'What are you doing? It's almost midnight! Who are you with?'

Vince was saying again, 'I'm in Paris!' as if he couldn't quite believe it either.

'You haven't called me in months, and now this!'

'Yeah, yeah.' Vince was drunk. 'How are you keeping, pet?'

Andy felt tears spring up. 'Oh . . . smart. How about you?'

There was a pause as Vince decided to be nothing less than honest. Not even consideration for Andy could stop him. 'I'm having a lovely time. I love it here.'

'Who are you there with?'

'Ralph.'

'*Ralph*? Who the fuck's Ralph?'

'We've been together since October. Didn't Penny tell you?'

Andy pulled a face. 'She told me nowt.'

'He's a Jane Austen expert.'

'Smashing.' Andy scowled, imagining them reading books together. That would be right up Vince's street. He probably couldn't think of anything sexier than reading with his lover. On the rare occasions when Andy read anything, he couldn't bear to have anyone near him. Vince would notice him reading and wanted to be near him, as if proud, drinking that silence up. It embarrassed Andy and put him off. Vince loved to read a novel with Andy hugged to his chest, almost like a child, as if he wanted to read out loud to him, something else Andy hated. Andy also thought it was as if Vince wanted to push his lover's whole body into the book. He would be happier with his lover inside the book, wasn't that the truth of the matter?

That was why Vince was no good, Andy decided, with the expensive long-distance seconds zooming by: he was no good because he would rather we were all inside a book. It would be easier on his nerves if he could read about us rather than having to live with us. Andy wouldn't forgive that look of his – sheer disdain – when he came to live in Phoenix Court and found himself having to slum it. He thought we all talked about stupid things. He wanted to talk about *Madame Bovary*.

'Well, thanks for phoning.'

'Are you sure you mean that?' Oh, that arch tone of his! On this phone it was worse, crackling and Gallic. Knowing exactly how pissed off Andy was. 'I wish I hadn't phoned at all now. I've made you even crosser and depressed, haven't I?'

'Yeah, frankly, you have. How old's this Ralph?'

'Forty-six.'

'Vince, he's twice your age!'

'You've had older blokes.'

'And it was awful.'

'Yeah, well. Ralph is wonderful.'

'You're just playing the little whore to get a free trip.'

'Fuck you, Andy.'

'Ay – fuck you an' all.'

A pause. 'I wish I could, Andy. I wish I was there. You've made me want to be in Phoenix Court!'

'Yeah?'

'Nah. You should be over here. I'm in the loveliest café. I could do with a friendly face.'

'Is that all I am?'

'Andy . . . we can't talk about anything seriously here and now. We should just say *Bon hiver* and have done.'

Andy let himself down then. He sounded almost beseeching and hated himself for it. 'Will we talk later? Will you phone me again? Can we talk about it? You went before we could.'

He could hear the foreign party noise in the background. He thought, it sounds like a *Film on Four*! Listen to Vince! He's in a smart art-house movie with subtitles!

'Ay, Andy. We'll talk next year. Listen. Happy New Year.'

Andy steeled himself. 'Same to you. Give my love to Ralph.'

When he slammed down the phone he gave a jump as

58

someone pressed the cold of a lager can against his neck. It was Mark.

'Trouble?'

'Vince, phoning from Paris, with some old bloke he's fucking.' The words were out before Andy could tailor them for straight consumption. Andy was so cross he'd forgotten the usual edit. Mark didn't bat a painted eyelid.

'Who's Vince?'

Andy shrugged. 'He was my last boyfriend.'

'Oh.' Mark looked down, making a deliberate 'Oh' shape with his mouth. Andy thought he was embarrassed. Oh, he must be mortified – this tattooed, single father of one, at having been shanghaied into spending chatty hours, whole mornings, nude in a sauna in the amber light, the air scented like ginger snaps, sharing his time and intimacy with a big fag. Mark looked up and asked, 'Is he treating you badly?'

'Just a bit. He walked out on me months ago.'

'So it's over.'

'I reckon so.'

Now it was Andy's turn to feel embarrassed. Mark was doing the sensitive straight man act. He was doing it well and it made Andy want to cry. The few soft words Mark had said, the way he looked and seemed concerned, all of it conspired to gather Andy up. Mark was taking his relationship with Vince as seriously as he would a straight one, a straight marriage, and Andy wasn't even used to taking himself that seriously. Was that why Vince couldn't be with him? Because he couldn't give them that self-importance?

'Come on,' Mark was saying. 'Let's talk somewhere quiet.'

Boney M were back on in the hallway. Big Sue and Nesta were dancing around and miming to 'Ra Ra Rasputin'.

It's coming on to midnight over Phoenix Court. It is the

focus of the night. It is time to think about the way the year will turn. Time concentrates the main events as they go off – one, two, three – around the chimes.

Either side of the main road the two parties are peaking and tumbling out of control. The bad lads are coming out of the house, spilling into the yard, into the clean snow of the street.

Sheila and Simon's daughter is picking stones in the snow. How she can find them in the dark and the snow is anyone's guess. She is a lumbering figure in her anorak, on the grass verge. The bad lads have seen her. The town clock, across the estates, across the Burn, starts to chime midnight.

Craig follows on behind the others as they run from the house, towards Phoenix Court. They're shouting and kicking at each other, as if they can't get there fast enough. Craig's wondering what they're going to do. He's just feeling slow and unhappy. Someone gives a tug of his ponytail. The road is almost obliterated with snow. The bad lads are churning everything up. They've got – and he starts to run when he sees this – they've got Sheila and Simon's daughter on her back in the snow.

Hardly stealthily, they've crept up on her and pushed her down on her back. Her collected stones lie scattered all around her head. When Craig reaches the bad lads and her, there is a silence none of them can quite figure out. All of them staring down at her massive form, her hair fanned out, her anorak zipped up. Craig looks down at her – Donna, they call her Donna – and she isn't screaming or saying anything. Donna looks too depressed to say anything.

Andy is in his bedroom and he's telling Mark, who sits listening patiently, that Vince means nothing to him now. He can't bear people sounding pleased with themselves, as Vince does when he's happy, and never even asking how the other person is. Sulkily Andy flops back on his bed,

60

which is dark and strewn with mess. Mark is perched on dirty laundry on a painted wickerwork chair. He's wondering what he's doing there. Andy's still dressed as a cowboy, rubbing his palms into his eyes. On the walls there are posters from *Pulp Fiction*, *The X Files* and Blur's *Parklife*.

Mark reaches forward and eases off Andy's boots. They aren't real cowboy boots, just his normal ones. Andy stops listening to the tired squeaking of his eyes as he rubs them. He tenses.

Mark leans over him. 'Andy . . .'

'Are you putting me to bed?'

Marks shrugs.

'Am I that drunk?'

'I don't know. Are you?'

'So why are you putting me to bed?'

Big Sue is looking for the loo, not used to the layout of these houses with upstairs landings. Even on a small trip out like tonight, she can start to miss her own bungalow. There's nothing like your own place, she's telling Jane as she hauls herself up the stairs. Jane is sitting with a Fuzzy Navel, made with Pernod instead of orange juice.

'Are you looking for the loo?' Jane asks after her, following her. 'Because there's a queue . . .'

Big Sue has flung open the walk-in cupboard at the top of the stairs and with a great sigh it disgorges its contents into the hall and down the stairs, taking Jane with it. Jane vanishes under squashy bags of old clothes, stacks of vinyl LPs and floppy paperbacks. She gives a squawk and is silent, buried under what looks like a car-boot sale. The stuff keeps on coming out of the cupboard, as if pushed. Nesta and a few others standing at the bottom of the stairs are screaming. Jane sits, very calmly, in a heap of old *Look-in* magazines, and discovers that she has twisted her arm.

Penny comes out of the bathroom to see all these old

belongings strewn. She groans and snaps at Sue when asked where the toilet is. 'How am I going to get this lot back in there!'

Elsie is at her elbow. 'Give it to the spastics!' she says, gleeful again. Her hair smells of vomit, Penny realises. 'Give me it all to give to the spastics!' And Penny remembers that Elsie does voluntary work in the week.

'Penny?' A deep voice comes from the downstairs hall, someone new making themselves heard above the music and kerfuffle. 'Is Penny here?' the voice asks crossly. 'Is Penny Robinson here?'

Her head jerks up as she starts kicking her way through the old records and tangle of musty coats. She skids her way to the top of the stairs and takes them at a run, almost pitching herself headfirst. 'Who is it?' Penny daren't admit to herself who she hopes it might be. In her heart she knows she has to be right. This year, this New Year, her mother has to have returned.

At the bottom stair there is a man she doesn't know. He is in a tank top and nylon trousers and he wears a taxi driver's numbered badge. 'Are you Penny Robinson?'

Standing on the middle stair, Penny nods.

'I've brought someone from the station,' he says.

Liz is bundled up in the back of the black cab, smoking a quiet cigarette, tapping the ash out of the partly opened window. That cold shushes in and she snuggles into her fur, sighing. Soon she's got to go back to the house that used to be hers. Will Penny be cross that she sent the taxi driver in ahead? Liz wanted to make a big entrance but, when it came to it, she couldn't do it alone. She wants to return with her daughter at her side.

Liz stares at the low, square houses and the play park, the humped shapes of parked cars, the lit windows. Phoenix Court seems so small to her now. But she's got to fit back in. No more flitting about. Nervously she smokes the ciggy down to its filter. She stubs it out on the old-fashioned metal ashtray and tosses the filter out the window. The town clock begins to chime. She wanted to be indoors for this, there in the thick of the party, among her own kind. Are they my own kind? she wonders. She straightens and glances out over the street. Everyone, it seems, is round number sixteen. Penny has made herself the centre of it all. Shit, thinks her mother, I needn't have worried about Penny being lonely.

She lets herself out of the taxi and steps carefully, as if testing the slipperiness of the snow. Then she braces herself and starts to hurry across the gravel as the snow starts falling again. The music from her house is getting louder, pulling her in.

Between Liz and her house, there is Donna, flat on her back with the bad lads round her, still weighing up what best to do with her on the stroke of midnight. Donna wills herself the strength to move just one hand a little, pick up one of the rocks she has collected, and throw it at one of the lads. The one closest to her. The bravest one, or the one who thinks he's bravest, who's chuckling now, low in his throat, as if he's decided what to do with her.

Donna doesn't even think it's worth yelling out. Everyone she knows in the world is in the loud house, having a party. She's fallen out of her orbit. She clenches her teeth.

Craig has closed his eyes and he wishes she would start to yell. He could yell, but where would that get any of them?

'Penny?' a voice calls to them.

In a long white fur coat there is a figure trotting carefully across the gravel of the play park. Her hair is shaken out, wavy and golden white. As she approaches, she is lighting herself another cigarette and her thin, awkward body looks ready to bolt and flee. The woman approaching, as the lads look up and watch her, seems suddenly terrified.

'Who is that?' she demands, her voice sounding smoky and broken.

The worst of the bad lads, Steve, tosses his head at her and says, 'Who have we got here?'

While Liz takes up their attention, Craig crouches over Donna, rolls her up and over like someone bedridden and tells her to flee.

Then they are all around the older woman, the new-comer. The lads seem to sense there is more fun to be had from her. She is more nervy and excitable, she has more fight. And her glamour, too, attracts and repels them. They think her ridiculous and long to drag her down. Liz is being baited. Her fur coat is plucked at, her cigarettes are taken from her, passed around. The boys surround her in a ring she can't escape and she remembers this from years ago, at school, when they played piggy-in-the-middle. She wishes she'd gone into the house in the first place, with the taxi driver. And where has he got to anyway? Why can't she ever do things the right way? She starts yelling out threats and this panics the lads, but doesn't make them let her go. When they panic they start to do worse things. Someone holds her chin and looks into her eyes. 'Give us a kiss, then.'

'She's old enough to be your mam!'

And before any of them know it, her wig comes off in their hands. She drops to the ground, clearing an angel-space of snow a few yards away from Donna's. The boy with her wig in his hands gives a yell and drops it. It falls, as if drawn, back onto Liz's head, but looks dislodged and crazy. Steve kicks her in the stomach.

'It's not even her real hair!'

Someone stands on her hand, crushing rings into the flesh of her fingers. 'Pick her up,' Steve commands in that easy way he has. Craig hates himself even as he finds that he does what Steve tells him.

'Did you hear that, Craig?' Steve snickers. 'Did you hear what she called you? Under her breath?'

Craig is confused. 'What?' Did Liz call him something? Her head is down.

'She did!' Steve crows. 'That bitch called you a pegleg.

64

She said you're a spacker. She called you a fucking spacker!'

A rushing fills Craig's ears. He can't believe this. He gulps down his breath. His pulse races.

They brace the frail weight of Liz between them, her wig slipped askance. 'Smack her one,' Steve shouts. 'Fucking smack her one!' He shouts it in Craig's face. 'She called you a fucking cripple, didn't you hear?'

'What?' Craig whimpers this, but his body is tensed against them all, he can see nothing but Steve's face and Liz's face and all he can hear is Steve's voice screaming at him.

'You! Fuck'n spacker! Crack her one!'

Craig shouts and lashes out. Next thing they all know, Liz has toppled once more to the ground.

Craig lurches forward to do something and, in that instant, there is a resounding crack as Liz's head hits the pavement. Her body jolts, convulses and lies still.

It was a sickening drop. He wants to tell the others the sound it made. He looks, although he doesn't want to, and there is something dark and oily coming out from under her head, from under the wig.

Craig grabs Steve's arm. Holding the crook of his arm as if for support, he points at the blood and says, 'We've cracked her head open. She's fucking dead.'

'Yeah, yeah.' Steve backs off.

'We've fucking killed her.'

Steve backs further off, then turns and runs. The others run with him. Craig shouts, 'We can't leave her! We can't leave her lying like this!'

Steve comes back. 'We can. You're coming with us. If you stay, they'll know you did it.'

'I did it,' Craig echoes.

'Right. Come back. Get indoors. Just look what you've done.'

Craig takes one last, frantic look at Liz's body, on which snow has already started to settle. Then he turns and runs after the others to the Forsyth house.

Will this ever happen again? is the first thing Andy wants to ask him.

Mark slides back and rests there.

Will we ever do this again? is what Andy was thinking even in the moments before either of them came, because he realised he wasn't making the most of this time. They were in the thick of things, it was all going on, but somehow, he couldn't quite grasp the situation. It wasn't real enough. He wanted to see Mark's tattoos, see the designs he had come to know in recent weeks, flexing and working, shifting their outlines as the two of them had sex. It wasn't enough, just this, it might be anyone.

He hears Mark rustling about, thoughtfully silent and then frozen, as if he has found something. Andy shrugs off his quiet. 'What's up?'

Like a footballer, Mark has his hand cupped over his cock. 'Condom's split.' He hoists himself up. 'It split.'

'When?' Now Andy is sitting up. They are both staring at each other, the sheets, the mattress, as if one of them has lost a contact lens. 'Inside of me?' asks Andy. 'Did it split inside of me?'

In the hallway Penny bangs hard on Andy's door. 'She's back! Andy! She's back! My mam's back!'

By then it is midnight.

Five

The Fantastic Four had a skyscraper all to themselves. What did they call it? The Baxter Building, that was it. And there was the Batcave, of course. And the Avengers had the Avengers Mansion, and the Justice League of America had a satellite station floating around the world. It was like a staff room, a futuristic staff room they could all adjourn to from their separate cities. The Justice League of America would beam themselves up to the JLA satellite and have meetings about what they had to do to save the world.

Who was in the JLA? Superman of course, who just flew up to the satellite. It was no bother for him, who didn't have to breathe and could do anything. He had a secret place of his own, too, the Fortress of Solitude, in the North or the South Pole, where he'd go and make his own plans for himself. It was like an ice palace. I remember the stories when someone would get in and there'd be a real panic on. Superman would be furious, someone in his fortress. There was one I remember, but it was a daft story and the intruder was only Batman. It was Superman's birthday and he was making him a cake. I fucking hated the stupid stories. The jokey ones like they couldn't be arsed any more taking it seriously.

Who else in the JLA? Aquaman, who lived underwater. Hawkman and Hawkwoman, who had bird powers. Wonder Woman, but she was crap. I hated Wonder Woman. What were her powers? A lasso. And Green Lantern and Green Arrow. I could never tell the difference between them and never knew what they were meant to be anyway. And the Flash, who was dressed all in red and he could run like a bastard.

We used to walk right across town to the newsagent by the Dandy Cart to get American comics. Now, mind, you can buy them everywhere. You get big shops in places like Newcastle, Forbidden Planet and Timeslip, shops like that, and they sell hundreds of comics really expensively. When I was reading them all the time in the seventies, say, you'd get only a handful of them on the spinning racks in the newsagents. The dirty newsagents by the Dandy Cart. That bit of town was even rougher than where we lived, Mam said. I used to go over and buy comics at fifteen pence a time, which was more than English ones cost then. Now it's like three quid for a bloody comic. The English ones then, even the ones that reprinted the American strips, were in black and white. The Americans were all colour, and small. They were often on yellowed paper and crumpled up. As if they'd been dampened on the boat or plane coming over, and dried on a radiator. On the spinning rack in the Dandy Cart shop they were in direct sunlight and they dried yellowy. You could never buy issues in sequence. It was pot luck. I just bought whatever was there, so I never saw a complete story. Issues began with the pick-up of a cliffhanger and ended with another nail-biting finish. You just had to make up what came before and after. The Dandy Cart stank of the cheese counter. When I think of reading comics and choosing which ones to buy, I think of rancid cheese and the glass counter, scratched by coins, over the Dandy Cart, where you'd pay and get a ten-pence mixture of sweets as well.

Sometimes I wonder, if I asked Steve, what he would say. If I said, Aren't we like one of them team-ups of superheroes in the old comics? Isn't that what we're all like in this house? He would just say I was cracked. He thinks I'm cracked anyway.

I'd like to ask him, though, because he used to read those comics as well. We were at school together and we used to swap them. I got one weird comic off him once about a walking tree in a swamp that went round just killing people. It wasn't a proper hero comic at all. I wonder if Steve remembers reading those things.

I think that we're a bit like a super-team when we're down the gym, especially on a good day when we're working well, everyone's muscles all pumped up. When I was little I used to wonder what the superheroes' costumes were made of. Like rubber or something. But now the material's common and we all wear it down the gym, even the old biddies and the tarts down there wear it: Lycra. In Lycra everyone's a fucking superhero. These days it isn't so hard. So maybe I'll mention it to Steve one day, remind him, make him laugh.

For a moment tonight it felt like we were a super-team. A bit out of it, running out of the house over the snow. When you're skidding about and piling after each other in the snow and you can hardly see two feet in front, then that's a bit like flying. When we came pounding out of the house at midnight I could see us all, like in one of those full-page frames that each comic begins with, streaking into the sky with wings and masks and cloaks streaming behind us. When the superheroes flew, the artists always drew a faint trail behind them, to show how fast they were going and where they had been. Last night I saw us all leaving those trails. And the heroes gritted their teeth when flying or fighting. Their mouths were wide rectangles with the teeth bared and that's how we all were, the seven of us, running across the estate.

What they thought they were doing, I'm fucked if I know. Suddenly we were out there and it was all going on. They had that lass, that Donna on the ground. And then there was the other woman there.

I made sure that Donna got away from them. Donna's soft in the head. She was scared of them. I helped her get away. I did that much.

The other one, Penny's mam. She's been away. She came back all of a sudden. She got mixed up where she shouldn't have.

They dragged her body out onto the playground, where she'd be found easy. I was going to stay, to make sure. Steve said no way. We'd get the blame. They dragged her over to the play park. Pulled on her fur coat. She was bleeding. A hank of fake fur came off in Steve's hands.

I watched tonight from the upstairs window of the Forsyths' house. I wanted to see them find Liz. I wanted to see her all right. There was more snow. When they drew snow in the comics, it was like blots of old paper. I was dozing off, waking with a jolt, drifting away again, my head on the cold windowsill. I watched the lights of Penny's party house ... and heard our own party downstairs.

I dreamed I phoned Penny in the middle of the party. I've never talked to the lass before. I phoned her and told her, 'They attacked your mam. They made her fall and hit her head.'

If I phoned Penny's house, they'd never hear the ringing anyway, because of the party's noise.

A taxi driver climbed into his empty cab. Its doors had been left open like wings. Black on clean white. He drove off.

What vehicles did the superheroes have? Mr Fantastic of the Fantastic Four could invent anything. Cars like spaceships, with a seat for each of the four, that would transport them through the scary Phantom Zone that connected their universe with the fucked-up Skrull universe.

My chin resting on the cold, white-painted windowsill, watching over the road. The room behind me smelled of lager. I started dreaming about the Justice League and thinking, they wouldn't have done what my lot had done. But the Justice League were squeaky fucking clean and that's why I hated them. Why were Marvel comics always better than DC?

I could see people leaving the party, crossing the road, drunk and stoned and hopeless. I could see the snow getting ploughed up. I could see Penny in the street, wrapped up, yelling at the others, 'It is her! It is her!'

And the whole party crowded around Liz. Light from the opened doors of all the friendly, open homes shone on the recumbent Liz. Everyone gathered and watched her regain consciousness. She stretched and yawned. Sleeping Beauty. She sat up. Penny helped her to her feet. 'Mam, you're back!' she must have been saying.

Liz supported herself on the walk to her house. Everyone followed. She appeared tired but unharmed. I was glad. The door closed behind them all. Liz was safe.

'Where is she, Andy? Where's she gone?' Penny has forgotten to put a coat on. She's standing in the main road with Andy, who has dressed himself hastily. Mark has gone home. The party is breaking up. Someone said Liz was back, but she hasn't appeared.

The taxi driver leads Penny to his cab. They come hurrying over the snow. 'She was here! She was here! I drove her from Darlington!' The driver is furious. He never got his money. Liz has left his car door open. 'That's twelve quid that!' he shouts.

Penny and Andy won't pay him. They watch him leave.

'Maybe he was just trying it on,' Andy says. 'Maybe she never came back at all.'

'No, she must have,' Penny says. 'She just changed her mind about seeing me. She's come back and lost her nerve.' Penny's face is grim. She sets off, back to number sixteen. 'She's nicked off again.'

Andy follows her back to the house. Some fucking party. His body aches and he's shivering now, the cold and anxiety are starting to get to him. Happy New Year, he thinks.

They pass the play park without a second glance. Liz's white fur coat is camouflage in the snow, which falls heavier and heavier, covering her face.

Six

In a past life, thought Elsie, I must have been a homing pigeon.

She struggled to sit up on the settee on New Year's Day. One of them brave home-loving birds. And what were the other things that got themselves home at all costs? Salmon – returning to their place of origin in order to spawn. She used to be quite interested in wildlife, although she wasn't quite sure what was meant by spawn. 'All God's creatures,' Tom would say sententiously, 'All God's creatures must spawn.'

Elsie woke up on the Dralon cushions, her face stiff and reddened, and realised that somehow she had brought herself home last night. She went into the kitchen and saw that it was past ten. Actually, that was quite a decent hour for the first day of the year.

Tom always said that the way New Year's Eve finds you will be the way you'll stay all the following year. It was one of the few superstitious nonsenses he allowed himself. So you had to be bathed, immaculate, smart, sober and prepared on the stroke of midnight. One good thing about his spoiling all the recent New Years was that Elsie had enjoyed a few pleasant, clear-headed New Year's Days. This morning was tender like her distant past.

On the old squashy armchair in the kitchen, the one that smelled of dog, Big Sue was fast asleep, snoring steadily. Her home-made skirt was rucked up so you could almost see her pants and her hat was still firmly on her head. In the corner, between armchair and fridge, the inflatable reindeer grinned at Elsie. It was saying, 'Where did this old wife come from?' Elsie wondered if anyone else from Penny's party had ended up here.

Craig hadn't turned up, that was for sure. Fancy, New Year's Day and he wasn't here to see his old mam. She started shuffling around with mugs and spoons, making some tea. She was glad the do hadn't been at her house. Imagine the state of number sixteen this morning. Nachos trodden into the carpet, lager on the cushions and up the walls. All the stuff from the cupboards littered down the stairs. And vomit . . . oh, God! She'd thrown up and Penny had been the one rubbing her back in the bathroom, talking her through it.

Elsie, man, she thought, staring out of the kitchen window as the kettle boiled. It's exactly what you weren't going to do. You said you'd never let yourself do that again. And you hardly even know the girl. Still, she thought, it took scenes like that (but whatever had they talked about?) to bring folk closer together. What did they call it on *Vanessa*? Bonding. (Now, that Vanessa was a sensible lass. Elsie liked her and wished that she could have sense like Vanessa. Elsie didn't have the gift of the gab like she had.) They called it bonding, what she and Penny had been doing when Elsie was ill and getting the shakes on the bathroom mat. She couldn't remember at all what they said, but the aftertaste was one of shared confidences. They had shared a moment, those two, Elsie and her future possible daughter-in-law.

Oh, Craig, if you'd been there, son, I could have said, proudly and smiling –

Penny, this is my lovely son –

Son, this is Penny –

And I could have taken a tactful step or two backwards –

And meanwhile the two of them would have been staring rapt at one another, unaware of me by then –

They'd be dancing close to Boney M –

God, remember Nesta and Big Sue dancing in the hallway to Boney M! Them big tits of hers jouncing about all over the place. They were kicking heedlessly through all the old toys and records and books and stuff that came sliding down the stairs. Spoiling all the old stuff, probably, when it would have come in good, donated to the spastics shop. And God, yes, Jane had hurt her arm, dropping down the stairs. Elsie had been too out of it to check on Jane – she was her pal, as well!

Big Sue let out a groan.

'You're awake then,' Elsie mumbled, still looking out across the play park.

The old lady groaned again. At least she's not dead, Elsie thought. That would be terrible, a neighbour karking it in your kitchen.

'I'm awake,' said Sue. The two of them didn't think much of each other. Elsie had heard round the doors that Big Sue kept saying that she, Elsie, was slack.

'How come you ended up back here?' Elsie asked. She had a brainwave and fished out her emergency fags from the cupboard where she kept the bleach and furniture polish. She fiddled with cook's matches.

'You never had to help me home, did you?' she asked with sudden dismay.

'Nah,' said Big Sue. She hadn't moved an inch yet, not even to adjust her skirt. She was gathering her strength to stand up but it looked like she just couldn't be bothered. 'Tell you the truth, Elsie,' and here Big Sue gave a sigh. 'I didn't want to find my way alone, all the way to my house.'

Elsie gave what she hoped was a sympathetic tut, but she didn't think that Sue had *that* far to walk. She thought it was soft of her. Fancy imposing on someone for the sake of dodging the walk home.

'Oh, that's all right.'

'God, I'm stiff,' said Sue. 'Are you making a pot of tea?'

Standing by the window, Elsie suddenly squawked. 'It's Craig! Our Craig! He's coming over to see his mam!'

Even before she could make out details of the figure plodding over the main road though the snow, she could tell it was him by the jointless, lurching walk that she knew by heart. And it was mother's telepathy too, she thought.

'Happy New Year, Craig!' she called out in the kitchen with no hope of being heard yet. 'Oh, look, he's definitely coming here to see his mam!'

'Ee, you do sound pleased to see him, hinny.' Big Sue hoisted herself up to neb through the window. She was actually warming to Elsie for once, hearing her sound so fond of her son. Elsie might be something more than a raddled floozy.

Craig was crossing the play park, the dry snow halfway to his knees.

'Look how much snow there's been!

'Oh, doesn't he look handsome?

'He's got his Gladiators ponytail in –

'And his new Christmas ski jacket I got him –

'Oh, doesn't he look like a Gladiator? One of the nicer ones, I mean.'

Big Sue went to the sink, suddenly brisk. 'Shall I finish off making the tea then?'

'What's he stopped there for?' Elsie asked.

Craig stopped in his tracks. He was in the middle of the play park. The morning air froze in his throat. He had the momentary, sickening impression that he was in a dream. There was a body, limbs flung out, sprawled before him.

He dropped to his knees and started clearing snow off the body. It was almost two inches thick.

From a distance he seemed to be stooping over an anonymous hummock of snow, the size and shape of a sleeping policeman. For now, only he knew what was inside. He couldn't believe he had been so stupid. He had believed his dream. His fingers stung with cold. Her face was frozen stiff.

'What's he found? Craig . . .'

Big Sue turned to watch as Elsie unlocked the kitchen door, fiddled with latches.

Outside, beyond the back yard, Craig was kneeling now and moving with the horrible, lagging inevitability of a dream. He was running his hands through the snow, scooping it away, ploughing it like a dog into a rabbit warren.

'What's going on?' said Sue.

Elsie flung open the door and stepped into the yard. 'Craig?' she called over the fence and something in her voice betrayed her worry. She knew something was up. Even from the kitchen Big Sue could see that Craig had turned white.

He worked feverishly in the snow, unearthing that bump.

First he uncovered the stiff fur of Liz's coat. His numbed, red fingers encountered the spikes the fur had frozen into. Her long hands lay squashed to the gravel. When he came to it, her face was like a death mask. He was careful not to move her head, but he thought anyway that it wouldn't move, that it would be glued in its wig to the ground under the snow. His fingers met the slick, frozen pool of blood.

Elsie came running up, ruining the clean snow and the silence with her yelling.

'It's like the start of a film!' was the first thing she thought to shout. 'You've found a bloody body, Craig!' And then, overwrought, she burst into tears.

They'll blame Tom, she thought. I bet they'll blame Tom because they all know he's a loony.

'Get the paramedics, Mam,' Craig snapped. 'Get back in the house and phone.'

He held his ear close over Liz's face. Her mouth was partly open and her painted lips were glossy, but seemingly frozen hard. If you kissed them they would be hard like boiled sweets. Craig thought, I'm holding my face close over Penny's mother's mouth.

'What if –' Elsie began, but Craig waved her back. He couldn't listen for breath, for heartbeats, with his mother flapping round him.

'Go on!' he shouted and she went.

Craig held his face close to Liz's and placed all his concentration on her signs of life. Yes. A light fluting whisper of breath. Somehow, by force of will, she was sucking in the slowest, the slightest of breaths.

Five minutes before, less, it had been so peaceful here. She lay like Snow White under the snow and New Year's Day found her quietened, almost asleep.

Snow White gobbled down the fatal chunk of apple, choked and had to lie still.

Five minutes after, there were a good ten people standing around Liz. They didn't know what to do. Elsie had phoned 999 and ran back to say they were coming. They'd be fifteen minutes coming from Bishop Auckland, round all the winding, drifted roads. 999 seemed like something off the telly, something full of adventure that shouldn't be real. Dialling it felt like a dare.

What were they meant to do in the next fifteen minutes? Elsie wanted to go back indoors and get dressed, but she knew she couldn't. She'd have her tights halfway on and then she'd hear the sirens. She'd miss it all. More neighbours were joining them; here came Fran in her padded, flowery housecoat, one of the bairns following her with a dummy in its mouth. It was too old for a dummy.

Elsie allowed herself a flush of pride: her Craig had taken charge. Right beside Liz he sat on his haunches and kept talking to her. There was no response, of course, but he kept on talking in a slow, measured voice. He sounds such a grown-up feller, Elsie thought. Where does he get that assurance from? His bad leg lay out awkwardly on the ground and her heart gave a twinge when she saw it.

Liz looked terrible. Her face was blanched, but not magnolia like the snow. She was a dirty white like her scabby, frosty fur coat. She looked like a clown the morning after. Her lost blood had matted some of her golden wig and that added to the effect. Elsie was trying not to look too closely as Craig went on talking to her:

78

'We're all here, Liz – don't sleep – don't go to sleep – wait till we can get you warm – we're all here, Liz – your Penny's here – if you open your eyes you'll see her.'

First thing this morning Penny had set to work with black bin bags. Going round the house and chucking in beer cans, paper plates, wine bottles. The house was a wreck inside. She stumbled about, thick with a hangover, thinking it was just as well Liz wasn't here.

Then Elsie was banging on her door. 'It's your mam!' she cried, before Penny even opened the blinds or found the key.

To Elsie's eyes, it seemed as if Penny was hanging back. Perhaps she was ashamed of her mother, laid out like this in public. Or it could be shock.

'Penny,' Craig said. 'You've got to talk to her as well – don't let her go to sleep.'

Penny was trying not to look too hard at her mother. She stared at Craig and wanted to ask him, How do you know my name? Andy touched her elbow, prompting her. She couldn't think of a thing to say. That thin, pale face didn't even look familiar. Besides she felt shoved out of the way by Craig. He was exerting a charm of dogged protection around Penny's mam.

Penny tried to make a step forward and found there was no room. 'Mam,' she said, finding the word strange to her after only a year. 'I'm glad you came back. What happened? What went on?'

Still not looking into Liz's face, Craig said, 'She must have slipped up on all the ice and snow last night.'

Andy spoke up. 'Slipped, my arse! Does this look like someone who's slipped over?'

'She's banged her head,' said Elsie.

Fran couldn't bear hanging about, not being helpful. 'What can I do?'

Craig said, 'The paramedics will be here in –'

'Ten minutes,' said Big Sue. 'You've got to keep her warm. She must have lost loads of body heat.'

They all stared at the tarmac and its dense layers of snow.

Craig's resolve was weakening. 'So what do we do? We can't touch her or move her . . .'

'Get some blankets. We'll get some blankets.'

Behind Fran, Nesta was already turning back to her house. 'Mine's closest,' she said. 'I'll fetch blankets.'

Fran watched Nesta going off to be helpful. Wonders will never cease, Fran thought.

A weak, guttural voice came from Liz. It sounded as if she was laughing in slow motion. 'Huurrrr. Huurrrr.'

'What's she saying?' Bending forward with her hands on knees, Elsie shuffled closer and almost had Big Sue over.

'She's not saying anything,' Penny said, sounding almost disgusted. 'She's not saying words.'

'It could be "hurry",' Big Sue put in.

Nesta arrived with armfuls of blankets and pillows from her airing cupboard. That was what she said but in the crisp, clean air of the morning they smelled fusty and unwashed to Fran, who helped her spread them out and lay them over Liz. The pillows were useless because they didn't dare move her head.

When the blankets were spread out – pink and scratchy, their hems ragged – they all looked down at Liz lying under them. Her head was staring up out of one end, sightlessly, almost proudly, and that was when Penny started to cry. Andy hugged her. He was very quiet, looking as white and shocked as the rest of them, still in his tartan cowboy drag, minus the leather chaps. There was no sign of Mark Kelly and his tattoos this morning. He'd told Andy that today there was a New Year's Day lunch, a gathering of the Kelly clan, and so he had to be away. Andy hugged Penny and mumbled into her hair, unconsciously. The crowd around Liz was even larger now, as Jane and Peter, Frank and Ethan, came to join them.

When the paramedics came, they were efficient and

frazzled. It had been a busy night in Aycliffe. Penny and Craig went with Liz in the ambulance and there was hardly room for them. Andy called a cab from the box on the corner and he was joined by Fran, Elsie and Big Sue, following behind the ambulance all the way to Bishop. Others would be coming later on the bus.

In another five minutes the play park was still again. Nesta gathered up the used covers.

'Go on, lad. You sit in the front.'

The three women crammed themselves onto the back seat and, when the taxi arrived at Bishop General, they made Andy pay. 'Lad,' he thought miserably on the drive out; they don't even know my name.

All the way there they tagged along behind the ambulance and, through the windows in the back, he could see shapes moving and blurring and he was glad he wasn't inside there. Imagine sitting with Penny, looking down at her battered mother.

It was a half-hour drive and, behind him, the three women talked among themselves. They were deciding that it was impossible to fall and hurt yourself as Liz had apparently done.

'But she's been out all night,' said Big Sue. 'Out in all the weather.'

Fran said darkly, 'Ay, but I reckon there'd been, what you call it, foul play.'

'That's a big accusation,' said Elsie, looking out at the fields of snow sliding past. Andy glanced back and saw that all three of them had their handbags on their knees.

'I wasn't accusing anyone,' said Fran. 'Who is there to accuse?' She fell silent for a moment. 'But I don't think you bleed all over the place like that just by slipping over.'

'To me,' said Big Sue, trying to get more comfortable, 'it looked like she'd been clonked on the head.'

Elsie was still looking away. 'So it was a wig she had on all that time.'

They all thought about this. Under the wig they had

glimpsed smooth brown hair, plastered down to her scalp. They don't know, Andy thought, turning back to watch the road, they don't know why she wears that wig. There's a relief at least, he thought, though he wasn't sure why. Lying on the ground, Liz had seemed too exposed, too open to their view. He knew that that was what horrified Penny most. Liz with all her secrets open to the street.

The taxi driver was chain-smoking as if he was concerned, too. He was in an Arran cardigan that was stained with nicotine and he wore diamond-patterned pyjama bottoms as if he hadn't been bothered to dress properly. It was his own firm, Tiger Taxis, and his orange car was painted with brown stripes. 'It's distinctive, isn't it?' he said to Andy, when Andy started up a conversation to make the trip go faster. 'Tiger Taxis stand out in the taxi rank, because we've got a gimmick.' Suddenly he looked into his rear-view mirror and raised his voice. 'You gotta have a gimmick, haven't you, ladies?'

Elsie scowled at him, Fran shrugged and smiled and Big Sue, who wasn't quite sure what he meant, said, 'I suppose you do.'

He had to drop them round the front of the hospital, the main entrance for visitors, while the ambulance went straight to the back. 'The tradesmen's entrance,' said the driver gloomily. 'I hope your friend is all right,' he said when Andy paid him and the others were clambering out.

'Shall we buy flowers?' asked Big Sue, watching the Tiger Taxi steam and shunt its way out of the car park.

'He's a terrible driver,' said Elsie. 'We should get a discount for his driving. Our Craig never passed his test, but he was much more careful than him.'

'Let's not get flowers now,' Fran said, leading the way to the sliding smoked-glass doors. 'It seems morbid.'

Andy disagreed. It seemed quite the thing to turn up with armfuls of white lilies, say. He was sure, from all he had heard about Liz, that she would appreciate them, but Fran was busy finding out where they could wait, where they could get information, and the moment for finding flowers had passed.

In the waiting room Big Sue and Elsie smoked, Elsie fiddling all the while with the dirty-looking toddlers' toys in the bucket in the middle. Fran leafed irritably through issues of *Hello*, tutting at the affluence, and Andy lulled himself into a waiting trance. He often found himself going off into one of those, forgetting, almost, the reason for being there.

No sooner did he think, I've got myself an older man! than he felt a stab of anguish, almost like guilt. It was guilt and panic and he recalled all of a sudden the gashed and useless condom Mark had tweaked free, held up for a moment and then slung away. They had barely had time to register it before they were dressing and taking in what Penny was shouting through the door. Andy's chest had been hammering. He didn't know what to think. He dragged on his clothes faster and wordlessly watched Mark's more methodical re-covering of all his tattoos. Mark looked at him and said, 'It'll be all right.' When he was pulling on his shoes he said it again; 'Honest. It's all right.'

Penny shouted from the hallway, 'Come and meet my mam! She's waiting outside to make a grand entrance!'

Andy thought back to the headiest, most extreme moment of their sex. He felt as if things had got out of hand. He couldn't believe it and felt, for a moment, as if he had let himself down somehow. He never fucked with Vince, it wasn't something they did. What came back now was the exact moment of penetration, the snug and gagging seconds that Mark spent inside him. He could even recall what must have been the exact second of the split, Mark biting into his shoulder as he thrust harder, and that must have been it.

'Honest,' Mark said, over more of Penny's shouting.

'So you've been tested,' Andy said, not letting the question sound, wanting it to be a statement. Anyway, he's had a bairn, he told himself, and she's all right, so Mark had to be healthy. Of course it was all right. They could do it again right now, risk as much as they liked, and it would still be all right.

'I haven't,' Mark said. 'No.'

That could be all right still, Andy was thinking as they went out to the landing. If he hasn't taken the HIV test, then he can't think he has any need to. Mark was leading the way downstairs and there was some other bloke there, Penny was saying this was the taxi driver. They had to go outside to meet Liz. She's always like this, Penny was gabbling excitedly: my mother thinks she's bloody royalty.

'But where's Cliff?' Penny was asking. 'Where's my mother's sexy bus-driver boyfriend? Has she come back alone?

Andy watched Mark straying into the crowd, into the living room. He was off to fetch a drink but it felt as if he was running away. Andy could still feel him, still feel the absence of Mark inside himself, as if his muscles had been stretched too far. Like when we work out together down the gym, he thought, and ache deliciously the following day. We've just been stretching each other a bit further again.

This was as midnight approached. Rose was telling Jane to hold her horses: they could get her busted arm sorted out after they'd seen the New Year in. It was only sprained. Jane was snuffling to herself, cradling her arm, and her pageboy son Peter looked frightened.

Mark's a family man, thought Andy. And what does that mean? It means that usually he's straight and tonight was just a branching out – but was that true? Andy couldn't believe it was his first time with a bloke. He remembered the awkwardness, the mechanics of his own first time with a man. No, Mark had known exactly what he'd been about. And anyway, what did his predilections have to do with risk? Except . . . Andy was looking through the bodies for him. They were sweaty and jostling and roped in streamers of tinsel. The party was counting down the last three minutes.

The risk was the same whatever, Andy decided coldly. We fucked up. Suddenly Mark was beside him with a fresh can of lager, handing another to Andy. Whatever was in Mark was in Andy now.

When the clock struck, Mark pulled him into an alcove where the coat rack bulged out with the party's freight of outdoor clothes. Everyone was kissing everyone else.

Mark kissed Andy in the alcove in the hall, out of sight, and Andy asked, 'You said it would be all right. How do you know?'

Elsie was coming down the hall, rakish with gleaming eyes, looking for others to kiss the new year in with. She stood watching Mark consoling Andy, pressed up against her own anorak and Sheila's fake fur. Wordlessly she stepped backwards.

It was the first time, she thought blearily, that she had ever seen two men kiss each other. There was a moment of doubt, as if she had seen something entirely fabulous, a made-up animal. And then, with a bit more thought, it seemed all too obvious and real. It was just the first time she had seen it in real life. She shouldn't be surprised, she supposed. They had it on telly now sometimes.

Andy went through all these scenes the following day, in the waiting room at Bishop General. The women weren't talking much. They were staunch and practised, settling with ease into the slog of hospital waiting. Andy wasn't used to this at all, but there was something at the back of his mind provoking dread. He hated the antiseptic and used furniture of hospitals, the plastic seats and, on the walls, arrows pointing busily everywhere. It was an instinctive dislike, but one that he also traced back to his waiting with Nanna Jean, the night his parents died. He had been eleven then, but the dread was still there.

He told the women that he had to go off for a walk. They were so implacable it drove him crazy. They just nodded and he sloped off, down the immaculate corridors, not even trying to keep his bearings. If anyone asked him or stopped him, he would just pretend to be daft and then they'd be nice to him. That always worked. *When will I be too old to play the daft lad?* he wondered and realised he'd walked into some kind of maternity wing.

He stood in front of a glass wall and beyond were rows and rows of freshly filled cots. Babies red in the face and tossing about angrily under blankets. All their yelling made the others worse. They had name plates and bracelets attached, but to Andy looking in on them, it seemed arbitrary. Oh, he'd heard before about people getting the wrong baby. Twenty-five years later they went on *Ricki Lake* to talk about it: how the children in question always *knew* that they never quite belonged, that there had been a mix-up. They felt a nagging. Genetics pulled on them like magnetism, taking them back where they belonged. Andy couldn't quite imagine that easy sense of belonging. Mind, there was Elsie and her Craig – how much they looked alike with those big facial features. Her face was a little-old-woman version of his, and her features looked more natural on him.

How many of the bairns in this room beyond the glass would grow up queer? He squinted along the rows for early signs. If there was a gene involved, then they were already queer. Gay babies.

The room was like a field, he thought. Or a battery-hen farm. It was completely fascinating. He remembered *Logan's Run* and a scene early in the film where they look at a room of babies like this and it turns out that in the future no one knows whose baby is whose and all child-rearing is communal. There was no fuss, no nonsense and no need for straight parenting. He couldn't remember what had made Logan run.

His favourite film of all time was still *Escape from the Planet of the Apes*, which ended with the death of a swaddled monkey baby; that scene broke his heart every time. *So I must have a sentimental streak about babies*, he thought, frowning. In *Logan's Run* they executed all the adults when they got to thirty, he couldn't remember why. Some weird, fucked-up science-fiction reason. They dressed the thirty-year-olds in red frocks, stood them in an arena and they got sucked up into a giant red crystal in the ceiling. It was like a rave. Dead by thirty, he thought.

It made him angry, suddenly, that last year Vince had tried to kill himself. He tried to poison himself with embalming fluid. He swallowed the whole bottle and only just made it. He was the healthiest, safest person Andy knew – how could he even have thought of doing himself harm? Ruining that perfection? Perfection that the clever Ralph, the Jane Austen expert, was getting the pure benefit of in Paris right now.

Andy closed his eyes, his forehead to the thick glass wall. When he opened his eyes, he thought one baby in particular was giving him a dirty look. Little bastard, Andy thought. He's looking at me almost patronisingly. Then the child seemed to sigh and roll over, turning its face away from him. Andy felt the blood burn in his cheeks.

When Craig joined them in the main waiting room, he kept scratching himself. He worked his fingers through his jeans into his shins and thighs as he told them about Liz's progress – or lack of it.

'And then they chucked me out. Next of kin only. So here I am.' He shrugged and rubbed at the back of his knee.

'Next of kin,' tutted Elsie. 'That means poor Penny is in there by herself. Anyway, you did smashing, pet.' She smiled proudly at her son. 'I wouldn't be surprised if, when that Liz gets out of here, she doesn't give you something. A reward. He deserves it, doesn't he?'

Fran smiled tightly and Big Sue just looked disgusted. Craig said, 'I just did what anyone would.'

'No, you were a star,' said Elsie. 'You were masterful.'

'Oh, get away!' He was scratching himself again and his mam noticed that Big Sue was frowning at this. He ran his hands nervously through his hair. His ponytail was out and his hair hung down all over the place. He went to the coffee machine in the corridor and his mam followed him.

'What are you itching for?'

'You what?' He punched Bovril.

'Oh, you don't want that. What about mad cows?'

He rolled his eyes. 'Mam, you've always, always bought the cheapest Walter Wilson own-brand beefburgers. One cup of Bovril won't kill me now.'

'Cheapest!' she cried. 'Listen, tell me, why are you scratching all the time?'

He pressed for sugar by mistake. 'Shite.'

'Craig!'

'I'm not scratching all the time.'

'It's like you've got fleas. Oh, Craig, it's not crabs, is it?'

He blushed. 'No, it's not. I've had crabs, I know what –'

'You haven't!' She looked shocked.

'And I used that lotion stuff that smells like pear drops.'

Elsie grimaced, remembering a bout of her own.

'But I *am* itching,' he said. 'Like there's something under my skin.'

She looked scared. 'You want to get down the doctors'.' She looked around. 'Maybe they'll look at you while you're here.'

'Don't be daft.' He lowered his voice. 'Everyone in the house is like this. I reckon it's something in the beds, in the mattresses. Someone said something about scabies.'

Elsie could only think about dogs foaming at the mouth. She said, 'Isn't that rabies, when they go mad and turn homophobic?'

'You what?' He frowned. 'This is scabies. It's like having itchy worms under your skin.'

She looked sick. 'Oh, my God!' Elsie had never had much, but she'd always been clean. Her house had always been spotless and there had never been vermin. Never. 'That does it then, Craig. You're not to go back there. It must be filthy. You can't go back to that den of vermin.'

He threw away the sugary Bovril and she realised she

was holding her breath, awaiting an outburst. It never came. When he looked at her, he just seemed obscurely pleased.

'Look, we'll see, Mam. We'll just see.'

Penny didn't want to see her mam like that. Tubes up her nose.

They had let her into her mother's room to watch all the urgent fussing around. Penny was content to sit in the corridor. She couldn't watch what they were doing.

She flipped through the tatty magazines left lying about. *Mysteries of the Mind*: UFOs, abductions, spontaneous combustion. She bloody hated mysteries. What was the point of the unexplained if no one explained it to you at the end?

It had shocked Penny that, while the doctors and nurses were working on her mam, they left her dressed in her golden frock and high heels. She was the most glamorous victim Penny had ever seen. She was bald and her wig was propped on the cardiograph machine like a mascot.

To Penny her mother looked blue. It was as if she was still getting colder, and she couldn't stop herself from turning blue.

She listened to the muted hospital-corridor sounds. She couldn't believe they were so stupid as not to see her last night. Her own mam, unconscious in the snow. The image of Liz being snowed on and blotted out preyed on Penny's mind.

She'd been mugged, there was no doubt about it. You didn't slip and end up like that. Someone had hit her. Penny made a quiet resolution to find out what had happened.

She had stared now for some minutes on end at a page in her *Unexplained* magazine. It was a page of ghostly apparitions. Grainy, probably faked photographs. There was a whole magazine dedicated to wondering whether they were real. It made her sick such effort was made to prove these shabby ghosts true.

Seven

'I'm not sure where my time goes. It just goes. It's not as if I'm doing anything special.' Mark was peering into the grill at their cheese on toast. The red element was reflected on the cheese's oily surface. 'And I can't even find time to cook a proper meal.' He looked up at Andy, who stood holding the bottle of Hardy's Nottage Hill he'd brought, feeling daft. 'Sorry.' He pulled the grill pan out and looked at the toast. 'I bet you thought this was going to be a proper meal, didn't you?'

Andy, who had indeed expected something more, shrugged and put his bottle down on the kitchen surface, screwing the tissue paper into a pink carnation. 'Oh, I haven't been eating properly for days, anyway,' he said. 'It was just nice of you to invite me round.'

Stiffly Mark plonked their toast on two plates. He handed Andy his. 'Shall we go through there?'

They were being strange with each other, the way they would have been a week ago, when they still knew each other only from Completely Fit. A week ago it was Christmastime, Andy thought. At home he and Penny were taking turns at being the optimistic one, while the other sank into despondence. Penny had no idea why Andy looked depressed. She thought he was simply sharing the way she felt over Liz.

'It must be . . .' Mark paused, choosing his word. 'It must be hectic round your house just now.'

'It's not *hectic*,' Andy said.

They had to choose between sitting on the settee or at the dining table. The settee. Would Mark switch the telly on? Would they make it as informal as that? They kept it off. Mark wanted to talk to him.

'It's not hectic,' Andy said again. 'To tell you the truth, it's like the bloody morgue.' His heart leaped daringly inside him. This was treachery.

'Is she still in the coma?' Mark asked, although he knew fine well that she was. Only that afternoon he had been round Fran's house getting the latest. Fran looked worn down. Hers was the most recent visit to Liz and she came back telling everyone that, even hooked up to life support, Liz still looked like the Queen of Sheba. Tubes gurgled into her nose, lights pinged and monitors skipped, and among it all Liz looked indomitable. She'd come out of this soon. Over tea and Battenburg cake this afternoon, Fran had told Mark she imagined Liz coming back from the brink of the next world and telling them all about it. She could see her sitting at the kitchen table, just like this, regaling them all with the lowdown on life after death. Liz would be just the type to have an out-of-body experience.

What did they tell you? That you floated up to a high luminous white point in the ceiling and when you looked down you could see your own body in repose. Like an empty crisp packet. Of course Liz would be the type to come back.

Something of what she saw at Bishop General had depressed Fran. It was to Mark, and no one else from Phoenix Court, she explained this. Mark wondered why she could trust him with her anxiety. He wondered about this as she was telling him, and he thought maybe it was because they had already shared tragedy. They had a shared history of tragic, true-story films and they knew all about hospital bedsides. She said to him, 'Remember that film about the coma patient? I remember one thing, they return to being like a bairn in the womb. They curl up. From lying down they curl up and even suck their thumbs. They make themselves small as possible.'

'Horrible,' Mark said.

'I can't imagine that happening to Liz,' she said.

91

'No,' he agreed, though he hardly knew her. He just thought of her as the glamorous woman round the corner, a little bit older than him. She'd vanished one night and walked out of her life, apparently striding into the unknown beyond Newton Aycliffe. She looked like something out of an eighties soap opera, over the top.

'Really,' Fran said, 'she does look like a queen . . . you know, lying in state.'

'She won't die, though, will she?' Mark asked Andy now.

'No,' Andy almost snapped. Despite himself, Andy was irritated by all the talk of Liz. He felt terrible about it, but it was getting on his nerves. In the first three days of the new year it had been Liz Liz Liz. Couldn't she do anything quietly, that woman? She hadn't said a word to any of them, she'd hardly done a thing, and look at the entrance she'd made. An impact on everyone in Phoenix Court. Currently she had a different person visiting every day of the week, sometimes two. There was a rota organised.

Andy was thinking that his own life registered very quietly in all of this. He wanted to shout out, But look what's happened to me, too! Abandoned by Vince! Phoned by Vince! Maybe I'll lose my home now! And I got fucked dangerously by an older man! An older tattooed-all-over man! And maybe now I'll die! He could catch an echo of that song – there was an old woman who swallowed a fly, or something, that was it – perhaps she'll die. I swallowed a man with tattoos, he thought miserably, and that event – the single most risky, potentially catastrophic event of my young life – hasn't been noticed here at all. Hardly an eyebrow raised. But what do I want? At least for Mark to acknowledge the fact. What they had made between them was like a pact. A pact in blood. Here they sat, eating cheese on toast, and they hadn't said anything much of any importance. Except about Liz, who seemed to Andy to be frozen in perfect inviolability. Bizarrely, out of everyone they knew, Liz seemed to be the safest of them all.

*

I was listening to him going on and my mind was not really on it. 'So tell me,' I said – and I'm a master of small talk – 'tell me about your New Year's Day.'

'Oh, with the family.' Mark pulled a face and the tattoos got pulled out of shape with his frown.

As he told me all about it, I wanted him to gather me up . . . and do what? Take me off to bed?

I just wanted him to gather me up.

Andy, man, I was berating myself. Get a grip. Who else do I know weak as me? Penny's strong. No one fettles her. Vince always gets what he wants. Here's me hanging on Mark's every word.

'Well, you know I've got this ex-mother-in-law, Peggy. She took it upon herself to cook for everyone. She wanted the whole family together and that included me as the father of her granddaughter – Sally's my daughter.'

Was he saying that pointedly to me: 'Sally's my daughter'? I already knew he had a daughter.

'And of course Peggy's got her own baby to look after, just gone two. Sixty-six and looking after a bairn like that and she's wanting to cook for everyone.'

'She sounds like a star.'

Mark snorted. 'Peggy's a star all right.'

'Where did she get a baby from at sixty-six?' I asked.

'Oh, well.' Mark threw up his hands and looked as if he didn't want to explain. I didn't mind. I could do without all the complications of his life. 'Put it this way,' he said, 'she had a baby last year when she wasn't expecting it. It came as a bit of a surprise to all of us.'

'Right.'

Now I was looking round at the living room and to me it seemed tidy. It hardly looked lived in at all. Mind, I'm used to number sixteen which, while it's never dirty exactly, we're not dusting everyday. And there's a kind of rumpled chaos about the place. I like that. It's homely. 'Rumpled chaos' was Vince's phrase for it, by the way. Things lying about. Always there's clothes horses up with shirts and pants drying. A pile of CDs and tapes out of their cases on the floor in front of the stereo.

In Mark's flat you got the feeling that whatever he used he put back in its place immediately he was finished with it. I think that's unnatural. The more I thought about it, the more it felt like something had been excised from the place. Maybe signs of other people. His wife and daughter, of course, and I felt sorry then for analysing what he had or didn't have lying about. This environment was so obviously the result of his being left all on his own. He made the best of it and for him this meant a crippling neatness. I went to the bathroom and noticed that round the edges of the bath he'd neglected to remove all traces of his ex-family. There were a number of those plastic characters you get bubble bath in: Ariel the Mermaid, Minnie Mouse, Robocop. I was almost tempted to check if he'd cleared out his daughter's old room. I don't know why. I knew he had her staying at weekends, so it stood to reason that her room would be kept the same as ever. It was something perverse in me that wanted to see her room like a shrine.

Honestly, I think I'm turning into a sick bastard.

I reckon I do need to get out of Aycliffe for a few days, I thought. They're all doing my head in. I'm sick of seeing Penny with a face like a slapped arse. Sorry, Penny, that's not fair. I owe Nanna Jean a visit anyway. I didn't go and see her during the festive season. Festive season! I've had more festive shits. Nanna Jean was in Corfu anyway with the girls from the club. But she's due a visit. See her tan.

I went back to the living room and Mark was putting his jacket on. 'Listen, I'm still starving. Do you want to come and fetch fish and chips with me? We can have them here with the wine you brought.' That smile of his held an infectious enthusiasm. It was like when he put me to bed on New Year's Eve and, in so many words, unbuttoning my tartan shirt, he came out to me and made the loveliest pass that anyone ever has. He made it all into a wonderful joke with that grin.

94

I said, all right. But I only had, like, one pound fifty on me. 'My treat,' he said. 'Like I said, I should have cooked properly for you. These are guilty fish and chips.'

We walked out in the snow. It was dark again and I thought about Liz lying in the play park all night. You can't help thinking about it. Her blood is still frozen there. You can see it. The kids were playing with it the other night. Dirty little monsters, playing with Liz's frozen blood. I watched out the window and it made me want to run out and tell them, 'Don't play with her blood!' I saw a dog lick it, too.

We walked out to the Redhouses. I always thought that the fish shop there was dirty and I wouldn't have gone there if it had been my choice.

I said to Mark, 'Was the other baby there on New Year's Day?' I meant his ex-wife's new baby, the one he had been roped in to deliver. He sighed and said yes.

'I'm getting attached to the little thing. Another little girl.'

'Was her father there?'

'Bob the policeman?' He scowled. 'We tried to make more of an effort to include him in the conversation. My ex-wife gets cross when we leave him out.' He shrugged. 'He's so boring.'

'But your wife loves him.'

'Well.' For the first time he looked perplexed. I had probably overstepped the mark.

I said, 'It's amazing you're all still so much a part of each other's lives.'

'It's the bairns,' he said. 'All the bairns keeping us together. Making us eat family meals and watch the big film on the bank-holiday afternoon, while Peggy fusses round, making us tea as well as dinner.'

I said, 'It's got to be more than the bairns. There are lots of divorced and split-up families and they don't carry on like you lot. I think you lot are quite unusual.' We were at the fish shop by then. There was a queue inside and it was steamy. I leaned against the far end of the counter and ran

95

my fingers on the dimpled metal. A sign said not to burn myself on the glass.

'Unusual?' He smirked, but not as if he was really listening to me. 'Compared with my lot, Andy, you don't know what unusual is.'

Now I smirked. 'You reckon?'

And we were smirking at each other until it was our turn.

Back at his flat he put the telly on while we ate. I picked at the fish, teasing off its yellow cardigan of batter and eating it in strips. The wine was rough and it seemed to cut through the claggy grease that lined my throat. We watched a bit of the film that was on that night, *Big*. I bloody hate that film, Tom Hanks acting daft. I said to Mark, whenever I really want to see a smart film and I'm depending on there being something good on the telly, it always turns out to be *Big* with bloody Tom Hanks. Or *Three Men and a Little Lady*.

Mark asked me what my favourite film was.

I said, *Escape from the Planet of the Apes*.

He went, 'Oh.' He hadn't seen it.

I must have kept making bored noises all the way through the film. He picked up on them and realised I wasn't enjoying it. He drew the curtains and took away the plates, which had been resting at our feet, smeared in grease and tomato sauce. I could hear him washing up. I went to stand behind him at the sink. I was being bold, I thought, standing right behind him.

'So there's been no word from Liz's boyfriend, has there? That Cliff?' he asked. I watched his blue hands moving about in the suds. The air was scented with vinegar from the chips and the red wine.

'No, there's been nothing,' I said. 'We don't know where he is. He should be here, though. Taking some responsibility.' I kissed the back of his neck clumsily and he flinched at the contact.

'He used to live in the flat above this one,' Mark said. 'Until he ran away with Liz last year.'

96

'Did he?'

'He's a good-looking bloke.'

I watched him finish the few dishes, dry his hands and screw the tea towel up. He stood still, facing away from me, and I started to feel a little silly, leaning in close like this.

'Will you let me stay tonight?' I asked and was wondering as I said it why I asked like that. I sounded so subservient. What did I think I was doing?

'Andy,' he said, turning, 'I . . .'

I stepped back. 'Right.'

He could see the look on my face. 'It's not that I don't want to. I think you're a great bloke.'

'Right,' I said stupidly, again.

'You know I fancy you,' he said. 'Obviously you know that.'

'Yeah,' I said. I couldn't remember where I'd put down my coat when we came in with the chips. I wanted to go back to number sixteen. I'd rather put up with Penny being miserable than this.

'It shouldn't really have happened on New Year's Eve,' he said, and sighed. 'It was like I took advantage. Andy, how old are you?'

I turned to go. 'Fuck you.'

I wanted to scream at him that his finer feelings weren't the issue here. Whether he felt he had taken advantage or not, I never cared. I wanted to tell him we were bonded in more than just one mistaken night. It was something I felt in the pit of my stomach and it wasn't that I thought our complicity was a good one, a healthy one or a positive one. I just felt we should . . . I don't know . . . cling together for a bit.

But when I made a rush job of saying goodbye and leaving then and there, he just looked relieved. And I didn't see Mark Kelly again till I came back from Tyneside. That was more than a week later. The time-scale we work on, well, it might as well have been a year. By then things had moved on – what do they say? – apace.

97

Andy dreamed for much of the night about the animals he knew were on Mark's body. Were there really seahorses and centaurs? Had he seen them? Great, splashy butterflies on his shoulders; cherubs and turtles malformed with age. Was he making it all up and giving Mark's body more credit than it deserved?

There was no leopard, he was sure about that. He'd have noticed any leopards a mile off. After a while in that dream the creatures in their tattoo colours cleared away and made space for Andy's favourite.

In a weak spot the leopard will come back and give me that baleful stare.

Mostly his eyes are green and blue and I'm sure that he's a he. He has that hungry look men get.

And women don't get that hungry look? Oh, don't quote me on this. I'm only talking from my experience.

Green and blue, eyes like clocks. Eyes always at twelve, always at dinnertime. This is the eye of the leopard that comes back to look at me.

I have fallen out of bed because the leopard looks at me. He doesn't do anything else, he gives me that hungry look and, in a weak spot when I'm not feeling my best, it's enough to startle me out of bed.

I woke tangled in my sheets. I woke wrestling them, damp, and I thought they were his pelt, glossy and wet, coming flayed and free in my hands.

His mouth hangs open all the time, he's frozen like that. Not stupidly like a dog's mouth, panting and sloppy. His mouth is open in a grin that cracks his head wide open and his ears stand on end, his whiskers all a-tremble.

I haven't described his spots yet. The leopard's proverbial spots.

Look! that black-lipped, pink-gummed, bloody and ivory grin proclaims. Oh, look at my proverbial spots!

Tonight I veer my eyes away from his marks, as if at a defect. But how can I? His spots are everywhere. A pox on him! His covering is comprehensive, from the ends of his whiskers to the tip of a tail that twitches and coils to punctuate the sentences I invent for him to say. Oh? he purrs. Ah! he murmurs. Oooh . . . he concedes, jabbing the air with that tail of his, dot dot dot.

Under, between and round the spots his fur is tough and golden. It cascades over muscle. If you opened him up, you'd expect him to be golden through and through. But he's not, inside he is fibrous red meat, like me and you, my leopard.

Those black spots, now that I can gather myself up to stare uninhibitedly, are the exact size and shape of lip marks, all over him. Someone in black lipstick has taken him and kissed him all over. As if with equal parts passion and possessiveness, they have laid a claim to his pelt and marked it for their own. They have kissed his twinkling golden ears, his fairer, tightly muscled sides and even the soft, dimpled pads of his feet.

Have I mentioned before that I dream of my leopard at times like these? When I feel like this?

It comes from the time I lived in a taxidermist's. Before I lived in Penny's house I had rooms above my uncle Ethan's taxidermist's shop in Darlington. Downstairs in the gloom, surmounting mildewed pedestals and scratched glass cabinets, were stoats and kingfishers, everything you'd expect. The cupboards were full of all his stuffing paraphernalia. There was a back room where he would set to hollowing the poor beasts out and patching them up again.

In the front window, sunning itself in the meagre light, his leopard surveyed the length of North Road with that same baleful stare. He said he never would sell that leopard. It was as broad across the shoulders as I was and from its nostrils to the end of its tail it almost spanned the width of the shop.

I used to do bar work and when I came back late to the empty shop and flat there would be only my leopard to greet me. To say, How was your evening? Why are you so late? Who is this you've brought home with you?

Look what the cat's dragged in! he'd go, and I would laugh.

Uncle Ethan let his taxidermist business go and I had to move out. 'It was a liability,' he said, 'and believe me,' he added, 'a man with a wooden leg knows a liability when he sees one.' All the animals went and I wanted to keep the leopard for my own. Yet at that stage I didn't even have a home. I could just see myself on the streets with a leopard in tow. *Bringing Up Baby*. So I just lost sight of him.

Some nights he's back, looking at me, giving me advice.

Often I tumble out of bed, all sweaty, when I see him in the night.

He jumps up on his hind legs and presses his paws into my shoulders. The retracted nails dig into my skin but never break the surface. All the while I get the feeling my leopard is trying to impress something on me. His advice.

When I dream of him tonight, the night I've been round Mark's, the leopard's telling me I was right to think I should get out of Aycliffe for a while.

Go north, the leopard is saying, pressing his paws on my shoulders, his mouth gaping wide, his clock-faced eyes implacable.

All right, I say, I'll go north.

Then I wake myself up by sneezing and realise I've come down overnight with germs.

More snow has settled, it's six o'clock and I can hear Penny knocking about in the kitchen downstairs. When I get down there she's making up some sandwiches for my bus journey north. Somehow she already knows I've decided to go. I thank her, though sometimes it unnerves me, the way Penny just easily, unquestionably knows exactly what I have been dreaming of.

Eight

Elsie's incentive for working at the spastics shop was this: getting people to look in. After all her years on the town she knew nearly everyone who came through those doors. Some came in especially to see her. It was what she liked best about the job. It wasn't paid work. It was all for charity and she wasn't one of those who expected to get something for nothing.

'There's also something else,' said Charlotte, when they stood listing incentives to each other over the counter. 'There's also the fact that we get the pick of the best stuff. That's our best perk.'

Charlotte was a bit posh, Elsie thought. The older woman put on this accent, even though she had lived in Aycliffe for years, well before her man died and she was widowed. She came to the spastics with a clean, pressed pinny every morning.

When Elsie was on the till she could hear Charlotte crashing and stumbling about in the sorting room upstairs. She always got there first, rooting around in the donations, setting stuff aside, pricing things up with the yellow stickers. Elsie hardly ever got a look-in. She found herself thinking unkindly of Charlotte getting to the best donations with those hands of hers like claws. The old woman was twisted up with arthritis and her hands were purple, so that Elsie could hardly stand to look at them. Charlotte had difficulties pushing the till buttons. It was terrible and embarrassing to see. That was why, usually, it ended up with Elsie stuck behind the counter serving people, taking money and chatting away. Meanwhile Charlotte fussed around the racks, straightening and sorting, then ducking upstairs to poke around for the cream of the crop. Elsie knew for a fact the old woman put 20p stickers on the things she wanted for herself. And grudgingly she paid this nominal amount, going home with bagfuls of goodies every teatime. God knows how she got it all to fit into that bungalow of hers. She lived just off Phoenix Court, in Catherine Cookson Close, and thought she was a cut above.

'Someone asking after you,' Charlotte called, waving one of those hands of hers in front of Elsie's face. She knew Elsie went off into these dozes and she clicked her fingers under her nose to bring her round. Elsie hated it when she did that.

'Hm?' I want to stay daydreaming, Elsie thought. The shop was overheated and it was empty, which was strange, because the January sale was on. She was enjoying being able to drift off in the relative quiet, buoyed on that dry, dusty air and the scent of washing powder and other people's houses. Their shop had that particular smell, whatever the stock was. Elsie thought of it as a compound of the smells of all the homes in Aycliffe.

'Someone's asking after you,' said Charlotte, and pointed to Penny, standing awkwardly next to the rack of blouses Charlotte had spent the morning arranging. She had put them in order of the colours of the rainbow. They shaded gradually from salmon to poison green. Penny was clutching a carrier of Red Spot groceries and she held a family box of cornflakes under one arm. Elsie hurried over and wanted to cuddle her or greet her fondly – do something nice, anyway – but there was something that held her back. She was never quite sure how to say hello. People could be funny about things like that and anyway, there was something about Penny that kept people at a distance. Elsie had forgotten that since she last saw Penny. A few days of fondness and absence had softened Penny's edge.

The girl looked pale today, her hair unwashed, her legs

bare and mottled with the cold. She wore those clumpy boots and what looked like a feller's old duffel coat.

'Are you all right, pet?' Elsie asked, and made her smile. She was glad someone was asking after her, for a change, instead of her mam. For a week that was all they had said to her, friends, faces she knew, complete strangers: 'How's your mam doing, pet?' These days Liz and Penny were public property. Penny was nothing but the unconscious mother's press agent. Just because they'd seen Liz lying out there on the ground, they thought they all deserved these constant updates. Penny imagined putting up messages on letter-headed paper like outside the gates at Buckingham Palace. She thought it was just bizarre that people who had never bothered with them before were suddenly wanting to beetle over to Bishop Auckland General to see Liz on her life support and connected to her drip. Were they just ghoulish? Was that the fascination? At least Elsie had the sense not to go asking about Liz again. There was nothing to tell her if she had; there'd been nothing to tell for days.

Penny said, 'I thought it was about time I thanked your Craig for everything he did the other day.'

'Ah,' said Elsie, and bit her tongue. She thought, Let the lass take this at her own pace. Don't jump in and spoil it. Her heart set up a mad tattoo because somehow she knew, she absolutely knew, that she was going to get what she wanted.

'Do you know where he is today?' The poor, washed-out girl hardly had any tone in her voice. It was like she could hardly be bothered to speak. Elsie was flushed in the face, as if she was the one being courted.

'Oh, he's . . . um.' Think! Elsie snapped at herself. 'He'll be at the gym, this time of day.' It was early afternoon, exactly the time that Craig and the lads would be doing weights in that place up the ramp, above the precinct.

These days Elsie could be a little more certain about Craig's whereabouts. All his movements and routines she found herself suddenly, wonderfully, privy to once more. This gave her a glow of pleasure too, that she was able to tell Penny without doubt where he was when she needed him. She felt she had got him back. As if he had been away, or ill, or living abroad, and then something went wrong – as it always did when you tried to break away from things – and here he was, returned to his mam. He was back in his room at Phoenix Court. Only last night they had enjoyed a full evening together watching telly, Findus Crispy Pancakes for tea, then helping each other take down the Christmas decorations. Almost wordlessly and working in complete, relaxed accord, mother and son had unhooked, refolded and boxed away the streamers and festoons of tinsel. They popped globes of painted glass into their yellowing cardboard boxes. Craig said, 'Mam, they were *mince* Crispy Pancakes we had.'

'So?' she asked, ravelling up yards of fuchsia tinsel. She realised. 'Shit! We're both vegetarians now, aren't we?'

That was a new thing too, as of the New Year. They were back together in the house, with no sign of Craig's rough friends or her Tom acting mad about the place, and they had both given up eating meat. Mind, meat was everywhere, as Elsie was just finding out. On morning telly they were telling you it was in all sorts you never suspected. Fruit pastilles! Cheese! Polos! She couldn't even bite Sellotape without thinking it was made from the skin of fish. When she used Sellotape at work she cut it deliberately with scissors. And the thought came to her: We live in a world made of meat! Which made her shudder. She remembered being told at school about Nazis making lampshades out of people and at the time she thought, What a thing to teach kids! She told her mam after school and her mam said, 'What a thing to teach kids!' Elsie looked around, thinking, You don't know what the world is made out of.

Penny was saying, 'Will they mind if I just go stomping into the gym? Don't you have to be a member?'

Distractedly Elsie said, 'I don't think so, pet. People are glad of people calling in. Any time of day.' Yet really she had no idea. She was talking from her own experience of shop work. She had no idea of the clunk and grind of the gym, its grim camaraderie, its seclusion from the world.

When Craig worked out in the gym, all he heard of the outside world was the voices of his mates, MTV thumping out of sets above his head and, floating up from the precinct below, the chirpy, repetitive jingle of the Mr Blobby kiddies' ride outside Red Spot.

In the small changing rooms downstairs, all it takes is one person who stinks to come in and it's awful. Everyone gets in and out fast anyway. You don't hang around. Though I have a sauna on Sunday mornings. It opens all your pores, Mary says, she's the manageress, and it lets the badness out. The steam is so good for you. What does it do? Tighten or loosen your skin? One of those things. I do that on Sunday mornings and every day, otherwise I concentrate on what's underneath the skin. I work on the muscle, on making it all muscle, all that potential fat.

You have to isolate, Mary says, the manageress says. To make it work you have to isolate the bit you want to work on. She knows all about it, so I listen to her. The other lads would never listen. She tries to tell them, they laugh her off, she's a canny lass and wouldn't show them up by knowing much more than them. She knows when to leave well alone.

She slinks about the place in her shiny leotard thing. The crotch goes right up her bum when she's working out and she wears it all day. We usually have a laugh about that, though I hope she doesn't know what we're laughing at. I think she'd be mortified. She works all day doing demonstrations on the gym equipment for the women, the lads who come in by themselves, and the older fellers. Anyone who will listen. Our lot wouldn't take instruction, they know it all, and get on with it.

Like the Justice League of America, training on their satellite in space.

I listen, mind, to what Mary has to say and I think I benefit by it. I've come on better, stronger and more developed than the other lads. Just recently they've been commenting on it. I get those funny, rough compliments we make to each other: 'Eh, Craig, man, your legs are getting massive' or 'That's some chest you're getting on you.'

I do my workout like a routine now, that's what it is, not much talking. The others take the piss a bit because I won't go messing on with them, but what's the point in that? We're paying for this. It's not just a social thing. In the back pocket of my shorts I've got my workout card that Mary made out for me. She did a list of fifteen different exercises in order and each, she promised, isolates and works on a different portion of my body. Put together, a full rotation of the exercises makes a comprehensive plan. An all-over body plan. She tailored it for me, even allowing for the slight weakness in my right leg. After the name of each of the fifteen exercises it says X20 and they're how many reps I have to do. And I do that every day. Mary sees me come and go every day and seems pleased I keep to her plan. She takes a pride in my development. Steve took the card off me one day as I was putting it back in my pocket and he looked at it. Steve is bigger than me and although he only ever farts about in the gym, it's like he hardly needs to pay any attention at all. He just keeps as big and as powerful as he is. 'Look, lads,' he said. This was in the free-weights corner, so a few of the lads from our house were gathered round. 'Look, his card's written out by Mary's own fair hand.' He gave it back to me with a laugh. 'He'll be wanking over that.'

This was quite recent. Something's come between Steve and me. I'm not sure what it is, but he's using every opportunity he can to take the piss, to turn the others against me. And they don't take much turning. Maybe it's because my mam's feller's a nutcase and everyone knows that now. Maybe they think I'll turn out a nutter too and I end up wanting to tell them, But it's not blood! He's no blood relation of mine. Other times I think it's my foot and the way you'll catch them looking at it sometimes. It's why

I won't sit about in places like the sauna for long, when they're all about. Downtown once we saw an old woman, she was quite small but she had huge, swollen legs. She had that elephant disease and I could hear what the other lads were thinking, I thought I could sense them, itching to say that her legs were bloated up like my foot. That I must have an old woman's disease. I knew that if I hadn't been there, that's what they would have been saying.

Steve says to me as we're getting changed, 'That lass you've got hanging around you – that's the daughter of the woman you punched out, isn't it?'

Steve is staring at his own full-length reflection, hoisting up his arms, flexing them like wings, watching the stretching of his pecs. He's dripping wet from the shower and he's pulled on his pants without drying properly.

'Penny's not hanging around me,' I go and, as I say it, I realise that's exactly what she's doing. She came to see me today, as I worked out.

'I want to say thank you,' Penny said, walking up to me as I sat on the pec machine. You have your arms spread out either side over bars like James Dean and I was kind of trapped there as she said her piece. I couldn't shrug like I wanted to or look cool like that. Actually, she looked minging, her eyes all bloodshot, with these awful bags under them. She was dressed like a mess too. I was hoping the other lads hadn't seen her visiting me like this, but they had, it turns out.

'Canny bird you've got there,' Steve says with a smirk, pulling on his shirt, and it irritates me, the way he won't put on deodorant or dry his back. I hate the smell of sweat in this tiny wooden room. It smells like the pie shop down the precinct.

Penny said, 'It's because of you that my mam's still alive.' And I gulped.

Now Steve is pulling a face at me. He mocks Penny's voice, does it like bad acting, 'It's because of you that my mam's still alive.' He comes closer. 'Are you gunna tell her it was you who punched her mother out?'

107

She was waiting for him down in the precinct. She would never put it like that, God knows, but she thought, if he comes by after the gym, then we'll bump into each other. And that's all right.

Penny spent some time looking in the other charity shops, not Elsie's. There were ten in the town, out of only about thirty shops in all. She was always up for bargains and she remembered fights with her mam. Liz had always refused to dress her daughter in anybody's castoffs. Liz couldn't bear the thought of it but as soon as Penny was of an age to buy her own things, she was straight down the second-hand shops. And the things she would come back with . . . Even Penny had to laugh now at the thought of those bargains. Bargains she had picked up and worn, almost out of defiance – as if defiance could make these clothes stylish. At thirteen she was dressing in old women's things, willing them back into fashion. But those particular shapeless black dresses, those exact flowery polyester blouses, never came back. Penny wore them layered, like a bag lady. When she turned vegetarian and cooked each night, tossing all her sliced and diced vegetables, her herbs and her spices into a wok, Liz had said, 'You know, you've started to cook how you dress. Shove everything on at once and hope for the best.' At the time Penny had thought this acute and dreadful. Her mother was never anything less than fastidious.

Nowadays Penny was free to heap as many old castoffs on her back as she liked. She could block out her mother's old horror of second-hand clothes, the thought that someone might have died in them. She could go round dressed in old men's clothes if she liked and no one would object, no one would bat an eyelid. Going round the drab shops this afternoon, she thought about making herself into a real fright – Stig of the Dump – and visiting Bishop General, sitting by Liz's bed. Hair stuck all over the place, odd socks, lumpy old jumper and yesterday's pants on. She could imagine Liz's eyes flying open: 'A daughter of mine visiting her mother like this!'

She sat on a bench under a tree in the middle of the precinct. It was freezing. She couldn't pretend she was just passing the time of day. She had to admit, at least to herself, that she was watching out for Craig. She lit a cigarette and her eyes scanned the walkway and ramp leading up to Completely Fit. The Mr Blobby theme going on and on outside Red Spot was driving her mad.

Then he was coming out of Stevens the newsagents, the *Northern Echo* rolled under his arm. He was in tracksuit bottoms, lurching towards her on his bad foot across the slippery flagstones. It was pattering on to snow, hard, dry flakes that wouldn't melt on your skin when they landed there. He was grinning and that made his hobbled progress even more pathetic to her. Penny had forgotten that his limp was so bad.

'You're still around,' he said, coming in close.

She hissed out her smoke. She'd done her bit and said thanks already. Now she could afford to be cool with him. They didn't like you to gush. At least, not at first.

'It's a bit miserable, back at home,' she admitted and blew her cool by shivering.

'How about some tea?' he asked. 'Have the Health people closed down the Copper Kettle yet?'

They looked across the town centre and saw that the café was still open. It had been given a month to sort out its hygiene problems or it would be forced to shut down. Its loyal customers kept on going. They had organised a petition to save their town's only café and it said they would organise a sit-in if the Health people tried to shut it.

'All right,' Penny said.

At this point in the afternoon Craig often went for some tea at the Copper Kettle. Today was when he bought *2000 AD*, a British comic he had been collecting for years. It was folded up inside his newspaper like a dirty magazine. He followed Penny to the café, deciding to forgo his usual hour or so alone with his comic.

Nine

When I woke up the first morning, it was with a terrible pain in my gut. For a few minutes it stabbed and just held in there. I sat up in bed and I couldn't move, I sat there shocked by the pain. It went off like someone throwing a switch and then Nanna Jean knocked and came in with a tray.

'Lemsip for the invalid,' she announced, plonking the tray on my knees. It had two cups and saucers on it, one of Lemsip, one of black tea. I looked down at the clear green and the clear orange, bits swirling round in both, and neither looked inviting. The nice thing about Nanna Jean, though, is that she always serves tea in the best china, whatever the time of day. I remember when I lived with her in my teens, when she started going out nights again, she'd come back tipsy from dancing and still make tea in china cups at four in the morning. She and her cronies sat round her kitchen table, cackling and tapping their ash into a spare white saucer. I'd watch from the stairs sometimes, loving the homely smell of the smoke.

When I told her about the pain, she surprised me.

'Aah, you get all sorts of pains when you're growing up.'

And I didn't remind her that I was twenty-four, that all my growing had been done, that this pain must signify something else, something new besides simple growth. I let it drop.

She still lives in the same place she always did, and I find that reassuring. When I think, it's the single thing in all my life that has stayed the same. Nanna Jean lives in Hyde Street, a terrace of dark turn-of-the-century houses on a gentle hill in South Shields. When my dad worked in

Shields town hall for a year during the sixties, he used to go round Nanna Jean's in his dinner hour. Ham and a bit of salad. He said Nanna Jean never talked to him much, just gave him his dinner and watched him eat it, weighing him up.

Nanna Jean had this cat, Lucky, who used to slink about the place. Not a hair on it, Mam said. A few bits of fluff on its back. She and all her sisters used to hate that cat. It used to wobble about all over the place, and perch on the antimacassars. She made Dad take it away one day when Nanna Jean was out, down the spiritualists' church. He got rid of Lucky and it was his first act as a member of our family. He moved into the front parlour and then I came along and we all muddled in together. Auntie Olly lived under the stairs, behind a green curtain. She had a bed like a bunk on a ship and she was nearly seven feet tall. Up on the top floor lived Auntie Jane and her Brian and our Steve, but you never saw them.

Nanna Jean was a proper old lady. Mam always said it was something to do with her generation. Always going about in those long coats, clumpy shoes, fruit on their hats, and their handbags held under their bosoms, arms folded.

I remember Mam saying that Nanna Jean was a funny woman. Repressed. Like many of her age and class, she couldn't quite deal with the world of the sixties. This world that came to claim her children. They started staying out all night in clubs like the Chelsea Cat. When I was tiny, Nanna Jean was this imposing presence all in black, often under a duvet in her armchair. She seemed a real old woman, but she must have been only about fifty when I was little. And all through the sixties and seventies she was blind. It happened very suddenly, just before her husband died, in 1960. She was working in the scullery, doing something to kippers, when he called her from the parlour, where he was watching the telly. 'Come and look at this, Jean! It's like real life! They're talking like real people on here!'

They had a telly quite early and they were proud of it.

The programme he was on about was, of course, *Coronation Street*. I never saw my granddad. My mam used to call him 'my dad who would have been your granddad'. He died at the end of that week. When he called Jean about the telly, he started to cough, and when the fit passed he heard Jean wailing in the kitchen and saying she'd turned blind.

They got the doctor straight in – doctors were different then, they came out. Jean said she sat on the chair in the scullery and wouldn't move. She could smell the nicotine, the thick yellow of the doctor's fingers as he waggled them in front of her face, but she couldn't see them. And she could smell the kippers, which, it turns out, were off. She would never shake the idea that offish kippers had robbed her of her sight. While the doctor was there, all she could think about was the awful smell. 'I worried he'd think I'd wet myself in shock.'

She stopped seeing things until 1979. She was at her daughters' weddings, five of them shared out between three sisters. Never saw a groom, a gown or a flower spray. She couldn't look at her grandchildren, whose number steadily multiplied over the years. She sat in her stiff-backed armchair holding baby after baby, staring straight ahead, smiling a funny smile. In 1979 I wasn't quite ten. Mrs Thatcher had come in and we were living in Darlington, my mam and dad and me, in a beautiful Victorian house in the terrace by the park and the Arts Centre. We had space for a granny flat downstairs, which my parents argued about. Living in that house, my mam said, was one of the only times in her life when she felt she had arrived somewhere. Set into the wall up the stairs we had fish tanks brimming with exotic fish, which Dad collected.

One day in 1979 Nanna Jean turned up in Darlington under her own steam, which was unheard-of. She had come over thirty miles in a taxi and had to pay a fortune. But, unflustered, she stepped out of that cab all dressed up in a new suit, fashionable and pastel blue, with a ruffled collar. Her hair had been eased out of its usual bun, coiffed up and dyed amber like Mrs Thatcher's. When we opened the front door and stared, we realised that her eyes were wide open and she was looking straight back at us. Twinkling, even.

'It came back! My sense of sight!' she shouted. 'It's like the scales have fallen from my eyes! Look at your faces!'

The years had dropped off her, too, and it was a sprightly, somewhat raffish Nanna Jean that inspected our house and ourselves. She cast a quick glance around the granny flat we'd hoped to convert for her, sniffed and said it would be impossible. She could never live with us. We needn't worry about her.

She spent the eighties having her home in Hyde Street modernised. New windows, inside loo, bit of a conservatory. The yellow wallpaper went in favour of big, cheerful floral prints, borders and dado rails. She even took the nets out of the windows and fitted venetian blinds. Then she took a big interest in the new colours that had come in for make-up. Almost cruelly she ribbed her daughters for not keeping themselves up to date. For letting themselves go as they headed for middle age.

Nanna Jean started going out. She got herself a gang of cronies she went dancing and gambling with and the next thing was that they all went on holiday together. She went all round the world. She started in Marrakesh at the age of sixty and she's still going strong. Trogging round bazaars, having continental breakfasts in places I've never heard of. She's filled that little house with knick-knacks from all over and you can tell each one has a story behind it. Every jade sculpture, every pot and carved little effigy.

After Mam and Dad died when I was eleven, Nanna Jean took me in and set busily about looking after a teenage boy. Feeding me up, jollying me along. As it turned out, I never took up that much energy in the looking after. I wasn't as demanding as some.

I've still got a lot of stuff at Nanna Jean's. I wake in the back room, look around, and it surprises me, the stuff I've got. It's funny. Photos of school friends on the walls in little frames, which she has left up. There's even a picture of Vince with me in about 1987. We've both got hair with streaks, gelled up. It was taken here, that picture. She used to let him come and stay at weekends. She must have known what we were up to.

I moved out to my uncle Ethan's shop when I was eighteen. Back to Darlington, to live alone above a taxidermist's. It seems wherever I live I'm surrounded by exotic things.

Nanna Jean didn't miss me, I don't think, when I moved out. She started travelling for longer periods to ever more far-flung places. Then, on a white sandy beach in Australia, she did her hip in. I didn't ask what she'd been up to. She had one hip replaced and then, a year later, the other one followed. 'That's cooked my goose,' she said to me, sitting up in her hospital bed. Bupa, of course. She voted Tory all through the eighties; it was the only note of discord between us. She went through this again that day on her Bupa bed. 'What you don't understand, Andrew, is that they've sorted things so that ordinary people like me can buy our own houses and do what we like with them. It's free enterprise. It's a very important thing. You'll see that. And, actually, I *do* think the pendulum's swung too far. On *lots* of issues.'

At eighteen I would feel myself blush and go cross and have to leave the room. But this time I felt obliged to stay until the end of the visiting hour. 'You'll see, you'll see,' she said. 'It's human nature. Maggie's got it right. The first right thing she did was take away the free school milk. That's setting the bairns up wrong, thinking they can get something for nowt.'

It always got back to the free school milk and how it bred a generation of ingrates. That was my mam's generation. Her sisters were remarried, doing very nicely, thank you, with six cars and seven bathrooms between them, both living in the south with different accents. Nanna Jean still couldn't quite approve of them. Full of the spirit of free enterprise they might be, enjoying holidays in Tunisia and all the rest. 'But the joy has gone out of them!' Nanna Jean moaned. 'Before they've even hit forty!' My parents were killed in the first plane ride they ever took, to Hong Kong. They had been on Bruce Forsyth's *Play Your Cards Right* and won the holiday. Only Mam was above Nanna Jean's criticism. She was an angel.

I can't imagine what it must be like to lose a child. Sometimes I think it hastened Nanna Jean's reinvention of herself. As if regaining her sight and seeing her daughter die were things to make her seize what remained of her life and shake it for all it was worth. Every time I come here and wake in this room full of my old things, I think about this stuff. I look at the wardrobe of clothes left behind. I always had too many, none of them quite right. I thought I was a funny shape. Every *Dr Who* novelisation Terrance Dicks ever wrote, about two hundred of them, are lined in a bookcase on top of which stands an almost complete set of *Star Wars* figures. Only Princess Leia is missing. Every time I'm here, going over all these old thoughts, I think, if Nanna Jean thought the generation after her, her daughters' lot, were wasting their time, footling it all away, then what must she think about my life?

At twenty-four I'm sitting up in bed wondering what to do with the Lemsip I've let grow cold and toying with the bare Action Man I've found under the bed. Listen to his joints squeal!

Then she pops her head round the door, smacking her lips to get the fresh lipstick even, pulling on some lilac gloves and asking, did I want to come into South Shields with her? She had an old friend dying she felt she ought to visit and there were a few things to pick up for tea.

On the Metro going into town we have the following conversation.

I say, 'I like this train system. It's like a little London.'

It's homely, I think, with a map that isn't at all complex,

115

and much of it, unlike the tube, runs overland. The Tyneside Metro whistles and shunts over scrubby wasteland, through docks and estates, across town centres. And there are thrilling moments when you glide on bridges over the Tyne. All the trains are an off-yellow colour, that of the juice in the cheapest of baked beans.

'You haven't been to London much,' she says and it's not really a question.

'No,' I say, knowing full well that Nanna Jean can't see the point of London or the south of England at all. The south is where she has to pass through on her way to travel the world. Gatwick, Heathrow, these are the south to her and they are just waiting rooms, stepping stones. Everything in the whole world, she says, you can find here in the northeast. Now that she's been everywhere, this is her solemn declaration. More than once I've sat on the Metro as we've rattled across Tynedock and she's told me without a glimmer of irony that all human life is here. Any human drama can be played out in South Shields. There's room for everything, she's said.

'I thought you'd end up going to London,' she says. 'You lot often do that, don't you?'

And I don't know what she means. She might mean young people generally, or she could mean queer fellers specifically. And now there is an ironic cast in her eye as she sits opposite me, bouncing slightly on her seat. Oh, I'm not *out* to Nanna Jean. Whatever that means. I can't make that phrase sound right in my mouth. That I'm out to anyone at all is more by luck than design, I suppose. Easier just to be self-evident, no questions asked. But sometimes you want more. You want questions, interest, you want – I suppose – explicit acknowledgement. I want Nanna Jean to ask about Vince, now, on this day out; have I seen him, how is he, will he be coming back to me? I want her to divine, with her wise old womanly instincts, my unhappiness and to tell me I was silly, insane, lucky or entirely right to get involved with Mark Kelly, the tattooed man. I even want to tell her about his tattoos. Nanna Jean's husband, my granddad as would have been, was in the navy and he probably had tattoos. We could share that.

'You don't think about going to London, then?' she says.

'I've thought about moving,' I say. 'I wanted to last year.'

'Ah,' she says simply, gazing out of the window at the grey shelf of the sea. In that 'ah' I can hear as much understanding as I want. She's given me that much space. It's true, though, I have thought about moving to somewhere bigger. I was going to go to Edinburgh and live in the gay village part of town, wear tight T-shirts and go out dancing every night.

She changes the subject.

'It was in the *Gazette*, the day before you came. They've closed down Lampton Lion Park. You used to love it there.'

I wince because I can't remember and I've always wished my memory better, especially of those years. I have that sharp digging in my stomach again. A stitch, trapped wind, a claw in my gut.

'When you were very small we took you round the park. Your little face pressed against the back window. Your dad was going mad because the filthy baboons were jumping all over the bonnet, pulling and twisting at the windscreen wipers. Your mam just laughed and laughed. She threw back her head and laughed until the tears rolled down her face, she was always like that. Screaming at the monkeys' pink little things sticking up. We were held up by one of the rhinos standing right across the road. Ten minutes and it wouldn't budge, wetting all over the tarmac. Imagine wetting for ten minutes! It scared us. Your mam said it looked like it was made out of rock.'

I could picture Nanna Jean as she would have been then, unseeing and buttoned up hugely in her thick winter coat. We would have had to describe to her everything she is describing to me now.

She says, 'What you loved best was the big cats.'

117

I flinch.

The train is whispering and clunking into South Shields station.

'How big they were. You kept telling me, in ever such a serious voice, "Nanna Jean, the big cats are as big as this car." They came right up to the windows. And you gave a yell, I remember, because this one pushed its face up to the glass. A big cat's face filling all of the window, your mam said. And you howled that it was staring right at me, its nose inches away from my nose. Of course, I couldn't see a thing then. I just stared back. That stuck in my head, that story. I thought you would remember.'

'No,' I say. 'I'd forgotten completely.'

We get out. The passengers around us are mostly old women who get to travel anywhere on Tyneside for five pence daily. Whenever I have been in London it surprises me how young and busily energetic all the commuters are. Nervously watching stations notch by. The ladies on the Tyneside Metro system spin their train journeys out. They want to miss their stations on purpose for the fun of going back the way they've been. Sometimes they have their knitting with them.

We walk about town. All my muscles ache – they feel the lack of exercise. I feel stretched and then left alone, not knowing how to relax. And my pockets are full of crumpled toilet roll. This miserable cold, expressing itself in a stream of snot as we go round the shops. We look at ladies' slacks in Marks and Spencer's because Nanna Jean wants something comfy to wear on the plane to Corfu. We have coffee in Minchella's, an ice-cream parlour that's been there for years. The sugar cubes are wrapped in twists of white paper. I go to the loo to get new tissues. All my old ones are like papier-mâché. Some bloke in the loo is looking at me sideways. I hurry out.

It was funny to see Nanna Jean like that – indecisive and fluttery. We spent an hour walking the streets while she

118

ummed and aahed, trying to talk herself out of seeing Iris, her friend.

'We know what each other looks like. Why do we need to see each other? We're both on the phone.'

I gritted my teeth and wanted to ask, Why did we come out, then? Why did you dress up, lilac gloves, best shoes and all, if not to go and see your best friend?

'They reckon she's turning yellow. Her skin has turned yellow all over and she has to sit by the phone, ready to ring out.' Nanna Jean shuddered. 'I couldn't abide that. When it comes to my turn, Andrew, don't let them let me deteriorate.'

With that she trotted into the Shields museum, where she thought we might waste another hour or so. Inside it had been made into Catherine Cookson Country, a sign said. It was all reconstructions. Waxwork people dressed up as the 1930s on Tyneside. Milk carts and horses and kids with whips and tops. Nanna Jean clicked about on her heels with a glum expression. It was echoing and cool inside and we talked in reserved tones. There were racks of Catherine Cookson's novels on sale. Nanna Jean had read all eighty.

'They say she's a wonderful woman,' she whispered, gazing at a blown-up photo of the author in a bed jacket. 'Ah, look at her wrinkled old hands. She gives every penny she earns to charity.'

The main attraction turned out to be an indoors recreation of Hyde Street and how it was in the 1930s. This was news to Nanna Jean. She turned the corner into a dimly lit hallway and her feet scraped on cobbles. 'Well, you bugger,' she gasped and instinctively drew her handbag in under her bosom. 'This is like being on *This Is Your Life*.'

Beyond the street there was a cross-section of a house: the back parlour, the scullery. 'Look at the old stove,' she said. 'We had a cat die in ours. Oh, look!' It was her house before it was modernised, before she had gone blind.

After that, emerging blinking into the street, we decided

to head up the hill at the top of the town. We could have a poke around the Roman remains. I was interested in that kind of thing, wasn't I? She was harking back to a school project I did at twelve, but I didn't let on I wasn't interested.

The Heritage people had downed tools for the winter and the half-remade fort was quiet and still. We got up to the top with no bother. Looked out at the town. The view of the sea and the docks still took my breath away. I said, 'Imagine being a Roman soldier, the wind here shushing up your leather skirt.' She smiled.

I asked gently, 'Should we go and see your friend now?' Nanna Jean sighed. 'I suppose we should, if she's expecting us.' She was clasping her handbag, I noticed, upside down. 'It's not that I don't want to see her,' she said. 'Every time I do, though, she looks worse. It reminds me of the way things go.'

As we walked back down she told me how her other friend, Minnie, was the first to know of Iris's illness. Iris had visited with tea and cakes and vomited blood on Minnie's new three-piece. The stain wouldn't come out. Minnie said Iris had dropped to her knees to help scrub it up. After that she stopped visiting people. Nanna Jean said she couldn't look at anyone ill these days. She'd seen enough of all that business.

Iris's skin was almost olive in the late-afternoon light. After hearing Nanna Jean's lurid reports, I'd been expecting this poor old woman the colour of custard. She lived above a pub that she used to run, but that was all over now and it was a fun pub these days. While we ate our sedate tea with her, we could hear the video games and the jukebox downstairs. Iris had laid on tinned-salmon sandwiches cut in white triangles. Nanna Jean looked impressed and relieved. We ate sandwiches and angel cake and sipped tea almost wordlessly while someone in the fun pub kept putting on that Billy Joel song 'I Love You Just the Way You Are'.

120

Nanna Jean popped off to the bedroom to try her new Marksies slacks on. I was alone with Iris and suddenly aware of a rank smell.

'I'm not sleeping in my room now,' she told me brightly. 'I sleep in my chair. And, oh, sometimes I do feel heavy.'

There was a fruit bowl made of shiny metal wiring on the sideboard behind her. The fruit had turned brown and deliquescent, the shapes all humped into one, spreading into a puddle through the wires.

Nanna Jean came back to show off her slacks and we admired them. She kept them on for the rest of the visit.

'Did your nanna tell you that we're related, Andrew?' Iris perked up suddenly. She had flecks of white bread-crumbs on her lips. Her voice was rather posh, I thought, gentle and restrained in comparison with Nanna Jean, who, scarlet-faced and embarrassed by something, was braying out when she spoke. Iris went on, 'I'm some kind of auntie to you, I think.'

'I'm glad,' I said.

'There are all sorts of connections round here.' Iris smiled. 'I bet we don't know the half of it. It was only in recent years I found out I had all these cousins in South Shields. All of them black. An aunt of ours married a man black as coal in 1900. They had dozens of children and they all stayed here. Imagine that! So when I found out, I looked them up and went round paying visits. Ever so clean. And they all looked like members of my family! Except all of mine, the white ones, were dead. All the same faces, all the same personalities, almost. Different names – and all of them a different colour.' She clicked her fingers. 'Ha! What do you think of that?'

'Don't confuse the boy,' Nanna Jean said huffily. 'He doesn't want to know about all that.'

'He's a man!' Iris smiled gently and reached across the perfect tablecloth for her Embassy Milds. 'He's interested, aren't you, pet?'

I beamed at her.

'The family stories have to go somewhere, Jean,' she

121

said in a voice sounding as if she was falling asleep. 'He's the one who's got to carry it all on, and give it to his own bairns.' She was becoming fainter.

'It's a lot of nonsense,' Nanna Jean said, but kindly, trying not to hurt her feelings.

Ten

Penny found herself pushing Liz further to the back of her mind.

Every other day Penny went to the hospital. She listened to her mother's bedside machines bleeping. Was she meant to talk to her? Liz showed no sign of change. She lay there, straight, her features strong and implacable. She was bathed in the lights of the displays that showed how she was getting on. Elsie said that she talked to her, chattered to her about all sorts. She couldn't stop herself. She said that the other visitors did it too – all the women of Phoenix Court. This made Penny feel inadequate.

She would arrive in the late afternoon and sit down in the uncomfortable chair at Liz's side. She'd have spent the whole bus trip through wintry fields thinking up things to tell her mam. And she'd sit down and there would be nothing. Suddenly she felt stupid. If she opened her mouth, the air would crack. Her voice was sucked away by the dull machines lining the room. She looked at Liz and thought about speaking, coming out with caring, cheering, supportive things, and it felt like talking to a plant.

Things were moving on with Craig. Andy called him 'your straight boyfriend' and this gave Penny a warm glow. Was she proud of him? He came round to fix a problem they had with wiring. And then the toilet wouldn't flush. He went in and sorted it, not in the least put off that the toilet was chockablock. He was very handy. In the Forsyths' house across the road he had been an asset because somehow he knew how to do things. To make things, fix things, to sort them out, without really being aware of how he came by such knowledge. Craig just somehow knew. Penny adored this about him. She was used to living around people who relished their own haplessness. Andy would tut and wave his hands at problems like these, practical concerns. Liz would treat them with a derisory sneer. And because both were so set on behaving like ladies, both would call in a plumber or an electrician.

Craig, on the other hand, would stick his head into the source of the problem, ask for his tools and start to poke around. Once in January Andy tried to switch the telly on. It was just after he came back from his nanna Jean's, his cold germs were ebbing and he spent whole days watching the telly. It had been left on stand-by all night and it wouldn't come on properly for him. He was wanting to see something particular and Penny watched, almost cruelly fascinated, as he worked himself into a fit of pique, into stomping-up-and-down-the-room angry. She had noticed Andy becoming more temperamental recently. 'Hostage to my hormones,' he snarled once, when she pointed this out. More than half-seriously she put his touchiness down to the gym, which he was now visiting daily.

Penny tried to turn the telly on. Andy flung himself down in an armchair. 'You won't be able to do it,' he snapped.

'Oh, where's my lovely Andy that I used to know?' she sang mockingly, thumping the set. Trying the button again. Click. Click. It wasn't working at all. The screen was stubbornly opaque. Recently she had found herself thinking that Andy wasn't fun to live with any more. Now he went off into the kitchen, where she could hear him clatter, making a sandwich. Apricot stilton with whole-grain mustard. He ate these on the hour, every hour, in place of cigarettes. When he came back to the living room he said, through a mouthful of chewed sandwich, 'Before you say anything, I'm feeding up my muscles. I'm still a growing boy.'

She stared at him. And it was true. She hadn't noticed how much extra weight he was carrying. Today he wore his cropped black T-shirt. It said *Grrr* in glittery golden letters. A little bit of stomach was coming out from under it, above his extra-tight jeans. Though he bragged about how much he was working out, how much extra he was devouring daily during and between meals, she knew how prissy and mortified he would be if she drew attention to his increased size. Filled out, she decided would be the phrase she would use if asked. She would work to make it sound very attractive.

'I can't get the telly to come on,' she said.

'See,' he tutted. 'My programme's finished anyway.'

'Mine isn't.'

Andy rolled his eyes. She had become a fan of *Home and Away*.

She phoned Elsie's house and asked if Craig could come round to look at the telly – before half past one.

They watched through the living-room blinds as he came across the kids' play park. He carried his metal toolbox under one arm and dragged his bad leg in the snow.

'The cold must make it worse,' said Andy.

She looked at him, checking that he wasn't being cruel. His face was thoughtful and composed.

'Have you shagged him yet?'

'Andy, you're so blunt.'

'Well, have you?'

'Yes.'

He looked at her and she laughed.

'I'm not telling you what he was like.'

'Suit yourself.'

'You always want to know that stuff,' she said accusingly. 'What people are like. It's like you can draw up a big chart and point out their best features, their special skills.'

'Well,' he said. 'So you can.'

'Like the decathlon.'

'I take it he's rubbish, then.'

'No, he's –' She pursed her lips. 'He's lovely, actually.'

Then Craig was there. He brought in with him the

125

smoky, ginny, dog-smelly atmosphere of Elsie's house as he installed himself on the living-room carpet. After saying cursory hellos to Andy and Penny and giving Penny a chaste kiss on the lips, he applied himself to the proper task.

Penny took herself off to catch the bus to hospital. She warned them that she wanted to watch the second showing of *Home and Away* when she returned.

Craig unfolded the dark, cluttered compartments of his toolbox. Andy stayed to watch him work. He was careful and precise and something about his application and the way you could see one thought after another chase across his forehead kept Andy watching. His hands were scarred, dirty and skilled. Their nails were stumpy and nibbled. He wore thick white socks and trainers with a kangaroo motif. Soon he had the whole TV in pieces and scattered across the carpet.

'I hope you know what you're doing,' said Andy, wanting to draw his attention away for a moment.

Craig looked round briefly. 'Not at all.' He smiled. His teeth were very even. 'It can't be that difficult.'

He asked for the Hoover. Andy jumped up – oh, far too eagerly, he scolded himself – to fetch it from the hall cupboard and banged his funny bone getting it out.

Then he sat enthralled as Craig wielded the attachments and set about hoovering each and every part of the TV's innards.

'Will that do any good?' Andy breathed.

'Dust gets everywhere,' Craig grunted. 'It causes problems.'

When he was satisfied the bits were clean, he told Andy to put the Hoover away. It took him another hour to reconstruct all the parts.

'Amazing,' Andy said, once the telly was back in one piece.

Craig held up a single golden screw. It was tiny. 'I couldn't find a place for this bit,' he said sadly and went to put it on the fireplace.

126

He switched the telly on. The picture appeared like a dream.

'Huh,' said Penny, when she arrived just in time for *Home and Away*. Andy and Craig were drinking cans of lager in celebration. 'Maybe you should get up to the hospital,' she said. 'Take Liz to bits and give her a good hoovering.'

Eleven

On the table beside the hospital bed someone had left a box of Quality Street. What would Liz want with chocolates? Probably they were left over from someone's Christmas. They stood among the few flowers that visitors had brought.

Fran sighed and looked around the room. Funny that Liz had a room to herself. They must think it serious. For a month she hadn't so much as blinked. Fran found that she couldn't say anything to Liz. She couldn't talk to a body like this. It didn't seem right.

'When I was little,' Fran told Elsie, who sat on the other side of Liz, 'and my auntie Anne was dying in hospital, I got told off for chatting to her. I got my ear clipped for chattering away. I was only trying to cheer her up.'

Elsie gave a tight smile. Fran wanted to explain that this was why she couldn't talk to Liz now. It wasn't that she didn't want to. In fact, she'd give anything for a proper chat with Liz, even one-sided. But now she felt inhibited. Not least by Elsie, who for the past hour had been untwisting boiled sweets from their wrappers and sucking them contemplatively. Suddenly everything about Elsie was annoying Fran, even down to her green sweatshirt with the cartoon lamb appliquéd to its front. Elsie was talking to Liz with the ease of someone well used to not expecting replies.

'It gave me pause for thought.' Elsie smiled vaguely to herself. 'I mean, obviously I don't mind, but it did make me think. He's still my own little lad, isn't he? And there he is, running around with a woman, inviting her to stay over for the night – in my house!'

Fran wondered if she should be hearing any of this.

'I'm sure you don't mind me telling you like this, Liz,' Elsie confided as she scooped a heap of sweet wrappers and brushed them into the bin at her feet. 'But it's my job, I think, to keep you up to date. The fact is, your lovely daughter and my son Craig are very definitely an item. Already she feels quite the little daughter-in-law. She's stayed over at our house three nights this last week. And I thought it would be weird, you know, my son bringing back a woman to sleep in his boyhood bedroom. But it isn't. It's company. Your daughter is lovely company, Liz. I'm sure you're proud of her. She's washed up, helped me with the breakfast things, she's a sunny smile about the place. She's a tonic to me, to tell you the truth.'

Fran thought the irises under closed lids shifted. The eyes would fly open. But Liz stayed silent.

'What I would have given for a daughter like that!' Elsie said. 'You need a good daughter for your old age. Daughters are good to you.'

Fran thought, What's that poor girl doing to herself? That Penny, they reckoned she had all the good prospects. She could go off and have a college education, a career, anything she wanted. It would be no effort at all for her to get off this town. Fran couldn't imagine such a thing for herself. How would you set about leaving? But the likes of Penny, she would have no trouble, setting up a better life elsewhere. There she was, though, by all accounts lumbering herself with Elsie's son. Did Fran have anything against Craig in particular? True, he had separated himself from the rough gang of lads over the road. He had stopped running around with them at night, causing trouble. He'd moved back to his mam's house and seemed to have turned over a new leaf. But what were his aims in life? What was he going to do? If Fran had been a different sort, a better woman, she would take Penny aside and have a word with her. She would explain a thing or two. About what it's like to tie yourself down and deliberately ignore the other, more complicated options. Fran wasn't one for interfering,

129

though. She didn't instigate events; she mopped up afterwards.

Elsie was looking at her. She had run out of things to say.

'Shall we let her rest?' she asked. And Fran felt a twinge of sadness. Elsie looked so pleased with herself. Pleased at taking over another woman's promising daughter.

'I'm parched,' Elsie said, and they went to the canteen.

Elsie asked, 'What do you know about scabies, Fran?'

'Well, nothing. Not a lot. It's like nits, I think, isn't it?'

Elsie shrugged and looked about. 'I don't know. I wish I did know. Who do you ask about things like that?'

The canteen was mostly empty, apart from a boy of twelve, hugging a toddler to his shoulder, waiting for his mam, who had been in the ladies' a full half-hour. The twelve-year-old looked anxious, as if preparing to ask one of the women at the canteen counter for help. The canteen women put chips on plates with small golden shovels like those in McDonald's. The tea came in the smallest of aluminium pots, which made it taste metallic, Fran thought. These trips out to Bishop to see Liz were becoming routine; they were always rounded off with a pot of tea in this bleak canteen.

'You don't think you've got scabies, do you?' asked Fran, prompting.

'I'm itching like crazy,' said Elsie, her lips pursed in self-disgust. 'It started off and it was just our Craig. When he moved back from that rough house of lads.'

'Ah,' said Fran. 'You think it's come from there.'

Fran's heart was thudding crossly. The idea of Craig and Elsie passing scabies on to the whole street! It was like living in a slum. How did you catch scabies? Was it in the air, or skin on skin? Could it be through brushed contact of sleeves or leaving your coat hung up in someone's hall? Unreasonable anger welled up in her throat as she watched Elsie pour herself a second cup of tea from the metal pot.

'I saw a bit on the telly about it once,' said Elsie. 'And, like nits, they said it's nothing to be ashamed of.'

Fran leaned in closer. 'Isn't it more like crabs?'

Elsie blanched. Her own worst itching came around her pubic hair and just above. The doughy white folds of her stomach were red and inflamed with the itch. She had been like this for the past few weeks. This discomfort was something she'd grown used to. She clenched her teeth against it. Her inner wrists and ankles seethed and tiny boils had poked up under the surface of the skin. She was covered in a poor person's rash. And this morning Penny had said in a loud, appalled voice: 'What's this I've got all over me?' She'd forced Elsie to look at the inflamed skin of her wrists and stomach. Shame-faced Elsie looked and didn't dare tell Penny: Well, I think our Craig's given you a kind of rash. So what was she to do? Find an answer, a cure?

'You want to get down the chemist's,' said Fran. 'It can't be very comfortable, or healthy.' She sat back in her seat thinking: or clean. 'They'll know what to do about it.'

'You're right,' said Elsie and it seemed possible, somehow, that this could be dealt with. The worst thing with itching, she wanted to tell Fran, was that you could never be sure it was really there. Even if you had a red, sore rash to show, it didn't prove much. Even that could be – what did they call it? – psychosomatic.

They were standing up to go. 'It's funny what you can catch, isn't it?' she said, as they left the last of the clean-smelling corridors.

Then she set about begging Fran to come with her to visit Tom. After the last, disastrous visit there was no way she was going alone.

'It'll only be an hour or so,' Elsie said. 'You'll be back for the kids being home. I can't go up there by myself.'

Fran gave in. They crossed the road outside the hospital to catch the bus that went to Sedgefield. What am I doing? Fran thought. She didn't want to get caught up in the lives of Elsie and Tom any more than this. Yet here she was, on

131

the bus to Sedgefield. Elsie sat beside her trying to chat brightly. Fran stared at the fields, on which the old, crusted snow was starting at last to thaw. She was only too aware of the press of Elsie's overcoat and the rest of her clothes against her.

When you live together all the time, there are a million things to do. You neglect each other, that's what Tom's said before, and I suppose that's true. We never made the time to sort things out. We had so much to do! I like my house nice and he was good with his hands. Paint this, Tom! Sand this down! Put this new unit up! And he was good, he was, he was meant to be an architect and so he was always good with things about the house.

What he hated, though, and this was the hard bit, what he hated most was the way I would let Craig get away with things. When Craig would take to his room and stay there, Tom would get at me and say I'd brought him up funny. He hadn't turned out right. I'd go round the house, doing my chores, and Tom would follow me round, telling me all this about my son. How I had spoiled him for the rest of the world.

Once, when Craig was out – when he first started hanging about with that gang of his – I found Tom poking about under the boy's bed. Hundreds of comics were pushed over all the carpet. I said, 'But Tom, what are you looking for?' And he looked up furious to be disturbed like this.

'It isn't fair,' Tom would rant at me, 'that I have to paint the hallway, do all this, be the master of this house, and that son of yours doesn't have to do a stroke of work.'

So Tom would remind me that Craig wasn't his and that would make me ache inside. At mealtimes we would eat round the kitchen table and the two of them wouldn't speak a word. It would set all my nerves on edge. I could hardly eat. I'd jump up halfway through my dinner and have to throw it in the bucket. I'd put on the radio to drown out their silence as they ate. TFM, where they play the hits of the seventies.

Tom said all our time was ruined by my son and the things I wanted doing to the house. I just wanted it decorated. I thought he enjoyed decorating. He took such a pride. I knew Tom was sinking into depression the first time because the dining room took such a long time to finish. He slowed to a rate of one strip of paper a day. He did one, very slowly, and you could see him fret over how straight it was. Then he would go and watch Sky Sports for the rest of the day. Then he stopped leaving the house, and that put more strain on the rest of us. He said he thought he was anaemic and he had gone very white. I said, 'Have you gone off the church? Because you used to love going there, you couldn't keep away before.' And he loved running the club for the kiddies, but that was all finished with now. He didn't get out much at all and it took him two months to get the dining room ready.

'Talk to me about something, woman,' he begged me the night he finished. I'd come in to see how the new room was.

'What do you mean?' I admired the wallpaper.

'Talk to me about something that isn't your house or your son. Tell me something.'

He looked strange and like he wanted something else off me. I was scared almost, except that it was only Tom. I didn't know what he wanted from me. I look back now and I think, that was the moment things could have been different. If I'd known what to say to him then. But what was the right thing? And what do I know? Compared with Tom and his grammar-school education, I'm an ignorant woman. I told him I was doing chops for his tea and he laughed in my face. He laughed high-pitched, like a boy.

The last time I went to the hospital, he said, 'I decided I would never decorate anything else for you.' We were taking a walk around the grounds of the home. It's a beautiful old building. It's like something out of a film. Lovely walks. He took me on a turn around the lake, pointing out the deer across the misty fields. I almost felt relaxed. Until he started talking, talking with almost no gaps for me. 'I decided that was it,' he said.

'That was all right,' I said. 'The house was finished. We've a lovely home together and it's all down to you.'

'You almost crippled me, woman.' He looked at me and what was in his eyes stopped up my voice. 'Do you realise what put me in here? Do you?' He stopped in his tracks. 'You've bored me stupid, you pathetic woman! You've got nothing to give me. You're all curtain rails and cups of tea and cheese sandwiches and the *News of the* bloody *World*. And mowing that rubbish bit of garden out the back of your house. Is that all you want out of your life? Keeping that house of yours nice? Forcing me to make it right for you? Couldn't you see what you did to me?'

'Tom,' I said, and I wanted to say more. He looked at me, waiting.

'You've no excuse, have you?' he snapped. 'You don't know any better. You don't know what else to expect out of life.'

His face was all contorted. He burst into tears and then he ran away, back into the main building.

What was I meant to do then? Go in after him again? I have my pride. I wouldn't beg him to listen to me.

He thinks I'm an ignorant woman. He thinks I've nothing to say to him. Well, maybe I haven't. I came away and caught the bus home. Left it a full week before I came to see him again. Then, this time, I brought my pal. I brought Fran.

When he was shouting at me, when he was saying, 'Couldn't you see? Couldn't you see how miserable I was with you?' I wanted to tell him, Yes, Tom, I could always see how miserable you were. But I didn't know what to do about it. How was I meant to know? Why does everyone want to know the answers from me?

They were made to wait in what looked to Fran like a rather grand hall. The woodwork was dark and shiny, like

134

toffee hot from the oven. The floorboards creaked under-foot and there were stuffed animals lodged high in the walls. She could imagine coming down those stairs in a frock, Scarlett O'Hara, maybe music playing for a ball. Again that antiseptic smell, which spoiled the atmosphere. Beside her Elsie was scratching herself. Both sweatshirt sleeves were up to the elbows and Elsie rubbed the skin fiercely. When Fran looked the skin was blotchy. She wanted to tell Elsie to pack it in.

'They've never kept me waiting out here before,' Elsie said. 'Something's happened. Usually they've let me straight in to see him. Something has been going on.'

'I'm sure it hasn't,' said Fran, though she wasn't so sure. Every time she heard a yell or the thudding of feet from elsewhere in the building, she flinched. But the only other soul they had seen so far was the nurse who showed them where to sit.

The nurse was back. 'You're Elsie?' She smiled, and Elsie looked up, wondering why they didn't have these nurses in proper uniforms.

'Has something happened to him?' Elsie asked, clutching both her elbows and hugging herself.

It was the fair on the waste ground that came every holiday weekend. They set up on Friday and there were three nights of noise and music and everyone trampling through the heavy dirt. Elsie always loved the penny arcades. She took Craig after school on the Friday, and then the next two nights. He watched as she played for ten-pence pieces and, when she made enough, he was allowed to run off to jump on a ride. Nothing too dangerous. Elsie would train herself not to go after him and watch, not to call him down and show him up. Once she had asked the man in charge of the shuggy boats to switch it off, to bring down her son, because as he was going round and round, she could have sworn that he looked upset. Everyone had laughed as she ran up to help

135

him down. Afterwards she kept to the penny slot machines and wouldn't look at him enjoying himself.

It was on the slot machines she met Tom. He had only just started out with the Rainbow Gang, helping the underprivileged kids on the estates to find God. He brought his Friday-night kids to the fair because they had all insisted. He abandoned the games and the songs he had planned for that night in the Methodists' hall and gamely walked his flock of forty over to the waste ground instead. 'Stay together!' he called when they arrived and as they dispersed suddenly, noisily, he realised he had no hope of rounding them up again. The Rainbow Gang for that night was ruined. As he walked around the fair, the sun going down and the coloured lightbulbs strung between booths and canopies coming on, he kept glimpsing the different members of his flock. They waved and yelled at him from dodgem cars and swinging chairs on the rides that reeled above him. Tom always waved back and shouted a greeting, but he wasn't sure if they were taking the mickey out of him. When he saw his children at other times, in shops, in the post office, slouching on the corners of streets, and they shouted out loud hellos, he wasn't sure then, either, whether he was the butt of their jokes. On the whole he didn't mind. He was bringing them together. He gave them a place to meet every week. Kept them off the streets.

Elsie watched him work the one-armed bandit to her left. She admired his greased-back hair and his worn black leather jacket. He had dark-blue jeans that looked new and he seemed the sort of man that shaved very carefully. You could see just by looking. His sideburns were straight and level. He would shave, she thought, in very hot, soapy water, with an old-fashioned razor. She breathed in and, through the sawdust and sweaty smell of hot dogs, she could catch the scent of his Brylcreem. He looked up at her as he collected his winnings. She must have inhaled too loudly.

136

'I'm new to the town,' he said to her. 'Would you mind coming round the fair with me?'

So even for a man of God, she thought later, he wasn't backward at coming forward. She'd be delighted, she said, and they left the amusements behind, to walk through the busy fairground. When he grinned at her she saw he had very pointed wolfish teeth. 'My vampire teeth,' he said, smiling, when she pointed them out and she thrilled at this.

Elsie found that she could talk to him easily. He was an interesting man, he had travelled, he knew many sorts of people, he had studied and he knew a thing or two. She loved to hear him talk and the way his sentences had fewer gaps and mistakes than hers. She wanted to ask, Do you make up what you're saying beforehand? There was something fluid and easy about him. She felt led around and light on her feet and she found that his arm was at her back, urging her along. Then she shamed herself by hoping that they wouldn't bump into Craig. She didn't want to have to explain – not just yet – to Tom that she had a son of twelve. She imagined Tom looking her son up and down. Craig at twelve was chubby and his clothes ill-fitting. He covered his mouth with both hands whenever he smiled and he walked slump-shouldered, which only drew attention to that foot of his. Elsie was ashamed of herself, but she didn't want Tom to see Craig yet. First she wanted to get used to this new feeling of lightness, of swishing through the fair with all its crowds and its black mud. She was wearing a long, flowery cotton frock, which billowed round her in the breeze. They came to the edge of the crowd. Diana Ross blared from the distant carousel. As Tom led her round the back of a chugging generator, they had to step gingerly over the brightly coloured cables that wound through each other in the grass. He kissed her long and deep and pressed himself up against her. She was surprised. He'd already told her he did something like Sunday school for the bairns. Things had changed since she was a bairn, of course.

'Can I be your vampire?' he asked, and laid his head on

her breast. She was taken aback. Then she thought, He'll have that hairgrease on my frock.

'Let's see your teeth again,' she said.

He grinned at her and they were really frightening.

'I have a son,' she said.

'You hardly look old enough.'

'He's twelve.'

'Never!'

'I've had a life already, Tom.'

'Good.' He kissed her again.

'You're not really a vampire, are you?'

He hugged her and she felt the bones down her back – was it vertebrae? – she felt them click, one at a time, not unpleasantly. 'I am, I am,' he said.

This time there was definitely something different, something wrong. They had to go to see the woman in charge of the hospital. Elsie seemed to go inside herself as they entered the smart, book-lined office. She stared at the heavy green lamp on the woman's desk. Fran had to do the talking. The woman in charge had neatly cut hair, no make-up, a dark jacket and skirt. Fran thought she looked like a woman in control, like a woman off a Lynda La Plante TV show. The woman smiled pleasantly and explained that she had been trying to contact Elsie all day.

On the way up the stairs, up the green carpet that was so soft you felt obliged to save it by walking on the edges, Elsie had been chuntering away to herself. She had said, 'The thing I couldn't stand would be that he's dead. That he's gone and done himself in, like he always said he would. He always threatened me with doing himself in. I even hid the scissors from him. But the last time I saw him he was so angry he ran away from me. I'd be so guilty if that was the last I saw of him.'

Now Elsie stared past the woman in charge at the black tree through her window.

The woman said, 'The thing is, he's vanished.'

What a draughtsman he was! He could draw you anything. He used to draw all the time, on whatever was to hand. If you left an old envelope lying about, the leccy bill or a magazine, you'd find it again with a little doodle on. He always had a pen in his hand. Like I said, he should have been an architect. 'Draw me! Draw me!' I'd say, and strike a pose. If I was being too demanding, he would quickly draw something hideous, like a monkey, and tell me that's what I was. He would do that to make Craig laugh, and sometimes Craig would. Other times Tom would spend hours drawing me carefully, with pen and ink, with pencils, with coloured crayons and everything. Careful hours staring at me and I would let him, imagining what he was setting down. One of them drawings we've got framed on the wall. Me in my white blouse. It was the one that looked most like me. I watched him work and he did it biting his bottom lip, so you could see his pointy teeth as he concentrated. They were digging into his skin and I could feel myself melting just looking at that.

Some of his drawings, mind, they made me look hideous. I found some he'd done and they gave me the creeps. They didn't look like me at all. Like some horrible woman. But what a draughtsman he was!

The first time I brought him home, to see the house and to meet Craig, he used his drawing skills to break the ice. That's what it must be like to have a talent. You can use it in social situations like that. That must make things a lot easier. I have no talents. Tom shouted at me once, in one row we had, that I had no gifts whatsoever. And I haven't. No, that's wrong. Everyone has gifts from God. That's something Tom told me too. And I think I've the knack for talking to people. But Tom's talent was something that could draw him closer to children especially. At the Rainbow Gang he would have the children queueing when he drew cartoons for them to colour in. Mickey Mouse and the Power Rangers and what have you. Anything they could ask for and he'd scribble it down in a flash. The kiddies thought he was marvellous. I said, 'You should sell them drawings.'

When he came to tea with Craig and me the first time, we ate iced buns and salmon-paste sandwiches. Craig was being quiet. The telly was on in the corner, like it always is, but with the sound a bit lower. Next to his plate Craig had his Etch-a-Sketch out. Tom stared at it with interest. I thought Craig was too old for it at twelve, to tell the truth. It was one of the few toys of his that had lasted the years. Something his dad had bought him. It was a kind of plastic board, full of grey, shifting sand. You twiddled knobs to make a black line appear on the screen, you could draw things on it. All through tea Craig was twirling patterns on the screen of sand. And you could see it was just a mess he was making. Just to make a point, just to annoy me, when he knew I wanted him to pay attention to Tom.

'May I have a go?' Tom put his hand out.

Craig shrugged and passed over the Etch-a-Sketch. I watched Tom's strong hands take it and place it before him. He shook it briskly to make the screen blank and ready. Smash it, I thought impulsively.

Tom pushed aside his tea things and set to work. He twiddled those buttons and knobs and soon he sat back, satisfied. He held up the screen for us both to see. I gasped. He had drawn the most wonderful giraffe.

Later that night I said goodbye to Tom at the front door. We thought it would be pushing it for him to stay the night.

'Let him get used to me slowly.' Tom smiled, holding me. 'We've got the time. I'm going to be around a while.'

I couldn't help smiling back at him. When Tom spoke to me like that it was just like hypnotism. I watched his mouth and his teeth and those deep eyes of his and I couldn't dispute a word he said. There was a slow, magical charm to him and I know it was all to do with sex. And how do you explain that to your twelve-year-old son? How do you explain that it's important to you to feel sexy now, when you haven't for so long? Craig would look at me resentful and I'd want to explain, but I never knew the words for it. When Tom wasn't there I'd start to feel ashamed of myself. That was why it was easier, at first, when Tom did move in. Alone with Craig I would feel accused of things. He'd be looking at me and thinking that I was a silly, middle-aged woman trying to be sexy. I wanted to say, What's wrong with being sexy? You have to keep yourself sexy, and nice and healthy. It's all good for you. He couldn't see that then. I think he can now. It's about how life goes on. I took that chance with Tom. I fought my son to keep him.

That night I went to clean up the tea table and I saw that Craig had gone back to his room. He hadn't even moved his own plate and cup. Everything was left lying around for me. His Etch-a-Sketch was left on the table, too. He had given it a vigorous shake and cleared the screen.

They went back home on the bus bewildered. The woman in charge of the home had told them she would keep in touch. Perhaps Tom had just wandered off. He might soon be back. This had happened before. Confused people became lost in the woods, in the grounds, in the fields about the house here. It wasn't unknown. It was only this morning he had wandered off. Perhaps he would be home by nightfall. They would let Elsie know what was happening.

'I was certain they were going to say he'd died,' Elsie said to Fran.

'Oh, don't say that,' said Fran superstitiously.

'But you know what it's like. When something's wrong, and you dread the worst.'

'Yes.'

'If he's out in this cold all night, he might die.'

'They'll get him back.'

'Exposure. Hypothermia.'

Fran couldn't believe the people at the hospital were being so casual. Who knew how many people they let walk away. There could be any number of missing patients.

'Our best days,' Elsie said, 'were Sundays, when he was still big on God. Some of the Rainbow Gang would be invited to our house. The favoured few. Tom would invite these kids and we would have a big family Sunday dinner. Some of those kids had hollow legs. They ate and ate and ate.'

Fran thought she was talking about Tom as if she'd never see him again.

He had wrapped himself up warm, knowing that he would have to traipse the whole distance to Aycliffe across fields. Hitch-hiking didn't even occur to him because he didn't hold with it. It put people – hitchers and drivers both – in compromising situations, which Tom hated. It was dangerous, he used to warn the children in his care, and pleaded with them never to try it. Newton Aycliffe is a town beside the wide motorway leading north. It lies between a whole number of roads elsewhere. What a temptation to stand at its perimeter and let someone take you off.

The fields were frozen again as night started to come down. He fastened up his coat, tugging his scarf into multiple knots. The coat was stolen from a room at the home. He checked the pockets for gloves and found some balled-up leather ones, and some rolling tobacco and papers. If he knew how to roll he might have had one, to warm the space of air around him. Instead he held the envelope to his nose and inhaled the scent of soft, brushy tobacco. When he started to walk again, he followed the ruts in the ploughed field, crunching through the ice. It was like thin spun sugar, cracking under his heavy shoes.

He made his way by the lights of Aycliffe, of the industrial estate, far ahead.

I'm not even from Newton Aycliffe, he thought, but he recognised it as a place that always drew him back. No one actually came from that town, except children born since the sixties. It was too young. It was a place that took people in and made them all the same. You all had to go to the same shops. It made no one better than any one else. It dulled the goodness out of people. It filled them with the same old concerns. It bored him.

In the free local paper he had seen an announcement. It had puzzled him, but it had summed something up.

> Bill is seventy.
> We have no time to stand and stare
> to stand and stare beneath the boughs
> to stand and stare like sheep and cows.

People were always making up rhymes for that paper. This one seemed to be about the way people in Aycliffe stood about doing nothing with their lives. When Tom was in the town precinct with Elsie, she stood about talking to just about anyone. Because she worked in that shop she knew loads of them. They stopped her and talked drivel. Standing and staring. Tom would feel like tearing out his hair. They went, 'This is it' and 'Uh-huh', reassuring each other with their dullness.

She has made me feel my life is over. I have spent it waiting for the future to begin.

When Craig failed all but two of his GCSEs, there was a row. I made the mistake of saying, maybe it wasn't so bad. I tried to hint tactfully that he wasn't the brightest of lads. That maybe his skills weren't the sort that showed up in exams. Elsie said that she wanted Craig to have all the chances in the world. She snapped at me, as if she thought it was me taking them away. She wanted someone to shout at. Craig just looked embarrassed. I said, of course he would have other chances. We always have other chances. Then she turned that back on herself, like she always does. 'What other chances have I ever had?' she sneered. 'I'm always stuck between these four walls. I don't expect any better. But Craig should.'

'We can always expect to have another chance,' I said.

She blew up. 'We don't need anything else. Craig does. We've had all our chances. Our lives are over.'

I got angry. I said my life certainly wasn't over.

'What else are you going to do with it?' She was practically laughing in my face.

I stared at her, and I couldn't believe she was being so cruel, so certain. There wasn't a flicker of doubt there. I was looking at someone who firmly believed that her life could never improve or go anywhere. In her forties she had accepted that she had seen and done everything she needed to. I was astonished and scared to be with her then. Craig left the room, aware that this was now a private row, and I got the blame for that, too.

When I looked at Elsie's face she looked old, but also like someone resigned to being trapped in the past. She was speaking categorically and depressingly from a point of absolute certainty in the archaic past. And this is when I realised what I believe to be one of the great differences between the sexes.

Woman is always of the past, and Elsie is no exception. She is the mother, viewed always from the present and seeming somehow behindhand. This was never clearer than in that row. I suppose this was why sex always made me feel nostalgic. The hankering for the past. The man is always in the present moment. That is why I – he is for ever thinking and moving and can reflect back on things and put them in perspective.

Between Man and Woman the future is made. But there was never to be a future from Elsie. She never wanted to have any more children. She was knocking on, she said, and her waterworks were problematic. And Craig might be jealous of a half-brother or sister. Any reason, any reason, she wouldn't have a baby. Denying me this, she has trapped me in the present for ever.

The town seems no closer and it's dark now. Is there a garage near here, so I can get chocolate and crisps? When I get to Newton Aycliffe, will I go home? It isn't my home.

She has made me into a man-child. I will leave nothing behind me. I'll be in the present for the rest of my time. Frozen, undead. She wanted me perfecting her house for ever.

Twelve

Don't let this be a grimace. As Craig talked to him, Andy was trying hard to look interested. They were working out together. Craig was explaining the benefits of having a work-out partner. You egged each other on.

'I think we're naturally lazy. We all need some discipline. You can do that for each other.' Craig nodded at a couple using free weights nearby. The older, bigger man stood poised over the one lying down, ready to pull the load away from him if it proved too heavy. He yelled, 'Go on, lad!' into his face.

Craig called everything he did on machines his 'reps'. As Andy followed him about Craig hardly dropped his conversational stride and he didn't seem out of breath either.

'I always thought my stepfather was Dr Octopus,' he told Andy. He lay on his back in a crouching position, pushing weights up a slide and bringing them down with a regular, satisfying clunking noise. 'My mam's feller, Tom. I thought he was Dr Octopus. Do you remember him? Spiderman's deadliest enemy?'

Andy nodded absently. He stared at Craig's weak leg, held in place by the machine. In that grip, clamped upside down, it looked almost normal. Andy knew, though, that the stronger leg was doing all the work. On that leg the muscles bunched and tensed twice as big.

Craig was on about comics again. A week ago Andy had made the mistake of mentioning that, as a boy, he read Marvel comics. Craig's eyes lit up. This bonded them, Penny said, and she listened, laughing, to the pair of them reminiscing about the X-Men and Marvel Two-in-One.

Soon she became bored and started to mock their enthusiasm. They were talking about the Incredible Hulk and how sad that story always seemed. Andy had noticed Penny's boredom and tried to change the subject. Every few minutes after that Craig would remember something else to remind Andy of. 'Did you read that one when all the Avengers were killed off in one issue?' or 'The story when the Goblin threw Gwen Stacey into the Hudson River and Spiderman was powerless to save her?'

At the end of the night Penny said to Andy, 'Well, you've made a friend there.' Andy rolled his eyes. But Penny was pleased they had found something to talk about. The night before, Craig had been fretting. She woke to find him staring at the ceiling. 'What do I talk to a queer bloke about?'

She laughed at him. 'Anything you want. He doesn't talk a different language.'

To Craig, though, that was exactly what Andy did. As Penny went back to sleep, he stared at her hair mussed up on the pillow. Imagine not wanting her. It was seeing the world a completely different way. Yet they must have something in common, despite that. Craig made himself imagine not wanting Penny. Hating things about her. Thinking that he didn't want her breasts or want to push himself easily inside her. He made himself think about fancying men. Captain America. All those superhero bodies were the same: toned-up muscles, small nipples, everything on show as they flew through the air. There was no mystery in a man's body. It was all up and down. But that was just men's bodies, that's what they looked like, that's what they were. At one level Craig couldn't see what the fuss was about. That's what I am, he thought and stared at Penny again. Look at her, he thought. She could talk about anything. It knocked Craig sick to think he would seem daft to Penny's friends. They'd think he was thick and boring. It was his mam's fault, not pushing him on to be clever, to better himself. Steve and the other lads, the company he kept, they made him stupid too. But look!

Now Andy was interested in what he said about comics. They had shared all this past, all these adventures. He wondered if Andy had kept his back issues.

Craig was taking a big chance here. I must think Andy's friendship is worth it, he thought. And Penny. I must be doing it all for her. Because here he was, hanging around the gym with an obvious queer. It was such a risk. He had been the one to suggest they work together. Andy looked pleased. What would happen when the other lads came in and saw them together? What would be said?

Andy was on the machine now, watching as Craig set the load much lower. He tensed himself, ready to start. Craig looked at Andy's too clean, neatly ironed black T-shirt and orange gym shorts. He thought Andy was all right really. They hadn't said anything pointing out the difference between them, but it was there all the same. As if Andy had a funny accent. He hadn't said anything puffy yet. What would Craig do then? For friends, he supposed, you had to grin and bear it.

'Do you remember,' he said, 'the story in the old Spiderman comic when Dr Octopus discovered his secret identity?'

Andy gritted his teeth, hissing out breath, exhausted already. 'Not sure.'

'He found out that Spidey was really Peter Parker and that his auntie was this sick old woman. Dr Octopus pretended to be Auntie May's real doctor, who would cure all her ailments. He came to her front door, rang the bell. He had hidden his six extra metal arms inside his overcoat.'

Andy said, 'Maybe I remember.'

'It was fantastic. Spidey was away fighting the Green Goblin and by the time he came back home he found that Auntie May was getting married to Dr Octopus. How could he tell his auntie her fancy man was evil? If he did, he'd give away his secret identity.'

Andy said, 'I think I read that.'

Craig nodded. 'I forget what happened at the end. I remember wondering, did Auntie May have to go to bed with Dr Octopus? Would she see his other arms?'

Later, Andy went downstairs to shower first. They had between them a tacit understanding about not seeing the other naked, as if they weren't quite of the same gender. Andy stood aching in the shower cubicle, his head against the tiles. He felt closed in, worn down. 'This every day!' he moaned. His exercise programme had stepped up. He felt stronger, flushed, but all his energy was going into it. He was doing nothing else. Without looking he felt down his arms, his chest, his newly tautened stomach. He was coming on fast. Everything felt so connected, so concerted. He should be glad. He just felt tired and sickly. He lifted his arms up to stretch.

And there it was. He blinked away the warm water and stared. Under his left arm, printed boldly across the numbed muscle. About the size of a ten-pence piece and a kind of glossy purple black. He had a single leopard's spot staring back at him.

Andy turned off the shower. He stepped out to dry himself, almost slipping. He thought quickly and hard. He wouldn't look at the spot on his arm again.

Craig walked in as Andy dried himself. They both looked confused. Craig said, 'Look how your body's coming on.'

Andy stared at himself. His muscles seemed suddenly hard and heavy to him. But he wasn't sure why. He looked down at himself, but he no longer felt like his own man.

Penny was in the arcade in Darlington when she saw Mark. He was in that clothes shop where everything was on offer with a 70 per cent discount. She realised that she hadn't been in that shop, just because Andy reckoned there must be a rip-off involved. You didn't get something that cheap, he said. Penny went in. It's funny how people can put you off things.

Mark was with his daughter, who was about ten. The

girl was standing by, looking bored as Mark folded and unfolded rather bright shirts and tops. He noticed Penny.

'What do you think?' He held a tight yellow T-shirt against himself. She saw at once that it was too young on him. But his blueness and the sharpness of his tattoos looked stunning.

He pulled a face and shrugged. 'No?'

Penny couldn't help asking, 'Do you have to buy plain clothes, I mean, clothes without patterns, so you don't clash with your designs?'

His daughter gave a snort of laughter. Mark smiled. 'I do, actually. At one point I never even thought about it. I wore checks and all sorts. Then Sam, my ex-wife, said I looked like a dog's dinner. I've got better since then.' He pushed through a rack of velour tops, frowning. Penny thought that she, too, would grow neglectful of the sort of clothes she wore, if she were covered with tattoos. Clothes would seem too prosaic.

'Are you helping your dad?' Penny asked the child.

Mark's daughter gave Penny a look. 'Dad, can I have my pocket money now? I want to go to Smith's.'

Then she was gone, cutting through the Saturday crowd. Mark shrugged. 'She's at that difficult age.'

Penny thought back to being ten.

'She's getting a filthy mouth on her. She answers back. She's foul-tempered. She half understands things. And she throws tantrums like she never did as a baby.' He sighed. 'Sometimes I feel treacherous. I wish she was little again. I preferred her that way.'

'That's natural.'

'And sometimes I think, I'm even glad she lives with her mother and not me. It's a relief sometimes.'

Penny smiled. 'We're allowed treacherous thoughts.' She was thinking, Since when did I know this man well enough to hear him talk like this? He was looking at her as if they were always meeting up.

They caught the bus back to Aycliffe together. They had a forty-minute wait for the 213. Outside McDonald's they

149

queued and chatted. He asked the inevitable questions about Liz. Penny stood with her groceries from Marksies between her knees.

'You've got posh shopping,' he noticed.

'I'm doing a nice meal,' she said. 'For Craig and his mother.'

'Craig's your boyfriend.'

Penny nodded. She still found it odd to hear him called that. She felt vaguely proud and distressed by the term. But she put these qualms to the back of her mind. He seemed to adore her and he was attentive and so, for now, he would do. What grated was the rest of his life, which Penny found herself taking on wholesale. Elsie had become a mother-in-law in a way Penny could see she had longed to. And now, with the extra stress of Tom's disappearance, Penny felt even more heavily leaned on. Elsie turned automatically to her clever, dependable Penny to see her through and to say the sensible things. And I'm playing up to that, Penny thought. I'm cooking them dinner and keeping the family together.

'So don't you see as much of Andy these days?' Mark asked. Penny could have sworn she saw, as he said this, the creeping of a blush behind his tattoos.

'I still see him every day, of course,' she said. It wasn't the same in the house, though. They used to do every day together, consult the other about everything. Now Penny drifted off round Craig's and ended up chatting with Elsie and hearing her woes. Andy was in a world of his own. Penny hated to think she had made him worse. He had turned almost secretive. Something was up and she no longer felt in a strong enough position to ask what it was. He wouldn't take her seriously, she thought. We aren't fond enough of each other at the moment. When people live as close as we do, they have to be tougher and quieter sometimes.

She thought Mark had a nerve, though, asking about Andy.

'You really pissed him off, you know,' she said.

He looked taken aback.

'I know what went on,' Penny said, keeping her voice down for the sake of the child. She wished she hadn't started this. Now there really was a flush between the markings on his face.

'I don't know how much Andy's told you,' Mark said. 'But it was never meant to be more than a one-night stand. Honest. I thought he was clear on that. It was just –'

'You don't believe that,' Penny said flatly. 'He's a lovely bloke. You just fucked him over.'

'I know he's lovely.'

'You've hardly said a word to him since.'

'Is he really so upset?'

'Would I be telling you if he was turning cartwheels?'

'Maybe I'll go round.'

'You should have told him in the first place that you weren't interested.'

'He's lucky to have you to worry about him.'

Penny shrugged as the bus arrived. Last night Andy had woken screaming. He ran out of the house and across the damp, slushy play park to bang on Elsie's door.

Elsie hoisted herself onto her windowsill. She opened her window, terrified at what or who she might see banging on her door.

'Tom?' She hissed. 'Tom? Have you come back to me?'

Andy stared up at her from the garden. He was in his boxer shorts, hugging himself. Penny went out to fetch him. Craig made them a cup of tea. He watched Penny cuddle Andy, who had tears streaming down his face.

'That's what he was like last night,' Penny told Mark on the bus next day. 'That was the state he was in.' She thought Mark should know.

Andy kept saying, over and over, 'I was dreaming of the leopard again. I always dream of him when I'm not well. He stands on my shoulders. Only now he's eating my insides.'

Craig and Elsie stood back, baffled, as Andy clutched at Penny and told her this. He looked helpless. As Craig stared at him, he saw the scattering of black furry rings up the flat of his back. They were quite distinct, shuddering with the rest of Andy's body as he sobbed against Penny.

Everyone was out so Penny could make a start on tea in peace. She had her own key to Elsie's house. The smell of the place as she let herself in was familiar and homely to her. The kitchen cupboards as she opened and closed them, putting shopping away, smelled of tomato ketchup and burst tea bags. She put on local radio and stacked up her boxes from Marks and Spencer to read how long each thing took in the oven. She hated using Elsie's microwave because its door didn't quite fit. Penny had heard a story about a woman whose door didn't fit and who stood too close to the radiation in her small kitchen. She ended up microwaving her own insides.

Am I a fag hag? She ripped open the boxes of vegetarian lasagne and pricked the plastic sheeting, as instructed, with a fork. Was it going too far to harangue a one-night stand of my gay friend on the bus back from Darlington? No, it's not going too far, she thought. Andy was upset and I would harangue anyone for that. But she supposed she was a fag hag anyway. My natural element, she thought glumly, plumping up the sealed bags of mixed salad and shaking the various dressings, is with queers. How can it not be? And maybe that's why life just recently with Elsie and Craig seemed so exotic and desirable. I'm living in the straight world, Penny thought. I'm taking a holiday in the world of the straight. But it wasn't where she belonged. I'm straight, she thought, but there must still be something queer about me. She stared at Elsie's kitchen. The ceramic dogs and chickens she kept her knick-knacks in. The corn dollies nailed to the walls. I'm on holiday in someone else's life, she thought again, and turned the oven on.

Elsie came back when dinner was almost ready.

'That smells lovely, pet. Bless you, aren't you clever!' She went to hang up her coat. 'Craig's out with the lads. He won't want tea. I saw him before I went out.'

Penny tutted. She took the wine from the fridge.

'Eeeh, wine! Aren't we wicked!' Elsie grinned. She rolled her cardigan sleeves up. 'We're like the continentals, having wine with every meal. You're starting me on bad habits, pet. Now, what can I do?'

'It's all ready,' Penny said. 'It's nothing special. Just stuff ready-made from Marksies.'

'You still had to put some thought into it!'

Elsie was grinning at her as Penny passed her a glass of white wine. The older woman smacked her lips. 'Lovely. Not too sweet. I'm sweet enough.'

Elsie had been cheerful these past couple of days. If Penny didn't know better, she'd think that it was a relief to Elsie that Tom had vanished. It meant she could think of him less if he wasn't there. But Penny had been seeing lately the various layers of self-protecting nonsense which helped Elsie through each day. Elsie had thrown herself into her job at the spastics shop. She had brought Penny back a pair of scarlet patent-leather shoes.

They fitted. 'If I click my heels three times, will I go home?' Penny asked.

'You what, pet?' said Elsie.

'Have you been at work today?' asked Penny. She noticed Elsie checking to see she was wearing the new red shoes.

'Not today. I went to Bishop. I popped in on your mam, actually. Still no change.' She mouthed the last few words respectfully. Penny felt stung, as if Elsie was accusing her of neglect. Elsie was beginning to sound like Liz's very own High Priestess. Tending to her altar, sitting by it every other day, leafing through *Take a Break*, watchful for changes.

On the bottom of her boots Elsie had snow chains which, she had once explained to Penny, came from an offer in the *Daily Mirror*. Their metal teeth gripped through the black ice of pavements. They were a lifesaver. If Liz had had them that night in the play park, she

153

mightn't have cracked her head. Penny stared at Elsie's boots and felt like throwing them out of the window.

'Dinner's almost done,' said Penny.

'I'm off for a widdle.' Elsie jumped up. 'I get all excited when food's ready, don't I?' With that she hurried through the living room.

Penny was pulling the silver trays out of the oven, a tea towel bunched around her hands, when Elsie yelled out.

'What is it?'

She found Craig's mother staring through the window at her back garden. She was shaking from head to foot.

'Some vandal's been in and destroyed my garden!'

Penny looked.

Every paving stone in the patio had been extracted and stacked neatly to one side, as if they were ready to be taken away. The dirt underneath was dark like rotten gums. The trellising up the fences had been dismantled and lay in splinters of blond firewood, and the rose bushes had been hacked systematically into useless thorny bits. Pink and yellow flower heads were heaped in a corner. Even the small pond had been drained. The orange bodies of the fish were lying to one side, as if resting. It reminded Penny of when vandals broke into the *Blue Peter* gardens and turned them upside down. That had made the evening news and the old man who tended them cried on the telly. All that work.

'My sweet peas are up, too!' Elsie cried and dashed outside. 'Who would do a thing like that? It wasn't like that this morning.'

It was so neat, Penny thought. Someone had taken great care to take it all neatly apart.

I still don't know what to think. The truth of it is that I came home high as a kite. I was out of my skull, but I never imagined it. This is what I saw. It was true. Penny was out in that garden in the middle of the night with her arms raised above her head. Her hands were black and the rest of her was lit up.

I came home from my night with the lads. That was a successful night. I was back in with the lads. And there'd been me thinking I wasn't part of them any more. Since I'd moved out and taken up with Penny, since I'd started working out with Andy, I was sure the lads would think I'd turned my back. But I should have known better. They're loyal in a way you can't put in words. At least we don't talk about it. Our night down the Turnbinia and the Acorn just happened, we didn't plan it, but suddenly we were all together again and it was like nothing had changed. I was relieved. I got drunk because I was so relieved. And they were happy to have me back again. We trogged back over the Burn singing Oasis songs at the top of our voices. Only Steve wasn't there. I asked where he was. I got a shrug from Rob. 'He doesn't come out as much now,' I was told. 'It's different.'

We ran through the trees, still laughing and singing. My head was pounding, but the kind of pounding that makes you shout louder, run faster and you don't care. It's good for me, that. I stop thinking I'm going to trip over. And we were running through the trees and there's all the hills and tree roots and if I thought about it, I could kill myself with this leg and everything, but when you're like that and you can hear all your mates yelling out and everything, you don't worry. I don't.

They left me at the corner of Phoenix Court. I got invited back to the Forsyths' house for a smoke. They all watched to see what I would say. But I thought I'd go home. Penny and my mam waiting. I said that and waited for someone to make a skitty remark. But Rob clapped my back and said, 'See you, son,' and they all moved away, waving me good night. I was relieved we were still a team, but in a way I was more relieved to see them go home, the night finished, unscathed.

I walked past our house and I saw the back garden. Penny with her hands up in the air. She was concentrating.

All I could think at first was of the Invisible Girl in the Fantastic Four. With the powers she had gained from

155

being struck by cosmic rays, she could generate invisible force fields. Make matter do anything she desired. When artists drew the blonde, willowy, beautiful Invisible Girl, they indicated her force fields by inking in dotted lines that radiated from her forehead as she frowned and made things happen. Now I cursed the darkness and my ten pints of Stella because, try as I might, I couldn't see the dotted lines in the air coming from Penny.

Yet she was making things happen. My mother's back garden was up in the air.

Rocks and stones of different sizes, clumps and tussocks of grass all dribbling bits of wet frozen soil were sailing and dipping through the air. Bulbs and shrubs and half-grown roots tangled and whirled in the dark, brushing by one another as if working out where to go, where to set themselves down again. The roses, my mother's roses she was so proud of, transplanted from one council-house garden to another over the years, danced about each other, and reattached themselves to the bits of twig and branches that clicked back into one piece and snuck their roots into the ground.

At first I thought Penny was using these unknown, diabolical powers of hers to destroy my mother's garden. I almost shouted out for her to stop. But then I realised, as the rockery and the shrubbery and the sweet peas were sucked back into the cold earth, that she was rebuilding it. She was making it better than it had been before. Like giant dominoes, the paving stones slapped onto the ground, one after another. Then she was finished. Her body sagged with exhaustion and that glowing light ebbed away.

I wanted to dash over and give her a kiss. My own girlfriend. My new, clever girlfriend. With superpowers!

Thirteen

'There was a little monkey,
ran across the country
fell down a dark hole
split his little arsehole
What colour was the blood?'

'Frank!'

She grabbed her son by the arm and shook him. She shouted indoors again.

'Frank! Come and listen what this son of yours has learned!'

For good measure Fran shook Jeff again and the tears bubbled up in his eyes. He wouldn't let them go, however. He set his face in defiance against her.

Fran didn't know where her kids learned it from. There was her eldest, out at nights and only fourteen. Frank said she was a little tart, the way she dressed. He said he hated his own daughter.

'Come on! You're coming inside to tell your dad what you've just told me!' Not even four and coming out with things like that. 'You're not playing out for the rest of this week!'

Jane turned up for a pot of tea and she commiserated. The kids were getting cheekier. 'But what role models do they have? The little bairns look at the grown-ups and look what they're getting up to!' She looked round at the other houses in the close. 'If I was a kid today I wouldn't know if I was coming or going.'

They went in to sit in Fran's kitchen. Jane wanted to talk through plans for her Peter's birthday. She had read something in *Bella* magazine about making your garden into a circus and fairground by painting cardboard boxes. She liked the idea of a party with a theme. Fran thought Jane liked the idea because it meant she wouldn't have to have anyone in her house.

'So I might have to ask you for some help,' she said, 'painting the boxes in circus stripes.'

'Right,' Fran said. But none of us can paint, she thought. She imagined how it would all turn out. Jane would end up with a pile of rubbishy painted boxes in her garden and that would be the party. Her soft son would be disappointed and cry, Jane would get cross and hit him, then send everybody home. Fran wanted to say you were better off having a clown party at McDonald's. They did all sorts for the kids there.

'Have you been to see Liz recently?' asked Jane.

'Have I not told you about visiting with Elsie?'

Jane nodded. 'It all got eclipsed by the story of you going to the loony bin with Elsie.'

'Don't call it that.' Fran pursed her lips.

'Elsie's gone bloody daft now,' Jane said. 'She was out in her garden this morning, sobbing and shouting and waving her arms in the air. I leant over the fence to see what the matter was.'

Elsie had looked desperate and worn out, still in her housecoat and nightie. Her hair was out of its bunches and she was raking her hands in the soil.

'I kept my voice as normal as possible and I asked her what was going on.'

'And?'

'She said her garden was back to normal. She said that the day before it was ruined and now it was all better again.'

Fran said, 'I think she must be under some stress.'

'She would be.' Jane stared out of the window. 'Hasn't that Penny let herself go since taking up with her Craig?'

'Do you think so?' Fran asked. 'I thought she looked happier.'

158

'That's just sex.' Jane sniffed.

'Maybe I should go over to Elsie's,' Fran mused. 'Talk to her. See if she wants anything doing.'

'I'd keep well away. That husband of hers. You don't know where he might be lurking.'

'That's awful!' Fran gasped and gave an involuntary shiver.

'Well. He gives me the creeps. He could be hanging around anywhere.'

'I think he'll have left Aycliffe behind,' Fran said. She looked at Jeff, her young, sulking son in the corner of the kitchen. 'They all do.'

Mark Kelly turned up. He was in his jogging outfit, a more neutral blue than his tattoos. Jane was quieter with him there.

'Do you think Penny and Craig will last long as an item?' Fran asked.

'Who?' he asked.

Fran explained, smiling. Sometimes Mark was slow on the uptake. He couldn't keep up with everyone's business.

'That Penny's an interesting lass,' he said, looking for his cigarettes, patting his pockets. Jane saw that he had one of those bum bags on. She didn't like them. Mark, she noticed, was the only person Fran let smoke in her kitchen. When he sucked on the cigarette she watched the tender bit of his temples move and dimple.

'Have you been to visit her mother in hospital?' Jane asked him. 'Have you been to see Liz?'

He frowned. 'Should I? I don't really know the woman.'

'It just seems like everyone's going up to see her,' Jane said. 'Like a bloody shrine. All of us touching the hem of her gold lamé frock.'

Fran cackled. 'That's good, that!' Then she was ashamed of herself. That poor woman, in a coma. She told Mark the poem her son had come out with. Mark spoiled it by laughing long and hard. His laugh was so infectious he started Fran and Jeff off too.

'I still don't think it's funny,' Jane said. 'If my Peter said that, I'd –'

'Jane, man,' Mark said abruptly. 'Sometimes you're a pain in the arse. You think you're so bloody proper.'

Fran loved this about Mark. He said exactly what he meant. Plain as the tattoos on his face. With a final slurp of tea, Jane took herself off home.

'You'll have started something now,' Fran said, who would bend over backwards to avoid falling out with Jane. Jane could be quite nasty.

This is like a story I'd forgotten. Was it one of the Ladybird books? Sometimes I'll remember those stories and see the picture exactly as it was. I've still got all those books, on a bottom shelf at Nanna Jean's. But I needn't open them to see the pictures. They're all in my head. How all those characters chased the Giant Pancake, or pulled the Giant Turnip out of the ground, or got swept up in the molten deluge from the Magic Porridge Pot. I liked the obscurer fairy stories. Chicken Licken proclaiming disaster everywhere. And the one I have forgotten, but am reminded of tonight by my dream, is the one where the dog runs through the streets of a town with a princess strapped to his back. Every night in the story the dog has larger and larger eyes: the size of dinner plates, of cartwheels, of round towers. And the princess is always strapped to his back.

In my dream of course it isn't a dog with gigantic eyes roaming the streets. It's a leopard. I'm leopard-dreaming again.

The city is unfamiliar. The leopard is pounding down a long, empty road. The tarmac shudders as his paws crash down, one after another. His tongue lolls out of his mouth and he slavers, with much less self-possession than usual. I'm used to seeing my leopard looking dignified. Here he's dashing about like he's been set free.

The shops are all shut and dark. Opposite them there is

a vast rock like a ruined wedding cake. On top of it a castle slumps and squints down through the chilled mist.

I'm following my leopard as he leaves the main streets and, moving slower now, more stealthily, patrols the older part of town. Where the streets crisscross above and below each other. My bearings are lost. He pads to a standstill in an abandoned marketplace. A drunk old bloke sits against a pub wall. He clutches to his chin a bottle of QC sherry and sings into it: '*Vol – aa – re, uh uh uh – oh . . .*' The leopard stares at him from across the street until the old man notices. The old man's anorak is shredded all about the sleeves. It looks like it hasn't been off his back in years. Stuffing's coming out like upholstery. When he sees the leopard, he panics and can't move. He yanks out handfuls of his stuffing and throws it, sobbing, 'Shoo, shoo!' And I know how he feels. In my dreams I'm always shooing away the big cats. And my limbs get full of dread and I can't move fast enough. Every second I think I'm going to be eaten. In my last dream that's exactly what happened.

And how can I be so lucid when I dream like this?

The old man reeks of stale piss. The leopard wrinkles his moist, leathery nose and moves on.

There's something exhilarating about the way he runs easily through the city. He's unimpeded. He's liquid amber, slipping cursor-quick up alleys and stairways. The city is old, it seems old and continental, but cold and unforgiving. You can feel the air shiver with alarm at the leopard's incongruity.

I'm pleased that, in my dream tonight, I can keep the cat at an arm's distance. I feel like an observer, tailing him. Tonight he isn't into mauling or molesting me. He has other concerns.

Down another main street the nightclubs are emptying. Bouncers corral red-faced, sweating women and men along the curb, some into taxis. Some form clusters and gangs that roam off back into town, shouting, breaking glass, tumbling into the road. The leopard sweeps past. When I follow I feel worried by the crowds. I hate going past straight nightclubs as they close and empty. I feel menaced. Vince told me I go about with a sign on my forehead telling fellers to beat me up. And they can see me too, in my dream. Some bloke lifts a bottle to hit me, a soppy grin on his face, but I manage to dash on.

I stumble into a park, through a small graveyard, in the shadow of the castle I saw earlier. The leopard is by a fountain, all golden heroes with torches and lutes. There's a fine mist of spent cold water. He jumps into the fountain and gleefully submerges himself. He knows I am watching. I wait. The night closes in around me. The street noise has faded away by now and I no longer feel scared.

With a sudden burst of laughter and noise, the leopard jumps back out of the green water of the fountain. He jumps right over me, and I get showered. When he touches down, somewhere over on the grass, I see that now he has a princess strapped to his back. A sleeping princess in a golden frock, who barely moves a muscle as the leopard thunders off into the trees, back to the long main road. Mind, she's knocking on a bit for a princess. She must be in her forties. And, as I watch, she stirs and wakes, jolted alive on the leopard's back. She clutches her bouffant wig to keep it on straight. It's Liz.

Across the Burn the ground had sheeted over with the dirtiest, most walked-on ice she had seen. It was hazardous, climbing up hill into town. Cars zipped by on Burn Lane and it took Penny half an hour to walk in the same direction. She had to leave the path and struggle up the hill, finding footholds, clinging to branches. It was like taking hold of the trees' fingertips, snapping them off when she leaned too hard, when her feet slipped. If it had been up to her, she'd have stayed indoors today. Hidden in the house with a good book. It was one of those very black February days.

Elsie wouldn't leave the house. At first Penny suspected she was just lazy. Then she remembered that Elsie was the type to gad about town come hell or high water. When she was happy with Tom, it had been their favourite thing to traipse the streets in all weathers, knocking on the doors of friends or acquaintances, getting themselves brought indoors to talk about God. Elsie had always been less keen on the God bit. She just liked the visiting. But these past few weeks, she was more inclined to stay indoors. After that business with the garden she was often to be found staring out of her windows, as if waiting to see what would happen to it next. She confided in Penny, saying she thought it was haunted. Now Penny wished she hadn't set it all to rights again, and just left it in the mess it had been. It was only to cheer Elsie up, but her small spell had caused more harm than good. Elsie thought that she was cracking up now. She sent Penny to fetch her messages from town, and had decided to stop work at the spastics shop for the time being. That was one of Penny's jobs for the afternoon; telling Elsie's colleague Charlotte that Elsie was planning to stay away.

Penny reflected on how caught up she was in Elsie's and Craig's lives. Soon she would be doing everything for them. It was so easy to get sucked into where other people were headed.

Already it was getting dark. Friday tea-time dark. This time last winter she used to go shopping for groceries with Andy. They would walk back this way, through the Burn, along a route that she would never dare take alone. It was sinister down here in the dark. A curious vegetable gloom which a couple of years ago she would have found mysterious and exciting. Now it was terrifying. Would Andy have been much help anyway, if someone had jumped out on them? Funny, it was only now that she thought of that. They had their own stolen shopping trolley from Red Spot and they wheeled it unsteadily up and down the icy hill, laughing and shouting in the dark as they followed Burn Lane by its dirty yellow streetlamps. Andy was probably depending on Penny's help, should anything have happened.

This was one of the big changes to her life lately. She

now had something she'd never had before. A man's man. She smiled to herself. Craig was what you would call a man's man, and you wouldn't be saying it with an ironic smile, a wry lilt in your tone. You wouldn't be making a sly jibe about his sexual preferences. You'd be saying quite plainly and honestly that he liked to go out with the lads. That his dealings with the outside world were all located in the world of men. And home was where the women were. Penny wondered if fag hags grew up. She wondered if she could think of Andy and Vince as . . . well, not childhood friends exactly, but people she'd played with on the way to growing up. And there was something in their adventures and their love affairs that seemed juvenile to her, once she thought about it. They were flippant about the whole thing. They laughed about all of it. They were so careless with each other, as if they'd never grow up. Because, now that she thought about it, they never had to grow up. They wouldn't have a family life like others had. They could stay boys like that for ever. And that wasn't something Penny could do. She had to find something of her own. These past few weeks Craig had been looking like an alternative. A man's man, who knew how life and mechanical things worked.

She had reached the long road at the top of Burn Lane. Now the streets were flatter and safer all the way to town. Maybe this felt a little like betrayal. She had lost her interest in Andy's life, in Vince's. She was there if they needed her. And besides, Andy must know that she'd already moved on. She couldn't hide it. Couldn't pretend she hadn't spent all her time with Craig. The other night, she'd been proud of Craig going out with his mates again. Actually proud he never came home till the early hours, stinking of lager. She'd been pleased that he was back in with his mates. He made them sound fearsome. Esteem meant a lot to them. There was a pecking order. She wondered if he would show her off to his gang.

Esteem. Penny stopped. She was in the middle of Faulkner Road, a street of pensioners' bungalows. Was this all about her self-esteem? Here Craig was, apparently doting on her. Was she accepting this for the sake of her self-esteem? Was she changing everything she ever thought just to bask in the compliment of all his attention?

Crap. This was just the way it was. She was having fun and maybe some security, too. The sense of somebody being there for her. He lay against her at night and his body was hard all the way down her side.

Charlotte had taken it upon herself to shut up shop. Penny banged hard on the spastics door. When the old woman let her in, she looked pinched and red.

'What's happened in here?' Penny gazed around the shop's inside. It was like a bomb site.

'You tell me,' Charlotte snapped. She snatched up her dustpan and brush from where she had left it on the counter.

'Have you been burgled?'

'The till was open. I was stupid. I hadn't emptied it last night. It's not like we get a fortune coming through.' She sagged inside her clean pinny and had to sit down. Obviously she was blaming herself.

'Did they get away with much?'

'Oh no,' Charlotte said. 'Look.'

Penny went to the till to look. All the paper money was still there, but shredded into tiny pieces. Green and orange confetti littered the floor all around. The coins were partly melted, fused into each other like a pocketful of chocolate buttons. Penny reached out to touch them, to see if they were warm.

'Who could do this?'

'Don't touch them,' the old woman said, standing up again. 'I haven't had the police in yet.' She drifted over to the clothes racks. She had kept everything beautifully hung and colour-coded, almost so that you'd never know it was a second-hand shop. The blouses had been slashed with knives and they hung in tatters. They looked odd, still colour-graded like that.

'Has everything been ruined?' Penny asked. 'How did they get in? Why would they do it?'

Charlotte shook her head. She had tears bubbling up. 'All this shop does is raise money for them poor crippled bairns,' she said. Penny was shocked to see her cry. Charlotte seemed to work at keeping her feelings in. She acted hard on purpose, as if life had grieved her. Penny went to her and the old woman put out one of her clawed hands to keep her at a distance. Or maybe it was for Penny to take. She couldn't tell. To be on the safe side, she stopped. Charlotte dabbed at her eyes with her other hand and the gesture was clumsy and childlike. 'Sorry for crying. This is my work, you see. It makes me feel rotten, seeing it like this.'

'I bet.'

'Has Elsie sent you?' Charlotte was trying to make her voice sound normal again. 'I wondered where she was.'

'She said she won't be coming in for a while,' Penny explained. 'She's not felt herself just recently.'

'Hm.' Charlotte picked up a china shire horse. Its head had been cracked off at the neck. 'She'd had her eye on this.' She set it down. 'I could do with her help, cleaning this lot up.'

Penny bunched up her sleeves. 'I'll help.'

'That's good of you, dear. I was going to phone Big Sue, too, at the Christian Café, see if she'd bring some of her cronies. They're always well-meaning.'

When Big Sue arrived, full of purpose and with a roll of black bin bags and a few of her religious pals, she was shocked by the mess. 'I'll bet it was those rough lads who took my underwear,' she breathed. 'This is the kind of thing they get up to.'

'Now, now,' said Charlotte. 'It doesn't do to cast aspersions.' She was back to her brisk self.

Penny was thinking; what if it *was* the lads from over the road, from the Forsyths' old house? Was it the kind of thing they would do, just for a laugh? And a worse thought: had Craig been with them? Last night was another night having a laugh with the boys. Was this how they amused themselves? Yet surely Craig couldn't have been party to any of this. It was his mam's shop. He couldn't spoil that.

This was Andy's idea, the step machines and the rowing machines. I never used them before. They recommend aerobic exercise as part of your work-out plan, but I always thought it was just the lasses who did all of that. But Andy was into it and said we should warm up on the step machine. You're up on a height and it's like running in slow motion. You've really got to push down as you run, and the music from MTV helps. Andy always goes like the clappers when Take That or someone come on and you've got to laugh, really. He's not very strong or fit but he can give the step machine hell. He goes scarlet and the sweat streams off him. I'm on the stepper beside him, paying close attention to what the computer and its little green displays are telling me, when to speed up, when to cool down. Some of the lads in the next room, doing the weights, are taking the piss. They think you lose muscle and bulk, exercising like this. The woman in charge, Mary, went past a few minures ago, and gave me a smiling nod of approval. So I'm doing it right. She plucked her Lycra pants out of her bum as she went by, thinking no one could see. Like a fuchsia thong. Gave me the horn and I sped up to take my mind off it, but that made me worse. My fifteen minutes is almost up, but I can't get off here with this stiffy showing through my shorts. That Andy for one is bound to notice.

He still gabbles away even when he's exercising. He doesn't understand that you don't always want to talk when you're doing the biz. He's saying that being on a step machine is like running in a dream. All that effort getting nowhere. Mind, I know what he means. Then he's telling me that he dreamed last night of chasing a leopard and it was like running on this. He tells me all sorts these days and I feel uncomfortable when he does. Like I'm preparing myself for what's coming next. Like it's something that's gunna embarrass me. I don't know what. I think he talks so much because he sees less of Penny. He's stuck in her house by himself a lot of the time. I'm most of the company he gets. So he crams in all his talking when he's down here. I let him go prattling on.

This machine's good for my bad foot. I never thought of that. Since I'm running on the spot, my foot strapped in secure, it isn't getting any stress. I'm getting the benefit of running without having to move. That's smart.

Him going on about his dream reminds me of mine last night. I woke up and felt sick, like you do when you've dreamed something awful. When it takes five minutes to convince yourself it wasn't all real. Penny never woke up and at first I was pleased, because I woke up with a cry. Then I wanted her to ask about it, but she didn't, of course, because she sleeps like anything.

I was on a shingle beach, a small one like Robin Hood's Bay. Dad took me and Mam there for a holiday. It looks like someone's pushed all the buildings right up to the shore, and they all topple one into the next. Quaint, my mam called it. I was on the beach and there was a boat going down, just that bit further out than would be safe to swim. Even though it was that far away, I could see who was aboard. I put my hand up to shield my eyes and saw it was a black dinghy and its rubber was punctured all the way around. Like someone had sunk their teeth into it. Dracula, who came ashore nearby in Whitley Bay, had jabbed his vampire teeth into the rubber.

I was on a jetty and trying to run to its end, see if I could help from there. My foot made me lag behind. My mam was with me, shouting that I had to hurry up.

And who was out on the dinghy?

People from Phoenix Court. They were waving and shouting, their mouths open like goldfish wanting feeding. Liz and the tattooed man, Penny and Andy, all of them shouting at me.

But I can't swim. My foot is like a weight tied to me. It

168

would never flip like a proper foot. In school swimming lessons I could never propel myself. And I burned with shame throughout because everyone could see that foot in all its glory. When we jumped in the heavy, warm, chemical water, the crazy distortions made its ugliness leap up at me. Of course I couldn't swim.

My mam said, 'They're going to drown, Craig.'

And I hate having dreams like this, where they put guilt on you. My mam turned away in disgust. She spat into the water. In real life she never spits. So I must think this is how she really thinks of me. She tossed off her cardy, the one I hate, with the pink embroidered cats, and leaped into the sea. She dove straight and looked so graceful. But the sea was green and cold and dark and somehow I knew it had just sucked her in and she wouldn't be rescuing anyone.

The step machine lets out that heart-stopping bleep. Fifteen minutes. I'm relieved. I slow, slow, stop, automatically checking out how many staircases I would have climbed if this was real life. How many calories I've burned. Andy is already off his machine. He's over by the rubber plants in the corner, talking with Penny, who's come to meet me.

Fourteen

Craig thought he was going to die and that was why the future wasn't worth thinking about. Once he startled Elsie by saying something along these lines. They were at the fairground; Craig was ten, an age when he stayed close by his mam. She said he needn't grow up poor and uneducated like his mam and dad. Craig came right back with, 'We'll be dead by then anyway.' Elsie was shocked.

'What does that mean?'

'There's no point in thinking about when *I* grow up,' he said with a shrug, gazing dispiritedly at the lights of the dodgems. 'Can I go on them?'

Only if Elsie could come in the same car and keep an eye on him. She drove and let him place his hands on the steering wheel. The air smelled of rubber and crackled with the static that powered the cars. Someone rammed them and jolted Elsie's neck. Her concentration was off because she was thinking over what her son had said. He came out with odd, gloomy things. She thought it was them funny comics he read. Once he'd told her he wouldn't feel guilty shooting her in the heart if she was taken over body and soul by a Swamp Thing.

'Is it because of your bad foot?' she asked him, as sensitively as she could manage, swinging round in a dodgem car, grappling the slippery wheel. Maybe she should wait till after, but she was anxious to know what was going on in her son's head.

'You what?' He looked at her, scowling. She knew he hated mention of his bad foot. 'No, it's nothing to do with that.'

Elsie thought, He might think that. He might think his

foot will spread, that the crushed, diseased flesh will kill the rest of him. If I was a kid with a foot like that, I'd look at it, clutch and feel it at night and think that it was going to kill me. Especially if I read the weird kind of comics Craig reads. They're always about monsters and things.

'Then why do you think you're going to die?'

He sighed; she could almost hear it above the noise of the fair. Sometimes he looked so frustrated with her. 'I never said just me. I said we're all going to die.'

So that was it. 'This isn't about nuclear war again, is it? Because if it is, I've already explained to you about that.'

He tutted. 'No, it isn't about nuclear war.' Though he hadn't really believed Elsie's saying that it was all right if you hid under the stairs and ate tinned peaches. It was at this age that Craig started to feel he knew more about the world than his mam, and each thing she tried to tell him from then on only compounded that impression.

'We're all going to die anyway, aren't we?' he said with a bright smile. It was something he'd learned in comics. The superhero comics never flinched from deaths. Someone was always getting it. Look at Gwen Stacey, killed by the Green Goblin. Chucked in the river. Spiderman had been distraught. It had taken years for his alter ego, Peter Parker, to learn to love again. That was when he started knocking about with Mary Jane, who always called him Tiger. Craig had his first wank over Mary Jane. In his recurring daydream he'd been dressed as Spiderman and she felt him through his red and blue Lycra. 'You've helped me love again,' Spiderman told Mary Jane in the comics, and she smiled, pleased. On the bathroom floor Craig stared at the widening pool of his white sperm and hardly dared touch his numb cock. His first sex was fraught with the idea of rescuing love from the jaws of death.

And the Green Goblin himself had been killed, the inadvertent victim of Spiderman, a bittersweet revenge. Found dead, he was unmasked and revealed to be the insane father of one of Spidey's best college friends. The irony of life! Something else Craig had gleaned from comics, alongside the inevitability of death, was that your oddest, deadliest enemies are often just around the corner. Anyway, how could he explain this to Mam? She always wanted to bring all his worries and frowns and nightmares back to his broken foot or his absent father. I don't care about either of those things, Mam, he wanted to say. But the wet way she asked and guessed around him made Craig angry with her.

When their go on the dodgems was over, one of the Gypsy fellers jumped on the back of their car, clung to the pole and drew them to a standstill. When he grabbed the pole, he took some of Elsie's flyaway ginger hair and yanked it by accident. She screamed out. This and her subsequent muttered complaints took her attention off her son's morbidity as they wandered through the rest of the fair.

Fish and chips on the way home and that was their Friday night out. In bed Craig listened to his mam play Shirley Bassey and he thought about why it wasn't worth bothering.

One morning that December he came down into the kitchen. Mam had been making her milky weak tea for them both and the radio was on. Some New Wave band was on, just before the news, he couldn't remember who. His mam started saying something bright and cheerful about the snow that was coming, how they might go sledging, when the news started up and the first story was that John Lennon had been shot and killed in New York City.

Then the news was finished and the first song after that was 'Help!' Elsie's face was wet with tears. She finished making the tea and sat down heavily at the breakfast bar.

'Who was it, Mam? Who's died?' By then, though, he recognised the song as one by the Beatles.

'John was the cheeky one, he always said something to annoy the interviewer and make them look daft. It was Paul I liked, because of his eyes.'

'So why are you crying?'

'I don't know.'

Elsie was thinking, You're a morbid little bugger. Kids have no heart.

Craig wanted to know all the details of the shooting. Who, why, where, how and how many bullets did it take? After his mam had finished with the papers, he kept them and pasted the clippings into a scrapbook.

'And he'd just got back with his wife,' Elsie said sadly. 'That awful Jappy wife. But still, they were happy.'

Craig thought, They get you in the end. Don't bank on too much. Doesn't matter what your special powers are, your number comes up some time or another. He tried to tell Elsie this as she played her copies of the Blue Album and the Red Album that night.

'Hush your mouth, you heartless thing!' She looked shocked at him. How dare he tell her life is futile? What was she raising here? And she sang 'Strawberry Fields' to herself.

These were the convictions that Craig grew up with: that it was all going to end soon anyway, wherever or whatever you were. It made him set his goals within manageable limits. He worked on his body and he sought out a girl. And here Penny was.

With Penny all this unquestioned stuff of his had to alter. He started looking at things differently for the first time he could remember. It wasn't what she said that changed what he expected out of life, though she never shut up about things like that. She was for ever questioning things. What made Craig think again was her very presence, how much he loved to be with her. He felt full up and hungry all the time. He started to think there would never be enough time. For what, he wasn't sure. Thinking about this showed him that he believed this time limit was on everything. They were doomed and Penny would go. So when he looked round after thinking this, at his mother's house, their lives on this estate, in this town, they all looked too shabby for what he imagined he and Penny had going. There wasn't enough life here for everything he wanted.

I've started to want too much, he thought, and this frightened him. There was a danger in wanting too much. This was the one thing Elsie had succeeded in drumming into her son. Hubris, she called it, with a sneer. Don't get greedy like your father, she warned. It'll end in disaster. Though neither of them knew exactly what disaster had befallen his father when he swanned off to his new life in Leeds. Perhaps things had gone wonderfully for him. What Elsie had meant, he realised, was that his father's greed had meant disaster for *her*. Now Craig was thinking he could play with greed. He could allow himself to want things.

That night when Penny went to meet him at the gym, they returned to find that Elsie was out.

'I thought she was nervy about going out now,' he said.

Penny frowned. Sometimes Craig talked as if his mam really pissed him off. 'Maybe she wanted something at the shop.' Penny was relieved Elsie wasn't there. She wouldn't have to tell her just yet about the state of the spastics shop.

There was a note on the pinboard in the kitchen. 'She's gone to Fran's,' Craig said. 'We've got the place to ourselves.'

'Yeah?'

The house was gloomy. They walked through it without switching lights on as they went. It was like being intruders. Elsie had left the place messy, which was unlike her. Not messy enough to be worth making a comment on, Penny thought, but the place bore evidence of Elsie's distractedness. The living room looked as if a tide had swept in and out again, subtly dislodging and disarranging things.

Craig pulled Penny down on the real sheepskin rug in front of the fire, which he switched on. The fire-effect cast orange shadows on them; Penny watched them creep back and forth on his perfectly sculpted chest when he sat in front of her. She felt the sheepskin tickle up her crack as Craig went down on her. He hadn't done that before and he was clumsy. He lapped right into her like a mother cat cleaning a kitten. Penny said, 'Is that all right?' when he came up for air and could have kicked herself for asking. Did he ever ask the same when she sucked his dick? Was this any more alarming or exotic? He grinned and went back down, as if he'd discovered something marvellous. Penny squashed his head between her legs and relished that gym-trained stamina. His ears smarted and burned as if someone was talking about him. He licked around and up inside Penny as if he was taking in some magic elixir.

Elsie's key rattled in the door and she let herself noisily in, shouting, 'Yoo-hoo?' sounding nervous. 'Why aren't the lights on? Yoo-hoo?' Hurriedly Craig and Penny dressed themselves, straightened themselves to greet his mother.

Elsie hardly noticed how flushed they looked. Penny was sure she would smell the sex in the air. Everything smeared across her son's rueful, grinning, daft-looking face.

They watched some telly and went to bed.

They had hard, longed-for sex and it wasn't as good as the run-up had promised. They had spent too long watching *Wheel of Fortune* and all that stuff. They lay together, dishevelled and cross. This was the first bad sex they'd had. It was the moment Craig chose to tell Penny he had licked her innermost essence. She had transformed him magically with her superpowers.

'You what?' Her voice was hard, but there was a tremble in it. As if she had been caught out, Craig thought with satisfaction.

'You've passed on your powers to me,' he claimed.

'I don't know what you're on about,' she said, turning away from him to where the bed was cooler. She was pressed up against the wall, right into that horrible *Baywatch* poster. She considered ripping it down and telling him how demeaning she found it. Penny scratched at her stomach, at her inner thighs. Tonight she was alive with itches, which she put down to Craig's scratchy stubble. But that's kidding myself, she thought. Lately I've always got these itches and I've got to sort it out. Find out where they're coming from.

'You do know, Pen,' he said in a low voice. It was the voice he used when they had sex. She let him get away with that then. He thought she thought it sexy, but it wasn't really. Like that bloke off the aftershave advert. He said filthy things as he thrust into her and she let it in one ear and out the other. If that's what got him off – she shrugged. Now he was talking like that without the excuse of sex. 'I've seen you, you know. I've watched you use your powers.'

'My powers?' she repeated, and hoped she sounded sceptical enough.

'Your superpowers.'

Penny made her hands into fists under the blankets. Her black fingernails tingled, a quite different itch to that under her skin. This was an older tingling and one she hadn't told many people about.

'Craig . . . I don't want to talk about this.'

'I watched you the other night. When you were out in the garden. I was pissed, but I know what I saw.'

'I'll tell you things in my own time, Craig. You've no right spying on me.'

'I wasn't spying. I caught you. You can make things happen. Like magic.'

'I know,' she said quietly.

'It's like having superpowers.'

'No, it isn't.'

'But it is! Who else can do that?'

'I don't know.' She sounded surly. I sound stupid, she thought. I should just tell him to fuck off. Or I should explain, calmly and rationally, that my powers, if that's what he wants to call them, are something that I've always had. The power of making things fly through the air, mend themselves or to come to life has been something I've nearly always practised. To me it isn't out of the ordinary.

If that's superpowers, then it's Craig's superpower to be able to fix tellies. It's Andy's superpower to desire other men. It's Elsie's to have ginger hair and work down the spastics. If Penny could have been bothered, this is what she would have explained to Craig. Instead she said, 'Oh, man. Look. Life isn't a comic strip.'

He lay quiet. He moved apart from her. That side of the bed sagged with his silence.

Oh, great, she thought. I've put him in a huff.

'I had a hideous cunt of a teacher tell me that when I was eleven. She thought I lived in comics. I did live in comics. I told her that. And that it was better than living in fucking Newton Aycliffe. That scraggy bitch laughed and told me that life wasn't a comic strip. She lived on a farm somewhere out beyond Darlington. She came to school filthy, smelling of sweat. My mam was disgusted at such a dirty-looking teacher.'

Penny hadn't heard him say as much as that before. Maybe the superpower he'd picked up from her was talking.

'Anyway,' she said, after a thoughtful silence. 'Even if I do have superpowers – which I don't want to say I have or haven't, or even discuss right now, right? Even if I do have some kind of . . . power, then what makes you think you've picked them up off me?'

He turned round in the bed to face her again. 'Because I love you, Pen,' he said.

She thought he must have gone mad. Or he was taking the piss. It was too awful. Here was a man professing his love. It was something she had waited for. He was offering her his ordinariness, his safety. But at the same time he had made himself seem mad and dangerous, talking about superpowers. It was like a cruel joke.

'I'm sorry, Craig,' she said, and sat up. What time was it?

'What's the matter?' he asked, alarmed.

Penny was out of bed in a flash, hunting around on the carpet for her jeans and shirt. She was crying, she realised.

177

'No one's ever said that to me,' she sobbed. 'I'm going home now. Right now. Where's my boots?'

His mind raced. He went, 'But . . . but . . .' and it was as if the effort of telling her had robbed him of the power of ordinary speech. Inwardly he shook, full of adrenaline and disappointment. It was like being someone in a film. This was Craig, he had vowed never to say anything like that. And the other part couldn't believe that Penny had reacted as she had.

'Fuck, bollocks, shit!' she cursed, hunting out her remaining clothes. She was like a scalded cat. 'Look, I've got thinking to do. OK?' And with that, she opened the bedroom door.

'Penny, you can't walk out in the middle of the night.'

'I can't?' She paused and seemed to weigh this up. To her mind it instantly became one of the disadvantages of accepting his love. She stared at him, half in and half out of his bed. But I don't love you, she thought. And I won't. He was expecting her to say the same back. He wanted them playing snap with similar sentiments all night long. Penny couldn't take someone's love and be unsure what to do with it. She didn't want to crush someone like that.

'Are you going home to Andy?' he asked, and some bitterness crept into his tone.

'What?' She blinked. 'I suppose I am.'

'Right,' he said. And then he couldn't think what else to say.

When she closed the door he listened to her creeping down the stairs, through all the rooms, then out. Every noise was charged with her presence and her magic. Craig stared bleakly at his ceiling. But I'll get her back, he assured himself. Now I've got powers too. I can win her back with the magic I must surely have taken.

Andy had been to the hospital.

As he arrived, Fran was just leaving Liz's bedside. It was like the changing of the guard, she said with a smile as they crossed over in the corridor.

'It's funny, I've sat there for hours,' she said. 'And it's, like, hypnotic.'

'I know what you mean,' Andy whispered, staring through the glass panel of the door. 'She's so beautiful.'

'I suppose she is.' But that wasn't what Fran had meant. 'I reckon it's because I've been run off my feet all day, at home with the kids and Frank . . . and then I come here and it's so peaceful and relaxed.' To Fran, sitting by Liz's bedside and hearing the regular beep of her life signs was the most restful bit of the week. She found she was almost looking forward to her visits. She came alone now, making polite excuses to Elsie, and found she could talk to Liz without embarrassment. She told her neighbour all sorts of things about her life and what she wanted. Was she imagining it or did Liz look concerned? It could be the way the light worked. Fran felt they were closer friends now than in the few weeks when they had lived beside each other. Fran had told Liz how often she thought about leaving Frank and leaving her own kids. Thrilled, she voiced her most serious plans about maybe starting a new life somewhere else. Liz didn't look at all shocked, that was the best thing.

'Good night, pet,' Fran told Andy with another quick smile as she set off down the corridor. She left the building wondering what Andy would tell Liz about. Fran laughed to herself. When Liz woke, what a lot of stuff she would know!

Andy chucked out some of the older flowers, replacing them with a handful of anemones. Their stalks were tough and haired and their heads looked sullen, peering over the lip of the glass. But were you allowed to place flowers on the life-signs machine? What if water got into the machine? So he moved the vase onto a side table.

Chitchat first. Bring her up to date with the everyday news. Maybe Liz didn't even know who half these people were. Andy was going on about Judith at the shop and how she'd had a fight with her boss's son, who'd been left in charge for a week. She was over twice his age and had

had it up to here taking orders from a snotty kid. In the end her daughter had gone round there, waited outside in the dark for the boss's officious nineteen-year-old son, and given him a good slapping in the alleyway. For a day or two that had been the talk of the street. What else to tell her? About the spastics shop getting done over? About the social services going round to see Nesta and it turning out that Nesta was seven months pregnant and she never even noticed? Andy could see Penny's face now as she passed on this gossip. Penny looked sour and her tone was censorious. 'How could she not know she's in the family way?' she had sneered and to Andy it didn't sound like her. It was only afterwards Andy realised that Penny sounded just like Elsie. He didn't tell Liz that bit. He didn't think she'd want another Elsie for a daughter.

Then, when he'd exhausted recent gossip from round the doors, Andy broached the subject of himself. His voice was unsteady, but he was warmed up now, used to the way his voice sounded in the cosy gloom. It might just have been inside his head. He looked at Liz and thought she looked as she had in his dream.

He found that he was telling her how worried he was. It came flooding out. In a matter of minutes his throat caught and he was crying. He let the worst of it out in great gasping sobs and wiped his eyes on one corner of Liz's sheet, since he didn't have a hanky.

'I'm so selfish,' he said. 'Because all I'm worried about is myself. But I've bottled this up inside and who can I say anything to? Somehow it's like I can't be upset if it's just for my sake. It's just ... I think these spots mean something terrible.'

Spots? Liz's death mask seems to wear a quizzical frown.

'Spots.' He nods. 'The size of coins. Like leopard spots, and they're under the surface of my skin, all over my body, they look permanent and blurred ...'

He pauses, then untucks his denim shirt and unbuttons it. He removes it to show his new, gym-toned body. He

180

twists round to see his spots and to demonstrate them to Liz. He is fascinated to see, in this clinical light, how they march in irregular rows up his sides, round his back in increasing sizes and denominations. The middle of his chest is almost bare, like a leopard's tender underbelly.

'What's going to happen to me?' he asks Liz.

When he looks her way this time, that perplexed frown has subtly altered and become a look of dismay.

Andy pulls his shirt back on before the nurse catches him.

Fifteen

At the bus stop Big Sue looked nervy. Jane sighed. Sue's still not getting out much. It's like Elsie; by all accounts she's afraid of leaving the house, too. What's happening to people round here? She tried to get Big Sue talking, which wasn't hard usually. Today all Sue wanted to talk about was the state of the world. How the young people were running amok. Big Sue pointed out the graffiti on the bus-shelter wall.

Phil Says: Tina I love you
Tina Says . . . Phil fuck off
Sandra loves Tiger Taxis driver (Kevin Costner look-alike)

Someone had drawn a TV screen with an aerial on the top. They'd drawn a newsreader next to a picture of a fat person made of circles. The headline was *Fat Fuckers Take Over*.

Big Sue had a point. Bairns would be reading that kind of language. Filthy language written down struck Jane as worse than that said out loud. When she read it she never failed to blush. Jane loved to read romantic novels, tumultuous, thick blockbusters which, on some wary, insomniac nights, she could finish before dawn so that in the morning her head would spin with passion and adventure. But she would snag and trip over, jolt out of her spell if there was bad language. It made the blood burn in her ears and she would go back to reread, trying to justify it to herself, mouthing the words.

There was no excuse for this in the bus shelter.

'That'll be them lads over the road,' Jane said.

'We're not safe in our beds,' Big Sue said, though she

182

said it all in one rush, as if it was just a thing to say. 'Are you heading into Darlington, pet?' she asked Jane. 'Where's your little boy?'

'School,' Jane said and felt a moment of guilt since, as a teacher's helper-volunteer, she should be there too. She couldn't face it. Spring was in the air. The sky was bluer than it had been for months. The tarmac was wet and sizzled with melted ice water, as if the sun was deliberately sucking it all back up. Jane wanted to be off round the shops. She was meeting her mam in Binn's café, mercifully minus the one-legged stepfather.

Jane said, 'What about Nesta having another bairn?'

'Eee, yes.' Big Sue bit her lip.

'I don't think she looks after the others proper.'

Big Sue looked pained, as if she wasn't the type to pick fault. 'I think the thing with Nesta is that she's subnormal.'

'You what?'

'Subnormal in the mental department. She was adopted, you know, by a lovely couple. Very clean, from over Faulkner Road way. And Nesta grew up like she is, quite different from them. I don't know what they think about her. It just shows, it doesn't matter how you get brung up, it's all in your genes. I suppose.' Big Sue clutched her handbag under her bosom.

Jane thought about how Nesta's daughter came running out of the house at eight every morning, seeing herself off to school. By all reports Nesta was still in bed at that time. She had Vicki, who was eight, and one who was little more than a baby, and Vicki had to get herself up and fed and deal with the baby as well. And if you saw Vicki . . . she was like a street urchin.

'I wouldn't be surprised,' said Jane, stepping half out of the bus shelter to watch for the bus, 'if they got reported and social services came and took that new baby off them straight after it was born.'

Big Sue looked shocked. She tried to remember which fairy tale it was, when the wicked fairy takes the princess

183

as soon as she's born. The queen knows this will happen even as she gives birth. 'Oh, that would be terrible!'

Where was this bus? They'd been waiting over twenty minutes here. 'You worry about bairns being kept in a house like that,' Jane said. 'It's a kindness, I think, to report the parents. Look at Fred West and Rosemary West and the House of Horror. That was allowed to go on because people didn't think to phone in. Nesta shouldn't have been allowed to have any bairns.'

'Oh, now,' said Big Sue worriedly.

The bus had appeared at the bottom of Woodham Way, down by the private houses.

At the back of them there was the clang of a gate and Penny came running. She's dressed up too warm for the weather, Big Sue thought. What a mess she looks! All them layers of cardies and shirts! Pretty girl like that, spoiling herself! Penny was just in time for the bus, breathless as it drew to a halt before them. Jane gave her a tight smile and thought, Typical of a daughter of Liz to swan up to the bus exactly at the right moment. When the likes of me have to wait nearly an hour!

They got tickets and Jane turned to ask over her shoulder, 'How's the great romance?'

'The what?' Penny scowled. 'Well. That's over with.'

Jane hurried down the gangway to sit with Big Sue and tell her. They watched Penny find a seat near the front. Then, as the bus shunted off, it stopped abruptly to let on a latecomer. Mark Kelly was wearing a white T-shirt and tight blue jeans. He grinned at Penny and sat down with her and immediately they started chatting. From the back of the bus you couldn't hear a word they said, but they looked thick as thieves.

The bus heaved off on its trip to Darlington. Big Sue and Jane turned in their seats to look at each other at precisely the same moment. Jane raised an eyebrow. 'I never realised them two were friendly,' she said.

'They seem to be,' Big Sue said, her lips pursed.

*

'It was in Darlington that I had all of my tattoos done,' Mark said. They were heading up North Road, the long street that went into the town centre. It was the street Penny thought of as the exciting one: all pubs, cinemas, sex shops and taxidermists. 'The shop was called Tattoo You and it's still down here somewhere. I've never been back for years.'

Penny stared at the designs on his face. She hadn't had a very clear look at him before, or dared to ask many questions about them. He'd brought the subject up today, so she felt free to ask. It took her mind off Craig. 'How old were you when you first got done?'

He laughed. 'Pardon?'

'You know what I mean.'

'Oh . . . I forget, really. But I reckon I was under the age you're meant to be. I used to come on the bus with my best mate, Tony. It was all his idea. I was so scared the first time. You've no idea.'

'Did Tony get tattoos?'

'He never did.'

'Was he scared?'

'I don't think so. He never looked it. And he loved to watch it happen, loved to watch me get it done.' Mark smiled. 'It ended up with him designing my tattoos. He was a wonderful artist, you know, though he never did very well at art in school. They didn't think much of what he did. But he'd make up things, work them out on paper. Then he would draw them on my skin in biro, the nights before we went to Tattoo You. The woman there – Marjorie, they called her – used to go over Tony's lines and colour it all in.'

'Show me one he drew on you.'

Mark lifted up his T-shirt sleeve to show his right shoulder. Underneath, reaching into his shaved armpit, he had a centipede in scarlet and gold, its legs twisted in all directions. Penny thought, What a thing to have crawling into your armpit! It was like an optical illusion because the insect jigsawed precisely with a bird on one side, some kind of eagle, and a furled orchid which went round to his chest. She could see only parts of these things down the short sleeve of his top.

'But why did you get so many?'

'I dunno. It's like an addiction.' He thought. 'But it's also like balancing up. You get something on one arm, then you need the other one doing. One leg, and the other needs the same. With a clock on one tit, the other will need a balance. You spend all your time weighing yourself up, making it all balance . . . next thing you know, you're on your way to being covered.'

'Right,' she said and could see how it happened. 'I still don't think it's fair that this mate of yours, Tony, wasn't brave enough to get any done.'

'That was just Tony.' Mark was about to add, 'And besides, you don't know what it's like.' He stopped himself and the words froze in his throat. Penny had pulled up her many layers to reveal her taut, pale stomach. There she had a hummingbird, its fine green beak pointed at her navel. 'I got this in Whitley Bay last year,' she said.

'Smart,' said Mark, leaning in to see.

'What's he doing now?' Big Sue asked, hardly daring to look.

'I can't see,' said Jane. 'But she's lifting up her clothes and he's bending to have a look at something.'

'This is disgraceful!' Big Sue fidgeted with the clasp on her handbag.

The bus swung round the last roundabout before the town centre. Jane was up on her feet, ready to get off. 'I'm sure Elsie's going to be pleased to hear about this. She thought a lot of that Penny.'

'Oh, you can't interfere . . .' Big Sue began, but Jane had already set off for the front of the bus, where Penny was still exposing her belly for Mark.

Jane slipped past trying not to look.

Mark saw her and grinned, turning away from Penny.

He was about to say something when he remembered what Fran had told him. Jane had it in for him.

Penny waited downstairs in the café while Mark went to the loo. It was chintzy and genteel, full of pensioners. The waitress took her order and she said coffee for Mark, as he'd asked.

'Now, does he want milk, hot milk or cream?' asked the waitress worriedly.

'No idea,' said Penny.

'Let me think.' The waitress tapped her teeth with her pen. 'He has hot milk, does Mark. Normally.' Then she was gone.

Penny sat thinking. She wished she'd asked Mark if he'd had his whole body tattooed. Perhaps the moment had already passed. Could you ask a question like that without blushing and seeming prurient? She had read somewhere that it was impossible to put a tattoo on the penis. Its poor tender shaft bruised the instant you started to apply that kind of pressure. The more she thought about it, the more she wanted to ask.

He reappeared and smiled, taking his place at the green marble-topped table. 'Now,' he said. 'Tell Uncle Mark all about it.'

She found that was exactly what she wanted to do. She started with New Year's Eve and told him bit by bit how she'd ended up settling for Craig.

'Is that how you think of it?' Mark frowned. 'That you've "settled for" him?'

She thought. 'I suppose I must.'

'You're tying yourself down and you're not even sure.' He sipped at his coffee, but it was still too hot. 'Listen, I could tell you a thing or two about settling for things. Sometimes it seems like the best thing to do.' He stared at her and the effect was mesmerising. 'And whatever you settle for, there's always something to be salvaged out of the situation.'

'And there was!' Penny burst out. 'There is! When he

187

wants to be, Craig can be a lovely bloke. He'd do anything for you, for me. I felt . . . protected.'

'Did you need protecting?'

She shrugged. 'Not really.' Then she added, 'But it was nice anyway. And I liked feeling part of a normal family, just for a bit.'

'There's no such thing,' Mark said sadly. 'I hate to tell you, but there's no such thing as a normal family.'

'Don't patronise me, Mark.'

He laughed. He was twice her age, he supposed. Almost, anyway. Really, he had every right to patronise her.

'All right,' he said. 'We'll pretend, for argument's sake, that life with Craig and Elsie could be like normal family life.'

Now she snickered. 'Well, maybe not. But don't you know what I mean? Don't you hanker after a bit of ordinariness?'

'I don't know any more,' he said. 'I really don't know what I want any more.'

Penny was silent for a few minutes. They blew on their coffee and started to drink, stuck in their private thoughts. What he'd said sounded so bleak. She hoped she wouldn't end up like him. And it seemed awful to think that.

Penny said, 'When I think, what made it impossible to be with Craig was the way he fixed our telly.'

'Hm?' A smile played on Mark's face. The thought struck her that they were both enjoying this conversation more than they'd like to admit.

'He was so methodical and dry. He took it all to pieces and hoovered all the parts –'

'He hoovered your telly?'

'Then he put it back together and it was mended.'

'That's amazing!'

'Yeah, but how can I shag a bloke who thinks like that? I'd have much more respect for someone who got in a flap and chucked the bits around, or who made it blow up or who . . . I don't know . . . wanted to *read* instead.' She stopped and laughed at herself.

Mark shook his head, tutting. 'Fancy hoovering the telly!'

'Don't you see what I mean?'

He grinned. 'Craig sounds like a handy feller to have around.'

'But can you imagine having sex with him?'

'You'd be watching for that nozzle coming your way . . . listening for the hum as his Hoover bag inflates . . .'

'Oh, shut up,' she said, with a grimace. 'The sex was all right.'

'Only all right?' he asked mischievously.

'Sometimes it was smashing.'

'Good,' said Mark simply.

Talking like this reminded Penny of the night before. It reminded her that when she had returned home and told Andy – diffident, quiet, worried-looking Andy – all about it, she had become furious with Craig. When she stamped off to bed, all she could think was that Craig went down on her only because he was mad and thought that he could become infected somehow by her fanny juices. That he would get access to what he called her superpowers. That was all he wanted out of me, Penny thought glumly.

She shook these thoughts away and said to Mark, 'Craig couldn't tell me anything about myself. He liked my mystery, he said. Some fucking mystery.'

Mark pulled a face. 'Did you like his mystery?'

'It sounds awful, but I think I knew everything about Craig the first time I met him.'

'He's that superficial, is he?'

'I don't mean that exactly.' She felt hateful.

'You're right. You sound awful.' Mark shrugged. 'Maybe you're not the right person to see into Craig's depths. He's certainly not going to see yours.'

She wanted to thank him for that. He looked at her straight on and she was discomfited. She said, 'I was starting to feel guilty about him. How do I tell him all this? I have to finish with him, don't I?'

Mark smiled and tipped the rest of the coffee down his throat.

Jane didn't have much to do in Darlington. Really, it was for the run out that she went. She had to be back in Aycliffe for three, to meet Peter at the school. They liked you to be there to pick up your kids, what with funny people wandering round. In the past year school security had improved tenfold. Dunblane.

So Jane had time enough for a pot of tea with her mam in Binns. Rose said she was off soon to Tunisia with her newish husband.

'I don't know where you find the energy . . . or the money.'

'Neither do I!' Rose laughed. She looked like a jolly person, Jane thought, gloomily twiddling the plastic carnation from the table's centrepiece. My mother's a jolly person, jiggling her breasts under her mohair jumper, tucking into cream cakes in Binns cafeteria. How could I have come from her?

'I don't know very much about Tunisia,' said Jane.

'Apparently it's extremely hot,' Rose said. 'Ethan's been before. He went most places with the navy.'

'Of course.'

'I'll come back all bronze and lovely for the spring.'

'Lovely.'

Rose stopped talking about her holiday and fixed her daughter with a stare. 'So what is the problem?'

'There's nothing.'

'Oh, come on.' Rose let out an irritable sigh. 'You could be pleased for me. I'm having a life at last. Don't I deserve one?'

'Of course you do. I –'

'You look narked.'

'Maybe I am.'

'It doesn't do to get jealous, Jane.' Rose reached for her Regals. 'Especially not of your old mam.'

Jane snapped, 'I just wonder when it's all gunna come to

me. I want my luck to change. I want my life to be different. I'm not even thirty and it's like it's all over.'

'It's not over!' Rose smiled. 'Look how young you are.'

'Oh, I've said that to mesel' for years, Mam. But I never do anything different. Nothing's gunna change now.'

'Look at my life!' Rose spread her massive hands in a gesture of wonderment. 'My life changed overnight when I met Ethan! And I was over fifty!' The look on her face said it all: she believed that everything could change for the better in a flash. 'You need someone to come along and transform you. That's all.'

'But that's *your* life,' said Jane, wishing she'd never started this conversation now. It was making her feel worse than ever. 'That applies to you, not me.'

Rose frowned. 'Why should you be any different to me? You're my daughter, for goodness' sake!'

'I'm not like you, Mam.'

'No harm in that!'

Jane struggled with this. 'You're . . . more *fun* than me. You're larger than life. People notice you more. Of course someone was bound to come along and want to change your life. I'm . . . I feel twisted up.'

'Nonsense.' Rose took hold of Jane's hands. 'You're still mine. I've watched you, these past couple of years, sink into yourself like this. You hardly feel you've got any worth left, do you?'

Dumbly Jane agreed.

'All the fight's gone out of you, Jane. Fight I put there. I'm scared to say it, but it's like you've no self-respect.'

Jane bridled. 'I bloody have!'

'No ego, then. You won't fight for yourself, speak up for yourself. You're absorbed in other people's goings-on.'

Jane fiddled for one of her mother's cigarettes. 'I don't know what's happened to me.'

Rose stared and thought, I don't know either, love. And I don't know what comes next for you. Your mother's a dab hand at making the best of things. Slapping on the make-up, putting on the glad rags. I wouldn't know how

191

to face the world as you do. Your life looks pinched and mean. How did you get like that? She took Jane's free hand in both of hers. 'Come to the desert with me.'

All the way home on the bus Jane thought about going to the desert. She had never been abroad. Imagine her and Peter on the golden sands in a place she'd never thought about before. She could relax into the care of Rose and Ethan, maybe even enjoy their company. For however long the holiday lasted she wouldn't have to be the grown-up. Rose and Ethan knew all the procedures. They knew how to travel abroad and how to do it in style. Jane needed their help. She wouldn't have a clue where to queue with her passport and tickets, how to travel on a plane.

They had the money for it, too. They could afford to treat Jane and Peter. He would miss some weeks at school, but it was worth it, surely. He would have some exciting tales to tell his pals and his teacher. He was such a quiet kid. He'd wow them all with his tales from the desert.

Jane saw herself packing two cases, one for him, one for her, with shorts and tops, new underwear, bikini, sun dresses, sun block, and how many novels might she need for a fortnight? Fourteen days in the sun with nothing else to do but read her books.

She thought about this all the way to Aycliffe. She got off the bus at Humphrey Close, just by Peter's school. When he came down the drive he looked upset. Something had happened today but, as usual, he wouldn't tell her anything. It was swimming day and she assumed it had to do with that. As they walked home across the Burn, she considered telling him the plan. But I won't, not yet. Just in case it doesn't come off. There was nothing worse than raising a kid's hopes and letting them spoil.

When they reached their estate it was nearly dark. They met Elsie scooting across to Fran's house.

'I'm going for my tea,' Elsie said. 'Fran's being ever so good to me.'

'Hm,' said Jane. Fran never invited her for tea these days. Fran always made it sound like she had the five thousand to feed, and that her family meals were sacrosanct. Elsie sounded so pleased with herself, getting an invite over the road to eat with Fran's mob.

'I saw your Penny on the bus into Darlington,' Jane said.

'She isn't *my* Penny.' Elsie smiled, but she was blushing with pleasure. 'She's my Craig's Penny.'

'Well, anyway.' Jane waved her objection aside. 'All the way there on the bus she sat with that Mark. You know, Mr Tattoos.'

'Oh yes?' Elsie's eyes narrowed. Jane was getting at something. Her voice had gone hard, her accent just that bit posher. She was meaning to be awful.

'They were friendly as anything,' said Jane. 'Laughing and carrying on all the way there.'

'Were they, now?' Elsie thought, Jane's trying to upset me. Why would she do that? She decided to ask outright. It was the best thing to do with people like that. 'What are you trying to say to me, Jane?'

'I just reckon your Craig should learn to keep an eye on his lass. By the looks of it, she likes the fellers.'

Elsie flushed with anger. She kept her voice steady. 'Well. Thanks for telling me that, Jane.'

Then, without saying goodbye or anything, Elsie stumped across the play park towards the lights from Fran's house.

'Wait a minute!' Elsie cried and went running back to Jane. Her voice sounded almost gleeful. Jane swung round and found her arms being grasped by Elsie, who was gabbling right into her face. 'You needn't worry about that, pet! Our Craig's Penny isn't carrying on! She couldn't be carrying on with that Mark! Mark isn't like that – I saw him on New Year with the other bloke – Penny couldn't do anything with him! He's a queer!'

Jane recoiled as if she'd been slapped. Peter looked up at her.

193

Elsie stared at Jane for backup. 'So it's all right, isn't it? Penny must be all right.'

'I don't know,' said Jane. She turned to go, leaving Elsie looking confused. God, thought Jane, what have I stirred up now?

Penny waited outside the shop where Mark's ex-wife worked. In the cool, white, crowded arcade, Penny wondered what she was doing, hanging around for him. The music piped through the speakers was faulty. Abba were doing 'Thank You for the Music' at twice the usual speed. When Mark came out of Sam's shop he was cross and flushed.

'Sam can still wrap me round her little finger,' he said. 'She's got me baby-sitting for her new baby again.'

By now Penny had decided Mark couldn't be the ruthless user Andy had said he was. She knew Andy liked to overdramatise things. She and Mark went to look at the discount home appliances in Wilkinsons.

'I'm in heaven here,' Mark said, cheering up, gazing at the racks and rows of primary-coloured kitchenware.

'Me too,' Penny said.

'It was my mother-in-law's lover who taught me to love kitchenware,' he breathed.

Penny said, 'It was Liz who passed the love on to me.'

They went to the bathroom section.

'Honestly,' Mark said. 'It's like being one of the Stepford Wives, but I don't care. I just love things for the house.'

'Me too,' said Penny.

They came home in the dark on the 213 and Penny realised that she'd had a nice day with him.

He said goodbye at her garden gate. Tactfully he didn't let her ask him in for tea, knowing he'd probably bump into Andy.

She kissed him on the cheek. 'I'll see you –' she began, and jumped backwards.

The instant they touched, her lips brushing the side of

his face, Penny came over weird. Mark, too, had straightened up, looking shocked. 'What was that?' he asked and, instinctively, they took a step apart.

'I don't know,' murmured Penny, but she did.

When she kissed Mark Kelly on the cheek it had been in a particular spot along his jawbone. This was a piece of his design she had been fixated on all day, a very beautiful tattoo she couldn't help feeling drawn towards. Just above his jawline, to the right of his mouth, there was a crimson butterfly, very small and tucked into the blocks of tidy colour. This is what Penny had kissed and, at this first contact, she had felt those thin, cottony wings stir and beat a brand-new pulse against her mouth.

Mark smiled at her. 'See you soon.'

'Well! You bugger!'

This was after tea and Elsie stood in Fran's kitchen, peering through the blinds.

'What is it?' asked Fran, who was busy washing up and weary with Elsie. All through dinner that woman had talked about nothing but herself. Frank and the bairns had gobbled up their dinners as quickly as possible, when usually dinners here were a long-drawn-out affair, full of family chat, business and argument. Tonight Elsie banged on and on about her poor, missing husband, his madness, her son's first love and her own bladder complaints. Maybe Elsie was embarrassed because she had to go to the loo a few times through the meal, but not everyone wanted a running commentary. Frank was a man, Fran thought crossly. Why would he want to be hearing about Elsie's waterworks? Eating fish fingers, listening to that. It was intolerable.

Elsie was supposed to be doing the drying now. But the Mother Shipton tea towel was still in her hands and she was clutching a wet plate to her chest. 'Just look at them!' She was staring at number sixteen.

'Whatever now?' asked Fran, but she went to see.

They both stared at Penny kissing Mark, just outside her garden gate.

'Oh,' said Fran.

'I'll have something to say to that little madam!' Elsie said.

Fran regretted letting Elsie have some of Frank's beers. He'd been pissed off but acquiescent. Fran was only too pleased to lessen his intake tonight – Spar lagers fifty pee a can – but Elsie was becoming red-eyed and reckless-looking. Fran had forgotten Elsie was meant to be on the wagon.

'It's just like Jane said,' spat Elsie.

'Jane said what?' asked Fran.

'Penny's been carrying on behind our Craig's back –'

'Oh, I'm sure she –'

'With that shirt lifter from over the way!'

'Elsie,' Fran said. 'You can't go round calling people shirt lifters!'

'I'm going over there,' Elsie said grimly, and was out the door.

At one glance Penny saw how drunk Elsie was.

'I don't want to talk about this now, Elsie.'

The older woman had barged her way into number sixteen. She was short but surprisingly powerful. When Penny looked at her she was shaking with rage, her hair all disturbed. 'You'll listen to me whether you like it or not.'

Penny sighed. 'What is it?'

'You're treating our Craig like a common convenience,' Elsie said, her mouth all twisting. Penny thought she might be having a stroke. 'And I'm not having it. I know you think you're better than us.'

'What's he said to you?' God knows what version of last night's row Craig had given Elsie. There was no way Penny could come out of it well.

'He's said nothing. He tells his mother nothing. He wouldn't hear a word against you! He worships the chair you sit on! But I saw you, you little minx. You're taking him for a ride. I saw you kissing that bloke from over the way.'

'You what?'

'That Mark.'

'So?'

'So, she says! Have you no common decency! You're going out with my son! You're practically his fiancée!'

Penny had heard enough now. 'Yeah, yeah,' she said airily and opened the kitchen door, readying herself to throw Elsie out.

'I don't understand you, Penny. You've got a lovely lad in my son. You're like a cat on heat.'

Penny raised an eyebrow. 'What?'

'You really think you're a cut above, don't you? You think you can mess about in our lives and then just leave us.'

'No, I don't.'

'Like your mother. Think you're so superior. Not like the rest of us. Even lying in a coma she still thinks she's *it*.'

Penny stood by the open door. 'I'm throwing you out now, Elsie.'

'Throw me out, she says! Listen to her!'

'I'm asking you to leave.'

Elsie gathered up her dignity. 'Little madam!'

'And you tell your Craig he can fight his own battles!'

'Oh, he can, he can.' Elsie cursed, shuffling past. 'And you'll find yourself sorry, you little bitch!'

Penny slammed the door behind her.

Elsie cried all the way across the dark playground to her house. The wind had picked up, forcing her to struggle against the garden gate to get in. She just wanted to be indoors and hiding now. What a horrible day it had been. She felt she'd run out of people she could talk to. Even Fran looked cross with her tonight. Elsie wanted to be in her house, watching telly, the fire going.

Something nagged at her and pushed her back, however. A feeling of gloom. Something like a warning.

She let herself indoors and the hallway was dark. There was an unfamiliar sound of rushing water. When she switched on the light it burst into life only for a second, then went off with a bang as all the lights fused. She leaped back against the wall and found it soaked. Water ran down the walls of the corridor in silver sheets. As she walked across the carpets, they squelched and sucked at her feet. Then she saw into the living room and, beyond, through the serving hatch, the kitchen.

The pale streetlight coming through the windows was enough to show that the furniture was overturned. Someone had taken a Stanley knife to the sofa and chairs and slashed through the upholstery as if they were looking for money. Elsewhere the destruction was more aimless. The coffee and dining tables had been dismembered and scattered, the bookshelves tipped and their contents shredded apart. Mirrors were smashed everywhere and all that glass kept Elsie from dashing into the room. She still had enough sense left not to fall on the glass. She counted in her head how many mirrors had been broken, how many seven years of bad luck that made.

Her pictures had been wrenched off the walls and dashed on the floor. On the mantelpiece the brass ornaments – the ladies who were bells inside, the Aladdin's shoe, the Scotty dog – were all melted into each other. The real-effect fire had been kicked in.

There was no message. Nothing written in blood or shit across the emptied walls. No clue.

'Oh, me house,' Elsie said.

She knelt and opened the cupboard on the wall unit. The wine glasses they never used were shattered and blackened, as if by fire. She reached past them for what she was looking for. A shoebox she had covered in lilac sticky-backed plastic. Her memory box. For a moment, as she grasped it to her chest, she didn't dare open it. But it rattled, it was heavy with the papers and photographs inside. That was something.

Elsie untied the purple ribbon to check. She squinted in the gloom at the pictures. The photographs were safe.

What would impress her? Nothing would impress her. Look at her powers, look at her intellect. She isn't a girl who's easily impressed.

And what can I do for her? Is there anything left? I thought I was good to her. I wish I could put things right, put things in a way she'll listen.

After gym that night I went to the Acorn with Mary. She came on friendly today. I don't know what that's about. The lads egged me on, so I went for a drink with her. The lads would rather me be with Mary than Penny. Mary's more our sort, Steve said. The first thing he's said directly to me in weeks. So he'd approve of me going with Mary. Mind, they couldn't laugh at her fanny in Lycra if I was going with her.

But . . . I don't want Mary. I don't want a skinny gym lass. I want Penny with all her softness and quickness, and them powers of hers.

In the pub after gym I had a few pints fast. After gym they go right to my head. It's good, though. I hate first dates with a lass. I never know what they want to talk about. My palms sweat on the glass and my thoughts go too fast. It wasn't a first date, though. But I drank and was on my third pint before you knew it.

Mary was giving it all this chat. I thought she'd been stand-offish before. Now she was coming on like I dunno what. I thought, if this had been a month ago, I'd be over the moon. Why did all my opportunities come at once? But I reckon it's like Steve said once. You get a charisma, a sexual confidence when you're knocking someone off regular and you feel horny all the time. The lasses come flocking round. They can't keep away, you're so confident and that. And here Mary is, in her going-out outfit, sitting on the edge of her barstool and she's making her little skirt ride up like that. Penny would never do that. I'm noticing little things about Mary I'd never have noticed before, because of Penny. Like how much make-up Mary's wearing.

When Mary goes to powder her nose, as she calls it, I'm away. I'm out of that pub and running through Aycliffe precinct before I know it. I've escaped.

I can run like the clappers. I'm not even limping. I'm drunk but even drunk I couldn't run like this before. Something has happened to me.

When Mary was singing my praises, staring up at me and saying how strong I was, she was referring to how much I was lifting this afternoon. Without any extra effort I doubled the weight I usually lift. Well, not quite doubled, but I added a fair bit on. Everyone noticed. I hardly sweated any extra.

Downstairs I showered and I sat in the sauna. I looked for an extra towel to cover my damaged foot, as I always do, when I heard someone else come in the room and I am naked. I felt my feet self-consciously, but my foot was a normal shape. My foot was foot-shaped for the first time I could remember. I set it beside the other and they looked almost the same. Spot the difference! Left and right mirror reflections! Snap! I had a pair, a pair the same!

I'm still not sure what's happened.

I run like a bastard. In slow motion, covering some graceful ground like Steve Austin, the Six Million Dollar Man. We have the technology – we can rebuild him. Here I am, Penny, here I come restored. Will Penny be my Lyndsey Wagner, my Bionic Woman? Will we be super-heroes together, do you think?

Mary will have come out of the bog, brushing her hands on her skirt, pushing her skirt into place. She'll come on tiptoes back to the bar, thinking about putting her hands over my eyes as she comes up behind me. Whisper, 'Guess who?' in my reddened ears. When I guessed she'd move her cool fingers down my bullworked neck, round my chest, brush my nipples hard. She'd be making her first move on me.

But I'm gone! I'm running! See me go!

Across the park, down Faulkner Road, across the Burn. If you looked you'd hardly see me. I'm just a blur, a pulse of light.

There's a pub here. I think of having another drink. More courage, and maybe I need it. The pub is the Robin Hood. Its sign is a painting of Kevin Costner as Robin Hood in that crappy film. Like on the cover of the video, he's firing a burning arrow right at you. It's a good likeness of Kevin Costner, that.

I run round the back of the pub and I realise I don't want another drink. I know what I want. To prove something.

When they made superhero TV series they always had a warning on at the end. They said, 'Spiderman – or whoever it was – has special powers and that's why he can climb up walls and that. Don't try it at home.' And of course I always did. Who was going to take notice of a warning like that? It made you want to do it all the more. But I could never bloody do it. I couldn't climb up walls. I couldn't even run straight.

That's why tonight I get the smart idea of climbing up the tallest side of the Robin Hood. Off go my shoes! Off with my socks! Look at my feet! I press my fingertips and my two bare feet against the brick. If someone caught me up this dark alley now it would look like I'm having a slash. But it would stop looking like that with the first step I take upwards. I brace elbows and knees and then . . . then . . . I hurry to the rooftop, to the eaves.

At the top I unfasten and unscrew and liberate their satellite dish. As proof I have been there. I imagine, as I scoot back down the sheer wall, that I can hear the groan of disappointment from inside the Robin Hood as the TV reception fucks up. They'd be watching the football.

And I'm away, with the satellite dish tucked under me arm. It's the dish that calls the superhero members of the Justice League of America up to their satellite which orbits the earth. That's what I reckon. And I can run!

Sixteen

The atmosphere was no better. It had got so that Judith dreaded going to work. And she was a good worker, she was never one for not enjoying her job. Shop work had always suited her because you saw people, but just recently the corner shop had stopped being a nice place to work. This was the business of the boss's son and his interfering ways, his ideas for upgrading the shop. 'It's a tatty little shop on an estate!' Judith shouted at him. 'What does it need upgrading for? We've got everything that everyone wants!'

The boss's albino son looked at her. 'Everything needs upgrading.' He was doing a business degree at the University of Sunderland and in his holidays his dad let him practise on the family business. All the threatened changes preyed on Judith's nerves so that she could hardly sleep at night. It had been her agitation that made her daughter waylay the boss's son one night after shutting up shop, and slap him one in the face. She wasn't usually like that. She had meant to give him a reasonable talking to, one business-studies person to another, but the boy was obtuse. She had made his nose bleed. 'Our Joanne,' Judith giggled when she was told. 'I didn't bring you up like that! Did he know who you were?'

It turned out Joanne had said this was from her mother: smack. Judith was horrified. 'Whey, now they'll sack me for sure!'

'That would be unfair dismissal,' said her daughter implacably. 'And besides, do you think that cocky little short-arse will want to tell his father he was clocked one by a lass?'

'I suppose not.'

'Well then,' said her daughter. 'Your job's safe.'

And she was right. Not a word was said. But the atmosphere in the place had turned awful. The boss's son treated her like dirt in front of customers. He wouldn't let her play the tapes she wanted over the speakers – she loved the *Pan Pipes*, she thought they were relaxing. He insisted they had a station with lots of contemporary, dancey pop music. Judith came home each night with her head throbbing.

'My feet and my head are throbbing!' she'd cry, throwing herself in a chair. 'I hate that shop!'

It was a shame. That shop had once been such fun. It had seemed like her own private shop. It was funny how things went downhill, how times changed. How you were never aware of your own peak.

She walked to work, ten minutes or so, with a heavy heart. First thing in the morning it was dark and the ground was silver. They said they could still have snow this year.

For the first hour of each morning the shop was hers again. The boss's son wouldn't be in till eight at the earliest. Judith was there for the early crowd wanting fags and milk and papers. Often she saw Fran when she was returning home from her cleaning job at Fujitsu. For that first, very early hour, it could seem that things were just the same. But then, when it became a more ordinary time of day, when the charm of earliness wore off, that brat would arrive to start shouting his mouth off.

This morning Judith unlocked the shutters and the whole series of locks that kept the corner shop safe. The lights on the deli counter and the fridges were left on all night, so the first thing she saw in the gloom each morning was, beyond the dark shelves and aisles, their lemon glow.

There was more light in there this morning. Her heart gave a twinge when she saw that the door to the back was wide open. Now that was always locked at night. Could she remember locking it last night before leaving? The backroom lights were blazing. They forced a wedge of cold light into the shop itself. The boss's son would go mad if she had started to forget to lock things up. That's where the safe was, in there. He'd have an excuse to sack her if she'd gone careless. She struggled to take herself through to the back, to check that everything was all right. She didn't want to go. She didn't dare look at what she'd find.

The lino was sticky. It was crunchy with pieces of glass. Lemonade bottles had been smashed up the middle aisle. Now that she stopped to stare, she could smell the thick sweetness in the air. Almost hear the distant fizz of spilled pop going flat. And lying on the floor in front of the meat counter was a boy. A grown man, in a T-shirt and pants, curled up as if he was sleeping. He lay in the debris. Judith wanted to run screaming, but there was also something vulnerable about him, the way he was lying, that drew her. His hair was smarmed to one side, stuck down with something. One arm was flung out in sleep along the floor and his fingers twitched slightly in time with his breathing, which sounded heavy and disturbed.

It was that lad from over the road. 'Andy?' she said. Why would he have broken in?

She stumbled closer and her heart was making a racket in her chest. She couldn't hear his breathing pick up as he started to wake. She looked at the spots up his arms and legs. Those limbs shifted, stirred under her scrutiny. One arm was clutching a heavy, wet object to his body. It had left dark smears on his shirt and his face. As his eyelids flickered he nuzzled this object, the size and shape of his own head, almost lovingly.

Judith had been bending to help him. What Andy clutched to him was slick with blood and it glistened. She could smell what it was before she could see for sure: a massive and fatty hunk of raw meat. He's pulled it out of the freezer, she thought. He's defrosted it by hugging it to him. She backed off.

His eyes opened fully.

'You broke in,' Judith told him.

He sat up. His face crumpled as he realised what he could taste. He dropped the joint. 'Blood,' he said. 'Where am I?'

'Why did you break in?' Judith asked. She went to turn on the main lights.

When they came on it was too bright, fluorescent. He stared down at himself and he was stained pink from the meat and his own blood. His palms, he saw, were shredded from climbing the walls, from breaking in.

'I don't remember coming here,' he said, as Judith came back up the aisle to get him.

'What is it you're covered in?' she asked.

'You mean my spots?'

They both stared down at him. Then Judith snapped into action.

'Listen, there's not much damage. I don't know what you did, or why, but I'll not say owt. You're a neighbour. Just go.'

Andy struggled to his feet. 'I don't know why I'm here.' He wanted to spit so badly.

'I can see you're not your right self,' she said. 'You could do without the police interfering. Just get yourself home, bonny lad.'

He didn't need telling twice. Judith led him to the back room and opened the door.

'Thank you,' said Andy. 'Judith, isn't it?'

She nodded, looking at his mouth, smeared in blood. His teeth were pink. Look at what I'm helping, she thought. He could be anyone. 'Go!' She pushed him out.

Andy ran.

Big Sue and Charlotte called for Elsie that morning. They banged on the door for twenty minutes.

'Even if she's gone crackers, her son should still answer the door,' reasoned Charlotte. But there was no sign of her son, either.

'And where's that Penny?' asked Big Sue, backing down the garden path and staring at the upstairs windows of

Elsie's house. 'I thought she'd virtually moved in with them. Give it another knock.'

Charlotte was wearing that dashing hat of hers, the one with the scarlet feather. It bobbed in time with the knock she gave the front door. Nothing. 'All the blinds have been pulled.'

Big Sue gave a sigh. 'She can't say we haven't tried to pull her back to the land of the living.'

'That's right,' said Charlotte. She'd wanted to tell Elsie that the shop was shipshape once more. That, no thanks to Elsie, they were up and running again.

'She must have gone into one of her depressed phases,' said Big Sue.

'Or she's drinking again,' muttered Charlotte.

'Could be.'

'She could be lying in a stupor. Choking on her own vomit.' Charlotte shuddered. The last time Elsie was drinking, she'd been doing it at work. She was too scared to drink at home, where her Tom could see. At first it had been quite amusing, Elsie livening the place up by trying on all the clothes. She kept dashing into the changing cubicle and coming out dressed up in the most ridiculous things. Layers and layers of multicoloured outfits.

Big Sue said, 'Where should we go, then?' They had banked on spending their shared day off at Elsie's, cheering her up.

Charlotte nodded at Nesta's house across the close. 'I think we should check on the mum-to-be,' she said. 'They say the house is filthy inside. I wouldn't mind getting a peek in.'

'Ha'way then,' said Big Sue, who was concerned too.

When they left, Elsie bent to peer through the blinds, making sure they were really going. She was in the kitchen, holding her breath.

Water ran down the walls. The floorboards were soaked through. The lights were still off. Craig hadn't come home last night, with or without Penny.

Elsewhere in the house the floor creaked. 'Craig?' she asked unsteadily.

Andy was caught red-handed heading off down the stairs with his rucksack. He had used all the hot water in the early morning tank and had hurriedly packed himself some essentials. In clean, fresh travelling clothes his skin felt scalded clean. This was his getaway. He had just enough money. No complications.

'Are you going somewhere?'

Penny called from the top landing. She spoke with that guarded, almost frosty voice she'd been using with him just lately. What have I done to her? he thought. Maybe she had been odd in anticipation of this moment. She'd known for a while I was going to walk out on her. If I leave number sixteen, he thought, then Penny is here by herself.

'Yeah,' he said, looking up.

She was wrapped in a towel, heading for the bathroom. 'Are you going to your nanna's again?' she asked. She looks scared, he thought.

'I don't know. I don't think so.'

'Weren't you going to tell me you were going?'

He smiled. 'Yeah. I was.'

'Were you?' What do I sound like? Penny wondered. He can come and go as he pleases. It's nothing to do with me.

'Listen,' he began. He didn't say anything else.

After a moment of staring at each other, up and down the stairs, she said, 'This time last year this house was chockablock.'

'I know.' He smiled. 'I'll phone when I get there. I'll give you the number.'

'Right,' she said, and watched him hurry down the rest of the stairs. 'Wait,' she said. 'You'll need some cash. You've not got anything.' She came down the stairs.

'What have *you* got?' he asked. 'You can't afford –'

'Liz left me a bit,' she said and, with that, went to the dresser and unearthed an envelope full of notes.

Wordlessly he took it. Once more he headed for the front door.

After it slammed there was a momentary silence in which she held her breath. She could picture Andy doing the same thing outside. Then he did what they both knew he was going to do, and put his house keys through the letter box. The metal flap clacked and the keys arrived in a sudden jangle.

Seventeen

If there's one thing I've had to become, it's self-sufficient. I don't need anyone in the house with me. Imagine living in a place where when you put something down, it stays there.

Here was Penny in the middle of the afternoon. She was sitting on the tyre swing in the kids' play park. These were good places to mull things over. Her boots were planted firmly on the gravel and she felt suspended, hunched up in her cardy. It was coming in cold. Here came that snow they were talking about. This winter was never going to end.

Penny looked at the houses around her in Phoenix Court. All full of people. People squabbled and grabbed things. They shouted in your face, exerted their demands on you. You had to take notice. My house was as busy as the rest, she thought. Now I could do with some time on my own.

This afternoon I should go and see my mother. She lies in Bishop Auckland, waiting. She doesn't know any different, but she's putting on that guilt. That easy emotional blackmail. Even the nurses there think I'm awful. They think I've abandoned Liz. Is she as good as dead? Andy said I shouldn't give up hope and I was shocked at the suggestion I had . . . but perhaps I have. Whatever's lying in Bishop Auckland isn't my mam. She's like someone made up.

Mark came out to see Penny.

She looked up from the swing. 'We're like kids, meeting in the park after school.'

'You're going to catch your death,' he said.

'Andy's gone off somewhere. He packed a couple of bags and wouldn't say where he was going to.'

'Right,' said Mark. He thought about Andy for a second, but didn't have much of a picture of him. I've slept with him, Mark frowned, but I can't recall much about it. He remembered more of what he'd seen of Andy in the gym. Sometimes sex was too close up.

'Come and have some tea with me,' he told Penny.

She smiled. 'Is that a good idea?'

Mark shrugged. 'I reckon so.'

He held out his hand. He wore a plain yellow shirt and the sleeves were rolled up. Oh, what a colour he was in this grey afternoon. She stared at the hand offered to her. What was on it? The thing with Mark's tattoos was that you could focus on one thing at a time. Something would jump out at you and snag your attention, then the rest would become a backdrop. Everything on him jostled and competed for your attention. On his palm, among other things, there was an eye. Which, as she looked, became a perfect blue egg wedged in the stretched jaws of a snake, which heaped its manicured coils around and around Mark's forearm.

'Take my hand,' Mark said.

She took it, prepared to hop off the swing. Under her own palm that drawn eyeball flinched. She felt its lashes brush the tender part of her wrist. The snake shivered and squirmed as he helped her up.

'Something happens,' she said, 'whenever we –'

'I know.' He grinned. 'Sssh.'

Penny touched her fingertips to the orange triangles she saw poking out from under his shirt. They were the petals of a tiger lily and the pollen was thick and felty.

In the days when they were happy they played some funny games. You do, don't you? Looked at cold, it might seem perverse or kinky. But that's not what it was like at all.

I loved Tom. When I first saw him at the fair, the day he took me round the back of the generator, I could see he had more to him. He had a mystique. He came from somewhere else. There was a power to him.

When we were happy he loved playing those games, too. Sex was something he blushed about. He was like a boy about sex. For someone so worldly like Tom, it was funny to see him get coy like that. He was clever and yet when it came to matters of the bedroom he stammered and didn't know the right things to say. Lucky I did. In some things at least, I was never backward in coming forward.

Look at him here.

Elsie had gone back to the memory box, pulled away the ribbon, and was flicking through the pictures. They smelled of Poison, the perfume Tom bought her each Christmas. She could see him at the counter at Boots, dressed in black, hideously embarrassed as he asked for ladies' perfume. No way he could have bought me lingerie.

In the broken fold-down cabinet Elsie had hunted out the emergency candles. They were old and cheap and kept there for power cuts. She set them in saucers and lit them and soon the wrecked living room glowed almost cosily. She found the half-bottle of brandy she'd stashed away and let her eyes slide past her ruined belongings.

In one power cut she'd sat up all night, terrified. This was before Tom. She had shouted at Craig to wake up. He came blearily to her bedside. 'Get the candles out of the cabinet downstairs,' she demanded, sounding scared.

The poor lad (where *was* he tonight?) hobbled down the stairs. She listened to his every move. He was plunging into the pitch dark. He was being lulled back to sleep in the dark. When he found his way by touch into the living room, he very carefully slid apart the wall unit's glass doors. Like a safecracker, listening to the heavy, dangerous swish of the glass. And then what he came for went clean out of his mind. He fished around in the cupboard and, instead of candles, produced a folded sheet of paper. Very carefully he returned to his mam's bedside and presented her with the red electricity bill.

'What's this, you bugger?' she howled, flapping the paper in the dark.

She hated power cuts. With no lights, no cooker, no telly, she felt abandoned by the world.

Tonight she had to squint in the gloom from the candles. She held the photos up to her nose. Here was Tom. Never photogenic. Craig as a bairn. Ah. He'd kill you for saying this now, but he looked like a little girl, right up until he was thirteen. He was too bonny for a little lad. When he was thirteen the woman in Greggs the baker stared at his long blond hair and asked Elsie what her daughter was called. That was the woman in Greggs with that disease that made her eyes bug out. Craig glared back at her with hatred. Then he went up the ramp in the precinct to get all his hair shaved off at Roots, the unisex salon. He was a proper rough-and-tumble little boy, whatever he looked like.

Now she had a handful of those square photos from the early seventies. The colours were thinning out on these old snaps. On the Polaroids she had from the early eighties, too, the colour was fading. Here was Craig in football kits, in tracksuits . . . he was never out of sports gear. On school photos he wore elasticated ties, sharply pressed shirts and the baggy bottle-green jumper of the Woodham Comp uniform. Year after year in these pictures he gave the photographer a sickly smile. Look how self-conscious he was, Elsie thought. I never saw that at the time. You always think boys are indestructible. That's how they go on. Oh, look, in this one he's at that awkward stage. He was all gawky, his hair fluffed up, his teeth sticking out. He's got a smile on like he's messed his pants. And the sweatshirt he's wearing is one I bought off the market. It says 'ET Lives!' and there's a picture of ET. That funny face of Craig's above it. He looks like bloody ET – how could I have been so cruel? Bless him!

Elsie started to laugh. It was awful, but it was funny too.

There was a heavy thump from upstairs.

'Craig?' she called, suddenly alert.

212

Elsie struggled to her feet.

Another thump. It came from her bedroom, directly above her. Well, who would be up there?

She put down the lilac memory box and the empty brandy bottle.

Upstairs he had lit candles of his own. He waited by the bedside. He was setting the timer on the Teasmade, like they always used to when they shared a room. That's what he used as an alarm clock. Every night he poured the clean water back to go round again.

'Hello, Elsie,' he said as she came into the room. Her bedroom hadn't been vandalised. She stared at him.

'I was just thinking about you,' she said. 'How we were happy. How we used to play.'

He was dressed all in black. He was lanky, skinny, his hair brushed back. He looked neat and sexy as he hadn't for years. When he smiled at her, the frail light shone on his sharp teeth.

'I'm glad you've been thinking of me, Elsie,' he said.

She took a step towards the bed.

'Wait,' he said. 'Hang on.'

'What is it?' Tears were beginning to roll down her face. I've got a complexion like a crab apple, she thought. How can Tom want me back when I look and feel like this? More tears ran in gratitude and dismay.

'We made each other very unhappy, Elsie,' he told her.

'Oh, Tom,' she said. 'I was never unhappy with you.'

'No?'

'When you had your problems and everything, it got harder but . . . you were still the same person.'

'I'm glad to hear it.'

There was another silence. Elsie felt like flinging herself on the bed.

'I've been going out of my mind, Tom. Someone's been getting at me. Have you seen the state of the house? They're destroying it all. They're taking every bit of my life and smashing it up . . .'

He shrugged. 'Do you know who's doing it?'

She shook her head. 'Oh, no. I wish I did. I thought . . . for a while . . . just for a bit, that . . .'

'Did you think it was me?'

Elsie nodded. 'Only for a second.'

'Would I really destroy your home around you?'

'You weren't well, Tom. You weren't responsible.'

'Maybe not.' He sat on the bed. Then he was more like his own wiry, creaky self. 'Come here, baby,' he said.

Elsie hesitated. 'Has . . . has the Lord helped you back to your proper self?' she asked. Somehow if he went on about God she felt safe. He believed in goodness then and wouldn't do any harm. He opened his arms to her.

'The Lord had nothing to do with it,' said Tom. 'I found my own way back.'

She went to him then and figured that she'd have to trust whatever he'd made of himself. She locked herself in his embrace and felt him rustle with pleasure inside his dark clothes. She even felt a pang of desire.

'My old vampire,' she smiled. 'My Dracula. Can we still get up to our old games?'

Tom smiled.

Eighteen

I miss Penny. I miss the things she used to tell me.

The things she'd been up to! We'd sit up in her mam's front room and divulge, all night. When I first met Penny, when I met her through Vince, I thought she was just a nice girl. But she'd been up to all sorts.

It was because of Penny I came up with my theory that everything teenage girls do, gay men in cities try to do ten years later.

Two weeks into my life in Edinburgh, this is my great discovery. I live in a flat in the New Town. Over restaurants, pubs and cybercafés I have found myself a tiny flat in a warehouse and from here I plan my new life. Everything that is going to happen to me.

And what will happen to me?

Another reason I need Penny here: to plan things, to talk things through.

I fling open the tall, dirty windows to see the city roofs. You can hear, but not quite see, the midnight fireworks in Princes Street Gardens. It's summer and the place is awake all night.

Tonight it's me – adolescent at twenty-four – leaving the house at midnight. Penny said she crept out to meet her boyfriend at night when she was still at the age of choosing O levels. Snogging off, she called it, in gravel car parks, in playgrounds, in shady woods. From here I don't have to sneak out. I've this whole flat to myself. In a way I do wish there was someone for me to creep past. Someone to put the lights on, shout out and stop me. And tell me I'm doing wrong, that I'm cheapening myself.

I leave the light on so you can see it from outside. In the

early hours the flat will look occupied and be safe. My meagre possessions will be all right. I clang down the red fire escape, six flights. Surely my steps must disturb the people in the three flats below. They must know I'm up and down all night. They all work, keep regular hours. They must wonder what I get up to.

They let me in and it makes me feel special. It's so easy, as if this is a place meant for me. All the bouncers are women, which is nice to see. All of them in black, in bomber jackets, each one holding a Vodaphone and nodding at me as I slip past into the bar. One's wearing tight tartan trousers, blue and yellow; I've seen quite a few trendy Wendys wearing those and I think I must get some. But will I still be trim enough to fit inside little trousers like that?

I don't know what I'm doing out on a Monday night, but it's madness staying in, within those four walls. This is a city. I have to be out. As soon as I came here there was a voice I'd never heard before, telling me to make the best of it. Use it up. Waste it all. As if I had a limit on my time. And I reckon I do have a limit on my time, but I'm not certain what kind.

At one of the tables by the door I sit down with my drink. The walls are sickly orange and yellow, stuck with fliers: they put a stripper on in the basement every Sunday after lunch, and Tuesday nights are Step Back in Time nights. Tonight the music is the blandest of techno, stretching some normal song well beyond its limit. Its verses and choruses have burst apart with the strain. The few punters here are a mixed bunch. I try not to stare. After a week I still can't get used to how ordinary they all seem to find coming to a gay pub. To me it's a novelty. They're popping in after work for a quick pint, or after midnight for last orders, or slinking in determinedly, looking for an easy lay.

And what do I look like? I haven't made much of an effort dressing up. I came as I was. I'm sitting with my pint by the door and getting the draught from Leith Walk. Cooler tonight, which is a relief. Like the bloke at the next table, I've picked up copies of the *Pink Paper* and *Boyz* off the twin piles by the bar and I'm having a flick through. One's full of rape stories and legislation, the other has pictures of soap stars and underwear. The man just by me seems to be a teacher type. I can see him look up and look around every time he turns his page, as if he's invigilating.

The bar is long and not very crowded. Three members of staff swish up and down in tight T-shirts, waiting for the crush. One drinks coffee and talks to a smart Jewish man who has perched himself on a stool. He's in a check suit and he looks like he's got eyeliner on. He flashes an appraising look around the bar. I wish I'd come later, or not at all. I've pulled my shirt cuffs down almost to my knuckles and I've surprised myself doing it. I've covered up the shining, healthy black spots under my skin. When I move to lift up my glass, one will poke out and it makes me wonder: do I mind if anyone sees my leopard markings?

If asked, I would say I'd had them tattooed on. What I'd like to do is wear slinky little tops and shorts. Show off all these muscles I've been gaining in recent months. I can feel them yearn to expose themselves and have the sun touch them. They also ache with disuse. In the week or so I've been in this town, settling in and becoming used to not being in Aycliffe, I haven't been to a gym. I haven't found a suitable one yet. Everything's so expensive. If you live in the city centre you're expected to be loaded. And I'm having trouble even signing on. What I want is one of those books and invalid benefit. I want to go to the post office every week and get my fifty quid in hand, no bother, no signing. I could say I've had a breakdown. Show my spots. Look – psychosomatic! Or I could tell them the truth. That I think I'm going to have a child.

Oh, but they look at me sceptically enough anyway. The morning I went to queue for my forms – in a building across town that was just like my old school inside – I told them I moved away from Aycliffe to look for proper work. The feller looked at me as if he thought I'd come to their city, to live in the middle of it, among all the noise and the tremulous, rainy lights, to waste things. My life, my time, their money.

Yet even without going to the gym I feel great. I thought the moment I stopped lifting weights it would all sag. I'd run to fat. I'd turn to jelly. I thought I'd regret even starting it all in the first place. But here I am, harder than ever. My muscles tense up and bulge without my even trying. Just sitting here. Look at me, someone! Look at this, if this is what you're wanting.

The teacher type looks over, as if I've spoken aloud. I can't even be sure I haven't. I spend too much time on my own. He looks about thirty-odd. Thinks he's cool as fuck. The man from C & A. I bet he's got a bit put by. He'll holiday in Italy and fly back with local ceramics. Slides his eyes away when I look back. Cheeky bastard! As if I was looking first. Looking over his glasses. Dressed sharp, a bit prissy. Maybe he's a university teacher like Vince got himself. He can take me to Paris for New Year. I want someone to look after me. Someone older and more sensible.

He asks me, 'Are people here always as chatty as this?'

He sounds shy, almost. I expected him to be cocky. So I'll talk to him. I say I haven't been here much, I don't know how friendly or unfriendly they usually are. But when I came to this town, I expected people to be friendlier. He shoves up along the plush seating. I'm saying, you arrive on this scene, come out every night with all good intentions, all trusting of a good time, and there's this apprenticeship. They won't talk. Sitting by yourself with a pint and the papers, like old men in the pub Sunday afternoons. He laughs. When he asks if I want coffee, I ask him if his crockery comes from holidays in Italy, but he reckons Ikea.

When I kiss him in his kitchen, a few streets away, high up over Broughton Place, he tastes of olives. He's been chewing them thoughtfully as we've talked, waiting for the kettle. Everything in his kitchen looks barely used. On the windowsill there is a row of very large oranges. He chews olives quietly as he watches me unbutton my shirt to show off all my spots.

'They're tattoos,' I tell him.

'They're wild,' he says, making me cringe for a second. I've come out dressed like a schoolboy. Striped tie knotted too tight, white shirt hanging out. When we go to bed he's put on an Enya CD and I can't come. He strokes my legs again and again, lying the wrong way up in bed. He says, 'How muscly your legs are!' and I'm pleased. He points out that my left calf muscle is more developed, and I tell him how observant he is. He smooths it and says, 'This muscle is huge.' It's very odd. I make him come twice and, on the second strike at four a.m., he's fallen asleep. Enya's on replay and I'm stuck with her wittering on till morning.

When I get home it's almost nine o'clock. I pass the couple from upstairs on their way down the fire escape. Immaculate, off to work. We all say hello and I check the communal post box. Nothing for me.

I watch them leave the alleyway and then I get this pain in my swollen leg. I have to haul myself up the rest of the steps and lie down in the living room. I stare at the stretched muscle, and watch something stirring under the skin.

I'm thinking about things that cheer you up.

Last Christmas Penny bought a two-foot-tall singing Santa from one of the cheap shops downtown. A tenner, in a red felt coat that went down to his skinny ankles. When you lifted the coat up, you saw that his legs were transparent plastic. He hummed four different seasonal tunes at random, waving an electrically lit candle in his tiny hand.

It worked fine at first. Then, the day we decorated number sixteen for Christmas, I was upstairs and Penny was shouting to me. She sounded fed up. He'd broken. I

219

came downstairs to look as she held Santa in her hands and I wanted to say, but didn't, You know what you get when you buy from those cheap shops.

As she stared into his face he started humming again, all by himself, 'We Three Kings of Orient Are'. Penny almost dropped him in surprise. I've watched her with those powers of hers: she's not always sure she's using them. She set Santa back down on the windowsill.

'Hasn't he got a creepy-looking face?' I said, and he stopped dead once more. Never to go again.

I was going downtown that afternoon and Penny asked me to take Santa to get him changed for another. I said no – there was no way I'd carry that thing down the town. I said it reminded me of that bloody Chucky, the devil doll in *Child's Play III*. I felt guilty, afterwards, about not changing Santa that afternoon, because when Penny took him herself the next day, they had all sold out. Maybe I'd have been in time.

'They were all faulty, probably,' I said, trying to make her feel better.

Penny scowled at me. I thought it was a real shame about her Santa, because when he was glowing, humming tunes, his candle lit up, she said that really cheered her up.

And what has made me feel better recently? What has been my consolation in Edinburgh?

Cameron did, at first. At the end of my first month here. He was around me for a week or two, a very blond boy from just out of town, who claimed to work in computers. He said he packed salads for Marks and Spencer, just part time for pocket money.

In the middle of one of the first nights he came back here, he said, 'I think you're like me. You're a naturally happy person, aren't you?' And I could have laughed in his face. I wanted to say, I'm really working at it. Can't you see how much effort I'm putting in?

I'd met him off the train on Friday night. Waverley Station was mad with rugby fans dashing about drunk. They'd come, like my boy, for the weekend, and they wore

220

tartan hats with fake ginger hair hanging out of the back. Cameron was the last one off the train, his white head bobbing through the crowd towards me. He was in last weekend's outfit: the cream jeans and, hanging over them, the blue check shirt. Both items were Calvin Klein, he'd told me, and they both cost seventy pounds. Cameron bought all his clothes from Jennes, saving up week by week the money he made putting mayonnaise in the potato salad at the factory.

He came up to me and I thought, This is when I'm happy. When someone's coming here just for me. He'd phoned me twice that night, making sure I'd come to meet him. Through the week we'd had hour-long chats at lunchtimes. He worked nights; lunchtimes found him alone in the family house and he told me he was sitting in the kitchen naked. He played dance CDs as we talked about nothing in particular. He said we'd dance to all this music when he came on Friday night.

His eyes were so blue. They fixed on me in my long black coat I'd bought cheap for the cooler nights. 'Oh no,' he said, swinging by me, 'that doesn't suit you at all.' He passed me a bottle of Stella. He'd opened one for himself and lit a cigarette the moment he'd stepped onto the platform. 'Come on then!' he said. 'We're going to yours!'

And that's what cheers me up now. Someone who will drag me bodily into their nights out.

This is the patisserie in Stockbridge. Everything is painted yellow and there is a sunflower motif. Look at how dear everything is. The waitress has recommended guava juice.

My new GP down here at the Stockbridge surgery says I've got tonsils like nothing on earth, black and ulcerated. I've spent a few days in flushes and burning up, waking each morning with my teeth black and my mouth full of fresh blood. The doctor even thinks the thing at the back of my throat is bleeding.

Tactfully he never mentioned my leopard spots. He looked in my mouth, nowhere else.

For days now I've been lying down in the afternoon, needing that extra rest. I thought I was just being lazy. I was just making it up. And you think about it and think about it and you can't remember what normal felt like. But that plunger of blood taken out of my arm this afternoon has set the seal on my having a real ailment. I've fretted for days and in the miserable, early hours, I've tried to decide what to do. Get myself seen to. Get a doctor.

My guava juice has arrived in a tall clear glass. It looks just like bloody piss.

Someone told me they had sex with a feller and, when they were really going for it, they snapped his cock right back. It bent and sprang back again. He couldn't touch it for days. The next morning he pissed blood. I've been getting that feeling, too, like a kicking in the balls. Spreading up from my swollen left calf muscle, the pain nuzzling at my groin. That horribly swollen leg was something else I didn't let the doctor look at, or comment on.

Poor Cameron, visiting me this last weekend. I wasn't at my best or my most inviting. I lay on the settee and shivered and sweated. He held me as we watched videos. *Breakfast at Tiffany's*, *Cabaret*, *Escape from the Planet of the Apes*. Before he knew me, he would come into town on the train after work each Friday and go straight to the bars, not returning to his family home till Sunday. He was always so sure of going home with someone. I feel he's been tamed, having him here on the settee, apparently content not to go out at all. As if being in the middle of the town and with me is enough for him.

So we were having less sex, too. On Saturday afternoon I lay under the duvet and we watched *The Chart Show*. He popped to the newsagent downstairs for crisps and sweets and magazines like *Eva*, *That's Life*, *Take a Break*. Those magazines are full of real-life tragedies, and Cameron claims to be addicted to them. He came under the duvet with me on the living-room floor. With all the blinds up it felt like we were exposed to the back streets, high over the roofs. He stripped and we rolled all over the rough carpet, once almost knocking the telly over. He yells out in pleasure more than any other boy I've been with, and I love that. It's as if everyone I slept with before was repressed. Men who keep quiet when they come, as if they're scared of getting caught. Cameron just yelps and howls out loud. He says he doesn't mind if he doesn't come. Sometimes he finds it eludes him, and he's happy to make the other bloke, as he puts it, 'spurt all over'. He says, for him the fun isn't in the spurting, it's in the initial copping off. This makes me feel older than him. At twenty-four I feel I belong to a different generation to my lover. As if my practices – my loving to come on a lover's chest and smear it into his skin – are already obsolete. Is Cameron part of a new breed who never need to climax? Who can just go on and on? And it strikes me that he fucks like he dances when he's E'd out of his head. Endlessly and noisily and without satisfaction.

That Saturday night he fed me oven chips and Linda McCartney sausages and Diet Coke. Halfway through this meal he realised that I was trying hard to choke all this down. He had given me the crispiest and fizziest things in the world. My throat was red raw. I longed to go to the Scarlet Empress, to have – oh, I don't know – tagliatelle and carbonara, pints of Guinness to ease my throat and pump me full of iron and goodness. He apologised for cooking me the wrong things. He says at home he never has to cook. His wicked stepmother does everything about the house. He says it's like living in a show home. They have to pretend to be a show family. But his fifteen-year-old sister is the blow-job queen of the town, he says, with sardonic relish, and he is what he is. And he said that in gloomy triumph, as if the only way he could be proud of himself was as revenge.

I grow anxious when I'm ill. Not on my own account, particularly. I was short-tempered when Cameron was around, and he thought I was wallowing. But it wasn't that. I fret about passing germs on. About passing anything on, anything I might have. And I think – I can't help thinking – I'm a gay man with bleeding mouth sores. What am I expected to think?

Cameron tried to talk me out of this despondency. I'd never heard him talk so much before. I realised he was no great talker, the first time we slept together. 'What shall we talk about?' he asked after sex. 'I don't know anything to talk about. I don't know anything about you.'

On Sunday he told me the story of how British Gas exploded the end of his street. Only he out of everyone in the street failed to wake up and when he did he found he'd been flung onto the floor.

He sleeps so deep. I sweat in bed beside him and watch him for hours. His white eyelashes.

He says he wants a proper computing job, wants to pass the driving test and his dad will buy him a car. I laughed, thinking, oo-la-la! Boyfriend-with-a-car! Which is what Vince and I used to say, trying to get the other to learn to drive. Cameron said he'd drive me out to places, take me to Edinburgh zoo to see the penguins. He said it would be fun – fun! – if he did have these germs after spending days with me at my most infectious. Then we could be ill together. But I shudder at the thought. And he's itchy, he says, which makes me think that either the bed, the settee or the living-room carpet has something nasty in it.

For Cameron I wasn't perfect, though at first he thought I was. When I first wore tight tops and trousers, dancing at CC's on Friday nights, all he saw was a body someone had taken to the gym to plump into shape. He thought my leopard spots were cosmetic. And it wasn't until we undressed in my living room, strewing clothes all about the floor, that he saw how my calf muscle bulged and looked grotesque. So I wasn't perfect for him. I was just good enough for those few weeks we had together. I would do.

I knew how important perfect bodies were to him. He told me about his weekly erotic successes, how each Saturday morning he would wake up and look at his bed

224

partner and think to himself, Fuck! I managed to get to sleep with *that*!

In the end he found my body too cold. He always complained that my fingers froze him. My skin was too cold. When I had my medical checkups it was a relief to see that my blood pressure was normal. His skin was warm and it felt like overly floury dough. You need cold hands, don't you, to knead and ply floury dough? But when he said my hands were cold I felt shrugged off.

I took the bus one morning from the centre of the city and travelled for an hour through gloomy green countryside, up into the hills. We passed through a village called – believe it or not – Darkness. When I got to his house I was furious with him because he would hardly stir himself out of bed to talk to me. And my heart went out to him also because he was fuddled with sleep, after working till five, packing salads. He sat up in bed and fiddled with cassettes and CDs, playing only half of songs, chain-smoking irritably in the tiny, boyish bedroom.

His sister, the blow-job queen, had let me into their house. She was bonny and pregnant, looking suspiciously at me as I stepped indoors. The dance music she played downstairs competed with that coming from Cameron's bedroom. Their parents were at work.

I had arrived in a cab. I'd made the last stretch of my journey by cab to the small estate on the hill. The shapes of the houses and even the garden fences were exactly the same as in Phoenix Court. As we drove slowly round the pointlessly winding streets I got a pang of sadness, of missing Aycliffe, and for running out on Penny. It seems so much has happened to me since I was in Aycliffe. All the lives I've been involved with since then. And I thought, What am I running after this boy for? Travelling all this way to his house? Yet I had a surge of enthusiasm, seeing the white little box shapes of the houses. It was like being in Aycliffe, being on home ground, in a way, and I felt like I could deal with anything. A feeling I've not had much recently.

The cab driver said, 'I know which one number ten is. It's right at the top of the hill. I've been there before. They take taxis everywhere, that family.'

His house was white and pebble-dashed, the windows double-glazed, and they had built a car port onto it. When I told him it was very like Phoenix Court, Cameron sat up in bed and said, 'But these aren't council houses. This is a private estate. This is the posh end of town.'

He shuffled about restlessly, wouldn't look me in the eye or talk about anything much. He was in the white T-shirt and shorts he'd slept in. That sleepy boy smell, his white hair all ruffled.

At two he was called to work and I had to go. He was nicer, sat himself on my knee, ruffled my hair. I realised I still wore sunglasses, even in his room with the curtains drawn. I told him, with a smile, that he was a little bastard. He opened his wardrobe to show me the clothes he'd bought with his wages. All Calvin Klein. He showed me a small stash of unlabelled videos; pirate hard-core porn from America. In them, you see everything, he said. They don't fuck with condoms and you see it go in. The one fucking slaps the other guy's ass to make him open wider. I paled, hearing this. I wondered why he was telling me. He even had on a bit of an American accent as he said it. But he still sounded Scots, even saying 'ass' and 'guy'.

He showed me to the bus stop but, as we walked through the estate, kept a few paces ahead, as if we weren't together. I felt ridiculous, tagging along. Not for years have I felt so daft, such a dangerously obvious queer. Cameron made me feel like that.

He explained that he wouldn't be able to phone me, because his dad had put on the phone something called a 'parental lock'.

I caught the bus and got talking to an old lady who was running into Edinburgh to buy headache pills. What they charged locally was a disgrace, she said. She would buy a bottle of three hundred in Edinburgh and that would keep her going. Only, at bingo, if word went round you had a supply of headache pills, you got a queue of old people expecting a handout. I listened to her prattle on like this all the way back to town, and it stopped me thinking about Cameron. I realised she was doolally when she started going on about the pills for the third time. The bus was empty apart from us, and she had come to sit right by me. I mustn't look threatening at all, I thought bleakly. That's good, if I look approachable and friendly. But wouldn't this old dear just talk to anyone?

'Have you been visiting family?' she shouted, over the roar of the engine as the bus laboured over hills.

'A friend,' I said.

'Friends are nice,' she said, and added that her name was May.

I helped her off the bus at the station in the middle of town. I watched her toddle off determinedly to the chemist's. I thought, Cameron is a nice weekend diversion. Someone to go out with and have a laugh with on a Saturday night. It's sad because it's not sex, company, talk or love in isolation that I crave – just *substance* in any one of them.

You're out, but you never meant to be. You're dancing and you've no idea how it is you came here. You don't even feel like dancing. Groggy with lager, heavy with your various ailments, you can't actually think of a worse thing to be doing. Yet you won't go home.

It's four o'clock in the morning, it's so crammed full in this cellar you have to dance touching at least three other people. Your clothes are steamed through with sweat and smoke. You dance with a ciggy in your mouth and a plastic beaker of gin. This gets knocked out of your hand at some point and you hardly notice as it sails over heads. It's Step Back in Time night, maybe that's why you're here. Every Tuesday you promise you'll only stay long enough to hear the Nolans' 'I'm in the Mood for Dancing'. In the odd way that certain songs at certain times attain anthemic status, this one has taken on a regular Tuesday-night sheen.

Usually you're here until the Nolans are finished. It's summer, so the place is open later. When you leave you find the East End lightening up. You cross Leith Walk, come down Queen Street and by the time you're home at the red fire escape, it's nearly daylight.

Tonight the Nolans have finished and you don't go. More cheesy late-seventies disco hits come on, one after another, and the trendy faggots and dykes squeal and clap in recognition of each one. They come dressed up for Step Back night, in easy-listening clothes, velour, nylon and PVC. Everyone knows the playlist.

You stand at a corner of the dance floor to watch them dance to the Carpenters. You're by the mirrors, which run with mist, and you watch how many of the dancers come to watch themselves, mime the words of songs at themselves. Or stand on the steps across the floor and stare, not at the dancers, but at their own reflections across the way. It's like football terraces. A boy, who looks under-age but probably isn't, goes round the edges of the floor, collecting glasses which he stacks in the crook of one arm. When he has enough to take back to the bar, he puts them carefully down and dances for a few seconds by himself. He raises his arms right above his head, straightens his back, shuffles his feet ever so slightly. Then his hands paddle gently at the air, cup his chin, slide back up again. He swishes about in a kind of Madonna trance. You remember Cameron coming back to your flat the first time, freeing himself of his jeans and, in all earnestness, telling you how Madonna gave him the strength to find his queerness: 'She teaches you that you have to be yourself. It's all about expressing yourself.'

Once upon a time when you were be-yourself Andy, dress-you-up Andy, go-out-all-weekend and be-off-your-tits Andy, you'd have solemnly agreed with him. Now that lad collecting glasses and the vogueing he's doing on his own just looks daft. Next to him is the mad bloke you see

228

here every week. In his forties, stripped to the waist, high as a kite on hallucinogens, pounding the air with his fists. 'On Top of the World' is the song and you wonder what he's hearing. He makes you want to say, It's retro night. It's meant to be fun, silly fun. Too many of them down here like to think it's hardcore all the time. You suppose they're down here every night.

Needing a piss again. It's such a drag. Everyone will think you're on drugs, the way you go traipsing back and forwards. On your way you catch sight of yourself, looking a state. Your newly grown hair is plastered to your forehead, your T-shirt is stuck to you. And that leg of yours is pounding something chronic; you've been dancing on it again. You remember your infant-school head-mistress, a terrifying woman like the prison governor on *Within These Walls*. She had a steel-blue perm that seemed huge over her body, which was petite apart from legs the width of tractor tyres. Your bad leg is almost as bad as that.

Why does the pain extend and lace up your thigh muscles? Separate out the tense strands and maliciously pull on them as you move? All your joints are churlish and stiff. Your balls ache like someone's grabbed them and your lower stomach is wound inside out. Occasionally it makes you want to throw up. Heading to the gents' now, you realise that you are going to throw up. You promise yourself that when you have, you'll go home. But that's happened once before and you couldn't manage the walk right away. Can't get a taxi from the rank. Money's running short. That time you sat on a scabby plush sofa upstairs and couldn't move, couldn't move. You imagined what would happen to you. Would they turn out all the lights and lock up after you? If you got locked in, by accident or otherwise, where would you crawl away to sleep? You couldn't sleep on the scabby plush sofa upstairs, because there you are in full view of the street, through the wide windows. Once when you were here, a brick came through one of those windows. So you'd crawl yourself over behind the bar and sleep there, out of sight of Leith Walk and the traffic and late passers-by, no matter how sticky and foul the floor.

You crash into the toilets and of course it's busy. There's a queue at the long communal urinal. They queue to use it one at a time. Sometimes the punters here refuse to piss side by side. It's funny what they'll choose now and then to be coy about. You need the cubicle, the single cubicle and you thump against the door and slide a little down it. You get glared at by a bloke standing nearby. You must look really out of it. Just hope that the cubicle isn't busy with a fucking couple. You need to be in now. If you could bend without increasing the pain you'd look under the door's gap, see how many legs are inside.

Then you slump to the tiles, yelling out.

Someone kicked.

I came to on the floor of the toilets in CC's. Piss everywhere. I still had the same pain, all up my bloated leg. I was half out of the cubicle and the queue had gathered round me. I had never fainted before in my life.

'He's fuckin' out of it,' someone decided, and the crowd started to disperse. The drumming at the urinal started up again and the traffic to and from the gents' resumed.

'No, he's ill,' said someone else. 'He needs help or summat.'

And here was Cameron bending down and kneeling in front of me. 'Andy,' he said, staring into my eyes. His eyes are Wedgwood blue. I'd forgotten how I'd missed seeing them. How grown-up he looked! As if he'd matured in the few weeks since we'd seen each other. His pale hair was fluffy with sweat.

'Hey,' I said.

'What's the matter with you?' he asked, frowning. 'What are you on?' He dragged me into the cubicle properly, for some privacy, and shut the door. By now the pain was building up again into another grand, crashing wave. I slipped into his arms and I was going to go again.

230

'It's my leg,' I sobbed, falling against him, and I wanted him to cut it off. I knew he always carried a penknife. For self-protection, Cameron had told me. You always have to protect yourself.

'Your bad leg?' he asked, and manoeuvred me to sit on the toilet seat.

Cameron could make me laugh when I didn't want to, or when I didn't expect it. Once we sat on the settee and he said, 'Look, we can kiss . . . but I've got responsibilities.'

I moved back. 'What?'

He shrugged and inhaled sharply. 'I've got a mug of tea and a fag on the go.' Then he tipped his tea all over himself, down his T-shirt and jeans, grinning, just so he'd have to pull them off.

Whenever we were together he stroked me and touched me all the time. He just held on, saying, 'Is that all right? It's allowed, isn't it? Hey?'

He was doing this again the night in the toilets, with me fading in and out of consciousness. I threw up, missing the steel toilet bowl. He splashed water on my face and shouted to someone to call an ambulance. I told him not to. I didn't want an ambulance. I wouldn't go to hospital.

'What can I do? What can I do?' he shouted at me, gripping me by both shoulders, shaking me as I slid to the floor. 'Tell me!' He slapped me hard to bring me round.

It was like I was going to burst apart. 'Cut me, cut my jeans.'

He took out that sharp little knife and, asking no more questions, slit the seams of the left leg of my jeans. The calf muscle beneath was shiny and purple like a sausage in the pan.

He looked me in the face. 'What's happening to you?'

Sweat was running down his face too. Was I generating heat that fierce? The pain reached up to twist my guts. It came in wave after wave and I wished I could pass out and just stay there. 'You'll have to cut me open,' I said, and thought about asking whether the blade of his knife was clean. He stuck it into my leg.

It just felt cool. Almost a relief. It took one jab of his knife and that whole shiny, bloated muscle slid open. It burst end to end to show a plush red interior.

A very white creature nestled there. It was curled into a sac of pale yellow flesh, folded inside the rich meat. Cameron drew back at the sight of it. It was no larger than the width of one palm. You couldn't even see its face.

'Take it,' I said.

There was blood everywhere. My ruptured leg was still pumping blood out onto the tiles. Perhaps now I did need an ambulance. My pain had lessened. A different sort was starting up. I just wanted Cameron to take up my child.

'I can't touch that,' he said, and flung his knife into the corner of the cubicle.

I looked at my child. I looked at Cameron and at the blood soaking down, filling my shoes. I had a brief, mad image of him rifling for change, going to the condom machine and emptying it. Making himself protective gloves with which to touch my child.

In the end, I took up the tiny body and pulled it out of the space in which it had lodged itself. It came away like a pit from a peach. The muscle and sinew seemed to suck itself back into one piece, but as I held the child up to my breast, held it up so I could see his face, I knew that I had a gaping wound still. But a very ordinary wound. One that might be inflicted by a penknife in a toilet cubicle. And I had my child, too. He set up a thin, mewling cry. His eyes wouldn't open, they were stuck with yellow, crusted mucus. He was a boy, I could see that much, and covered with fur.

Cameron had gone. He had fled.

Nineteen

They were taking up the paving stones in the precinct again. What was that for? In the morning the slabs were laid aside, revealing pale squares of sand. Nothing was put around the holes to warn you. What about blind people? They'd be straight down one of those shallow holes, breaking their legs. Elsie thought those gaps looked like scabs someone couldn't resist picking, and how odd to see the soil under the precinct, reminding you that shops hadn't always been here.

Mind, the shops used to be a lot better. Everything was closing. Monday morning Elsie was cross because they'd shut the last wool shop. Without warning, with Elsie halfway through her latest thing, the shop had gone. Its windows were Windolened out. What had become of the three old women who sat by their gas fire? The scratched glass counters, the musty, woolly smell? More importantly, what had happened to the six balls of pink four-ply set aside for Elsie on the shelf? What had become of her account? She had loved the routine of popping in whenever she needed a new ball, seeing one of the old dears go off to fetch it from the crinkly cellophane packet where it was kept with its fellows. Elsie couldn't believe all that had gone, over a weekend, with no warning. A whole way of life had vanished. Already it seemed an old-fashioned way to carry on.

'Boyes still sell wool,' said Big Sue when they bumped into each other outside Boots a few minutes later. 'In the upstairs bit. But you have to buy all you need at once.'

Elsie tutted. She bet that she'd never get the same wool again and she'd have to pull out all she'd already knitted.

What a waste! Knitting was an effort nowadays. She found it hard to concentrate.

'Isn't that Eric from over by you?' Elsie nodded to an old man at the Barclays cashpoint.

'It is. I didn't want to say hello to him while he was at the cashpoint. You can't interrupt someone doing their pin.'

'Is that hair of his dyed, do you think?'

Big Sue laughed. 'It's *pink*! Of course it's dyed.'

Elsie thought that was a bit cruel. She felt sorry for old Eric, who'd done his garden up beautifully. His seemed to be the biggest garden on the whole estate and he'd spent years working on it. A skinny old feller, out pruning things and digging with no shirt on. Elsie had been fascinated by his very pink old man's nipples hanging on his chest. He'd not done so much in the last year, he wasn't looking well, and the garden had slipped back. Someone had got in and ruined his rockery. Elsie supposed he'd have taken that hard. Just as she had.

Big Sue was telling her it was good to see her out and about again. She followed Elsie into Boots. 'No more trouble with your Tom, then? He's back to rights?'

Sighing, Elsie led the way up and down the medical counters. Sometimes it surprised her how Big Sue liked to tittle-tattle. She thought the woman was more religious than that. Her mind should be set on higher things.

'He's never quite right,' Elsie said. 'He's never going to be all right, exactly.'

'Oh,' said Big Sue and they came to a standstill in front of a display of 'Complementary Treatments'. Elsie looked as if she'd startled herself with her own candour. She went on.

'You see, I think what Tom's spent his whole life suffering from is disappointment.' Elsie shrugged. 'So it's never going to be easy.' She picked up a box. 'Look at these. Health bracelets. They're meant to touch your pressure points and do you some good.'

'Yeah?' Big Sue hadn't seen them before. Bangles in silver, copper and gold plate. 'They're expensive.'

'It says here it's like acupuncture.'

'Is that what you've come in for?'

Elsie nodded. 'For Tom to try. Fifteen quid isn't much, really, if it will make a difference.'

'Will a man wear a bangle like this?'

'I could have it engraved, maybe.'

Big Sue examined the box. 'Do they work for depression?'

Elsie said, 'If they got on your pressure points for disappointment and depression, then we'd all be wearing bangles.'

'Remember charm bracelets?' said Big Sue. 'I used to wear one that rattled, it was so full. I got sick of it in the end. I had a tiny glass box on it. It had an emergency five-pound note folded up inside.'

'That's a good idea, that. In case you're caught short.'

'I can't remember if I ever pulled it out when I stopped wearing the bracelet. Are you buying that?'

'Why not? He's got his birthday coming up.'

Full of gusto Elsie took on this new phase. She was taking care of her man's body and mind, conscious of all his differences. It was like tending to him; a cautious botany. She was down the chemist's, buying him pills to keep him pepped up, vitamins for his blood and joints, fish oils for his heart and bones. Even this silver health bangle to put on his wrist, to act upon his pressure points and keep him well.

Keep him well, pray God, keep him right in the head. And in one piece. Elsie's man had been restored to her and she wasn't about to let him go again.

Here, take this, she'd chivvy him earnestly and pop him a pill, a chewable something-or-other from over the counter at Boots. He would submit to this, to her nervy care. In his own way, Tom was glad to be back.

The cynical part of Elsie's mind was telling her, Of

course he's glad, he knows which side his bread is buttered on. Your man is one who, in his time, has been among the lowest of the low. He's drank, he's lived on the streets of London, several times they've locked him in a mental home. He can see that past lives like those are something you can go back to. Any time, any day, you can wake up and you'll be back the way things were. You should never lose sight of the bad old days, they're never gone for good.

This was the awful side of Elsie, which tried to trip her up at every turn and whispered speculation at her: Does he really mean that? Is he laughing behind your back? What is he really trying to say? It was the voice that would suggest, rationally and quite out of the blue, that she throw herself down the stairs in the morning. Or in the path of a bus on Woodham Way.

The good part of Elsie – the part she hoped she listened to most – was saying she should count her lucky stars. Elsie at her most optimistic let herself think chances came round like the painted horses on a merry-go-round.

She wouldn't let herself take Tom for granted. It became summer and she started to take pride in her garden again. She made her lawn neat as a billiard table. She would urge Tom to sit out in his deck chair; she rigged up a table for him and encouraged him to start drawing again. From their garden he could see all of Phoenix Court. Surely a man of his obvious, if neglected, talents could find a lot to divert him.

Pale, long-faced, tired-eyed Tom sat invalid-snug in his deck chair in those weeks of early summer. The sunlight gained strength and soon he asked Elsie to stop putting a tartan blanket over his shoulders when he sat outside.

For a long time he stared at the cartridge paper Elsie had taped to his worn drawing board. He remembered how he used to love taping down the paper. Unrolling a creamy sheet, stretching it out; the muted squawk of the masking tape when he ripped off four strips to stick down the paper's corners. In a studied, ritualistic way Elsie aped the way she had seen Tom do it, and that touched his heart as she fussed about. Her elbows jabbed into his stringy body as she worked, and he put up with it. He tasted her scent on the warm air, of talcum powder and dry sweat.

It was a week or so before he took up his pencils and started to draw Phoenix Court. The cars, the houses, the play-park climbing frame, the sapling trees and the people passing by. 'Why don't you start drawing me again?' Elsie suggested, bringing him out a pot of tea on a tray. But he didn't draw Elsie again. He concentrated on the square box houses with their roofs of isosceles triangles. He perfected them in crisp isometric projection and his drawings were clean, almost clinical, and each of them similar to the last. Outside each house, he'd put a small figure. Just a few lines, the finest of sketches. Elsie pointed out they looked like the free toy in a box of cornflakes. He ignored her and did his figures with eloquent dashes, as from a Chinese brush. Each one, you could tell who it was meant to be. Somehow Tom always caught them. Elsie saw how he would grab up his pencil as a neighbour came in sight for a few seconds. He got them with a minimum of perfect strokes. 'The way you all flit around,' he said, 'I've got to be quick.'

When he said this, Elsie had worn herself out shopping. 'Some of us have to flit around,' she said. 'We have to keep ourselves busy.' Then she wished she hadn't snapped like this, and she praised his neat stack of drawings. They lay in the grass and she sat beside Tom, both of them laughing as she went through the pile. Here was Nesta, slump-shouldered, glaring at the ground. This one Fran, galloping in slippers, looking for a misplaced child. Penny slopping artistically about, Big Sue hugging her handbag to her bosom.

'Can I show everyone these drawings?' she asked him.

Tom shrugged and smiled. She could tell he was pleased.

Things were getting better. They didn't talk about the things that pained them. They never forced themselves to have difficult scenes. In the evenings they listened to their records and saw no one. They took equal turns at playing songs for each other. A dialogue in their favourite tunes. Elsie dug out Shirley Bassey. As August came she realised that her song of the moment was 'As Long As He Needs Me'. Tom had rediscovered his westerns LP. For Elsie he played 'The Good, the Bad and the Ugly'. The waw-waw-waw part, the bit that sounded like being out on the prairie, thrilled her. It was August and they left all the doors and windows open, as did the rest of Phoenix Court. It was a sticky month, bringing everyone out of doors, moving slowly, reluctant to talk and stir each other up.

Elsie and Tom kept themselves apart, as they preferred now. They stayed away from anyone they might row with. Penny was someone they hardly saw at all. This hurt Elsie who, during the spring, had found herself very attached to the girl. But people don't always turn out the way you expect. When Elsie caught a glimpse of Penny now, across the way or round the shops, Penny seemed self-absorbed and different. Elsie couldn't imagine having anything to do with her. Penny didn't even seem to come from the same place.

It was Craig's absence that hurt Elsie most. For long stretches of the summer months they hardly saw him. His mother feared that, now he was apart from Penny, he'd go off the rails again. She thought he was too suggestible and the signs were not good. The worst thing was when they bumped into him, one night in August, at Nesta's fire.

Unlike many others round there, Nesta had never held a party. She went to everyone else's but she never returned the favour. It was no more than anyone expected. This was the woman who went borrowing milk and bread and eggs round the doors and never brought anything back. And it wasn't as though everyone was dying to get inside her house to see what it was like. Half the women in the street wouldn't be seen dead inside Nesta's house.

Chez Dixon things were changing. Something was happening to Nesta. Some would have said it was hormones, some would have said it was genes. Some might have said it was conscience, she'd realised that she was bringing up three little bairns in a home that wasn't a nice one. Most of the ladies of the Court, however, decided that Nesta was pulling up her bootstraps because of her new bairn, Keanu, born early that summer. By August Nesta was spring-cleaning madly.

With the baby in a papoose she stood in her garden and shouted out instructions to her husband and the two young daughters. And out they came carrying old rubbish: duff furniture, dirty clothes, rubbishy old toys. Everything looked as if it came from a car-boot sale, and most of it probably had. Nesta used to spend Sunday mornings rummaging up and down the rows of cars parked at the equestrian centre, but now that was all over. No more cluttering up their home. She had to learn new habits. And everything with pointed corners and sharp bits had to go, as well: she had a tiny son to protect.

Keanu watched all this from his mother's back, as she told the rest of her dazed family to build a stack of all their old stuff on the common ground at the back of the Court. A bonfire was inexpertly heaped and humped in the middle of the sun-dried grass. A curiously unsettling, pathetic bonfire, too, being composed of such ordinary things. Dolls' heads and lampshades stuck out, piles of old books and catalogues, the wound, frayed coils of curtains and used clothes. Word went round that Nesta would torch it all, one particular Monday night after it got dark. She had a certain sense of drama. The rest of the street conferred; they'd be out there to watch. Nesta's voluntary, purging house-fire was the closest she'd get to throwing a party.

Watching from her top window, Elsie saw Nesta set a torch to the unstable pyramid of her belongings.

Elsie was sipping a very strong gin and tonic. In the room behind her, Tom would glug back his in sharp mouthfuls as he dressed. He was going to some effort to dress tonight, for seeing the neighbours again. Elsie's heart warmed; she was returning him to the community.

239

Friday night she had come home with a bottle of gin. When she'd bought it, Judith at the shop had asked once again if she was back on the drink, even with Tom home. Elsie had answered her gruffly. Bringing booze back into the house was her test. She wanted to drink and Tom could lump it. He was dependent on her now and he couldn't kick up the kind of fuss that he used to. At last she could have her own way. Maybe everything she wanted. In full view of Tom she unpacked the Friday-night shopping on the kitchen benches and there was the bottle of gin. No tonic, no lemon, just the booze. And Tom hadn't said a word. He'd taken two glasses from the cupboard and they'd settled in for a night of serious drinking. Saturday and Sunday had been the same. Sitting across from each other, trying out only the most companionable of conversations, drinking steadily through bottle after bottle. Her housekeeping money was vanishing.

Maybe Tom was drinking only because it was time to see the neighbours again. Well, whatever it takes to see you through. Elsie had reached that conclusion once again. Life takes a lot of nerve, and whatever can give you nerve is all right.

Tom clung to her arm like an agoraphobe all the way across the street. But when other people bustled around them, when they entered the gathering crowd, he straightened up, let go of her arm, smiled and started to murmur hellos. Elsie was proud.

Here was the fire in full spate.

The street stood back in a ring and held their breath, watching Nesta's family's unwanted things turn black, turn incandescent, crumble into nothing. Plastic flayed off like skin and whirled into the updraught. They watched MFI flat-pack cabinets burst apart and shudder into useless pieces. There were pops and crashes from inside the burning pyramid. The neighbours looked at Nesta, standing with her arm round her husband (who still wore his anorak in spite of the heat) and her kids clustered about her. She had the satisfied smirk of things going according to plan.

Everyone thought about burning their own stuff.

'Why keep anything at all?' Fran asked her husband. 'Half the stuff we've got is knacked and unmendable. We should do what Nesta's done.'

'She'll get into bother off the council, having a fire so near the houses,' Frank said. 'You won't get a chance to burn your stuff here.'

'I wonder if she goes out and buys all new things.' Fran had started to think about getting shot of the accumulated junk of her cupboards and drawers. After four kids, the house was chockablock. Imagine having her kitchen drawers to herself again! Neatness and room.

'But it's like she can't live with her past, her old things,' said Penny to Mark. 'She's deluding herself.'

'It's worth a try,' he said. 'Are your eyeballs itching with the heat? Mine are.'

'I love going through all my mam's old things,' Penny said. 'Records and clothes and that. Nesta won't have anything to pass on to her kids.'

Nesta's kids looked awed by the flames.

Elsie was saying to Tom, 'Look at that filthy old mattress they've got. That should have been burned years ago.'

'Leave them be, Elsie,' he said and she thought she could hear in his tone that old authority.

Then the lads from over the street were there, their shapes hazy and threatening through the flames.

'Our Craig,' said Elsie. 'He's back with that lot.'

'What do you think you're doing?' Steve was shouting across the small crowd. 'Are you burning witches?' His mates all laughed, Craig with them. 'You can take your pick out of all the bloody witches round here.'

'Just ignore them,' came Nesta's voice. She lit a sparkler for Vicki, her eldest.

'Is this your stuff?' Steve asked Nesta, coming round to see her.

Nesta gazed up at him. She looked stupid and defiant and Fran thought, Good luck to you, pet.

'Is that stuff from inside your house?' Steve laughed. 'You must come from a fucking pigsty.'

'Eh, look,' said Frank, weighing in. 'Just you lot leave them alone.' He saw then that all of the gang from the Forsyths' house were out, gathered around the fire.

'We should burn some of these witches,' one of Steve's mates suggested.

'I'm going to talk to them,' Tom told Elsie.

'Tom, you're only just back on your feet,' Elsie began. Her throat was dry with soot and gin.

'You boys think you can carry on how you want,' Tom said.

'Oh, it's him,' said Steve. 'What do you want?'

'I want you all to go home.' Tom was standing his ground. 'I want you to stop hanging around like you do, scaring people. I want things to change around here.'

'Things aren't gunna change,' said Steve.

Craig was there. Elsie stared at him. She willed him to talk, to stand up for her Tom.

'You're just boys. You need something better than scaring old women.'

'Hark at fucking Gandhi.'

'You used to be at my Rainbow Club, Steve. Years ago. I remember. What about God?'

Steve laughed, and his mates followed. 'We only went to your crappy club for the cheap sweets and that. You know that.'

'Something rotten has happened to you all.'

'Maybe.' Steve grinned, tossing his hair. 'But you're the one who's crackers.'

Tom's face went dark. 'What?'

'I said, you're the fucking loony.'

Tom flew at him with both hands outstretched. He caught Steve off guard and knocked him down in the dirt, yards from the fire. He seemed to claw at his throat. Everyone pulled back and Steve was howling to get him off him. Craig was first onto them. He grasped his stepfather by the armpits and wrenched him up off the boy.

Before anyone could do anything else, Steve was kicking Tom in the guts while Craig held him hard. He got a few good kicks in before Mark, Tony and Frank could intervene. They got Tom away and Steve fell back on the grass, feeling his throat, which was ripped and bleeding. Over these few months Tom had let his fingernails grow.

Mark shouted at the lads, 'Why don't you lot fuck off home? You've done it again, you little bastards! You've done it all again.'

Elsie stood in shock beside Tom, who lay curled, clutching his stomach. She found her voice and yelled at Craig, over the noise of the fire and everyone else. 'Tom is like your dad! He's almost your dad! And look what you do!'

Craig was as angry and shocked as she was. He was turning, with the other lads, to go back to the Forsyths' house. 'He was never my dad. Not that old cunt. He's poisoned you, Mam, and you can't see.'

Elsie watched them go.

Fran took her arms. 'Elsie . . . do you want the coppers?'

'No,' she said. 'No coppers.' She said it like ticking the 'no publicity' box on a pools coupon.

Twenty

I know it's probably impossible, the whole time I'm doing it. But I've got to try. Can't have him like this. How can I keep him still, though? How on earth do you make a baby lie still? So I put off doing it because it's too difficult.

Until he wakes me in the middle of one particular night. It's the fourth time that night he's cried for me and I'm dead on my feet. He needs feeding. My feet thud heavily on worn carpets. I'm almost back asleep again when I go to the kitchen and feel about in the fridge. There's one sliver of chicken breast left. It's pale and wet, like an eyeless fish. I rock on my heels, almost passing out in the kitchen. I'm not used to living here yet, up in this flat. The streetlight is looking straight in the curtainless windows, like something off *War of the Worlds*. Down in the alleyway there's a road sweeper droning away. They keep this city immaculate. In the night its centre is almost silent. You'd think I was the only one alive, standing here, clutching a ribbon of chicken meat in one hand. You'd think there was only me and my baby alive.

Jep is standing up in the cot I bungled together from bits and pieces. Things chucked in skips. It's probably a death trap. I've tried to make it safe.

Whenever he wakes me I hate him. I get so tired. But the sight of him, bracing his weight on unsteady legs, makes my heart contract and relent. I touch him and there's all his soft, resilient bristles and I feel scared and angry, too. I press the meat on him and, closing those too expressive, too alert eyes of his, he nibbles it experimentally. And I feel rather than hear the satisfied clasp of his pointy little teeth as he gobbles up the flesh. His eyes open slowly, almost

244

shyly and look at me, I think, in gratitude. And I hate the way he can see in the dark.

It is then I decide to do the impossible thing. The thing I decided upon in the dead of one night last week. The cruel but perhaps necessary thing. I lift him up. He's turned so heavy. I tell him this, holding him up under his armpits as I walk to the bathroom. There's no window in the bathroom. The light comes on like the light inside the fridge and at the same time the air conditioner rasps into life. It has a grill of metal slats clogged with lines of dust, all heaped there. It makes you wonder how much dust you are taking in all the time. As I strip Jep of his baby things on the bathroom floor, I'm imagining running a finger through those lines of dust and dislodging them. How they would feel, soft and brushy, and trickle through my fingers.

What if I hurt him? If anything happened to him, I know I would feel it twice as bad. I hold the pad of one of his tiny hands between my thumb and forefinger and I feel the squash of it. I'm more scared of my potential to do him harm than he is. I run hot water, cold water into the basin. I'm glad there's still hot water left. The immersion tank here is rubbish.

Because he's so tired – and contented now that he's at last eaten his fill – he's quite compliant and lies nearly still for me. Oh, his underbelly's such a lovely, pale shade of gold. The rest of him is tougher and darker, autumn-leaf gold. I've got soap, lots of it and with my one free hand, as I use the other to stroke his tummy, I froth it into a rich green lather. Under my hand he gurgles and purrs. I work the soap into his fur, all over, soaping these little limbs, every inch of him. I am careful around his eyes, of course, and he blinks at me, watchful. Then I have to hunt around for a fresh, unused, disposable razor blade. By the time I have found one the soft, lathery bubbles have begun to pop, leaving his fur smarmed and sticky. I wet him up some more and, taking one little hand in mine, shave a first, experimental strip off his chest.

Even in a city full of queers, I still get panic attacks about standing out in a crowd. Nanna Jean once said, in one of her more dour and paranoid phases, 'Ah, you shouldn't be dyeing your hair red, Andrew. That's how they see you in a crowd. That's how they get you and beat you up.' Now, is it any wonder that I grew up like this?

Today, trolling round the shops and the sales in Princes Street, I had this awful, sneaking sensation of panic. I wanted to scream out in the record shop. I couldn't get home fast enough. Of course I couldn't scream out. Not now that I have responsibilities. I couldn't scream out for the sake of the child.

I took him out round the shops with me for the first time. He clung to my neck in one of those baby pouch things they design for parents. Walking the streets, not looking for anything in particular to buy, I felt proud and scared and worried and conspicuous. In the end I just had to come home. I used to love going round the shops. In the past few months everything has turned on its head.

Jep was asleep when I came back up the red fire escape. I put him in his cot and paced the flat.

Of course I have to learn to be happy and confident, walking about with him on the streets. I can't leave him here all the time when I go out. Though already I'm guilty of that. If I lived in Phoenix Court, the women would be reporting me for neglect. But I can't be with him twenty-four hours a day. Anyway, he's more resilient than a normal child.

When I first walked out with him, his slight weight pressing on my chest, his bundled legs squashed against my stomach, I was struck by a very odd similarity. It was something I'd never have suspected. The conspicuousness I felt walking around with my new child was very like what I feel, now and then, when I think people are giving me second glances and thinking, queer. What a strange and sticky comparison! I don't know whether I feel better, if it makes queerness more normal, or whether I feel sad, because I feel doubly on show. I'll have to have a think about that one.

I went to sit in Princes Street Gardens. I sat on a bench and watched the sunbathers, the roller-bladers, the ambling mums and dads. Jep's fingers were tapping at my throat and I unzipped my jacket so he could see out. Twist round and look at the world, Jep. His eyes were startled by all the light. How green they are! His slits of pupils were more unnerving, almost, in the open air. I hoped no one would come close enough to examine him. And I felt guilty thinking that about my beautiful child. I should want to show him off. His fingers still pressed at my throat and I thought, What sharp little nails he has. I wondered about cutting them off, but decided against it. Not after the ridiculous, futile, fur-shaving exercise.

That night I worked so long and hard, attempting to remove his gorgeous but too conspicuous golden plush. I carved into the shaving foam and at first he lay stunned, letting me stroke his fur away. I thought I could remove all traces of his leopard spots with a swift and trusty blade. After a few strokes I became less careful, and he turned fractious and twisty. I nicked his precious skin, bright blood welled up and he howled. His face was a tight mesh of anger and pain.

I flung the razor into the bath, horrified by what I'd been doing. What I'd been doing to my own flesh and blood.

I picked up my cold, wet, soapy child and licked the tiny wound on his stomach. His blood tasted, naturally, like mine. Soap got into it and he yelled and kicked some more.

I felt the naked, bristly flesh under my tongue where I had tried to shave him. I felt the neat straight line of where the resilient fur resumed.

I held him out to have a look, once his cries of protest had tired him out and he had quietened.

In that patch I'd shaved clean of fur, his spots were as bright and evident as ever. They stared back at me and I thought, I'm such a stupid prick. I've been shaving the proverbial.

I sponged him clean of soap and put him back to bed. So you're stuck with these spots for life, Jep.

He's humming into my neck in apparent contentment as I think this, as we sit in the sun in Princes Street Gardens. He hums rather loudly, deep in his throat.

The odd thing is – and I can't be sure yet if this is real or not – my spots are starting to fade. Each day they have grown a little less distinct. But perhaps I am making this up. Honestly, I don't know if I'm coming or going these days. Such are the joys of fatherhood.

The people passing by our bench feel tempted to come and see my child, to pet and examine him. It's a compulsion they have. I try to ward them away and luckily this works. I feel them thinking, What's this lad doing with a baby that small? It doesn't look right. He looks a bit rough, that lad. Where's the baby's mother? Shouldn't she be in charge of the child? He isn't holding that baby correctly. Look how clumsy he's being!

Of course I can't be sure of what they're thinking. But I do feel clumsy holding Jep. How am I supposed to know how to hold a baby? No one's ever told me. It isn't instinctive, at any rate. I imagine that it is for mothers.

I try not to think about the actual scene of giving birth. I feel like you do in those dreams where you are somewhere you know you shouldn't be. In a supermarket with no clothes on, upon a theatre stage in the wrong play and none of my lines learned. There are times between the moments of sheer panic when it's just me and Jep and everything's fine. He's a loving bairn. I can see that already. He'll be intelligent too, and strong. He stares at you when you talk to him, stares at how your lips work, as if deciphering your words. You can see by his eyes how intelligent he will be. That split lip of his, that cat's muzzle, twitches slightly in response, as if he's preparing words of his own. He has vestigial whiskers there, the short hairs stiff and brushy.

I gather him up and like any other baby he smells milky

248

and clean. Except when he's just eaten and you catch that whiff of dead, raw meat on his breath.

We walk further into the park and I decide I like it here. Funny to think it's so near the busy heart of town. It's so peaceful. We round the corner and there's the golden fountain, teeming with warriors, horses and trumpeters. The fountain I saw in my dream before I came here.

'That must mean we were meant to come,' I tell Jep. 'If I saw it in my dream.'

Then I have to go to the loo, even though I hate public toilets, how dark and messy they always are. I have to go to the loo quite a lot these days. Does having a baby mess your waterworks up?

I have to take Jep into the cubicle with me.

These toilets are kept quite clean, luckily. I suppose it's a very touristy area and they have to put on a show. The gents is busy with dads and their small sons and they're all chatting away along the steel urinal.

When I'm using the loo I read the graffiti out of habit. A fair amount is about football and some of it is about the Scots versus the English. Most of it is of course phone numbers and desperate-sounding messages suggesting times and places. Some vicious, homophobic replies. Bigger than all the other writing, in thick black marker, straight in front of me it says: GOOD COCK FUN. And it seems like a slogan, a simple advert. Jep's head is lolling against me as he nods off to sleep again. I realise, as I step out of the cubicle, that I'm blushing.

What would Nanna Jean think of me?

I can think of one or two things she'd have to say about all this. Oh, I want it to turn out all right.

To start with, I want to present Nanna Jean with her great-grandchild, because that is what he is. I can see myself travelling south to Tyneside, arriving at Newcastle station, carrying Jep bundled up in baby blankets. I cross the white marble, the cool, crowded expanse of the platforms, and get us onto the Metro. As the shuttle flashes between the crumbling red-brick houses and over the green river, I'll be having second, third, fourth thoughts about knocking on my nanna's door. What if she rejects me? What if she rejects my child?

So here I am, on the last leg of my journey back. She's had her front door repainted, I see. A glossy scarlet. I knock and it's then that Jep starts to cry. He doesn't cry often and the noise he makes is strange. It raises the hair on the nape of my neck and my stomach knots up for him.

I can see Nanna Jean through the door's frosted glass as she undoes all the locks.

When the door opens, she smiles. I suppose you could say her face lights up. Her hair's been tinted that tobacco colour. She goes to the place where they let students practise on you. She's in a flowery blouse and yellow rubber gloves. She is staring at the baby now.

I suddenly see how small my child is and I have this stupid thought that if maybe I'd given birth to a *larger* child, she'd be more likely to accept him.

So this is what she'll say. This is what she'll do. She'll make me feel at home. What am I thinking? I grew up here. Nanna Jean made her home my home when I was little, when my parents died. She denied me nothing.

'This home will be yours,' she once said fiercely. 'Till the day I die this home will be yours.' I knew then that Nanna Jean would fight for me, whatever came. Whatever was wrong with me, she would defend me. In the end that was the one thing I knew I had: this woman who believed in me. Vince never had that. He and his dad never got on, his mother ran away. Penny's mother ran away, too. I was lucky. Even though an orphan, how well I was parented! So do I feel secure about Nanna Jean?

She'll take my spotted child to her bosom. That magnificent, matronly bosom under layers of lace and silk and cardy. She's not had any great-grandchildren yet, no tiny bairns to lay on that breast. Will she let Jep clamber over her old-lady bulk? That small leathered nose of his, twitching, wet, inhaling the old-lady smell of face powder and sweet, cheap perfume.

Nanna Jean belonged to a generation that wore fur. Women of her class knew they'd never get this close to the real and lavish thing.

In that back sitting room, which is still her favourite room, the gas fire will be blue and orange, spitting, fluttering. The telly will be on. The pot will be mashing under an ancient, stained tea cosy, as if she was expecting us. She'll look kindly as she eases herself into her squashy brown armchair. But her eyes will look tired and knowing. At first glance she has worked out what's been going on.

Like an old woman who has seen everything, she will say, 'I know what you've come expecting me to say.'

I blink.

'You've come expecting me to say that everything's all right.'

I open my mouth to tell her that it's not forgiveness I'm expecting. I just wanted her to see my son. My son. My insides do a little flip when I imagine this phrase to myself. I get a little glow. A hard-on without having a hard-on.

Nanna Jean will shush me. 'I can't say that I like the way you've chosen to live.'

I want to ask her, How do you know how I live? But I don't push it. I remember the shameful made-upness, the living one minute to the next, the hand-to-mouthness of my current life and I shut up.

'I can't say that it's not a disappointment, our Andrew,' she says.

I brace myself to be told that I started out such a sweet boy. I had everything in front of me.

She says, 'I thought everyone had made sacrifices for a reason. We all had no money. We all muddled through. We lived ten to a house and no one got any privacy. No kind of life at all. And we all thought we were doing it for a reason. You had to. It kept you sane, to think that the ordinary, day-to-day suffering you were going through led to something. It was for the benefit of someone else. For your children and their future.'

Nanna Jean lets out one of those long, expansive sighs. The sort that seem to reach right back in time.

For some reason I don't feel like I'm being preached at. Before, I might have. I'd think, here we go again. All about the old days. Old days and sacrifice.

Nanna Jean wears that make-up she discovered and came to late in life. She's my glamorous granny, but now her mascara's coming down in long, gentle fingers. Her face is smudged.

'I lost your mam. You know she was my favourite. I never made any bones about that. It was for her I thought I'd put everything by. She was my new life.' Nanna Jean pulls herself together, as she always does when she talks about Mam, and moves swiftly on to the subject of me. It's always like this. We're Russian dolls, slotting neatly in and in and in each other. She says, 'So I placed a lot of hope in you, Andrew. I won't pretend that's not true. I had high hopes of you.'

Now I sit down on the low, uncomfortable couch along one wall. As if cross at not being talked about, Jep is restless in my arms. I squeeze gently: we'll be talking about you soon.

I ask her, 'What were you hoping for? What were you expecting out of me?'

For a moment her face clears. Now she really looks like she's thinking aloud and being honest with me.

'You wanted to see me married and with nice kids, didn't you? And a job, a proper job, and –'

With a sudden, sharp gesture she cuts me dead. 'Stop it, Andrew.' She looks hurt. 'Give me some credit, man. We both knew a long time ago that was impossible.' She stares at me. 'Didn't we? That sort of normalness. We both knew it wasn't going to happen. There was no point in waiting and pushing for it.'

'Oh.' I wish I hadn't shoved my oar in. I should have

given her more credit, she's right. Nervously I'm fiddling with the tassels on my baby's blanket.

She goes on, 'What my hopes were about was more general. I wanted you to find the way you could live, and be happy.'

Simple as that? I give her a sceptical look. Like, you don't believe all that liberal shit, do you? I can't really believe it of this Tory-voting, council-house-owning elderly lady. She can't really mean this.

'I thought,' she says, 'you might be the first in this family to start making your own life up the way you want. I thought you might not have to compromise . . . quite as much.'

Nanna Jean stares at my baby. 'Now you've landed yourself with a bairn and all the cares that entails. Same as the rest of us all did, going back generations. All right – you've waited till the grand old age of twenty-four. That's good. But you've still given yourself the job of being responsible for another human being. Did you do it just to have someone to love?'

'I . . .' I don't know what to say.

'I did,' she says. 'I married to have a baby, to get someone to love.'

I never knew this. I'd just assumed that in those days – when were they? – women just had babies because . . . because there was no pill. They had them natural and easy and they had large, problematic families. I don't say anything.

'Don't you love your life?' asks Nanna Jean. 'You live in that city of yours. It's cold and heaving with busyness and noise. The place where you live is dirty and you'll never have everything you want. You don't feel like a normal part of life at all. You've not got any of the normal things, the things that someone of your age might expect. The little comforts and consolations. But what freedom you've got, our Andrew! I can hardly believe it. You're in a place where anything can happen. The way you live, you're only ever a few steps from something new.'

She sniffs and looks at this room in which she has lived for most of her life. Refurbished, redecorated, done up and dusted, yet it still makes her give a long, fed-up sigh. As if there's only so far you can go, doing things up. 'Something new, Andrew! Have you any idea how much I've wanted my life to turn into something new?'

I hug my baby to me. 'Jep is something new.'

'Give him to me, hinny,' she says, putting out her hands. Her wide, chapped palms. Her fingers tremble as if she's been putting off this moment, delaying her pleasure. She takes his weight – how expertly! She puts her face right up to his tiny, exotic one. His hands bat gently at her nose, her slack cheeks.

'He's a beautiful bairn, our Andrew.' Her puzzled frown is also full of amusement. 'You clever thing! However did you manage it?'

These are the things she will do. This is what she will say. Should I take Jep on a trip to South Shields, should we catch the train from Edinburgh, from Waverley Station, and ride it to the northeast, through that wild and empty landscape, this will be our reception.

I'm in the Scarlet Empress, thinking this all up. It's a rainy Friday afternoon. The rain has taken everyone by surprise. I've made one cup of coffee last ages. Her from upstairs has taken Jep for a walk. She likes to walk him to Arthur's Seat, up past the palace, to the foot of the crags. And that's fine. At first I was resentful of the bond they're forming, Jep and that woman upstairs. But he needs other people around him. We all do. So I let him go out with her and I get this time alone, to think and brood. Nanna Jean says brooding isn't a thing you should do. You depress yourself. You should be like her, she said. Be up and about and busy, busy, busy.

A man with short, strawberry-blond hair has moved tables to come and sit by me. His legs are crossed, his coffee untouched. He holds *Boyz* magazine wide open and studies each page slowly as if there's stocks and shares on it. Whenever I look up, he looks up and it's an imploring look. When I look down I can feel his eyes still on me. I should go. I should go home. I look up and he looks up and he has absolutely no expression on his face.

If the woman from upstairs can take him on long, healthy walks, then so can I. Sandra walks my baby up to Arthur's Seat. They walk up the crags to catch the air, to stretch their legs. The air is so bracing up there, she says. You see it come in off the sea. Cool, salty, endless air and all that light!

If she can walk my son up there, then so can I. If that is his favourite trip out, then I should do it too.

Little mite, does he even know who is taking him out?

Marched himself to the top of the hill, and marched it down again. Look at the crags. Cinder toffee, how long and high and regular they lie, across from the city! What a distance! I'm not used to walking. Down Queen Street, Princes Street, down Leith Walk. These days I'm not getting my exercise in. So now there's Sandra telling me I ought to get out and about. Fill my lungs and the lungs of my son with air. Cheeky mare.

With the friends I've got, the people I'm meeting now, it's all too often me listening, then going, 'Oh yeah. Right. I knew that.' But I didn't. I'm waiting to be told things. Even I know that walking up hills like this, so you can see the city stretched out, even I know this is good for you.

When I lived in Aycliffe I never walked anywhere. What else were the Road Ranger buses for? And where would you go, apart from down the precinct, the shops and the gym? There was nowhere. Aycliffe is surrounded for miles by farmland, fields and motorway. Fields yellow with rape, grey green with scrubby pasture, tarmac grey studded with the squashed purple carcasses of rabbits and starlings. In the middle of nowhere. There's loads of space to walk in, but what do you look at? Where would you head to? I can't see the point in walking with no object. I like to think there's a shop or something at the other end of my journey. Something to view, to buy, to fetch back. That's why I got

255

sick of the gym. All that outlay and I wanted to see changes, changes, changes after every visit.

Up here there is so much to see.

The path goes up and up and it's a ledge only a few yards wide. Rocks are scattered across it and there are posters warning that they drop easily. I am in peril. A man was killed quite recently, knocked and tumbled off this ledge. He plummeted into the wide, green flats of Holyrood Park far below.

Now there's a thing. The palace is here, just below me, square, black and grey, fenced in with beautiful, tall iron gates. Eagles, lions. Only a matter of yards away are blocks of council flats, square and dark, 1970s. Who'd have thought they'd be so close? When she stays here and she pulls her bedroom curtains at night, can the Queen see into the lit windows of the flats? Can they look out of their flat windows and see what the royals have on their washing line?

I'm sitting for a rest on the bleached grass. Someone's left a hooded top behind. It's all right, doesn't smell. I tie it round my waist, the way they all do now.

Then I see that Jep has crawled onto the narrow pathway. I'm about to yell, to pull him back, but something makes me pause and watch.

It's so warm he's naked, overheating in just his native plush. He squints into the sun and I think, He's mine. His felted ears twitch. My own hands feel sore at the sight of his young footpads and fists on the rough ground.

I remember what Sandra told me in all her know-how. (But what does she know about bringing up babies? How would she know anything?) She said you aren't to cosset them or pull them back from things. You aren't to make them neurotic by fretting over their every move. She would say I have to let Jep set his own challenges, conquer his own apprehensions. Find his own way. So I hang back. Watch him on the yellow pathway, scratching in the dirt, then slowly hoist himself onto his hind legs. He staggers and swaggers and, with the same self-absorbed look he always has, he takes his first few steps alone. Up here, at this height, way above the city of his birth.

Twenty-One

They told Jane to keep the music down. A nurse put her head round the door to Liz's room and asked nicely. Jane felt foolish and quickly unplugged her tape player. She stashed it in her bag and flushed red as the nurse fussed around Liz, smiled and left.

Somewhere Jane had read that coma patients reacted to music. Jane had played Tina Turner's 'You're Simply the Best' six times, full blast, these past three visits. She thought it ought to be Liz's favourite song, she thought she'd once heard it round Liz's house. Now she felt she'd been doing it for nothing. Or that the nurses assumed she was playing music for her own entertainment. But she wasn't – Jane was here out of the goodness of her heart. She had better things to do than sit in Bishop General. She had a journey to prepare for.

Her suitcases had been packed for a month. She kept taking things out, washing and ironing them again, folding them with calm precision. She kept thinking of other things she and Peter would need when they went to visit the desert. When she thought about it her heart would give a jump of thrilled fear inside her chest. She had to get passports. Fran helped her. The forms were quite complicated.

'I hate doing forms for anything,' she said, sitting in the photo cubicle in Red Spot supermarket. Flash!

'These aren't too bad,' Fran told her, waiting outside the curtain. Flash!

'I hope I don't look horrible in these pictures!' Jane tried to make herself laugh, to smile naturally. Flash!

'Everyone looks horrible in these little pictures.'

'Have you got a passport, Fran?'

'Never needed one.'

Flash!

In her photos Jane came out blurred. Too busy chatting away.

'You look animated. Full of life.'

'Like a gobby bitch. I look like when they blur out someone's face on the news to protect them.'

They stood with the sticky strip of pictures held out between them.

'Look at these ones,' said Fran suddenly, reaching into her purse. It was her and Frank, ten years ago, squashed into an orange-curtained booth, grinning and red-faced.

'You look like little bairns!' Jane gasped.

'Did you and Peter's dad ever have pictures like this together?'

Now they were in the queue for lottery tickets. Jane was blowing on her pictures. 'Did we hell! He once wanted to take . . . like, mucky photos of me. I told him where to get off. He wasn't taking pictures of my arse. I know that woman in Boots photo counter. She'd see it was me.'

'It's nice having pictures, though,' said Fran.

'Not that sort.'

In Liz's hospital room, Jane was looking at her passport photos again. She compared her blurry, unformed self with Liz, who was so still and perfect. I'm jealous of a woman who's half-dead, she thought. No wonder I need a holiday.

Then she took out *Leaves and Angels* and started to read aloud at Chapter Forty-Two. Romance novels were something she and Liz shared a passion for. This was the new one by Iris Makepeace and it was all right. Not too much sex. A bit was all right, but nothing that rubbed your nose in it. Jane would have been embarrassed reading anything too sexy in a hospital.

The book was about travelling abroad, to Africa, for a romance. It made her feet itch to think of it. Listening to her own voice tell the story, it seemed as if she wasn't reading at all. When she finished she said goodbye to Liz and left for a coffee.

She knew that Tom was the next visitor in. He had put himself on the Liz rota, though Jane knew that he didn't know Liz at all. Funny old bloke. Jane felt a bit sorry for him – beaten up in front of everyone by his own stepson. They said he was a bit daft.

She bumped into him in the waiting room.

'You're Jane, aren't you?' Tom asked. 'You know Elsie.'

Jane nodded. 'There's no change in Liz. It's a bit boring in there.'

He looked like a shabby old gent, someone who had seen better days. 'It gets me out of the house, visiting,' he said. 'Otherwise it's the same four walls.'

Jane smiled and hurried on her way. Funny to hear him talking like a woman. But what sort of a man would live with Elsie, anyway? It would have to be someone pliable, who would listen to all the old rubbish Elsie came out with. Jane could take Elsie only in small doses. For some reason Elsie supposed that made them best buddies. If only the old woman would see that it meant nothing, that Jane, out of politeness, would spend the time of day with almost anyone who asked for it.

Jane hated the way Elsie sometimes swanned about, thinking herself a great social success. It was ridiculous. That night of Nesta's burning her belongings, the night that had seen Tom knocked almost unconscious by the bad lads from over the way, Elsie had thought she was a drama queen. She swore vengeance and damnation on the heads of the perpetrators. She tagged along, shouting her mouth off, as the men hauled Tom home to check him over and see he was all right. Elsie was too busy being self-righteous to do anything but gabble on. But Jane didn't hear her call her own son names. As far as Jane could see, Craig had been the worst one. He'd held Tom still for the other one to kick him. Craig was the worst of the bunch.

Once back in Phoenix Court, Jane walked straight into Penny. 'Well, you had a narrow escape, didn't you?'

'What do you mean?'

'From that Craig lad. Now we've all seen what a vicious pig he is.'

'I don't want to talk about this, Jane.'

'Did he ever hit you, Penny?'

'Jane, stop it! I'm not seeing him now. It's all history.'

'He's still a vicious pig. I've just seen Tom, visiting your mam. He looks like a scared old man.'

'What's Tom doing visiting my mam?'

Jane tutted. 'Just doing his neighbourly duty, that's all.'

'I've never liked the look of him,' Penny said.

Tom was an expert in visiting people. His mum had taught him how you went round houses that weren't your own, and how you put people at their ease. Then and now he felt safer in other people's houses than his own.

Here he was settling himself in a chair by Liz. He sat quite still and stared at her. He clasped his knees.

When he ran the Rainbow Club he visited people's houses with Elsie. They went to see anyone – Elsie's friends and friends of friends. He knew they weren't always welcome. He knew that often they were forcing their company on people. Sometimes Elsie complained, 'Why are we going to see people we hardly know? Sometimes can't we stay at home?'

Tom would say grimly, 'We're spreading the word.'

It was a crude way of putting it, of course. But he didn't think it hurt, going into homes and bringing up the subject of the divine. At one time he would have simply said 'God', but now he preferred to say 'the divine'. Just mentioning the spiritual life would keep it alive. Some of these people round here never gave it a moment's thought. Besides, at that time he never liked spending nights indoors with Elsie. What were those nights? *Catchphrase*, *Strike It Lucky*, *The Ruth Rendell Mystery*.

'It reminds you that we live in a world with other people,' he would tell Elsie. 'That we are social beings.'

Here they would go, traipsing the dark tarmac of the

estates, past the lit windows. How much you could see inside! Each window was a busy screen. Elsie, following Tom into other people's rooms, was enthralled.

Those days and nights were over, though. Tom felt safer indoors, even if it meant watching ITV with Elsie. See how contented she looked, in of a night, tucked up on the settee, drinking.

He still had the need to visit, even if he didn't want to walk the streets. So he came here. Liz would fulfil this need.

'Well, Liz,' he said, 'I don't know you, and you don't know me, but I've put myself on your rota. Elsie reckons they've got it so there's almost always someone with you. And I'm glad to help out. Will you listen to me nicely? I'll watch over you, if you listen to me.'

Tom thought he might pray. It was worth a try. Quite formally, like a child, he steepled his fingers. But he couldn't do it. His palms refused to go together. It felt like the tug of repulsion you get off two magnets held the wrong way. He couldn't bring himself to talk to God. He chuckled bitterly. 'I'll have to talk to just you, then, Liz.'

He said, 'Elsie tells me we could have been family.' If Craig had stuck with Penny, they might have been in-laws, that was what Elsie had said. Tom sighed, irritated by her plans. All these pretend-family ideas. Where was the blood link there? Craig was by no means his son. He'd never felt like that to Tom and now they all knew how Craig felt about it. Tom winced. Craig marrying Penny wouldn't make Tom kin to Liz. Tom felt about as related to . . . this chair as he did this woman. Yet look at how Elsie pushed and pulled at these relationships, to get them to come true. As if being related was the most important thing in the world. Tom knew there was more to it than that.

I started visiting people as early as I can remember. My mum took me round all the houses. And this was the country, it was different to here. It was up hill and down dale to all the houses. We were tramping over fields and

262

through stiles and it was a struggle when the snow was up to our knees. We weren't all living in each other's pockets. Not then.

Mum used to go round with her friend Sally. Plain Sally, with a worn, chapped face, her hair in pigtails. She followed Mum round faithfully and she believed, like Mum, that they were spreading the word.

What were they telling people? What they believed in their hearts the word to be. A childish version of what they heard and what they read. Father Dobbs used to laugh at them but he said, 'Their hearts are in the right places, those lasses, they won't do any harm.' Good, simple-hearted faith, he called it. Mum and her friend Sally were both a little in love with the handsome father. Mum passed me into his care and tutelage when I came to an age to learn properly what faith was about. She loved to see me go with him and to surpass the things she knew. She loved to hear me spout my learning and I was only a child, I used to love showing off.

Father Dobbs was a marvel. It was he who discovered I could draw. I drew Jesus for him, and all the disciples, and Mum wanted a drawing, and so did Sally, and so did everyone who lived nearabouts.

There was a ritual to a visit in those days. I remember the patterns and routines around those houses. I'd be given a glass of milk and a biscuit perhaps and listen to all the talk. Sally would be telling them the friend she had in Jesus and I could see them look at her thinking, A nice girl like that, what a shame she'll never get a man. Everyone had a front parlour for visitors to sit in. They listened patiently to the two girls and their simple-hearted faith. When they found that I could draw, Mum and Sally wasted no time in using my talents in the cause. I was to make myself useful and so I did, I sat with my drawing book and childishly sketched our hosts as they sat there, flattered and excited. I would draw them meeting Jesus in heaven; I had Jesus down pat. Usually I did it all in pencil, but sometimes they wanted themselves painted, to make it more real.

My mother was beautiful, you would believe anything she said simply because she was so beautiful. She didn't need cleverness or a plain friend helping her out. She didn't even need her son, drawing Jesus and the neighbours, to make those neighbours listen. When she talked about happiness her face glowed like clean china.

Father Dobbs went to London. He never came back to us. He made it plain that he didn't like the drawings of Jesus and the neighbours. Mum had made me draw him with Jesus, shaking him by the hand. Father Dobbs wasn't pleased and it was one of the few times he scolded me.

Mum died very young. Her faith never left her. Sally took me in. When I was fifteen, Sally was forty-five and you might say we became lovers. She was tender-hearted and curious. I was lonely and I didn't know what was what. This plain woman, growing hefty and old before her time, was almost more innocent than I was. She took me to bed and it was all a disaster, of course. We had no clue. I went to London, looking for Father Dobbs.

Sally was at the station, seeing me off. I was thinking I'd never be back in Yorkshire. She was telling me I had to get my education. I had to go to art college. I had to be Michelangelo. Getting on the train, I was embarrassed by this coarse, red-haired, frayed woman, in whose clammy, fleshy arms I had spent the night, telling me to turn myself into Michelangelo. I smiled and urged the train on.

I wanted to find the father and make myself an architect. I wanted to design the shopping precincts, the tower blocks, the housing estates of the future. That was my destiny.

I never found Father Dobbs. He'd gone.

Liz, do you think I should tell you all this?

Lying there, you're so receptive.

Yet you gleam, you give off light. You're like my mother's face. But you and her, you're just reflected light. You give it off without really understanding. Father Dobbs was helping me to understand. He went, like everyone else does. Who's left to help me understand anything?

Have you got anything to tell me, Liz?

You're poised between life and death. You reflect the light of both states. Tell me. Explain to me.

Twenty-Two

I'm at the station early today. Overeager. I don't like stations much. When I was a kid we never went anywhere by train. I only see this one because it's the quickest route between Darlington and Edinburgh. Straight up and down, like falling. I hate the mass of people. Last time I was here it was to meet Cameron, the last Friday night we had. There were rugby supporters everywhere. I hate the board with its spinning letters and numbers. They flap down and change and I'm never sure that I'm looking at the right thing. Aren't buses easier? You jump on when they stop by you, jump off when you arrive.

I'm too early but I hang about in Burger King.

It's Craig. He steps off the train with his big rucksack. When he comes up the platform we clap eyes on each other straight away. He's in a tracksuit and he's trying to look bluff and matey, to look like he's used to travelling about. But I can see he's relieved to find me straight away. When he comes up he's lurching with his bad foot. I'd forgotten what it was like. I always forget people's details.

A wary distance between us, though we're both grinning.

'Is Penny here?' I ask. 'I didn't know you were coming too.'

Craig looks abashed. 'Penny's still at home. She gave me her ticket.'

'What's happened to her?'

He shrugs. 'It was all last-minute. The hospital phoned. Something about her mam.' He shifts the weight of his backpack.

Has Penny sent him up to fetch the money? Is he here to nose on me? I help him with the bag. 'Tell me when we get sorted,' I say, sounding friendly, I hope. 'We'll get a cab to mine. It's not far.'

The cab swishing onto Prince's Street. That corner thick with tourists, where there's always a lone bagpiper having his photo taken. A Japanese husband is making his wife stand next to the piper.

Under the clock. Under arches. Onto Leith Walk. Craig's looking out, interested.

Craig puts on this serious voice. 'For some reason, me and you, we've always managed to see eye to eye,' he says. We're in the cold-floored kitchen of my flat. I make tea and coffee. I lay out warm tomato bread, different cheeses, pesto, olives. Giving him a posh kind of cheese sandwich. He's saying, 'Even though . . . even though we're different, we've still managed to talk man to man, haven't we, Andy? We've still been proper mates.'

I shrug. I don't feel like making it easy for him, whatever it is he's come all this way to say. I'm in a black jacket and T-shirt. Tartan Waverley Trust ribbon. My hair newly shaved. I look queer as fuck and he knows it.

Craig tries again. 'Everyone sends their love, you know. Penny, Mark, my mam, your uncle Ethan. They all want to know what you're up to. What's happening. How you are.'

I sit down. 'Have you really come just to pass on their love?'

He laughs ruefully. 'To tell you the truth, I had to get away from Aycliffe, too.'

'You and Penny . . .?'

'She can't be doing with me any more.' He looks out of the tall windows, makes appreciative noises over the view. 'Well and truly fucked and chucked. That's me.' He smiles. 'You've done all right here, haven't you?'

'Maybe.'

267

'I wanted to see where you escaped to. I wanted to see what it was like when you leave Aycliffe.'

'This is it,' I say.

Gamely he delivers himself up to my care. Entertain me, Craig says.

I thought about the things you did, the places you go with guests. It was only by showing off my new city to Craig that I realised that this is where I live. I saw how much I knew of it. How great it is here.

We walked to the Botanical Gardens, one of the last warm days of the year. Through the futuristic silver gates into rolling fields and dark, secluded trees.

Under the white crystal dome of the hothouses we sat and talked and looked at the orchids. They nestled behind the protective rubber of their leaves: hot pink, acid orange and green, fine white china trumpets of flowers. I had never been here before.

'Why didn't we bring the bairn?' Craig said. 'It would be a trip out for him.' He was talking more easily about Jep now. At first he'd been wary about even touching my son, as if he'd catch something. Now, when we were home, he'd sling him about fondly, tickle him, lug him around. What do they call it? Dandle him. I was starting to see that Craig would make a good dad. Rush of hormones telling me: he'd make a good father. I was nearly phoning Penny, telling her: he's good with bairns.

Today Jep was in the care of my neighbours. Craig didn't like my friends much. He thought they were posh. When they were round or we were out with them, he kept his head down. Glowered at them, which embarrassed me. It wasn't helped by the fact that they'd assumed for the first week that he was my new feller. Craig was mortified. 'Why do they assume that? That we can't just be mates?' I shrugged at that.

'It's amazing in here,' Craig said as we inspected the South American room. Lilies on ponds, their rubbery hides grown monstrous, covering all the water. In the room that

268

was meant to be a desert, Craig revelled in the cacti. He stayed there ages. I couldn't stand it. It was musty and hot. He was pretending to be in a western, scuffing through the sand, bending to glare at funny, stumpy things. The needles on them!

He pointed out the century plant. A dull-looking thing. At Easter, the sign said, they'd had to punch a hole in the glass roof for it, this cactus that flowers once a hundred years and dies. Now it was dying. At Easter – I bloody missed it, of course – it threw up this silly appendage, thirteen feet tall, and produced thousands of banana-yellow flowers. Now gone.

Craig stood up and brushed off his jeans. 'Apparently you can't tell a century plant is a century plant until it grows suddenly, hugely, and flowers like that. Until it bursts the roof.' He laughed at me, but not nastily. 'That's like you puffs. The way you suddenly come out.'

I thought, God – he's not going to tell me something, is he? But then, no, that would be too silly. Of course I'd thought of making a move on him. Of testing him out. But you can't, can you? He was straight, but being such a sport. Dancing at CC's, out all the time with me. He was game, old Craig.

We went back to the orchid house.

'You feel so safe here,' I said. 'The temperature will never drop.'

He stared at the lilies. It was funny. He's no queer, perhaps, but I've still got him spending afternoons looking at flowers. This hulking, muscle-building brute. 'Imagine if the wind got in. The frozen north.'

I said, 'I'm living the life of Riley, but it's not always a laugh, you know.'

He seemed to sag down. He looked older suddenly. 'Better than my life. I get a shag and it makes my year.'

'Is that what Penny was? Just a shag?'

He colours, because for a second he's forgotten that I'm more Penny's friend than his. 'You know what I mean.'

'Yeah.' I sit down beside him.

'I don't think there's much in me and Penny.'

'No?' I hold back from saying anything about this.

He changes the subject. 'I'm jealous of you, Andy. You've got it all. I came expecting your life to be a disaster. You make yourself sound like a fuck-up. Penny makes it sound like you've messed it all up –'

'Cheers!'

'But you've got everything I want! You've even got a bairn . . .'

'I've even got a bairn.'

He looks at me seriously. 'I don't know where or how you got him. I don't know why he is the way he is. I don't pretend to understand any of your life, Andy. But look at you. Sorted! You're a father, for God's sake! How does that make you feel? What's that like?'

I shake my head.

'It's like . . .' He hunts out his ciggies. 'I can believe in your life because of the weird shit I've had in my life recently. Last year I'd never have given you the time of day.'

I almost say something trite about how we all change. I bite my tongue. If he gets irritated he could punch me one. He's got a temper, this one. But I've also seen him work, measured and patient, that day he fixed our telly by taking it all to pieces. Breaking it into the smallest possible pieces. He's doing that with my life, his life, he's working his way round his own thoughts very carefully.

'You're so selfish!' he says at last. 'You've not let anyone hold you back! There's no one at home you feel guilty about! How can you be so selfish? How can I get to be like that?'

Hallowe'en on Leith Walk. There's me, scared of everything. Waiting at the bus stop, leaning on a lamppost, and it's humming in my ear. The whole thing throbs with energy. It's got me swaying on the spot.

The wind is picking up. It takes one of the bin bags piled at the kerb and flings it into the middle of the road.

Waiting to cause an accident. Traffic streams past. It never stops down here.

I'm waiting for the C3 across town. Stupid time to be out. Back in Aycliffe I wouldn't be out on Hallowe'en. When we were kids we used to run about everywhere, dressed in bin bags, banging on doors. A mate of mine crapped on someone's front path when they wouldn't give us Hallowe'en money.

Pub crawlers go past in gangs. One whole load dressed up. The women are all witches, one is a nun. The men find it harder, thinking up what to be on Hallowe'en. This one's decided to be a punk. They shout at me, some of the women waving. I don't know how to take that sometimes. People find it very easy to include me, to bring me in. They call me mate, pat my back, talk to me in queues, in shops, in bars. I'm pliable.

Dressing up. I should have my leopard spots on. Better than any make-up.

Some bloke goes past in an anorak, fetches the rubbish off the road. So there won't be an accident.

An old man goes zipping by in a disabled dodgem car. He careers all over the path, minding the dog shit. So his wheels won't track it into his front hall. He pulls up outside a closed toy shop and stares at the model spaceships. An Indian woman passes him, tinkling with golden hoops and pulling a child. She's looking in the charity-shop windows.

When the bus comes, everyone on it is drunk. Young men dressed to go out, in leather jackets, hair plastered back with wax. Women done up a bit tarty for a night out. We get underway, pulling through the fish-and-kebab part of town. All the grey fairy-tale buildings of Waverley, lit blue from beneath.

We let on a dirty man and his dog on a string. The dog's matted pelt is the same colour as his owner's hair. The Bridges. South Clerk Street. This city is filthy. I am sunk into its dirt. It is everywhere and I am included.

Twenty-Three

It was a long coming back. It was as if she was on a cruise liner, waving to the shore from the deck.

The decks of the *QE2* like tiers of a wedding cake.

Where was her groom?

Everyone came out to meet her.

Which day would she arrive?

Phoenix Court kept to the usual visiting rota. Everyone wondered if they would be the one to see her wake.

Fran thought it was weird. Who would really want to be a witness?

'Oh, I think it would be lovely,' said Nesta. 'Have you seen her recently? She's not moving much, but all her colour's come back.'

This was at the bus stop, in the rain. Nesta in a see-through headscarf. 'She looks like a princess.'

Fran thought that was going too far. She hoped it wouldn't be Nesta there when Liz returned. She'd need proper medical care. Someone sensible should be on hand. Nesta would be sentimental, excitable. She would fall on the floor, weeping and praying. She'd carry on as if it was *ET*. Liz the traveller returned from the brink.

'I wouldn't want to see Liz wake,' Fran said. 'Poor thing! She's been looked at enough, these past few months. She'll feel funny.'

Fran could imagine that being looked at in your sleep would be like being interfered with.

'I think it's lovely.' Nesta smiled. 'It's made me feel happy. Good news, for once.'

'Mm.'

That was true, mind. Good news at last.

Last week Penny burst into Fran's kitchen.

'They reckon Mam's coming back!'

Fran's lot were having their tea.

'Who reckons? Sit down, pet. Get your breath.'

'The doctors.' She couldn't sit. Pacing up and down the kitchen. 'They say she's coming back to us!'

Fran and Nesta went to sit on the back seat.

'Remember the sexy bus driver that Liz ran away with?' asked Fran.

'Ay, I do.' Nesta nodded. 'He was a hunk.'

Fran hated this expression. As though men were edible.

Nesta said, 'When Liz is back, she can tell us what she did with him!' She looked slyly at Fran. 'Just shows, you should never get involved with a younger man.'

'My Frank's a younger man.'

'Just shows.'

Fran pursed her lips.

'Penny should think about selling her story to *Take a Break* magazine,' Nesta said. 'You get hundreds of pounds for writing up your true-life tales.'

'You could mention it to her.'

'Somebody should.' Nesta stared at the rainy streets. 'People like real escapes and returns to life.'

Nesta thought of J. R. Ewing, of Bobby Ewing. All the Ewings of Southfork, Dallas, were shot dead at one time or another. Easy to go and come back. Easy to come back with a new actress in your shoes. A new, more beautiful and younger actress. Like when they ditched Miss Ellie on *Dallas* and brought a new one in. It was easy coming back, Nesta knew.

On Monday morning Penny took a deep breath and went to the spastics shop. At one level she thought it was tempting fate, telling people so soon. They said, when you were having a bairn, you should wait a little while before telling, before buying things. This was the same. Yet she wanted to tell everyone. She was thrilled by this news.

Elsie looked up from the counter, straight at her, when she walked in. There was that smell of starch and softener and spray-on deodorant. The shop was gloomy.

'Elsie, I've got something to tell you.'

Elsie just looked at her.

'I know we've not been seeing eye to eye these past few months . . .'

The older woman snorted.

'I've got some news about Mam.'

'Oh?' To conceal her interest, Elsie started folding cardigans on the counter, rapidly, making a mess of them.

'You've not been for a while to the hospital, I know. You don't know the latest.'

Elsie's eyes flashed. 'Can you blame me for losing interest in the doings of your family?'

'Elsie! Me and Craig split up! I'm sorry! But it was a two-sided thing!'

Elsie tutted. 'Little madam,' she muttered.

Actually, thought Penny, I do sound like a little madam, coming in here, telling her things she doesn't want to hear. 'All right. I'll go. I wish I'd never bothered.'

'Hang on, you,' Elsie said, coming round the counter.

God, she's going to punch me, thought Penny. She'd heard about Elsie in the old days, drunk in the factory and starting fights.

'I don't care what you say,' Elsie said. 'It's your fault our Craig's gone off to Edinburgh and left us. He had to get away so he wasn't haunted by the sight of you. You've driven away my only son!'

'Oh, get away! He's only gone on a trip.'

'He's never left me before,' Elsie said. 'What does he need with being away?'

'He's just gone away to visit his mate Andy.'

'Oh, *him*,' snapped Elsie.

'What do you mean, oh, *him*?'

Elsie was red in the face. 'That shirt lifter. Why's our Craig staying with a ponce?'

Penny looked around. All the shop's browsers and Elsie's elderly colleague Charlotte were watching now.

'What, are you saying that I've *turned* your son? I've turned him into a queer?'

Elsie bridled. Penny was jeering at her. 'I wouldn't put anything past you, you minx. That Andy was your boyfriend and *he* turned –'

'He was never my boyfriend –'

'And you're carrying on behind Craig's back with the tattooed man and . . . and!' Elsie laughed harshly, preparing to deliver her suddenly decided upon killing blow. 'I could tell you a few home truths about your precious, lovely Mark Kelly.'

'Oh, don't bother,' Penny muttered, heading for the door.

'I think you should hear this. You're in deep waters with all these queers, Penny Robinson. You should know the man you're sleeping with now is a queer as well. I saw him on New Year's Eve!'

Penny laughed. 'Kissing Santa Claus?'

'Kissing Andy! Where the coats were hung up!'

'So?'

'Oh, you brazen thing, you!'

'Elsie, to be honest, I don't care what men get up to. They always get up to things. They're dirty beasts. You know that.'

'I'm sure I don't!'

'Yes, you bloody well do. So don't blame me if your Craig isn't here to be mothered just now. I don't know and I don't care what he's doing in Edinburgh. I hope the poor lad's having the time of his life.' With that, Penny opened the door.

Elsie called out, chastened. 'What was your news?'

'Are you sure you want to hear?'

Elsie looked around at Charlotte and the customers. They had heard everything. Elsie felt stripped bare. 'You

275

know me.' She held her chin up, trembling. 'I don't like not knowing.'

'My mam's coming back to the land of the living.' Penny gave a wry smile. 'Now tell me you're not pleased.'

Nesta was hatching a plan. She wanted to leave Phoenix Court. She had set her sights on one of those Barratt houses they were building out of town. Red brick, three bedrooms, garage underneath. She had her new baby and now it was all change. She was wanting to go up in the world.

'They let them move in for a deposit of £99,' Elsie told Fran. 'They're practically chucking mortgages at anyone.'

Fran was ironing. 'It's a buyer's market,' she said. She looked at Elsie helping herself to more tea, cutting another slice of Battenburg. Fran had thought that, with Jane abroad, she might get her afternoons to herself. But here was Elsie, glowing and chatty. She kept telling Fran the lurid stories of the restoration of her common-law marriage to Tom. 'That devil had me up all night again!' she'd cackle. 'He's a wicked old thing!'

'I just hope,' Elsie was saying now, 'that Nesta has counted the cost and knows how much she'll end up having to pay.' Elsie pulled a face. 'Semi-detached.'

Fran knew that Elsie was jealous, knowing that she'd never get out of her council house, where almost all her rent was paid for her. Really, she was here for life. If she did any paid work they'd take benefits off her and it wouldn't be worth it. Elsie was dug in.

'I'm surprised they gave her a mortgage,' Elsie said. 'Nesta never paid a penny poll tax, when that was the thing. Her Tony gets that *Socialist Worker* paper. Says he's a socialist. They had bailiffs banging on their doors. Nesta said she was paying nothing, because it was against her principles.' She snorted. 'Principles! The likes of them!'

'Well, you can't blame her for wanting to better herself,' said Fran. 'For wanting to get off this estate.'

'There's nothing wrong with here!' Elsie said. 'The people round here are the salt of the earth!'

'Are they?' Wearily Fran folded her pile of pillowcases. 'You know yourself there are some right bloody horrors round here. The place is getting rougher and rougher. I'm telling you, if I could, I'd leave in a shot.'

'You wouldn't!'

'I bloody would. I think the younger ones have got the right idea.' She looked at Elsie. 'Any sign of your Craig coming back?'

'He's still in Scotland. He says he might look for work there.'

'I can't see it being any better there,' Fran said.

'I think he's enjoying the big city. Poor lad! He hasn't seen many places. He'll like the bright lights. I suppose he's like his dad that way.'

'Are you missing him?'

'It's lucky Tom came back to me! Otherwise I'd be on my tod!' Elsie gave a bleak little laugh. She couldn't imagine anything worse than being alone. Yet look how close she'd come to it recently.

There were two things Nesta knew for certain about the telly.

One was that on *Beadle's About* people did zany things for camcorders on purpose. There weren't as many silly-looking accidents in the world as Jeremy Beadle pretended. The world wasn't as funny as that. The people who got on his show staged their own ludicrous disasters, just to get on the telly and pocket some cash. Good luck to them. But Nesta wasn't taken in.

The other thing she knew for certain was that only men liked James Bond. Women liked real stories. Stories with real people and lives, not gadgets and guns.

She was sitting at Liz's bedside with Big Sue and for the past hour they had been talking about what was on the telly. What was good, what was hopeless, and what should be taken off. It was their great point of contact. Recently

277

the two of them had taken to visiting each other to watch telly together. They both liked the way the other interrupted and talked all the way through programmes. When they watched things alone it was this kind of ribald, deprecating commentary that they craved. Now, over Liz's body, they were agreeing on last night's *Heartbeat*. They thought the young policeman was lovely. And the music took you right back in time to the sixties.

'Back to the sixties,' said Liz. They both jumped.

They stared at her. She was quite still.

'She spoke!' said Big Sue.

'She said "Back to the sixties!"' said Nesta.

'Fetch a nurse!' said Big Sue, starting up out of her chair.

Nesta was on her way.

Twenty-Four

This was what she liked: getting some wellies on, wrapping herself up against the weather. Tying on a headscarf, plodging over fields. The matted yellow grass of the fields between Chilton and Ferryhill. When she could, Fran took the day to walk over the land between the small villages. This was how she visited her mother and brothers. No kids clinging round her, no shopping to be done. When she could, she dressed up like the Queen when she walks her corgis, and she would stride all the way to her mother's big house.

It was Fran's time to think. And the things that occur to you when you let them! Bubbling up from somewhere. She thought this morning that it would soon be the end of the year. The leaves were turning to orange paste on the paths. She was treading them into black mud. She had her first thoughts of Christmas. She could smell woodsmoke on the air. Funny to have the build-up to Christmas and no Jane around, going on about her present-buying. This Christmas Jane would still be in Tunisia. Eating turkey in the desert, she'd said and laughed.

Fran stopped to stare at the sky. Swifts. The trees were shrugging off thick pullovers. They stood half out of them. It did her good every time she walked out like this, to see how close she lived to the country. Newton Aycliffe was an illusion. It only looked urban. You could walk off the edge of the estate, through the trees, and then you were in the middle of a blond, green, leafy nowhere. The sky was huge. Aycliffe came from Aclea, a clearing in an oak wood. She'd been told that by her father. The old village of Aclea, a thousand years old, lay underneath Aycliffe town centre, which had lasted only fifty years. They had roots here, after all.

It was Fran's father who had taken the time to tell her things like this. Her mother, meanwhile, was all for her boys. Her strong two boys who would grow up to protect her. The mother taught her boys to care for horses. They were like Gypsies, her father said. That was where her mother came from, from Gypsies, he said, with a scowl, one morning walk they took. The brothers and mother thundered by, leaving the father and daughter to amble and talk. You come from Gypsy stock, he told his daughter sadly. Then her mother won the pools and bought the big house outside Ferryhill, bought stables, more horses. Father died of a brain tumour. He was gone in a flash. Fran was in her late twenties, working in an office, and she hardly felt she'd seen him go.

When computers took over offices, Fran never updated her skills. That was how she ended up cleaning.

If I wanted, she thought, walking on, I could imagine that everything leaves me behind in the end. She couldn't bear to think of her children going. Yet the eldest had a boyfriend already. She was making noises of complaint. The restless, triumphant sounds of a child wanting to escape.

Fran didn't want her children held in thrall to her. She hated going to visit her mother and brothers. Apart from the walk to her mother's house, these days were a chore. They taunted her subtly and made her feel stupid and wasted. She didn't want her kids to feel like that, dreading coming to see her. Resenting the binds.

My life, she thought, is very ordinary. When she went to her mother's she had to explain it. She felt compelled to talk it through, to justify it. Even when her mother didn't seem interested and Fran had to work to get herself noticed, she still felt the need to explain away the organisation and decisions in her life.

They thought she had thrown her life away, living with a ginger-haired man on a council estate. She'd given her life to four brats and a drinking man. Look how free her two brothers were! They were in their thirties and went everywhere on horseback. They lived with their mother in a house they'd bought for nothing and they could please themselves. To Fran it seemed that they lived on a different scale to her. Their lives were bigger than hers.

When she arrived it was lunchtime. Her mam was ladling out thick orange stew for her two boys. They both had newspapers out.

Fran let herself in and they barely nodded. Her mother had done up her kitchen like a country farmhouse. Everything was green. She'd bought copper pots and pans – or picked them up somewhere. The boys did house-clearance work round here and sometimes they picked up treasure. She watched their thick red hands ripping up bread, turning pages, thinking that they had the golden touch.

'There's some lunch,' her mother said. She was in a pinny with the sexy, naked body of a woman on the front. Her hair had been permed again and it was a shocking blue. Fran went to kiss her mother's proffered cheek and murmured something about it making her look very youthful.

Her mother gave a shout of pleasure and fiddled with one of her clumpy golden earrings. 'Hear that, boys? She says I'm looking youthful.'

One of the dark-haired brothers spoke without looking up from his paper. 'She must be after borrowing money again.'

'Are you?'

'No!'

'Hey,' said her mother, reaching for a plate, stirring the copper pot some more. 'One of your neighbours is in the paper. They've done a story about her in the *Northern Echo*.' She jabbed one of the boys in the back. 'Find the page. Show her.'

'Who is it?'

Her brother sighed and laid out the page. A full-page

281

spread. 'FIGHT FOR LIFE' it said. There was a picture of Liz, unconscious. Tubes. Eyes closed. Someone had put her wig on her for the photographer.

'They say she's making a miraculous recovery,' Fran's mother said.

'They reckon,' said Fran, feeling cross that she hadn't seen this spread first. She peered at the columns of print. Quotes from Big Sue and Nesta. Even, at the bottom, a smaller photo of the pair of them, looking concerned and heartbroken, outside the hospital. Their looks said, 'Our friend's in there.' Fran was piqued. Though she didn't really want to be in the paper, it would have been nice to be told.

'She's started saying things in her sleep,' said her mother.

'It isn't really sleep.'

They sat down to eat. 'Messages from beyond!' her mother cackled. 'I wonder if we can tune her in to your father! See what the old bugger has to say for himself!'

One of the boys looked over his paper, tutted, rolled his eyes. There'd been no love lost between father and sons.

'Get our lottery numbers checked out,' said the other brother. 'They say people half in, half out of life get the second sight. You should ask her. It could be us!' He snorted.

Fran was feeling more uncomfortable than when they criticised her personal life.

'She's very beautiful,' said the other brother. 'She looks serene and beautiful. She's like something out of a legend.'

His mother gave him a strange, appraising look. 'Yes,' she said.

'Do you know her well, Fran? Are you still visiting?' Fran nodded.

'Well,' said her mother sardonically. 'Fancy our Fran knowing a living legend in the flesh.'

Fran stared at the picture of Liz. She was thinking of her brilliance, the way she could catch your eye without even trying. Glamour, Fran's father told her once, wasn't just being made up, pretty and sophisticated. It wasn't just a film-star thing. It was a witchy spell that women pass across your eyes to draw you into their influence. You fall under them and their power, and you never even know it.

He said that was what her Gypsy mother had done to him. She'd taken hold of his soul, imprisoned it within the thick, crazed glass of her crystal ball. She'd never let him go until he cracked. He warned his daughter against glamour. She had listened.

Fran stared at her brothers and her mother as they went on to talk quietly, half articulately, about other things. About riding out to Barnard Castle. Selling bits of junk from dead people's houses to the greedy antique dealers. They were making plans, chuckling and hoarding. I haven't got anything to do with them, Fran thought, and had a pang of missing her father, dead seventeen years.

'I'm going home,' Fran said, after lunch. No coffee. 'I'm walking back.'

'You've hardly been here,' her mother said.

The thing about being under spells, her father said, is that you never know. You wake up one morning years after, and see that your life and your most crucial decisions have been made up while you were living half-asleep.

Twenty-Five

I took my knitting with me. But as soon as Tom opened his mouth, I knew I wouldn't get any done. He was compelling. Like he always was.

He said, 'I want you there, Elsie. Even if all you're doing is knitting, you are still by my side, giving me strength. I'll need your strength when I work with Liz.' Even though I wasn't sure what he meant by 'work', I went to support him.

Knitting relaxes me. It takes on a life of its own. When they get going the needles rattle and whirr, and it seems as if they're working *me*, instead of the other way round. Hospital bedsides are a good place to go knitting. You can chew up all the empty hours. Sitting by Liz I went through ball after ball.

I was making baby things. I said they were for a friend. Sexless yellow things, booties and little dresses. Only I knew who they were really for. I was embarrassed. When Craig and Penny were together and living round mine, those few, brief weeks, this was my – what do you call it? – subterfuge. I said I was stocking up with baby clothes for a friend of mine. And all the time I meant *them*. I was imagining a Christmas birth for their child. I was hastening them on with my needles. Grandmothers have to dream like this.

That's all gone now. Here I am, still making the stupid things. I can't seem to stop. They're perfect.

I have the beginning of new booties on my lap as Tom begins to talk. He's taking over from Nesta. Nesta has warmed Liz up. She's drawn her out into her half-trance. Now Tom can talk with her. Work with her.

284

What nonsense has Nesta been pouring into Liz's head? If what Tom says is right, then Liz can understand everything Nesta has been saying. They have a link.

I asked her, 'Nesta, what did you say to her? What did you tell Liz to make her talk?'

That was last night. Tom insisted we went round to Nesta's house. He had seen the piece in the paper. He wanted to know what gift the woman had, that she could speak with the afflicted like this. Tom was very eager. If I didn't know better, I'd have said he was covetous of Nesta's gift.

What all the women say is right. Even after the bonfine Nesta's house is a pigsty inside. It's like she never lifts a finger. The windows were filthy, brown with dirt, inside and out. In the living room where she invited us to sit on her manky old settee, I counted six half-emptied bottles of Coca-Cola. She was friendlier and chirpier than usual, glowing from her exposure in the paper. Already a clipping was in a flowery frame on top of the telly.

Tom repeated my question. 'Why was it you, do you think, Nesta, that Liz responded to? What did you say?'

Nesta looked him up and down. She knew she had power here. She could see how keen Tom was. She seemed to decide to help, and thought hard. 'I was just talking . . . with Big Sue, the first time it happened. We were just talking about the telly and that.'

Tom nodded, steepling his fingers under his chin. He looked like he was going to pray. That was how he carried on when he was religious. A great shadow would come over his face. His nose all hooked and his mouth grim. He has got that religious look back and it makes me wonder if that means God's coming back into our lives. I hope not. We've been getting on so well these past few weeks.

'The telly?' he asked.

Nodding sagely, Nesta said, 'We realised that she likes it when we talk about stuff on the telly.' She sat right back in her armchair, looking composed and pleased with herself. She looked like she was in a documentary. 'We were talking about *Heartbeat* – you know, with Nick Berry – and she joined in. She said something to us and that's when they were sure that she was coming back to proper life.'

'Do you think you are responsible for Liz coming back?' Tom asked.

'Oh, no,' said Nesta, full of meekness. 'But I think I've done my bit to help.'

Tom nodded. He seemed to struggle with an important idea until he told her, 'There is a bridge between this life and another. Liz was crossing that bridge. I think you have called out to her in a loud and friendly voice. And I think she has heard you, Nesta.'

'Good!' said Nesta.

'Her spirit has given pause for thought on its journey. She is caught on the bridge and can be coaxed either way. If she wants to, she can come back, by following your voice. You have shown her a way. Given her spirit the chance to decide.'

Nesta smiled. 'She must like the sound of my voice!'

I spent as long – longer! – by Liz's bedside as Nesta. I spent more hours there than anyone else. I talked to that woman about everything under the sun. I opened up my heart. I was unstinting.

And who does she choose? Whose gormless, mumbling, irritating voice does her spirit decide to listen to?

Nesta Dixon. Gob on her like a foghorn. Never talks a word of sense. Isn't that just the way of it? It's like I told that snotty Penny. Her and her mam. They think they're too good to speak to me.

'I want you to join with me, Nesta,' said Tom.

His most commanding voice, I noticed. Almost his vampire voice. The husky, deathly voice he would put on for our Christopher Lee black-cloak, pointed-teeth games. Her squinty eyes goggled under his influence. Why was he Bela Lugosing Nesta? What did he want with her?

'Oh yes?' She batted her thick black eyelashes. Now

she's gone all flirty and flattered, I thought. Now she wants to do everything she can for him. 'I have a special gift,' she said thoughtfully. 'I must put it to proper use.'

'That's right,' said Tom. 'You must come with me to see Liz. There is work to be done.'

'Work?' Nesta and I asked together.

'Liz is on the cusp,' he said. 'She is at the limit of experience. She is on the edge. While she is there, there are questions to be asked, before her spirit returns to us.'

'When she comes back, will she be normal again?' I asked.

'As normal as the rest of us,' he said.

'Good.'

'While she is on the edge, we must ask what it is like,' Tom said.

The room had become dark around them.

'Are you sure you want to know?' Nesta asked. Her white forehead as she frowned was the brightest thing there.

'She is approaching the totality of her experience on earth,' Tom explained. The shadows on his face were long and dark. 'Of course we need to know. I need to know.'

Andy is waving Craig off at Waverley Station in Edinburgh.

Craig stands with his bags in the train doorway. Andy has Jep in his arms.

'Are you sure you won't come back to Aycliffe?'

Andy shakes his head, grinning. He shuffles his feet and talks to his child. 'Wave, Jep.'

Craig has spent almost a month with them.

'I'll pass your love on . . . to everyone,' Craig says.

The guard is going by and checking on doors. He has his white table-tennis bats at the ready, to signal the train to leave.

'Good luck with your mother,' Andy says.

Craig pulls a face. 'She'll be all right.' He knows already

how she will try to make him feel guilty for staying away a month.

The train leaves.

Jep squirms in Andy's arms, to keep sight of Craig – Uncle Craig – and to wave. How he's grown! His sharp nails click on Andy's new tartan jacket.

Then the station is left behind.

The city flashes by. Savacentre. Terraces. The Meadowbank stadium. The land either side settles down to green. Then the sea appears.

Craig's mam isn't so bad. Elsie has sense. But he has to tell her that he's moving out of home. He's leaving Aycliffe. He doesn't know yet where he's going. She'll take it badly, but maybe she'll understand in the end.

He can't live with her and Tom. It's too sweaty and compressed with all of them there. Too many people on a long, breakless journey in a single car.

It's a step backwards for all of them, living together.

Seeing Andy has convinced Craig of his need for a new town, autonomy. Managing his own life. Paying rent and bills and fetching in his own groceries. Maybe he can put some of those skills of his to use.

Andy told him he should set up in his own business. Andy wished he had talents like Craig's. Craig could turn his hand to anything. You're a handyman! Andy told him, laughing.

I'm a handyman, thinks Craig, heading south.

Changing of the guard. Fran walked out of Liz's room, straight into Nesta, Tom and Elsie. The three of them sat in the waiting area, not talking, not reading, staring at the door. They looked keen. She wanted to ask them, what are you expecting? And why are you flocking here all at once? They wanted to see Liz doing handstands, jumping about. Tom would be putting it down as some great religious experience. It was too awful to think about. Elsie and Nesta pulled along for the ride, his handmaidens. Fran didn't trust Tom one bit. He looked manic and calm at the

288

same time. His eyes were silver. He was like a toad with silver eyes. Now he was pacing towards her.

'No change?'

'Nothing,' said Fran, buttoning her coat. 'I think all this ... expectancy will come to nothing. It's just raising Penny's hopes. There is no hope. I don't see Liz rallying.'

'Ah,' said Tom. 'You don't know the signs. The proper signs.'

'Don't I?' Fran looked at the two women, who were still sitting. How quiet and submissive Elsie was when Tom was there to do her talking.

'Forgive me,' said Tom. 'But you are ignorant. Liz is a person on the edge. The mistake people like you make is to treat them as dead already. Liz is on the verge of a new phase of life. She is in a very creative limbo. She is communicating with us in a host of different ways. We simply have to be sensitive and receptive.'

'Right,' said Fran, shouldering her bag.

The two women stood up.

'We must go and see her,' said Tom. 'We have work to do.'

Fran said her goodnights and left.

As she passed the reception, she wanted to warn the nurses that religious nuts were taking their turn to sit with the helpless Liz. Yet she couldn't do it. She imagined the receptionist – one of the organised, clever-looking, self-important, I'm-really-as-good-as-a-doctor type – staring back at her. Telling her wearily that they get all sorts in here. They've seen all the religious nuts in the world.

And who was Fran to criticise anyone and what they did at the bedside? She'd spent an hour with Liz tonight, going over in detail the state of her marriage, then her relationship with her mother.

Leaving Ferryhill, Fran had tramped miles cross-country just to spill out her feelings to Liz. She wished she had a horse, to bring her much quicker to the sickroom. She wanted to fly that distance at great speed. Liz was the first person she had wanted to talk with.

289

They drew up their chairs around the bed, Tom, Elsie and Nesta.

Didn't she look a treat? Under white blankets and sheets Liz lay very still and straight. Nesta was right. Her colour was back, peaches and cream. Those strong, mannish features. What a handsome woman. Tom felt the urge to pray, and suppressed it. When he looked at Liz he felt almost sexy. She was lovely, but it wasn't sexy in the usual way he felt. He was hungry for something bigger. This was different to the body and its usual appetites.

He looked at Nesta. She looked so dopey. Frustration rose in him. Don't let any of these bitches let me down. Liz is my bridge to another world. Nesta is my mediator to Liz. He hated being this dependent. He had to fight down the panic, learn to depend. Learn to trust these silly women. 'Nesta?' he asked gently.

Something went through her head. A beat, a message. That running of the beat of a song she had heard. When her adopted father died, she told her adopted mother that what she needed was a radio. They play you pop music twenty-four hours a day and that distracts you from thoughts of the dead. The ongoing music makes the time go fast. Fills up your thoughts. What you get into your head is a beat going on like this, like rap music, insistent. A kind of music Nesta never liked, but there you go. It was funny what got into your head.

She liked her mind because there was never a dull moment. Is everyone as entertained as this? As busy like me? Music and pictures and links between scenes and words over pictures and then all change. Nothing long enough to catch a hold of. When some time in the eighties, when the new computer technology took over the telly, when rap music and jazzy coloured graphics came on everything, for the first time she felt at home. Telly became more complicated, more demanding to watch. For the first time she had something to point at and say, There! That's how I think! That's what it's like in my mind all the time!

Music and pictures and changing, shifting one thing for the next. You can't unsnag the sense of things. Which was why Nesta found it hard to keep on top of the plot.

She didn't move at the same speed as other people. Her mind was faster. She worked at the speed of telly.

At first Nesta didn't know what to say. She looked down at her lap, the chapped hands resting there.

'Clear your mind,' Tom told her. 'Slow your breath, the pace of your thoughts. Breathe in time with Liz. Listen to Liz breathing and you match that. Be at one.'

Fat chance. This was like music and movement, all those years ago at school. Miss Simmonds clapping her hands in the school hall, which smelled of varnish, dust, dirty sandshoes. The record player would start up, the *Nutcracker Suite* crackling out of a box of blond wood, like a coffin with a grill on the front.

Everyone urged to dance round in squeaky sandshoes in their dark-blue knickers. Dance round like sugar plums, like fairies, dance round, use the space, feel the music, express yourselves. Miss clapped her hands to start, to speed up. Everyone moved. Someone giggled. Someone farted. Someone giggled some more.

'Talk with her,' Tom said. 'Keep your breathing even, Nesta.'

Who does that old bastard think he is? thought Nesta. He's like Uri thingy on the telly, Geller. Bending spoons and putting you in trances. Do us a trick, man.

Nesta stared down, shy all of a sudden. She didn't know what to say now. The talking she had done before, she had done because she wanted to. Big Sue should be here as well. She felt bullied by Tom.

She found she was staring at the silver locket she always wore. In her teens she had pasted in two tiny cameo pictures cut from the *TV Times*: Bet Lynch from *Coronation Street* and Meg Mortimer from *Crossroads*. They were her strong women icons. They were the faces that would inspire her to get what she wanted from life. She clicked open the silver locket and looked at the faces of these women.

Inspire. Inspire me and Liz. Breathe in with Liz, and out. If only she could shut out those faces of Elsie and Tom, staring, wanting a part of this. They were like vultures, them two. Like vampires.

'Do you remember how David Hunter was always trying to take ownership of the Crossroads Motel off Meg?' she said. 'Meg would never give in. She was saving it for her children. Crippled, ginger Sandy, who was in a wheelchair and died. And Jill, who was blonde and lived in that lovely house called Chimneys. She was divorced from a man who beat her. Meg wanted the motel for Jill, who ended up marrying another awful, slimy man called Adam Chance. Then Meg had had enough and you thought she'd committed suicide, swallowing an overdose of Valium while the motel was on fire. It was Bonfire Night, about 1980, remember? The motel in flames. Only Meg indoors. All the staff and guests at the firework display. Jill turned, saw the real fire, yelled out, "Mum!" It was terrible. But Meg survived. Went off on the QE2. Signed over her shares in the motel. That evil smoothie David Hunter – what a charmer! – took over. Adam Chance – another smoothie! – took over some of Jill's shares when they married. Jill went back on the booze. Funny how those awful men took over in the end.

'Like Bet Lynch on the Street, for ever trying to get away, pinning her hopes on another man. Leaving and coming back with her wings broken. She ended up in Spain. You never found out if she was happy, did you? You just have to imagine. Why couldn't these women be happy where they were? In their own programmes?'

Nesta draws breath. She is out of synch with Liz.

Something is happening.

Elsie shouts out, 'Do something!'

'Fetch a nurse!' Tom yells.

Nesta blinks. None of them know what to do. Liz is hyperventilating. She starts to thrash about on the bed.

292

Tubes plop out of her nose. She is disconnecting herself. She shouts something about the motel being on fire.

'Yes! Yes!' Tom shouts at her, overcoming his panic. Now he's fascinated and eager. 'Tell us more, tell us about the fire . . .'

'I'm on the boat now,' Liz says, lying still again. 'The fire has finished.'

'Where is the fire?' asks Tom, leaning close.

'They dragged me out of the fire. I'd left, but you never knew.'

'Where is the boat going to?' Tom asks.

'To the other land, the next place,' she says.

Tom nods smugly. 'The next place!' he echoes.

'You all thought I'd perished. You couldn't find my body. But I was on the QE2, ready for a long-earned rest.'

'Are you going to the next place now?' he asks, urgently.

'I am wearing a white headscarf and a white frock, and here I am, wishing to sail into the sunset.'

Elsie gasped. 'She thinks she's in Crossroads!'

Tom stared aghast at Nesta. 'You've brought her back to life!'

Liz starts to cry. She cries lustily, with all of her might.

Twenty-Six

'To me,' Fran told her husband, 'they looked shifty. I wouldn't trust them an inch.'

'There you go,' he tutted. 'I knew this would happen. All this hospital visiting.'

It was a gloomy night. Fran was glad to be indoors again, but she had brought the atmosphere in with her. She couldn't shake the feeling off. She wanted to sit down, put her feet up. Frank had the house upside down, up to his eyeballs in mortar. He was building in the living room in a little vest top.

She stared at his freckles, just fading from the summer. He had them all over his shoulders, too. 'I'm taking care of my mates,' she said distractedly. 'Liz needs looking after.'

Frank grunted and went back to work. He buttered each of the breezeblocks carefully. He'd put plastic down so he'd get nothing on the carpet. At least he'd taken that precaution.

He was in a new, industrious phase, building an indoor fish pond for their living room. He'd drawn up all the plans. There was to be a fountain, plants, weed, fairy lights. These days he always had his little projects going. He'd moved on so much from his days of drinking lager and doing bugger all else. To that extent Fran was proud of him. She wasn't keen on the fish-pond idea, but he was obsessed with fish. He'd put a tank in the bathroom. Watching fish, he said, made him drink less booze.

She wondered if Elsie was drinking less again, with her Tom back. She preferred Elsie pissed.

'The way they trooped into her room,' she said, more to herself. 'Like they were going in to interrogate her.'

He commiserated. 'Tom, Elsie and Nesta. What a bunch!' They weren't his favourite people.

'I think I'll pop out and see how Penny is getting on. I should tell her about this.'

He stood up and raised both eyebrows. 'Don't go stirring up trouble.'

She drew in an audible breath. 'It's never me that does the stirring! It's always me that wants things to settle down!'

On her way to Penny's she bumped into Mark.

'Have you seen Penny today?' she asked.

'Me? Should I?'

'Oh,' she faltered. 'I thought . . .'

Mark smiled gruesomely. 'You thought what, Fran?'

'Oh, you know.' She smirked, wanting the tarmac to open and swallow her up. 'The usual idle gossip. The usual bloody rubbish.'

He snorted. 'Ay, I know all right. You heard that Penny and I were an item. Well, we're not. That's Elsie, sticking her neb in and trying to cause bother.' He squinted at her in the gloom. They used to be close, him and Fran. As close as you could get watching sad TV movies together. 'Hey. You don't look right.'

'Frank's right,' she said. 'I do spend too much time running after people's lives.'

He nodded. 'Maybe you do, Fran.'

'Cheers!' She laughed, looked down and saw that she still had her slippers on. With her toes she could feel a worn hole the size of a ten-pence piece. Running out in her slippers. The pink fur was all wet. It was as if she thought all of Phoenix Court was indoors, her house.

'But,' he said, 'if I needed a good mate on my side – I'd wish it was you.'

'Oh, get away!' she chuckled, and submitted to a quick, clumsy hug from the tattooed man.

'Penny?' Fran banged on her kitchen door. 'Are you in?'

The kitchen was lit up inside and steamy with cooking. Penny's blurry purple shape came to unlock the door.

'Is it Mam?'

'It's something and nowt, pet.'

'Come on in, Fran.'

Penny had been doing herself a stir-fry. The kitchen was scented with ginger and soya sauce. Fran wasn't sure, but as they passed through the kitchen into the living room, she thought she saw the water chestnuts tip themselves into the spitting wok. 'Should you leave that cooking by itself?' she asked, following Penny. Penny said it was all right.

Fran started to take her coat off as Penny turned down the stereo. Carole King. The phone rang.

'It's the hospital,' Penny said, before she even snatched up the receiver.

This is a fairly warm night for the time of year. The boxy houses are chocolate brown against the evening's dusky pink. Mark thinks the estate looks like a chocolate box tied up with a ribbon – the triangles and oblongs of the rooftops.

When Mark returns home he has a sudden inspiration and changes into shirt and shorts. A quick jog around the streets. Twice round the estate is a mile. He's been missing the gym without Andy to goad him on.

He slips out into the near-dark. On the narrow streets between terraces, his trainers make hardly any noise. The pavements glisten under soft yellow lights. He remembers the night, almost two years ago, when his mother-in-law and her lover persuaded him to join them on a naturists' promenade round the streets of Newton Aycliffe. What a night that was! He flinches automatically from the memory. But it is bliss to be out with bare arms and legs, running till it becomes thoughtless. This must be one of the last nights of the year for being out like this. It strikes him how quiet the streets are. Are people that scared?

Mark thinks, I'm doing my own reclaiming of the night.

Whenever he sees someone by themselves, a woman alone or a child, he crosses the road so he's not coming up behind them or having to run towards them. He has to keep that distance. He hasn't seen any of the rough lads from over the Forsyths' house in a while. Whatever the phrase 'rough lads' means, anyway. Mark supposes that, when he was their age, he was a 'rough lad' too. He still has a shaved head. He thinks people are overreacting to these lads on the estate. It doesn't do any good to get too alarmed. It puts all the power on the aggressor's side. Those lads could rule the place now. Look how empty the streets are tonight. People prisoners in their own homes.

Tonight as Mark runs, as he starts to sweat, he feels like throwing off his gym kit and running naked but for tattoos. He feels free to run where he wants.

At last, coming round on his second circuit, he starts to plod, to weary. His legs shake.

He stops in the main road and, outside the Forsyths' old house, he sees a minicab slow to a halt. Craig clambers out with his bags and looks around at the street. He's looking smart and sure of himself. His gaze lights on Mark immediately. Unhurriedly he feels for taxi change.

'Now then, lad,' says Craig, tight-lipped.

Mark crosses the main road to see him. Mark feels light and loose-limbed, the opposite of the thickset, powerful boy. Mark comes to stand by Craig. *Now then*, Mark thinks. He hates this about Aycliffe men. Their bluff, bullying, obvious insecurity. He gets called 'lad' by Craig, fifteen years his junior.

'You're back then,' Mark says. He feels at a loss. Craig still hunts around for money. 'I reckon Penny will be pleased.'

'Do you know who I was staying with?' Craig looks at him.

'No, I –'

'Andy.'

'Oh. How's he doing?'

'You should go and see him, Mark.'

Mark smiles. 'All the way up to Edinburgh?'

Craig is insistent. 'He has something for you.'

'What?'

Craig shoulders his bags and turns to the Forsyth house. He hands the impatient driver the exact change. 'An addition to your family.'

'Don't let that taxi go!' This is Fran, running slap-slap-slap on her slippers from Penny's house.

Craig and Mark turn to stare.

The taxi has just pulled away. Craig darts after it. A burst of speed and he's rapping on the driver's window, forcing him to stop. Craig looks smug. They look startled at Craig. Where did that speed come from? Isn't he meant to be lame?

Penny comes up after Fran.

'We're going to the hospital,' she tells Mark.

'Did you lock up your house properly?' asks Fran. This is the kind of thing she frets about.

'Where did you come from?' Penny asks Craig sharply.

'Scotland,' he says, grinning even though he doesn't want to. 'I came back.' His month away seems like a lifetime. The longest month of his life. He looks at Penny now, her long, mousy, distressed hair, her shapeless dress, her thick socks fallen round her ankles. He's missed her.

'What's the hurry?'

'The hospital phoned. Mam's woken up.'

Craig feels this like a physical blow. 'You what?'

'They've known that she was ... coming near the surface ... but she's back!'

'Come with us!' Fran tells him. She bundles them all – Mark included – into the cab.

'Bishop General,' she snaps at the driver, plonking herself in the passenger seat and noting that the meter is already running. There is a sickly smell of forest-floor potpourri. It would be cheaper to buy a car, she thinks, than taking a taxi in every catastrophe.

All the way there, Craig feels ill.

298

'See?' Penny bursts out triumphantly as the cab negotiates the dark country lanes on the way to Bishop. 'Nesta and the others didn't do any harm after all! They did the opposite! They must have done Mam good!'

Fran looks round and gives a sickly, worried smile. A death's-head Hallowe'en grin of reassurance she'd be better off not bothering with. Penny sits uptight, scared, grinning madly back. She looks out of the window, feels Mark's hand on her lap. He sits tense and sweating between her and Craig. It occurs to her suddenly that since she last saw her mam she has fucked both these fellers. Craig looks less cocky now than she has ever seen him. What's his problem? It isn't his mother on the slab.

On the crackly radio Abba sing 'Voulez Vous'. To break the tension, the taxi driver starts to tell Fran why he called his firm Tiger Taxis.

'All that itching,' Penny says suddenly, 'was scabies!' She leans right across Mark's lap to tell Craig. She practically shouts it in his face. He looks so stubborn and dull she wants to shake him. 'I went to the doctors to get it sorted out. You bastard! That was scabies you gave me!'

Craig blanches, and so does Fran.

Craig asks Mark, 'If she had it, did you get scabies as well?'

'Who off?' Mark asks.

'Her.'

'Me?' gasps Penny. 'How would he get it off me?'

'Ha!' Craig turns to see her. His face all twisted up. 'Andy told me what you wrote to him. How you shagged the bloke with tattoos.'

'Oh,' says Penny.

They all sag back into the backseat. The taxi hurtles on. Over hills and bumps, jolting them.

'Yes, I *did* get the itching, actually,' Mark says.

Imagine! Fran thinks as she listens – imagine itching under all those tattoos! Your real self itching to get out!

Listening, she realises that she herself has started to itch.

'Have you got rid of your itch?' Penny asks Craig.

'Yes,' he says crossly, unsurely.

'I got some stuff on prescription,' she says. 'You have to paint your whole body covered from the neck down.'

Craig laughs. 'Did *he* do it for you?'

'Oh, man,' Penny curses. 'We only shagged once.'

At this the taxi wobbles slightly on the road.

'How's my mam?' Craig asks.

'Marvellous,' says Penny. 'Apparently she's brought my mam back from the dead. She's like bloody Jesus round here, your mam.'

'Maybe now,' Mark butts in, 'we can ask Liz who got to her. Who beat her up in the first place.'

For a moment – a shattering, self-condemning moment – Craig hesitates. Then, flustered, he says, 'Anyway, Penny, it's all true. Andy *has* got a baby. He's got himself a baby from somewhere. He's not making it up.'

Fran twists round. 'He's got a baby?'

'He says it's his own.' Craig nods to Mark. 'And his.'

'Is –' Penny starts. 'Are they all right?'

'Fine,' Craig says. But the car has pulled up in the dark hospital forecourt. Here already.

'Seven quid fifty,' the Tiger Taxi man tells Fran. 'Make it six. You lot are better than the telly.'

They bundle out into wind and rain.

'What a night to come back on!' Fran whistles.

That cold is coming off the fields and the open country. She realises that she too is talking as if Liz has been on a journey. As if she has been in outer space. She's talking like one of the superstitious ones. With her rational, everyday mind she knows Liz has lain still in the same place for month upon month. But how seductive it is to believe her to have been submerged in another world. Vital and living all the time, translated elsewhere. And now returned and full of news.

Mark is standing alone for a moment. I have a baby, he thinks. He looks to where north must be. Tomorrow he will check that he has money for the train fare. He is sorely tempted. If he can, he will go to Edinburgh.

Twenty-Seven

Tom is furious. He has appealed to the doctors and nurses and they brush him off. They are in the room now, shutting green screens around Liz. Putting the machines back on her. Surrounding her with the menacing paraphernalia of care. Tom is used to people playing doctors and nurses.

He kicks against the door they pushed him through. Nesta and Elsie are sitting back down. Elsie even has her knitting out.

'We are responsible!' Tom cries. 'It was we who provoked her back into life! How dare you – how dare they shut us out now?'

These are the crucial moments, when Liz has feet in both worlds. Maybe several worlds. Tom feels he is missing something he has striven all his life to be near. Beyond that simple grey swing door there are mysteries going on. They're keeping him out again. People with more money, more qualifications, more confidence than he has.

'They won't let me in, Elsie,' he says. His own defeated tone surprises him. He doesn't sound half as angry as he feels inside. She puts down the yellow baby booties she is knitting and pats the chair beside her. Come and sit, she tells him with one of those easy, eloquent quirks of her mouth. Then she mothers him.

He folds into her usual embrace and closes his eyes. They won't let him in.

'I tried, Elsie. I tried to get in. I tried to find out.'

'I know,' says Elsie. 'But they're busy in there, looking after Liz. You have to let the experts in. You wouldn't want to get in the way, would you?'

'No,' he murmurs into her woollen breast, while all his thin insides cry out, Yes! Yes!

Minutes pass. He gets back his calm. He thinks. Mulls over.

'Liz is at that special edge,' he says. He can sense Nesta listening from across the room. 'We all work to our own edges. Beyond which we can't go. Liz has gone further than any of us.'

Elsie smiles embarrassedly.

'It's the edge,' he goes on, 'at which we become unconscious or go mad or depressed or get sick. There we are hopeless. It's where we end up when we can't pull ourselves together any more.'

He looks up into Elsie's eyes. 'I had to see what was there. I had to see Liz at that edge.'

She looks sadly at her Tom. This isn't proper religion. It wasn't what he was like before. What's he been reading while he was away? This sounds American. Like those clean-looking young men who come round the doors in nicely pressed suits.

He also makes Liz's struggle for life seem like something she's best off losing. He even sounds as if he wants her to go further over that bridge. Funny thing to want. You want people to come back from the edge, don't you?

Elsie sees in a flash that Tom wants more than anything a glimpse of another world. He'd ruin anything to see that.

Elsie turns cold. She's besieged with worry. Across the way, Nesta looks as if she has fallen into a trance of her own. Elsie thinks that Liz might be better off not coming round. Not if she has to live like a vegetable. That's the worst thing. Not being able to see to yourself.

The best thing would be going in and out of consciousness for ever. A gentle up and down. Elsie could imagine ebbing and flowing and feeling happy. Sometimes you'd have to take responsibility, take a grip . . . other times let it go and let your nearest and dearest gather round you to take care. Liz is better off now, doing this hokey-cokey with her coma.

To Elsie, Liz is a porpoise, a dolphin, a mermaid.

Once, Elsie's doctor gave her a relaxation tape of whale song. It never worked, but she could see how it would for some. Liz swims underwater. Indigo and violet her element, streaked with weed and silver bubbles. Her golden frock tapers to a strong and luxurious tail. She crests and breaks the surface. Takes in a vast, replenishing breath. She dives again, and hesitates. For a while she delights in being amphibian. She loves her ambiguity. This can only last so long. But Elsie pictures Liz as she turns cartwheels, somersaults, Catherine wheels with exotic fish flitting off in terror. Taking a long time to decide.

Then, startling in that still waiting room, come Fran, Craig, Mark and Penny.

There hadn't been time for anything lately. The ordinary running of Elsie's house had gone to pot. She liked to get her messages in every morning. That way, she didn't have too much to carry back from the town centre. Just enough each day to fill her tartan pully-basket. Every time she walked down town she thought, if I had a car and drove myself, I could do all my shopping at once, on a Saturday, and fill the boot with everything I needed for a week. But what then? Where would I go on the weekday mornings?

With all the hospital visiting and the drama, things had got out of hand. On the night Liz woke up, Elsie and Tom came back to their house and found a scabby crust of bread and half a carton of rancid milk. Nothing at all to make a meal of. The middle of the night and they were starving, disappointed, dulled by the end of the drama. Elsie went off to bed and dreamed of owning a deep chest freezer, stocked to the icy brim with chicken Kievs, vegetable pies, toads-in-the-hole.

Before they left the hospital Elsie had snatched a few words with her son. She was breathless and overeager and thought perhaps she would scare him away.

'Are you coming home with us, pet?'

He smiled, not wanting to hurt her feelings. They were

by the sliding automatic doors, the midnight winds whipping through. 'I might follow on,' he said and let his mam go.

Elsie took this for an answer. She was glad just to have him back in her sight. And she was cross with Tom for virtually ignoring her son. Tom was back in that world of his own as he climbed unsteadily into their cab. Here we go again, Elsie thought glumly. He's going to get all morbid because of the way they treated him. They shoved his nose out of joint. Once the others arrived Tom hardly said a word. The atmosphere in the waiting room, although tense, became less sepulchral. Some of Tom's magic and mystery vanished. The others had been laughing and joking with a slight hysterical edge. They were tense with laughter, anticipation, fear. Elsie had stared at them almost jealously, and tried hard not to want to be part of that little gang. Fran, Penny and Mark and the way they had apparently taken in her son.

Elsie's cab drove away and she watched the hospital entrance vanish. She watched the blue of Craig's tracksuit until they were gone.

Next morning she got up, bustled about, and went downtown early to stock up the larder. When Craig came back she wouldn't want him thinking she'd run the home into the ground. He wasn't back yet. She wondered if he'd stayed all night in the waiting room. Elsie pulled on her thick winter socks. Winter drawers on, she thought ruefully, and found the first, early frost of the year lying across the street when she left the house. Her pully-basket wheels creaked and squeaked on clean frost.

In the supermarket she moved thoughtlessly between aisles, knowing where everything was. She caught a glimpse of herself and thought, I'm not looking my best. But what did that mean, anyway? Who looked their best when shopping? And who'd be looking at her? It was true she knew everyone, but that didn't mean she had to put on a show. And this morning she was determined, tossing things into her wire trolley.

She thought how much Craig had changed. How carefree he once was, how cavalier before, when he used to play out with the Forsyths' gang, the rough lads over the road. Even though they were up to bad things, perhaps, Elsie still knew where he was when he was with them. If she wanted him, she still knew how to get hold. And those lads were always polite with her. Fellers seemed to know by instinct to treat her like a lady. She was pleased with this thought.

When Craig was in another town, it was a different story. How could she know what was going on? He wasn't a sensible lad, really. He was too trusting. Didn't know the ways the world worked. How nasty people could be. He needed her there. There were things he couldn't do. And! This was the clincher! The reason he should never leave. His father had left for a different town and Elsie had thought of him, ever since, as dead.

Here in Red Spot they were branching out. Food was more exotic. She stared at racks and shelves of cook-in sauces. You just tipped these on top of your meat or your veg. She wondered if it was economical. She never liked those meals that came all in one pan. It didn't seem nice. Saved on washing up. But she didn't like all the spices. When Penny was in the house, she'd been cooking all sorts of extravagant things for Elsie and Craig. This was one: chicken korma. Sort of yellow. That had been all right.

There was something boyish and easy and uncomplicated about Craig. Now he seemed to be more serious and sorted out. It was something in the way he held himself. His common sense took her by surprise. Last night she'd let him just about dismiss her. She listened to him and did what he said. It was almost a relief to do so. Yet he was her bairn!

Elsie turned the corner with her trolley. She was nuzzling the fake fur trim on her anorak hood, lost in thought.

Big Sue was in frozen foods, looking at the vegetarian selection. She was going over to that way of thinking. Elsie had packed it in. You never knew what you were eating anyway. You might as well give up your resolutions and go with the flow. Like they said about mad cows, we've all been eating cheap burgers for years. We'll all be bloody mad by 2020. I'll be too old to know the difference, Elsie thought with satisfaction.

Big Sue nodded and mouthed across the chest freezers, 'I heard all about it.' She was behaving as if something mysterious had been going on. 'I heard all about last night's events, from Nesta.'

'Oh,' said Elsie, looking at the veggie selection without much enthusiasm. Bits of cauliflower and broccoli stuck in cheese sauces. Flans. She couldn't feed her men on that.

'Isn't Nesta a star? She could be a medium. Go on the telly.' Big Sue's wide mouth twitched, relishing her own irony. She added, 'I was sorry not to see Liz actually return. But I *was* there for the first moment she woke up and spoke, did I tell you?'

'Yes,' said Elsie blandly.

'"Back to the sixties!"' said Big Sue in a ghostly voice.

'Hm,' said Elsie.

'And,' Big Sue went on, unperturbed, 'I hear Craig's back from Scotland. You must be glad.'

'Very glad.'

'And –' Big Sue leaned closer – 'that he spent the night round number sixteen with that Penny. That must put a smile back on your face, Elsie. The thought of them getting back together.'

Elsie looked up and smiled slowly, thinking of half-finished yellow booties.

Penny lies in her rumpled bed and listens to the noises from down the hall. The bath is running; she can hear the drumming of water and the heavy padding of Craig up and down the hall. He always leaves the bathroom door open when he's in there, letting the thick steam drift down the landing. She thinks it's because he's used to the free and easy atmosphere of the gym, where it's all boys together.

She rolls over and groans. Now he'll take last night as confirmation that they're together again. Not that anything happened. Just before dawn they fell into bed and slept immediately. Fell into Liz's pink satin bed. With Liz lying in a natural sleep, no longer touching death, just six miles away, it might have felt strange to make love here. To lay a Rorschach test of moist blotches on her pink sheets. As soon as Penny thinks this, she wants him all over again. She loves the press of his warmth down her side as they sleep. She thinks about being wrapped up in bed with him. How cosy it is even in the headiest, hardest, most intense moments of their lovemaking. And that's because, with Craig, it is always comforting. With him she feels gathered up and safe.

'Craig?' she calls down the hall. The sloshing sounds of bath water have finished. There has been a concentrated silence during which she can imagine him drying himself. The curious, serious way he does this.

'Hm?'

Folding a corner of towel between all his toes on one foot. Lavishing a special care on that foot. Then rubbing his damaged foot briskly, as if he can't bear to look at it.

'Come back here and talk to me!'

He appears in a towel. His hair is wet and straggly and his face is white and worried. 'What is it?'

Craig looks at Penny as she sits up in bed. He looks at her small pale breasts as the quilt falls away.

'Come back to bed.'

He untenses slightly. For a moment he thinks she is going to say the thing he is dreading most. That Liz has already had a word in her ear. That she has said to her daughter, 'Lean closer, my dear, and I will tell you the truth . . . that Craig is the culprit. Your ex-boyfriend is the thug that almost killed me. Punched me in the jaw on New Year's Eve and pushed me backwards into a ten-month coma. That is the monster you have let into your pink satin bed.'

Evidently Liz hasn't said anything of the sort, yet.

Penny pulls him to her. As he scrambles back onto the quilt, she doesn't even notice that both his feet are perfect.

Last night there wasn't much chance for Liz to say anything.

Only Penny was allowed to go in and have real words with her mother. The doctors had finished their business and were waiting for the patient to sleep naturally, of her own accord. They drew back to allow the daughter five minutes' grace.

Penny came into the room unsurely. The light was weird, aquamarine and gold. It was like being in a fish tank. She'd once had a goldfish called Jessica, who dwindled and lay two weeks dying at the bottom of her unclean bowl. Penny expected to find Liz mooching in just that way, her scales turned the same dull gold.

Penny was aware of the watchful doctors stationed around the room like high priests. They must be student doctors for there to be so many of them. Fancy having students for my mam! She flushed with anger. They were experimenting on her.

Liz was propped on dark-green pillows. No make-up on. Her wig was nowhere to be seen. She had been stripped and lay apparently naked under the green sheets. Her chest was hairier that Penny thought it might be. No chance to shave it. The flat, haired, narrow chest shocked Penny as she came to sit by Liz. At first she thought, They've brought me to the wrong patient! Then, staring at the familiar features, she thought, They've brought my mother from the land of the dead, but with the wrong body! With an ordinary man's body! Where's all her studied voluptuousness? Her primped and powdered, shaved and made-up body? Where's her jewellery, her accoutrements? It was as if she had been robbed. Her arms were stick thin, lying listless over the sheets. The two large, pale nipples surprised Penny, too. She'd never seen her mother like this. Not since she was her dad.

Without the missing wig, her natural hair seemed so

short. They must have cropped it recently. It was fluffy and grey, like down on a baby pigeon.

A doctor came to stand between them. 'She might already be asleep,' he said. He seemed kind and concerned. His bald brow was sweating. She watched a single new droplet force itself out of a pore as he spoke with her. He was being tactful. 'Her name is down as Liz. Mrs Elizabeth Robinson. On all of our documents. We know she was living as a woman and taking hormones. We need to ask you, as her daughter, if you'd prefer her friends and neighbours to see her like this or not?'

Penny doesn't understand.

There is a fierce heat in the room. As if Liz has come back with an explosion. Or with the fires of hell at her back, like Eurydice. A flash of burning, transformative light.

'I mean,' says the doctor, 'we don't know whether her other visitors are aware of her biological sex or not. Do they know her as a woman?'

'Oh, yes,' says Penny.

'Then we'll have to cover up the more obviously male bits,' he says. 'When they come to see her. At the moment she's looking too . . . natural.'

'Thank you,' she tells him, pleased by his care.

Penny sits by her mother.

'I'm sick of this hospital already,' Liz says at last.

Penny doesn't point out how many months she has been here. She stares in wonder and simple happiness at her mother's face. She can't think of what to say.

'When will they let me go home?' Liz sounds older and querulous.

'I don't know,' says Penny, and her voice breaks. She bursts into tears.

'Hey,' says Liz. 'It's only concussion, isn't it? I was all right. Happy New Year! I just fell over! I just fell over.'

Tom comes clean.

He watches Elsie come up the garden path. He opens the

310

back door for her and watches her unpack all her groceries.

'Put the kettle on, be a love.'

He does so and that's when he decides to come clean.

'You know when . . .'

'You what?'

'You know when you thought maybe it was me who destroyed your garden and your house and all your things? When I was mad and I went missing for days?'

She stops, her head still in the cupboard for tins. 'Oh, Tom,' she says. 'I was upset. I was upset and lashing out at anyone –'

'It *was* me, Elsie. I came back a few times when you weren't home. I wanted to ruin everything of yours that you love.'

She comes out of the cupboard and stares at him. The cupboard is above the draining board, which she is kneeling on. She looks at him from this height, her knees aching and cracking.

He adds, 'I wanted to break it all apart. The petty, silly things you invest your time in. Everything you spend your love and money on. Your scraggy rose bushes outside. The ornaments you bring back from the spastics shop. All of it. I wanted to do it out of sheer, unmitigated spite. I did it because that's what I wanted to do.'

She takes the can of beans she has just set down and flings it at him. One of the six penny tins of beans, reduced to almost nothing in the baked-bean price war. More water than anything else inside. But still it gouges a red weal in Tom's forehead when it hits him, and he drops to the floor.

He stumbles back into the armchair, the one that smells of dog. The two inflatable reindeer are still there, having found no better home since Christmas.

Elsie takes another tin – spaghetti hoops – and throws this too. He yells in outrage as it thuds off his forearms, which he has put up, rather feebly, to protect his face. His twisted-up, ranting, loud, loud face.

311

Elsie cries out and reaches into the cupboard.

Marrowfat peas. Cream-of-tomato soup. Power Ranger pasta shapes. More beans. Tinned tomatoes. Ravioli. She chucks the lot. He can't protect himself against this remorseless barrage.

Pineapple chunks. Ambrosia custard.

Then she throws the jar of cook-in sauce. Chicken korma cook-in sauce explodes against his forehead in a gooey and bloody mess.

Just as well Craig isn't home to witness this. She clambers down from the draining board once Tom is unconscious.

Now let's see how he likes being at that precious edge of his. This is *your* limit of experience, lovey. *You* walk that bloody bridge of yours.

Twenty-Eight

The poor woman couldn't be bothered. You could see it in her face, the second the car pulled up to the kerb. Liz looked out of the back window and saw all of Phoenix Court waiting there. Everyone out to welcome her back. She smiled wanly through the window as Penny paid the taxi fare. You could see that the poor woman's heart sank when she saw all those faces waiting in Phoenix Court. She didn't want welcoming back. She couldn't be bothered.

Among the crowd, Fran felt ashamed of herself. It was she who had gone round the doors, alerting everyone to Liz's imminent arrival. Why hadn't she used her sense and thought on, in her usual way, and realised that Liz might want some privacy? Letting everyone know like this, getting them to indulge their nosiness and standing in a cluster, lining the path between the roadside and number sixteen . . . why, it was more like something Jane would do.

There had been a postcard from Jane this morning. Hot from Tunisia. Picture of silvery-white sands. A sunset. 'It's far too hot. We should have come back straight away. My mother's driving me scatty. Her hubby is a twat. Wish I was home in Aycliffe. Regards, Jane.' It was addressed to 'Fran and Family (Not Frank)'.

Jane would think this was a treat. Having the excuse to stand in the street and stare at someone's misfortunes like this.

Fran was standing by Sheila and Simon and their two kids. Sheila seemed more gargantuan than ever. She grew with every season. She said to Fran, 'It's like we should have little flags, shouldn't we? It's like royalty visiting!'

'Or a film star!' said Simon excitedly. 'She's like a bloody film star!'

This was the sentimentalised picture they all had of Liz. Through her absence and her coma it had hardened into legend. The Tiger Taxi door would be opened by a man in a suit. She would issue marvellously from its snug confines in a glittering evening gown. She'd be draped in fur, her jewels outrageous in the daytime, her golden hair beautifully coiffed.

'The door's opening!' Sheila said. 'Ah, look. She's getting out by herself.'

Penny was standing to one side, looking concerned. Maybe Liz was determined to do things for herself. With that indomitable spirit she was set upon looking after herself. Bette Davis in *Now, Voyager*. Joan Crawford in *Mildred Pierce*.

The door opens, the crowd shrinks back, and Liz stands up in Phoenix Court, clutching her vanity case.

Penny takes her arm.

They walk slowly to their garden gate in the silence of the gathering. The neighbours meant to clap at this point, but they are silent, staring. Liz looks down. She wears a friendly smile, but she is adamant she won't stop to speak. They pass the neighbours by.

'She's . . . she's . . .' This is Simon, standing next to Fran. He is the first to say anything. They watch the gate of number sixteen clash shut behind Liz and Penny. This is his cue to say, far too loudly, 'She's a bloke!'

Fran closes her eyes and stands stock still as the crowd gabbles away to itself.

Of course. Of course she's a man.

Liz is in a blue tracksuit, possibly borrowed from Craig. She has none of her adornments. Her hair is short and grey. She is a thin, prematurely aged man in his forties. How delicate she looks, how frail but determined. How familiar and unfamiliar. And how unmistakably male without the frock and the wig.

Someone is laughing. Someone shouts something at the door of number sixteen as it closes on the crowd.

'Well!' says Big Sue. 'I can't . . . can you . . .?' She gapes at Fran.

Fran shrugs and smiles.

She wants to bang on their door and pledge her support. But maybe Penny and her mother need some time to themselves right now.

This was news to Nesta. It was news she thought Tom should hear. She went straight round Tom and Elsie's house to tell them: all this time, Liz was a man.

Nesta had no idea what she thought about this. She skidded and slipped her way across the street. Her new baby was bundled up in her arms. She shushed it and tried to concentrate. She didn't know what to think until she could tell Tom. Tom would know.

Maybe Liz had come back from the other side transformed. There could be something magical in this.

'You can't come in.' Elsie has the door chain on. Her eyes look wild, her hair hangs in unwashed tatters. No one's seen her for days.

Nesta stands on the doorstep and stares at her.

'But I've got news!' Nesta says. 'I have to tell Tom.'

'Tom isn't well,' says Elsie, and for the first time looks Nesta in the eye. She recoils from Nesta's straightforward, unflinching stare.

'Has he been taken away again?' asks Nesta.

'N-no,' says Elsie. 'I don't mean in his head. I mean he has a cold.'

'Are you sure?' says Nesta.

'Yes!' Elsie looks like she might cry.

'If it's only a cold, why can't I come in?'

'Oh, Nesta . . . you just can't. That's all.'

'But it's important!'

Elsie sobs. 'All right, it's his head – he's gone funny

315

again. You can't see him because he's lying depressed in his bed and he won't get up.'

Nesta has to take this for an answer. She shuffles away.

Elsie goes up to see Tom, lying in his bed. She leans against the door frame. His pillows are pink and so are his sheets. This is the blood that is still damp. The older blood, the three-day-old blood, is brown, almost black. The room smells. It is claustrophobic, smelly, too hot. Just like the days when he used to lie, too fed up to greet the world.

Elsie worries about what she will do with him.

Craig calls.

'It's me! I'm back!'

Three days after his return he sees fit to come and see his poor old mam. 'You can't come in,' she says tearfully through the gap in the front door. She won't unlatch the door chain for anyone.

'Mam?'

The front door closes.

He's been three days in bed with that Penny. She knows it. Can't come and see his poor old mam. He's been in bed with that Penny all this time. Making babies. The only consolation.

I suppose, Fran thought, Liz is a very special person. She must be. That's why we all waited by her, for her, to see that she came back safe. She catches your eye and makes you want to *know*.

In that way Liz reminded Fran of the good-looking kids at school. The well-dressed ones, the cool, smart, popular kids. Fran thought about this, knowing that she herself was never that popular. She was never one for standing out in that way. Her life had been one of quiet effort, of carrying on. Of seeing things for what they were. If you stand out in a crowd, can you really do that? Can you still see things as they really are?

Fran watches her husband on the night he unveils his

316

living-room fish pond. He gathers the four kids and Fran to watch.

It is in the corner of the room, covered in green tarpaulin. It has mirrors along the back, spotlights and fairy lights. She has to admit, he has done a professional-looking job on it. If you like that sort of thing, which Fran isn't sure she does yet. She'll do her nut if the fish stink up her sitting room.

Frank even gives a speech before he unveils what he has built. He dedicates this pond to his 'lovely lady wife'. The four kids clap wildly and she smirks and curtsies. 'Tuh-dah!' Frank goes, and peels back the tarpaulin.

It's a nice pond. Four juicy orange carp roam around in the cool water. He's arranged it quite nicely, with flowers and green frondy plants hanging over the edge. Fran congratulates him and he glows with pleasure. Poor Frank.

Poor? she wonders, when they lie in bed, a couple of hours later. Why did she feel sorry for him as he fiddled on proudly with his fish pond?

Through the back wall of their bedroom you can hear Nesta and Tony next door, going for it hammer and tongs. 'They fuck like rabbits,' Frank grunts, his head muffled in the pillow. Fran lies still and listens to the bedsprings going mad on the other side of the wall. She feels like telling them to keep it down. This is ridiculous. Obscene. Nesta starts wailing out her pleasure like a ghost.

Fran supposes she's sad that Frank's dreams and ambitions come down in the end to a fish pond. She is startled by how proud he is. Later, watching a film, she noticed him looking round at his pond and his fountain, as if reassuring himself that it was still there. Fran hates the tinkling of the filtration system disguised as a fountain. It made her want the loo. But she supposes she'll get used to it.

In the end, she thinks, we all have sad lives. Even the popular kids at school have the same ordinary time as everyone else when they leave. By all accounts Jane was a pretty, sought-after girl in her schooldays. Look at her

317

now, alone. Taken on holiday by her mother to cheer her up. No one is 'cool', thinks Fran. But we all wanted to be that. She grew up in the sixties. Everything was a French film. She worked in an office but she learned to smoke her ciggies like Bardot. She was on the lookout for Marlon Brando in *A Streetcar Named Desire*. All a-sweat, all a-flame. At that age she thought desire made you special. She thought it made you magical and cool.

She looks across the bed at Frank. She tries to block out next door's racket. When she touches Frank, as she does now, the fine hairs on his legs stand on end, excitedly. He can't help his response to her. Or maybe he's turned on by the noise from next door. It's hard not to think of sex with all that panting and shunting through the paper-thin walls. But Frank turns to her with a hard-on and they push close to one another and this time she doesn't think it ridiculous she is so much bigger than him. They start to make love.

Even our rediscovery of each other, she thinks as he slips her straps down off her shoulders, is a quiet thing. A whispery thing. His soft red hair brushing her as he puts his mouth down to her breasts. When you lay these experiences of ours alongside those that others have . . . that's when I see my life is lived on a different scale.

Next door Nesta comes with a lion's roar. Her husband is silent, as if he isn't even there. Soon, however, they are heard bickering about putting the cats out, about who will fetch a cup of tea.

By then Fran is about to come. It keeps building and she keeps thinking surely *now*, but it goes on. Tonight is quite a shock to her. She had forgotten how she and Frank were, after all, experts in each other.

Twenty-Nine

This is us down the Copper Kettle.

It's the morning of the sit-in, a Saturday morning. Penny took the photo. It was in the *Newton News*, the free paper, the following week, posted into every letter box in the town. A bloody horrible snap of us ganged round coffee tables, looking terrible, protesting. They were going to close the place because it was filthy inside. I mean, it *was* filthy inside. But we liked it because it was a good place to meet up. I wouldn't have had their cakes, though.

Still. I got a copy of the original and I got it framed. I'm on the front table, lifting a cup of coffee in a toast. I'm with Penny, Liz, Fran and Nesta. We're all grinning madly.

I am the one with the tattoos all over my body.

At the time of this photo, I was about to leave Aycliffe. I got my own copy of the photo because I wanted a memento. In fact, I think the all-day sit-in was the last time we were all together. And whatever you might say, it was quite a gang we had. Look, even Frank's there, sitting behind Fran. He's drinking lager. The bodies are pressed ten deep, all the Aycliffe women, pressing in to get their faces in the free paper. Their bairns, teenage lads, single mums, old blokes, all those faces you'd recognise from seeing in the precinct and just going about the place.

That was a busy day, that. The day of the sit-in. It was shadowed by bigger events. Ridiculous events.

Penny turned up and told me that her Craig was being questioned by the police. They had torn through Elsie's house. They found Tom dead. Elsie and Craig were in for questioning. Tom was dead. Well, not many round our place mourned much for him.

319

Funny thing was, he'd lain there for days. Nobody knew. And, while he lay there, Fran had invoked his name in a white lie. In a ploy to get Liz out of her doldrums.

Fran went to number sixteen and stood in front of Liz. 'You know what they're saying, don't you?' Fran meant business. She stood with her hands on her hips.

'What?' Liz groaned. 'What are they saying?' According to Fran, Liz looked a sight. She hadn't washed her hair, she wore tatty, androgynous house pants again. She hadn't decided on whether to get in or out of bed yet, let alone which gender she was going to represent.

Since coming back from the hospital she had been lying on their settee watching daytime telly and old films, with a duvet over her legs and an old coat pulled on backwards. For warmth, she said. She couldn't keep warm. She still had dreams of the snow and that she was turning blue. She thought, when she closed her eyes, that she was under ice, under the polar cap. So she sat curled up on the settee and shivered under a backwards coat, her arms pushed down the sleeves. Penny waited on her mother, bringing her drinks and dinner and tea and snacks day and night.

'You'll pile on the weight if you live like this,' warned Fran. Fran thought how slim and svelte Liz had been.

'So?' shrugged Liz. 'Who does that affect apart from me?'

Fran tutted. 'That isn't the Liz I know.'

Liz bridled. '*I'm* not the Liz you know. Haven't you heard? Everyone has. I'm a . . . I'm a bloody travesty.'

'Ha!' Fran wouldn't let her get any more sorry for herself. 'We're all travesties. It's all a bloody travesty, Liz, man.'

There was an amused glint in Liz's eye at this. 'So tell me, what are they saying?'

'It's that Tom,' Fran lied. This was her great white lie, making use of poor Tom while he was lying dead across the street. 'He's been going round like an evangelical. Telling all and sundry that he reached into your perverted

320

soul and put you back on the straight and narrow. He brought you back to life and cured you of your sickness. He found for you your true self, and that's why you came back like this. Why you came back to us as a man.' Fran took a deep breath after this.

Liz's mouth hangs open. She looks down at herself. She shrugs off the anorak and the duvet, and dashes to the mirror in the hallway. She is in tracksuit bottoms concertinaed around her knees and a shapeless grey T-shirt. Her pale arms are mottled with mauve and blue.

'This isn't my true self!'

Fran comes to see what Liz can see. Liz's complexion is pale and she seems almost featureless. A pallid, empty man.

'This isn't *natural*!'

Fran shrugs. 'This is what that Tom is telling the world.'

'The little bastard!' Liz says.

'Why don't I . . .' Fran begins.

'Hm?'

'Help spruce you up?'

'Spruce?'

'We'll do you a make-over. Like on the telly.' Fran, watching Liz stare at herself, knows that she has won already. 'I don't suppose you've thrown out your old clothes yet?'

'Oh . . .' says Liz. 'No. Not yet.'

'So!' cries Fran. 'What are we waiting for? Let's get up them stairs! Let's get you dolled up!'

These were the dramas we had that morning of the sit-in. Penny arrived from the police station to announce that her lover and his mother were being held in cells. Pending an enquiry. Elsie had gone doolally. Penny sat with me and smoked my cigarettes for the rest of the day.

'Have you ever ended up involved where you didn't want to be?' she asked me. I shouldn't have, but I laughed.

'All the bloody time.'

'I want out,' she said.

321

And I hadn't the heart to tell her that I'd already booked my ticket. The next day, Sunday, I was bussing it up to Edinburgh. It was cheaper that way, but it took all day. I was going to see Andy. And going to see my son.

The next thing, into the busy café came Fran with Liz. Everyone stopped to stare. They all knew about Liz from the papers. They knew she had survived. They also knew she was a feller.

She came dolled up to the nines. It was the Queen of Sheba riding in, swanning right past the staring faces and plonking herself at our table.

She wore a fine white fur coat over a scarlet dress. Her look was imperious and she jangled with all those jewels. Her hair was up, quite different to how she was before. A more sophisticated look. It was as if she had been away all this time simply planning a new look.

Penny marvelled at her. 'Fancy dressing up like this just for a protest!' She grinned, hugging her mother.

'I can't let my public down,' she said.

Big Sue stood up and started the whole café on a standing ovation. They cheered and clapped Liz until she took her bows.

'This is ridiculous,' she hissed, but she loved it. 'Where's Jane?' she asked Fran.

Then Fran produced the card that Jane had sent, announcing she was marrying an Arab.

'She'd have married anything if they'd asked her!' Nesta cackled, but no one joined in.

'Good luck to her, I say,' said Fran.

Liz opened her handbag and slipped a bottle of Jameson's around the table, to top up everyone's tea.

'Get some music on!' she told the little waiter. 'Make it more like a party!'

Thirty

Ferryhill
Seventeen Years Later

She doesn't think of it as her new house any more. You could even say she is used to it.

As in the days when she woke up to go cleaning down Fujitsu, Fran is up with the lark. She likes to make coffee and watch the light come over the flat fields. Depending on the season, they get touched with different colours. Now it is spring. Field after field turns pink with the dawn. Leaning against the doorframe, Fran cradles her mug. Usually she fusses about in her dressing gown, the radio on. A local station, on which they play nostalgic pop songs of the seventies and eighties, for the young at heart. Fran will watch the morning start to happen and feel all shivery and full of memories.

This morning she keeps the radio off. She has a guest in this house of hers and compared with her, he is a late sleeper.

Does Fran get many guests here? Her grown children come to stay, all four of them; the three girls are married, little Jeff comes home from the army. He stomps about the hollow wooden floors in his army boots. The girls fill the place with grandchildren. At Christmas the old farmhouse heaves with life again. But there is lots of space. Fields all around. The children and grandchildren come for the horses, she knows. That'll be the Gypsy blood in their veins, she thinks and smiles.

She is surrounded by her family at Christmas and on other special occasions. They all live in funny places, Chester-le-Street, Penrith, Bath. They split apart and come dutifully back when they can. There is still a distance there. With her oldest girls especially, Fran can't really talk. When she tries to, on the phone, she finds that she is passing on the other children's news. She is a one-woman grapevine. To each other and to her face they accuse her of making trouble. Of telling tales. Of making nasty comparisons of what one sister is getting, of what they can afford, who is having a posh holiday or a new car, and who isn't. This isn't Fran's intention. She simply wants to keep them up to date with each other. They need to know, she thinks, what's happening in the family. She can't stand it when families break apart. She'd hate that to happen to hers.

The most loyal is the youngest, little Jeff. Although he's in the army, his room is still there at home for him. How much like his father he is.

Frank has been dead ten years. Fran thinks they would be a closer-knit family if he was still there. Last Boxing Day there had been a row. Her eldest daughter Kerry told Fran she'd killed her dad by nagging him about the booze. If she'd let him be, his heart wouldn't have given up.

This was over dinner. The whole clan at the large dining-room table. Fran had gone to such effort: napkin rings, candelabra, everything from her mother's posh cupboards. She was shocked, ladling out the bread sauce, stooped over, with her mouth hanging agape. At last she said, 'You know nothing about it.' She stared at Kerry. Kerry had no idea how Frank had secretly learned to hate and resent his eldest daughter. He thought she was a young tart. Fran had struggled to keep Kerry ignorant of her father's beliefs. Kerry has grown up angry without knowing why. Last Christmas she turned the full force of it on her mother.

That scene ended with little Jeff getting up, walking around the festive table and slapping his eldest sister full in the face. Anything in defence of his mam. Kelly's husband made a half-hearted attempt to get up and Jeff warned him, with a glance, not to even try. Kerry sat and quietly sobbed into a freshly pressed napkin.

'Your dad killed *himself*,' said Fran quietly, and then she went on serving up dinner.

That was last Christmas. Fran wonders what this year's will be like. If, after that, her family will even want to get back together.

She sighs and goes to open the fridge. She'll get some bacon going. An anticipatory growl from her stomach. She hopes the smell of bacon will wake her newest guest and bring him downstairs to keep her company.

Company. Fran is sixty-eight this year. She feels much the same as ever, and she craves company. Even Elsie is welcome to stay the odd weekend. She comes to drink Fran's gin.

This year's Christmas will be different. Even if her ramshackle family do decide to turn up and disgrace themselves by fighting, there will be other elements present. Fran has taken it upon herself to invite those from Phoenix Court who have moved away in recent years. It will be a reunion, of sorts, of a looser, even more dysfunctional family. Penny, Nesta, Elsie, Craig, Liz, Mark, Jane . . . whoever else she can contact. There's plenty of room in Fran's house. Before she popped her clogs, Fran's mother saw to it that there was a lot of room. The woman was obsessed with building extensions.

For once Fran is grateful to the memory of her mother. That ostentation and carelessness with money has enabled Fran to gather her invented family around her. The old white farmhouse with its pear and apple trees and stables, its sanded wooden floors, its furnishings and rugs and ornaments picked up from all around the world, is the place Fran can gather her gang.

The bacon in the frying pan hisses and spatters as she turns it over with her wooden spoon. It sounds as if it quarrels with itself.

Fran is now at the age her mother was when she died. She sees no gloomy symmetry in this. Fran thinks that you make life up as you go along. If you're not careful you can wish yourself to an early grave. It's all in the mind. Mind over circumstances.

And her brothers? They are somewhere exploring the wider world. Adventurously, having lives bigger – they say – than Fran could imagine.

Lives as big as Jane's, marrying her Tunisian man and living six months out of every twelve in a desert. That has lasted these good few years. She swears blind she's not in a harem, but Fran won't let the joke drop. Jane is happy.

Lives as big as Liz, who rediscovered glamour. And also her abandoned lover, Cliff. Who moved to London.

Lives as big as Elsie, who escaped a murder charge and lives, the one remaining neighbour, in Phoenix Court.

Lives as big as Penny, whose father once said she'd go to the moon. Who grew up with special powers and didn't know what to do with them. Penny is still deciding what to do with her life. She has three bairns, the first two with Craig. She's in Darlington.

In her cooking reverie Fran is interrupted by her new house guest.

He pads into the kitchen and startles her. She spins around and, when she sees him, sighs, smiling with relief. He gives one of his swift and unsure grins in reply and sits down at the small table, on the most rickety of the stools.

'Good morning,' Fran says. 'I knew this would wake you.'

The kitchen smells delicious. His nose twitches.

He's in bright-red pyjamas. He must have brought them with him. They don't look cheap. His eyes are still half-closed. He looks rumpled and sweet. His hair – his *fur*, she corrects herself – lies every which way. He reaches for the coffee pot and smacks his lips at the gurgle and slosh of thick black coffee into his waiting mug.

'My father says when I was tiny I used to drink black coffee out of my baby bottle,' he says.

My, Fran thinks once more, what a deep, sexy little voice this young man has.

326

She comes to sit opposite and proffers her own mug. The spots on his hand on the coffee-jug handle, the spots all over his face, down his neck, on the V of tightly muscled chest peaking through his pyjamas . . . these spots are the colour of black coffee. Irregular rings, like dark-brown lipstick marks, all over his body.

Why, Fran! she thinks mischievously. You're getting all sexy and silly over this boy child less than a third of your age. This visiting child who has entrusted himself to your care.

'Today,' Jep says, 'will you take me to Newton Aycliffe?'

He says the name as if it is something fantastic. Something magical out of a book, like the Emerald Palace in the Land of Oz. Perhaps to him, that's what it is. Names of unseen things can take on, through repeated tellings, a certain charm.

'Of course,' Fran tells him, finding that she is staring at his sharp, trimmed nails. His sleek, soot-rimmed ears.

'I feel like I know the place, you know. It's the place I'm really from. We moved around so much when they were bringing me up . . . we never stuck any town for very long. But I always heard about Aycliffe. About Phoenix Court. I can't wait to see it for myself.'

'You might be disappointed.' Suddenly, fiercely, Fran doesn't want this boy to be disappointed.

'My dad used to say a place is what you make it,' he says, with a self-deprecating shrug.

'Which dad?'

'Both of them.'

Fran chuckles. 'Well . . .'

Jep says, 'Whatever it's like in Phoenix Court, I'll love seeing the place I come from.'

Fran walks to her wide picture window. From here, in this intense north-country light, you can almost see Aycliffe's brown and silver buildings.

'Bonny lad . . . it'll be a pleasure taking you to visit. I've not been back for years, you know.'

Jep gives her one of his uncertain smiles.

Then Fran starts slicing bread for her toaster. She puts the kettle on, then the radio, for an old-fashioned song. She's enjoying this time with her new house guest. Breakfast with the bright, leopard-printed boy.

A SELECTED LIST OF CONTEMPORARY FICTION
AVAILABLE IN VINTAGE

☐	NIGHT TRAIN	Martin Amis	£5.99
☐	CANDY	Luke Davies	£5.99
☐	BLUE MONDAYS	Arnon Grunberg	£5.99
☐	HEADBANGER	Hugo Hamilton	£5.99
☐	THE FOLDING STAR	Alan Hollinghurst	£6.99
☐	ONE DAY AS A TIGER	Anne Haverty	£6.99
☐	MY BROTHER	Jamaica Kincaid	£6.99
☐	ENDURING LOVE	Ian McEwan	£6.99
☐	DOES IT SHOW?	Paul Magrs	£5.99
☐	HOMEBOY	Seth Morgan	£6.99
☐	BELOVED	Toni Morrison	£6.99
☐	THE SALESMAN	Joseph O'Connor	£6.99
☐	THESE DEMENTED LANDS	Alan Warner	£6.99

- All Vintage books are available through mail order or from your local bookshop.

- Please send cheque/eurocheque/postal order (sterling only), Access, Visa, Mastercard, Diners Card, Switch or Amex:

☐☐☐☐☐☐☐☐☐☐☐☐☐☐☐☐

Expiry Date:_____Signature:_____

Please allow 75 pence per book for post and packing U.K.
Overseas customers please allow £1.00 per copy for post and packing.

ALL ORDERS TO:

Vintage Books, Books by Post, TBS Limited, The Book Service,
Colchester Road, Frating Green, Colchester, Essex CO7 7DW

NAME:_____

ADDRESS:_____

_____

_____

Please allow 28 days for delivery. Please tick box if you do not
wish to receive any additional information ☐

Prices and availability subject to change without notice.